Cursed

to be

Mine

MIRANDA GRANT

BY MIRANDA GRANT

WAR OF THE MYTH
Elemental Claim
Think of Me Demon
Tricked Into It
Rage for Her

FAIRYTALES OF THE MYTH
Burn Baby Burn
The Little Morgen
Bjerner and the Beast

DEATHLY BELOVED
To Have and to Lose
Death Do Us Part
For Better or For Worse
To Love and To Perish
In Sickness and In Health

BOOK OF SHADOWS
Cursed to be Mine

CURSED TO BE MINE

TRIGGER AND CONTENT WARNINGS
(These are also spoilers)

Find them on my website:

https://mirandagrant.co.uk/cursed-to-be-mine

*To All Those Thinking Dark Romances
Lead to Twisted Desires:*

They really don't. I haven't once fucked any of
the people I've killed.

Want more of an experience while reading?

Scan the QR code to get access to an 'advent calendar' you open at certain points throughout the book.

Just a quick note before you read. There are two different spellings of 'hell' in this book.

1. Hell – which references the Christian Hell;
2. Hel – the Norse hel, a shortening of Niflhel

You can blame Christianity for stealing names (and a lot of other things) for any confusion.

ONE

HIM

I trail my knife over my girl's flesh as she sleeps. My pulse beats heavily in my cock at the thought of her waking, of her panicked blue gaze finding me in the darkness of her room, of the flush of her cheeks as she opens her mouth to scream. I will plunge my tongue in between her lips, lapping up every yell until she learns to scream my name.

Mine.

Not her fucking boyfriend's.

She is my girl, was from the moment I laid eyes on her two years ago.

And now her beautiful thighs beckon me to cut the heart-dotted fabric hiding her from view. Hiding what's rightfully mine. I imagine spreading her open and running my lips against her wet pussy, my hands heavy on her thighs, pinning her down until I'm finished with her.

Finished eating her.

Fingering her.

Turning her over to worship her ass.

And then fucking her hard in every beautiful hole.

A muffled groan pulls from my throat. I reach my free hand into my pants and grip my cock. It jerks against my palm as I tower over her, crying salty tears already, begging me to place it between her pussy lips and shove in deep.

The sleeping spell I've cast over her would let me do it, but despite my desires, I know she's not ready for me yet. Not primed.

And I want her awake for our first time. I want her looking into my eyes and screaming my name until her throat is so fucking raw and her mouth is so fucking used to being open that she takes my cock with ease.

Another groan leaves me as I squeeze my cock hard, imagining the muscles of her throat working around me like a satin vice. She's so beautiful with her round cheeks of innocence, with her long brown locks cascading over her face of purity. She's so fucking beautiful it hurts me to look at her without touching. Without claiming. Without connecting our souls in the oldest way known to man.

Unable to help myself, I press my knife in ever so slightly to her inner thigh. Just a scratch. Just enough to draw a thin line of blood that could be easily dismissed come morning as just one of those weird scratches and bruises people never remember getting.

Pulling my knife back, I bring it to my lips and run my tongue across its blade. My fingers tighten at the harsh cut of the steel, and the taste of her fills me with an elation that nearly has me coming before I even fully stroke myself.

I cut deeper, drawing my own blood. Irritation fills me when I wash away her taste with my own. I want to savor every part of her, but the blood ritual is necessary to stake my claim from my brothers. To mark her as one of us, offering her protection under my gang in a war she has no knowledge of.

Lowering my knife back to her thigh, I slide my blood

across her cut. Tightening my fingers, I moan again, and this time, I jerk down, then up. She sleeps through it all, the spell I've cast over her, perfected over these past three months, keeping her under.

At the sight of my blood smearing across her pale skin, I beat myself faster. My balls draw tight as I imagine her taking my cock all the way down her throat as I lick her pussy and ass. My hips jerk up into my hand as I sheath the knife and then run my finger over the scratched claim of my girl.

It's a small mark, simple. The ritual to bring her into the family will be more elaborate, but she's not ready for that yet.

And I'm not ready to share her with my brothers.

At the thought of them tasting her, having any part of what's mine, I push my finger hard against her skin, my teeth clenching, my rage building. For a brief moment, I think about not letting them fuck her when I bring her into the family, but I quickly dismiss that thought. The ritual requires it; I cannot claim her otherwise.

My girl twists in her sleep, rolling over as if running from my finger, but I don't let her, following her as she moves onto her back. The urge to grab her and hold her still while I fuck her courses through me.

But there's another occupant in her house just down the hall. And my girl will be loud, I know this.

She'll scream as she takes my cock deep in her pussy. And I'll grunt and groan as I release inside her, filling her with my love. The bed will smack into the wall like a war drum beating out a fucking conquest.

Mine.

Mine.

Mine.

My hand quickens on my cock, going up all nine inches, down to my base, pulling the head back, sliding my foreskin across the sensitive tip. My hips push forward again, and I can't help myself from touching her any longer.

Sliding my finger up her naked thigh, I linger at the hem of the heart-patterned fabric. My lips part, exhaling the urges I can't keep restrained. And then I'm pushing it aside and slipping between her lips, running up and down, not going in.

A little noise escapes her, and I still, my eyes on her face, seeing if she wakes. My blood boils in my veins, imagining the slow opening of her eyes, followed by that beautiful grin she always gives me during the day.

"Good morning, Khalid."

"How are you, Khalid?"

"Can you help me with this, Khalid?"

And then she would smile as she brings my attention to her large breasts in some way or another. She likes me staring at her. Her soul already knows she's mine, and the knowledge of that has me pushing my finger inside her.

She clenches around me, her pussy sucking me deep. She wants me to fill her, and I'm halfway leaning over her before I stop.

I can't take her yet.

Not now.

Clenching down my frustration, pulling on every bit of the control I am known for as the Family's reaper, I move back, keeping my finger inside her.

She doesn't stir as I jerk a hand up my cock in rhythm to the fucking of her pussy. I slip another digit inside as her arousal loosens the area. Her thighs spread for me, and I pant heavily at the instinct of her soul. She wants me so fucking bad. She wants me to fill her, claim her, fuck her until she's exhausted back into sleep.

With a breathy little moan, she starts riding my hand. Her hips roll on the mattress, chasing me and retreating as I lean back over her and beat my cock so close to her pussy.

I want to come all over her skin. I want to stain the hearts right over her pussy so she wakes knowing she's taken, so her soul can rejoice in finally being complete.

But she isn't ready to step into my world.

Soon though.

A few more weeks, a few more days...

Groaning, I shift back so I can lower my head to my fingers. I pull out of her, and she whimpers in distress as I suck my digits clean. *Fuck, I love the taste of her.*

"Khalid?" she says so softly, so mumbled, I know she's still not awake. But the fact that she's dreaming of me, wanting me during every moment of her existence causes me to orgasm hard. My cum threatens to shoot out and stain her sheets, to prove my existence here tonight, but I beat it back.

Control it.

I don't want to waste a single drop for her.

All my cum will be hers.

Only ever hers.

Withdrawing my fingers from my lips, I shake over her, my body trembling from my dry release. My lower back and legs buzzing, I pull aside the heart-patterned fabric and dip my lips to hers.

She groans as she rubs against me, her soft thick flesh cushioning my cheeks. My tongue licks her up and down, savoring her taste before dipping into heaven itself.

When I finally claim her, every morning and evening I'll eat my favorite meal. I'll spread her out naked before me, using her as a carrier for my food. She'll squeeze out every bite of my meal, coated in the most delicious flavor. And then I'll clean her and fuck her as I feed her in return.

Strawberries dipped in the cum dribbling out of her pussy.

Blueberries pushed all the way in and popped inside.

Pancakes after mopping up her thighs.

Her mouth will latch onto my fingers, her cheeks hollowing before moving to my cock to clean off the topping of syrup.

My cock twitches under such thoughts, wanting – needing to be inside my girl.

Licking my way to her clit, I suck it hard. She jerks beneath me, and the delicious pants sounding above me start to come out faster. My girl is close. So fucking close.

I want to finish her, but I need to leave, need to go help my brothers start a war with the Death Hunt gang.

With one last lick of her pussy, I pull away. My girl whimpers for me, and I capture that sound in my memory, holding it along with all the others. Then I grab one of her hands and place it inside her underwear, curling her own fingers inside her. I watch her face as I stroke her with herself, and I grow hard again with the need to claim her completely.

She's so fucking beautiful.

So beautiful it fucking hurts.

Telling myself I'll be back tomorrow, I slowly slip my hand out of the fabric, leaving hers in, leaving her to take what's mine as she continues to dream of me.

With one last look at my girl as she touches herself, I slip into the hall. I close her door slowly behind me before looking at one further down the landing.

The other occupant is in there, and the urge to remove them from her life, to just hide her body along with all the others I've hidden... I could do it. I could do it so fucking easily, my life as the Family's reaper giving me so many places to use. The docks. The butchers. The many estates our Family, a *respectable* business, landscapes.

But I don't. For my girl. Because she likes her family.

My silent strides take me to the side door. I open it slowly, then turn and dig the key out of my pocket. Sliding it into the lock, I twist it. My eyes lift back up to my girl's bedroom. A smile curls my lips as my tongue darts out to taste *her* on my chin.

Soon she will be mine.

Soon I'll be taking her, claiming her, slamming my cock deep into her wet, soaking pussy as she screams and spasms around me.

Soon.

So fucking soon.

TWO

HER

Awareness fills me, pulling me from a delicious dream. My thighs are soaked, my fingers sucked between them. I keep my eyes closed, trying to hold onto the image of my hot, sexy neighbor, Khalid Shadow, with his head buried between my legs, his long black hair no longer in that low ponytail it's always in. It cascades down his shoulders and against my skin.

My lips part.

My fingers push inside me.

And *curl.*

I roll my hips, riding my right hand. My left reaches up to my breasts, concentrating its attention on my erect nipples. He's young, scandalously young, younger than my boyfriend by about twenty or so years, but *damn*, his body is the definition of perfection – corded muscles with rich tan skin and with hands that are rough and used to working.

I think about him *working* my pussy, lifting my ass up so

he can go deeper. My fingers curl inside me as I clutch his hair in my mind, holding him there.

God, there!

I twist against my palm, his mouth. I pant his name, a quiet moan on my lips, breathing life into the fantasy that has my muscles humming with a heat that's twisting me up inside. Melting from its intensity, I imagine him staring up at me, the lower half of his mouth buried beneath my flesh. He has such beautiful eyes. They're a plain brown, not even golden in the sunlight like some go, but *God,* are they sinfully wicked. A fierce intelligence lurks inside, a hot focus that makes me want to just strip in front of him every time he looks at me.

Holding his gaze in the sharpness of my mind, I curl my fingers as I rub hard on my clit with my other hand.

I jerk, my back lifting off the bed.

My toes clench as I twist and curl. Twist and curl.

So fucking close.

My thighs bunch.

My hips buck.

And then I come *hard*, spasming around my fingers – *his tongue.*

I want to scream, but instead I bite my cheek as my body heats, then *floods.* My thigh muscles bunch together from the strong current pulsing through me. Controlling me. Holding me down, at its mercy. *His mercy.*

A scream builds in my throat despite myself, and I grab the extra pillow on my bed and smother it over my face as his name erupts from my lips. As I imagine his cum leaking down my thighs in place of my own.

God, I would let him fuck me raw. Down my throat, up my ass, whichever way he wanted me. As long as he kept his intense eyes on me and his large hard cock inside me.

Moaning, I remove the pillow and sigh into my empty room. My arm flops to the side, the pillow in its loose grip as I slowly withdraw my fingers from my pussy. Breathing heavily, I open my eyes, finally releasing his image, and take a moment to stare at the ceiling.

Fuck. Why can't Aaron make me come this hard?

He has a massive cock – longer and thicker than my forearm, but the only time I see stars with my boyfriend is when he leaves to take a shower or go to work and I finish myself off in his absence. Not even thinking about him most times either.

But I need to be seen as a family woman because as Benjamin, my 'hip' PA, keeps telling me, the voters respond better to a woman who 'honors the traditional role of family,' which doesn't include being a single mom. I need to be career-focused but also an involved parent, harsher on crime than my male opponents to prove I'm 'not too soft' but still warm and caring to the public eye.

Which means going to depressing hospitals to read to dying children. I would prefer to just give the hospital a giant check like Mark Reynolds, the democrat running against me does, but Benjamin is adamant I must attend and be photographed...hugging *–ugh–* the sick before the election in three months.

My alarm blares right on time, and I roll over to glare at it before smacking it off. Picking up my phone, I pull it off the charger and shoot Benjamin a quick message. The smear of my fingers coat the screen, and I smirk for a second, envisioning Khalid's face between my legs again.

Hannah: *You're sure none of the fruit is rotten?*

I stare at the screen, waiting impatiently for his reply. He makes us talk in code so if ever our phones get hacked, nothing incriminating will see the light.

Fruit: sick kids at the hospital.

Rotten: contagious.

Benjamin PA: *Yes, ma'am.*

But despite his assurance that none of the kids I'll be

seeing today will have anything infectious, I pull a face as I put down the phone. It's not that I don't like kids. I love kids. I just don't like spending hours in a clinical hospital room surrounded by them when I know most won't be breathing in a couple months. It's fucking depressing and taints my whole day.

But knowing there's nothing I can do to get out of it, I roll out of bed and head for my en-suite, phone in hand. Pulling off a piece of tissue, I dampen it and wipe the screen of my phone before laying the mobile down on the teak counter surrounding the white farmhouse sink. The phone's case is a light blue with a black edge. Nothing elaborate or overly feminine. But not too masculine either. This whole marketing myself business annoys the shit out of me, but it's a game I can't afford to lose.

Re-elections are coming up soon, and Mark Reynolds will see this city destroyed if he's elected. He isn't strong enough to deal with the monsters hunting our streets. He's one of those 'modern' men. Those 'feelings' men who willingly tie a rope around their own balls and give that lead to their girlfriends. He's too soft, thinks peace is a fucking option when dealing with the gangs terrorizing our beautiful country.

He keeps talking about rehabilitation programs and "cleaning up the streets at the source" – two options that will see hundreds dead during the time it takes him to attempt implementation, hundreds, maybe even thousands more before he accepts his foolish dreams will never work. Maybe they would work somewhere in California – one of the hippy cities that don't see horrific crimes, but they would never work here.

St. Augustine, Florida, is an old town with old crime. *True* old crime that goes back centuries, full of dark grudges and acts of revenge that see these streets bleed by the gallons. Death haunts this city, twists it so much even God himself has abandoned it to the devil.

But not me.

I love this city too much to leave it to monsters who'll watch it burn.

And there *are* actual monsters here.

Werewolves, vampires, and witches. Each head of one of the three old gangs terrorizing this city. *My* city.

Glancing up at the mirror, I shift uncomfortably as memories of massacred corpses and hundreds of news clippings assault me. Vampire bites and werewolf claws hidden under the cuts of knives and the thick spray of bullets. Blood-drained corpses simply 'killed elsewhere and moved.' Death by magic written off as undetectable poisons or 'natural' heart failure and brain aneurysms.

A shiver runs through me. If they just *suspected* I knew about their secret world, the truth behind their masks... I could be dead in an instant.

The security on my home would mean nothing.

Vampires don't need permission to enter.

Werewolves can change form at will.

And witches can be miles away, casting some demonic spell.

Holding the gaze of my reflection, I let the chills squeeze my lungs, the hint of terror making me want to flinch. But I need to face my fears. I can't afford to be weak in a world of such violence. I can't afford to be like Mark Reynolds in this. So I let the horrors fill my mind as I struggle to breathe.

I could be dead in a second.

I would've died fighting for my city.

Heaven will await me...

My blue eyes drilling into my skull, I hold my gaze unwaveringly as those newspaper memories repeat inside me, in the weakness of my legs, the tightness of my chest.

But I am strong.

Capable.

I will crush these abominations once and for all, eliminating their disease-ridden corpses from the streets of St. Augustine.

Breathing in slowly, I exhale my fear and straighten up at the sink. My eyes finally leave my reflection, and I reach down to pull off my dark-blue satin chemise.

Dropping it to the floor, I pivot for the shower. The perfect temperature already set on the knob, I simply turn it on and wait a second before stepping in. My thoughts instantly flood with Khalid under the hot spray, and I use his image to beat back the lingering fear that I could die at any moment.

My hand finds itself between my legs. Leaning against the cold tile wall of the shower, I spread my thighs and push in deep.

A moan whispers from my lips, quieted under the hot spray pelting my skin and bouncing off the white tiles. Ragged breaths leave me, mixing with the steam filling the cubicle.

I want him in here.

I want him fucking me against the wall, hard and fast and *deep* like he did in my dream. God, he fucked me a dozen different ways last night – ways I would never let Aaron have me, not that my boyfriend would even think to ask. All he ever wants to do is missionary.

Closing my eyes, I visualize my neighbor, the corded muscles of his back clenching and moving beneath my fingers as I hold him to me. Sharp lines of blood carve into his skin from my nails as he fucks me so hard I can't breathe.

I start to pant.

My fingers dip in further.

Lifting one leg, I brace it against the side of the shower and rock my hips up.

"Mom?"

My eyes snap open at the sound of my daughter's voice muffled through the bathroom door. All heat leaves me, replaced by poised frustration.

"Benjamin's here," Scarlett says.

Clenching my jaw, I breathe out heavily, hating my lack of privacy with her home for the summer holidays. Had she been at Flagler College, my PA would've waited outside, not rushing me to finish.

He *would*, however, have had a go at me in the car on the way to the hospital, complaining how we were going to be late. Bad publicity arriving late. Worse publicity if we are caught speeding given I just pushed for more road cameras to curb such 'mindless deaths.' Even worse if we crash into a car and kill someone...

Benjamin is always about good publicity.

So with a sigh, I remove my fingers and wash them under the spray. "Have him wait in the family room, Gen. I'll be out in fifteen minutes."

I grab the shampoo and squirt it onto my palm.

"He's already there."

I don't hear her footsteps as she walks away, but she rarely ever lingers. She just hides in her room, sleeping the day away. No drive. No motivation. What happened to my Little Genius (Gen) who used to talk non-stop about every little thing she learned? At six, she used to come into my room every night to read *me* grade-eleven books. At ten, she started researching which colleges she wanted to go to. Yale. Harvard. Oxford all the way in England.

But then she hit puberty at twelve, and she withdrew into herself as her chest expanded out. I was called to her school more and more often over her 'indecent attire' (her shirts were too tight around the chest – impossible not to be without reaching her knees) and 'distractions in the classroom.'

I wanted to burn the school down for blaming her for

being a *child*. It's not like she had control over how her body developed. And she sure as hell wasn't responsible for how teachers and other students looked at her or how they made her the focus of their 'pranks' and 'accidents,' ending up with her shirts wet.

The inability to truly stand up for my daughter, being new to the area and a single mom with no connections, no weight behind my name, pushed me into politics. And there's no better platform, no better way of gaining public support than by riling them up over a common hatred.

Red Acres High Supports a Thriving Pedophile Ring

'Beloved Teachers' at Red Acres High are Pedophiles

One in Eight Children Assaulted by Teachers at Red Acres High

Those were the articles I published online on my blog, printed out, and hung all around the district. The ones I got into the local news, then the national with changed titles.

I had dug into each and every employee at that school. With the statistical average of ten to twenty percent of children suffering an assault at school by a teacher, with that likelihood being a hundred times more likely than assault by a Catholic priest, I'd known that all I had to do was go looking for dirt. And in no time at all, I had found gold.

Disgusting gold in the form of six teachers assaulting a multitude of kids over the years but gold nonetheless.

The public outcry was intense – an inferno, a furious mob demanding justice. And once I was certain the fire could not be put out by the school's PR team, I released my next batch of articles online, wanting their contents to cause more of an uproar than what the local news would report.

Red Acres High Refuses to Fire Pedophiles

Red Acres High Tells Mother Her Ten-Year-Old Son 'Deserved to be Molested' By Mr. Anderson

Red Acres High Asks Pre-teen Girl, 'What Were You

Wearing?' Pants and Long Sleeved Shirt Saying 'Trust In God'

The entire school board was replaced within a week – though none of them lost their pensions. Of the six pedo teachers, four were arrested. The other two were beaten to death in their own homes. Their children were taken away by social services; their partners were run out of state. The state government ended up having to step in to keep the school running and to set up security for the other faculty. People left in droves. A lot of the teachers tried to leave for other schools too, but they couldn't get hired and so they became bus drivers.

The schools wouldn't let them teach in a public setting, but they'd allow them private access to children for hours. The logic behind that was shocking.

And with so many parents not getting off work until long after their children were to arrive home...I feared for the last students off the bus. From that day on, I always made sure to pick up and drop off Scarlett myself. On really busy days, I sent Benjamin, having hired him to be my PA not long after that. His older sister had been raped four years ago at seventeen, and on her graduation day, she'd committed suicide. He blamed himself for having never seen the signs.

My career rocketed after that incident. And when I sat on the school board, I made sure the dress code policy didn't encourage pedophile tendencies, giving them a free pass while blaming our little girls. Scarlett was never sent to the office for 'being a distraction' again, robbing her of vital class time.

But now, ten years later, her education was taking a dive anyway. I talked to my contacts at Flagler College yesterday and know she is failing half her classes. My Little Genius throwing her life away.

Sighing, I finish washing the suds off my skin, then turn

off the shower. I step out onto the brown bath mat, the soft fibers cushioning my wet feet, and grab a towel off the heated railing. Drying first my body, I then bend over and fling my long hair over me to twist it up in the towel. I straighten and grab my phone, turning it on briefly to check the time and to see if there are any messages.

My body heats at the sight of a notification from Derek Greene – a name I'm pretty sure isn't real considering the background check I ran on him came up empty. But I understand his paranoia. If I was the head of the Warriors Against Lycans and Lessers (WALL), a secret organization that went out every night hunting for witches, vampires, and werewolves to capture and kill, I would be paranoid too.

I quickly click on it. No previous messages sit in our chat.

Derek: *I can't wait to fuck your ass tonight.*

Benjamin would kill me for sending a nude, but I swipe the camera around on my phone to face me and hold it up at a flattering angle, cutting off my face and sticking two fingers inside myself. Although I'm fifty-one and have a scar from my C section, Derek and his son Daniel make me feel beautiful.

Hannah: *Maybe Dan can eat my pussy this time while you fuck me.*

I hit send, wait a few seconds, and then delete all evidence before turning off the screen on my phone. Then scowl as I turn it back on to check the time.

Eight-thirteen. I have fifteen minutes to get dressed, my make-up on, and my hair styled and dried.

Walking into my room, I grab the blue dress pants and white blouse Benjamin set out for me yesterday, having laid it over my chair still on the hanger. Throwing them on top of comfortable matching underwear, I settle in the chair and face the mirror.

Five minutes later, my make-up is flawless and natural,

and I work on sorting my hair. Blow dried and lightly curled around my shoulders, the style is approachable and fashionable. Feminine. Motherly – perfect for posing with children.

Benjamin is sitting on the white Oviedo chaise by the back windows, dressed in a crease-free gray suit as I enter the family room. Scarlett is, unsurprisingly, nowhere to be seen.

"Morning, ma'am." He rises to greet me, his southern upbringing combined with him being a military brat making him the definition of respect – a habit he hasn't been able to break despite being in his high twenties.

"Benjamin."

He offers me a paper bag with the logo *Schmagel's* on it, as well as a cup of steaming coffee with milk and two sugars, just the way I like it. I head for the door as he follows behind me, stopping to put on my shoes –dark-blue boots to match my outfit– and grab a small red bag off the hook by the door. Benjamin intercepts me, though, picking up the honey-colored bag beside it. "Cheerful colors, ma'am."

I glance at him, wanting to protest, but I don't. He's a damn good PA and has a keen eye when it comes to public imagery. He's been approached multiple times over the years by my superiors and competition, but his loyalty has never wavered.

Smiling, I nod at him. "Thank you, Benjamin."

Outside on the drive, the driver of my black Lexus is already standing beside its back door. He straightens off the car as we approach, his bald head flashing in the sun, and opens my door for me. No smile graces his face; he takes his job of security too seriously – not that I mind. I'd rather not talk about whatever shit he's into – boxing or football, assumingly. I scoot in, and Benjamin follows behind me.

As we drive through the narrow crowded streets of St.

Augustine, I open the bag from Schmagel's and pull out a warm breakfast sandwich: grilled egg, bacon, and cream cheese in a cheddar-jack bagel.

There's another one inside, so I eat quickly, the ride from here to Flagler Hospital only being a ten minute drive.

"Mark Reynolds rose a percent in the polls overnight," Benjamin says, facing me. His neatly styled hair flashes from brown to black and back again as the sun darts in and out due to the buildings and trees we pass. He scoots his glasses up as his phone dings. He pulls it free from his pocket and glances at it quickly before putting it away again, his full attention back on me.

"That still puts him what, eleven behind?" I say. "With today's photoshoot, I'm sure we'll regain it."

Benjamin nods. "I've screened all the patients, so there will only be ones that photograph nicely. A girl would be better than a boy, but the boys are all particularly cute and young. No acne."

Perfect, I think dryly as I nod. I hate this part of being mayor. The posing. The point grabbing. The need to get re-elected. It all gets in the way of actual work. Instead of dealing with the gangs destroying this city and saving the innocents caught in their crossfire, I'm playing doctor with a bunch of kids that are terminal.

My phone vibrates in my pocket twice, and my blood heats as I know that's a message from Derek. We're to meet tonight to go out hunting for the devil's children, but given the texts we exchanged this morning, I am certain whatever he's sent isn't decent.

Benjamin would be annoyed if he knew I have a sidepiece. He picked out Aaron for me, my image, himself. I was supposed to meet my boyfriend tonight instead of Derek, but I canceled on him yesterday, claiming I would be too busy working this close to elections.

When my PA redirects his attention to his own phone, I

casually pull mine out.

Derek: *Waiting for you.*

A picture of his cock in his hand comes through, and I swallow hard, heat hitting my cheeks.

Glancing at Benjamin, I breathe out slowly and quickly type.

Hannah: *Don't you two start without me.*

My pulse thunders in my chest and in between my ears drowning out the engine of the car as we travel the last few miles to the hospital. Teasing Derek is always a risk depending on what kind of day he's had. Given it's still morning, I reckon he's still in a good mood. A dominating mood rather than a punishing one.

When my phone vibrates again, my breath quickens. Benjamin is still attached to his own phone, so I open the message.

Derek: *We're going to take turns spanking your big ass and pussy for that.*

My lips parting, I stare for a long time at the screen. My thighs are filled with the urge to rub against each other as a wetness pools between them.

Quickly deleting the messages and picture, I put my phone away, then turn to the window. I roll it down a fraction, needing the cool air to hit my cheeks and wipe away all evidence of my arousal before we arrive at the hospital.

If Benjamin suspects anything as the Lexus pulls to a stop, he doesn't say anything. The hospital stretches above us, a multi-story white block building; its appealing and warm architecture belies the cold sterility inside.

I wait for my driver to open my door, and as I step out, I immediately smile at the flash of cameras shoved into my face as we walk to the door.

"What will you be reading to the children today, Ms. Davis?"

"What are your plans for dealing with the increase of crime?"

"Do you ever still think about Red Acres High?"

I turn to search the half dozen faces for the man who asked that question. Benjamin tries to gesture me forward, saying something about being late, but I ignore him.

"I think about that every day," I say, staring directly into his camera. "My own daughter went to that school, and when I learned how close Scarlett was to those sick pedophiles, that was the worst day of my life."

"And yet, you look well rested despite your outing of those student victims directly resulting in six of them taking their own lives."

I stare at him in silence, my brain too in shock over the bluntness, the cruel crassness of his words. I had saved hundreds of others. Six people, four of whom had been delinquents frequently in and out of the principal's office, was not a bad tra–

"Although those deaths were clearly tragic," Benjamin cuts in, standing between me and the dark-haired middle-aged man pointing his microphone at me, "Ms. Davis' actions during that time saved hundreds of future children from suffering that same fate. Now if you'll excuse us, we must head inside."

"One of those six was my daughter!" the journalist shouts as Benjamin leads me the rest of the way to the doors. I flinch as my PA falters one step. But then his strides are back to perfection as he grabs the door and gestures me inside.

"Are you okay?" I murmur as a lady in administration walks towards us, having been waiting for our arrival.

Benjamin nods once but doesn't look at me.

"I'm sorry I stopped," I say. "I shouldn't have –"

His brown eyes flick to mine. "Your fire is what I like about you, ma'am. You're one of the good ones. Don't let his words get to you."

I smile sadly at him. I never knew Rebecca, his sister, but Benjamin visits her grave every year. Her suicide thirteen years ago still weighs on him; I can see it in everything he does.

I reach out and squeeze his arm. "You're one of the good ones too," I say.

He nods, but it lacks conviction. Before I can say more, the administrative lady greets us and leads us towards the children.

THREE

HER

"Brown Rat, Brown Rat, where do you live?"

I sit with a child on my knee – a bald girl with cancer. She smiles beneath the haggard bags clinging to her blue eyes like little parasites. I force my lips up as I squeeze an arm around her bony waist, my heart breaking from the knowledge that she only has twelve weeks to live. Her parents stopped her chemo so she could enjoy her final moments.

Moments like today.

Her mother stands by the back wall with the other few parents, her presence an itch on my skin, her hand to her lips, her eyes wet with a courage she struggles to keep up in the face of her daughter's happiness.

Rare moments of happiness smothered by months of decay.

"White Rabbit, White Rabbit, I live in a burrow!" I say with a false excitement. My stomach tight, I hold up the book so the other kids can see the images of rats playing in their underground nest. The kids sit on their bottoms and knees, looking at me intently, each shifting to try to see the pages better.

A little boy at the back coughs. He's one of the 'less photographic' ones, one of the five Benjamin chose that look properly sick but not so much their presence will cause the public to not want to look at the pictures. Despite what even the democrats and far leftists say, few people are comfortable looking death in the face when it's raw and ugly instead of smiling and peaceful. A negative reaction to the pictures will lead to a negative reaction to me, then to a dip in the polls, and I cannot lose this re-election.

Mark, the democrat running against me, is one of those Christians that are only such on a poll or for public image. In truth, he is an atheist, and he doesn't believe in the devil. I tried to broach the subject with him over lunch a few weeks ago in case, God forbid, I do lose this election, but he stays arrogant in his foolish beliefs. If he wins, thousands will die in the coming months; the gangs have been increasing in activity recently, and I fear what is to come.

Turning the book back around to face me, I wait for the little girl to flip the page. She does so with a giggle. Her mother's tears slip free, and I feel as if they run down my own cheeks.

"Running out of his burrow, Brown Rat sees a Blue Bird pecking in the grass. 'Blue Bird, Blue Bird, where do you live?'"

"A tree!" The words barely out of his mouth, the little boy coughs again, this time setting off a chain reaction. As the girl on my knee joins in, her spittle flying across the pages, a splatter of red, I jump to my feet and set her down away from me. My eyes scan the room for the nurse in attendance.

"There's blood," I say, refusing to look at the girl's mother. The book fell onto the floor as I stood, and the little girl bends down to scoop it up even as she continues to cough.

A choked sob comes from the far side of the room. A silent one comes from me.

"I think that's enough for today," the administrative lady says, and Benjamin nods at me as he comes forward.

I don't want to leave, knowing this will be the last I see of any of them.

But nor do I want to stay.

Grabbing my cheerful bag, I look at the little girl. "You keep the book," I say. "Maybe your mother can finish reading it for you."

"But what about me?" an older boy says. "I want to know what happens too."

The nurse pulls the girl who was on my lap to her, checking her over as the administrative lady says, "We'll have one of the nurses read it to you later. For now, everyone say thank you to Ms. Davis for spending her time here."

A chorus of thank-yous ring out, and I hurry from the room before I can lose my composure.

A woman politician cannot be a bleeding heart.

Once out in the hall, Benjamin hands me a bottle of water, the lid already off. I lift it to my lips hurriedly, my fingers tight on the plastic.

"You did well."

"I didn't make it through the whole book," I say...because we had to get through the posed photos first, the publicity. I take another sip, then hand the bottle back to him.

"Their sickness isn't your fault, ma'am."

No. It isn't anyone's fault, and that's what I hate the most about doing these things. There are no monsters to fight. No one to *stop*. No one to bring justice to.

This place just forces you to accept death even if you aren't ready. Even if it isn't *right*, its victims innocent. Not delinquents or repeat offenders or criminals who got a light sentence or off on a technicality. It is too often little girls and boys who just want to hear the rest of a story.

Dammit.

My body burning with the need to move, I take a step forward, away from all the children I just spent the last hour with, the only hour we will ever share. As we head down the clinical halls to the main entrance, my phone vibrates and I pull it out to check the notification.

Detective Howard: *We have another one.*

My hand clenches around my phone. Henry Howard is one of the two men WALL has at the police department. He's second generation, raised on the truth of the witches, werewolves, and vampires infecting the veins of this great country. He is also the one who brought me into WALL after I'd witnessed a vampire bleeding a girl dry in broad daylight in the woods of Anastasia State Park.

At the time of seeing them, I hadn't realized what was happening. I'd thought he was just fucking her – his lips on her neck, his hand over her mouth, her silver slutty heels twinkling in the intermittent sunlight between the branches. Those heels had been splashed across the news, the police hoping someone would recognize her from them given her body had been so violently butchered, they couldn't get an identity, her teeth and fingerprints both dead ends. She'd never gone to a dentist. Never been arrested. An innocent civilian.

The official reports said she'd died from bleeding out after being stabbed over eighty times across her torso, limbs, neck, and face. Her body had been in so many pieces and with chunks missing that they weren't able to discern which of the stabbings had actually killed her. But found in a pool of her own blood, matched to her DNA, her cause of death was 'easy to discern.'

I would've believed those lies with the rest of the world if it wasn't for Detective Howard. He'd told me that if I wanted to know the truth, then to meet him at Derek's Clubhouse in the middle of the city. It was a bar owned by the WALL, their secret base of operations, and perched on a stool, I listened to the truth with a sickness in my stomach.

"The blood found at the crime scene wasn't hers," he said as he nursed a neat whisky. "Eight months ago, she filed a missing persons report on her twin. There've been no sightings of her, but the detective thinks she ran away to New York to become a star on Broadway. Her friends said that's all she talked about."

Detective Henry Howard reached down to pull out a file. Opening it, he slid a report of another young girl, Kayla Jackson, aged nineteen, to me.

"Six years ago, this victim was stabbed seventy-two times and found sitting in a pool of blood." He tapped the file listing her family. "She also had a twin who'd gone missing in the previous year."

Another file was pulled out. And another. And another, creating a horrible little stack in front of me. "In the last nine decades, sixty women have been murdered. All with missing twins. No killing wound able to be discerned..."

But every single case had been closed, a suspect caught with the murder weapon and charged with life in prison. The vampires were somewhere in the police department. Probably in the courtrooms too.

Inside WALL is the only true sanctuary, he told me, the only substance of truth. And with them, I will eliminate this sickness, these devil children, from my city.

"I need to powder my nose," I say to Benjamin, then slip into a handicapped restroom. Walking to the far end, I press *call* on Howard's number. He picks up after two rings, the sound of chewing coming from the other end.

"What's happened?" I ask quietly, the urge to pace making my muscles itch and flare.

"A werewolf's come in. Human form. Officially, the fucker died of a heart attack."

Fuck, that means it was killed by the witches. Out of the three gangs, I hate them the most. Werewolves and vampires are monsters due to their biology, something they can't change, but witches *choose* to be evil.

"And unofficially?" I ask, glancing at myself in the mirror. I jerk back, rocking onto my short heels as I see something grotesquely twisted crawling out of the glass. Black and smoking, it reaches one gnarled clawed hand through the mirror, which ripples rather than shatters. My fingers squeeze tight on my phone, and I miss what Henry Howard says over the rush of blood between my ears.

But then I blink, and the mirror flattens again, the thing I thought I saw just a trick of my hyper imagination. My skin itching, I head over to the tap. Each step towards the mirror makes my stomach clench tighter, but I ignore it, staying strong. Holding my phone against my shoulder with my head, I place both hands under the cold water.

"Sorry," I say to Howard, interrupting something about dolls. "Can you repeat all that? I lost you for a second there."

I swallow as his chewing vibrates down the phone. My pulse beating hard against my ribs, I hold my blue gaze in the mirror and tell myself the witches don't know I'm involved. I've only been out on three hunts so far, and each time, we killed all the sups –supernatural creatures–we came across. None of them had been witches either.

"The werewolf had a dozen pinpricks over his chest," Henry says, his mouth full with whatever it is he's eating. Probably a meatball footlong. The bin by his desk's always full of Subway wrappers.

"What does that mean?" I ask, pulling my hands out from under the tap and dabbing them over my cheeks. The itch consuming my skin lessens a bit.

"A voodoo doll."

A shudder runs through me as the presence of the mirror prickles my spine again. Not wanting to be alone in the restroom anymore, I quickly wave my hands under the dryer. My eyes keep the mirror in my peripherals, making sure nothing comes out.

"They tortured him for something," Henry continues.

"Any idea of what?" But even as I ask, I know he won't answer. All information goes through Derek first. He's given the members the green light to tell me about any deaths, but the specifics are all kept quiet. It's so we can't be tortured for information, he says. But I reckon it's more because of his paranoia. Derek doesn't trust anyone.

Not that I blame him.

Walking backwards, still facing the mirror, I head for the door.

"Nope, but I don't think the mutt gave it up."

"How can you tell?"

"They tattooed a death rune on his arm. Until this body decays, his soul is theirs to torture."

Ice spears my stomach. My blue gaze trembles on the mirror. "They can do that? Split one's soul from their body?"

"Mmm. Make a deal with the devil," Detective Howard says as he takes another bite of his lunch, "and you can do anything."

The glass of the mirror ripples again, and I jerk, hitting the restroom door with my back. Grabbing the handle, I want to wrench it open and tumble out. But I force myself to still. Benjamin doesn't know about the WALL, like most people don't, and I can't go out looking like I've seen a monster. If there are any lingering reporters, someone will undoubtedly twist the facts to say I was traumatized over being near sick children.

"I've got to go," Howard says as someone else's muffled voice comes down the line. "But I'll see you tonight if you want more info."

"Thanks," I say, my heart in my throat as I keep my eyes on the mirror. It's flat again. Normal. Shaking my head, I take a deep breath. "I'll see you tonight."

Hanging up the phone, I grope for the door handle behind me, then quickly twist around and exit.

Nothing grabs me to drag me back into the mirror. The door clicks shut. Benjamin looks up from his phone. "The car's been brought around, ma'am."

The hospital continues its routine of normality.

There are no demon children here. The witches don't know I know about them. Exhaling slowly as we walk to the exit, I try to get my heart rate back down.

But it's fucking hard when in the back of my mind, I know I'm a dead woman walking.

It's only a matter of time.

FOUR

HIM

My girl will be here soon. I have waited months for her, and now only a few more days separate us being together. The crawl of my skin beckons a shift in time, a use of magic that has her under me at this moment. *Now.*

My fingers tighten with unwanted control as the smell of her consumes me – beckons me like a phantom touch of her pussy grinding against my lips.

Like she did this morning.

Like she could be doing before the week is over.

But not sooner, as much as I wish it. Playing with time, although mentioned in the whispered tales of possibility, only comes with uncontrollable destruction. Magic is a volatile entity that pushes against one's command, a dark curse of power that wishes to see the world in its natural state of ordered entropy. To use it without specific focus, to let it run wild in all its possibilities (necessary to bend something as vast as time) would, at best, kill me. At worst, it would grab the attention of the archangels – the seven males responsible for keeping the universe in tight order. The seven males more feared than the wrath of the gods themselves.

So I fight the urge to attempt to bend time to my will. I will not be robbed of life before I even get the chance to slide my cock into my girl's gorgeous holes.

My lips roll in, and my tongue darts across them. I can still taste her there in the depths of my mind. But I have licked and sucked on them so much today, her sweet taste is long gone from my skin.

Tonight, I will have to bury my head between her thighs for longer. Until my entire mouth is full of her taste for the whole fucking day.

My cock presses painfully against the tightness of my jeans, but I ignore its prominence despite knowing my mother and brothers can see it as they keep an eye on the room, on me and the groggy soul of the werewolf just now coming to, through the black solid walls with their magic. Runes burn bright red, green, and blue across the floor, walls, and ceiling – a collection of old magic that increases my power (red), drains that of anyone not of our family's bloodline (blue), and contains the souls we've torn from the bodies of our enemies (green).

Lying on the floor in front of me, surrounded by a circle of magic, Cid Garcia flickers between his human and werewolf forms –both being his true identity– as his soul struggles to pick a state without a vessel of flesh binding it.

He jerks upright, half-werewolf, half-human in his translucent self. His green eyes widen, then narrow as he realizes the truth of his situation.

He will not survive this ordeal.

He is already dead, just on borrowed time.

Time I solely command.

As his eyes bore into me, the hairs on my arms and neck stand at attention. The circle of magic should keep him contained, but if he manages to break it, his soul will be able to attack mine.

He could drag me into the afterlife with him while I'm still technically alive, making it so I can never be reborn, forever cursed to walk the planes of purgatory alone as he continues the cycle of life and death.

Then my girl will be on her own.

Unprotected.

There for him to find and take his revenge on.

Rage consuming me, I pluck a pin from the air, shaped by the purity of magic, its smoky lime-green form both a solid and a gas, and slam it into the stone figurine I have in my other hand. The one that I crafted to look like Cid, the one connected to his very soul due to my magic and the drops of blood I took from his body before ripping out his soul.

His soul jerks on the ground as unfathomable pain arcs through him, twisting his body as he growls and snarls and flutters between man and beast.

The claws of a werewolf.

The teeth of a man.

The eyes of a beast that fasten on me when I remove the pin.

His chest moves heavily.

And then he's on his feet and lunging.

The circle of magic flares bright red and drops him to his knees, the barrier keeping him in. Contained.

For now.

Sweat beads on my brow as I pull on the magic of the runes etched around me, my system already becoming strained. Their heat feeds me, the energy of my ancestors who crafted this room flowing through me, rooting me with their strength.

Werewolves have natural resistance to magic, and Cid is a strong fucker even for their kind. He is the youngest son of the alpha – powerful, virile, respectable. He killed four witches while he was being brought in – experienced witches high up in our ranks.

The deep anger of his existence reaches the wall of my ears, and I look at him without emotion, pushing thoughts of my girl out. His pained and furious eyes drop to the stone figurine in my hand. The pin disappearing, I place the figure down on the floor in front of me and pick up one of the four other uncrafted alexandrite stones on my right.

The dark-green gems are rare and impossible to get hold of on Earth in the size and purity required even with our large financial reach. My ancestors brought a private collection over when they first passed through the portals from our home world of Blódyrió two millennia ago. Once our collection is gone, we will have no way to restock it.

But their extravagant use in this moment is worth the waste. In the last four months, the werewolves' violence against the vampires has been heating up, and we need to know why, if we're next, and how they're managing to wipe out the vampires all of a sudden, after two thousand years of a stalemate.

A growl emits from Cid Garcia as his ethereal shape flickers between forms.

My fingers work on the piece of alexandrite I picked up, conducting my magic to flow inside its brilliant green walls. It heats like a rock in a fire, and my digits move faster, attempting to stay cool. Filled with energy, the gem starts to change shape, molded into an image familiar to the werewolf.

I place it down on the floor in front of me beside the stone that looks like him.

"Tell me what your father is planning," I say as I pick up another piece of uncrafted alexandrite, but my words are lost under his howls of rage and the thrashing of his soul bouncing off the magic barrier.

Sweat pours down my neck as my fingers tighten on the alexandrite. Forcing them to relax, making sure I don't mold one part incorrectly, I draw more power from the runes around me. Working with soul dolls requires a high attention to detail. One wrongly shaped part can ruin the whole spell, giving the magic a way out of its confines to burn the world around me.

My body hums with volatile magic, and for a moment I am battered by both the werewolf and my own power. Sharp claws dig into my soul. Chaotic energy burns it. Blood blossoms in my lungs as both wish to see me dead, but I will not go and leave my girl unprotected.

Lifting my gaze to Cid, I slam out with my magic, giving it an outlet other than me. The tattoos of runes across my flesh light up with red energy – the color of our family's power. Wind rushes across the room, dropping him to his knees. His ragged breaths intermingle with choked snarls. The magic, for now, is sated.

"If you hurt her," Cid growls as he lifts his head to face me, having the nose of a wolf but the chin of a man, "I will hunt you down in the afterlife."

He knows there's no survival for him. I respect his instant acceptance – no pathetic groveling, no pitiful denial. Because of that, I hold up the piece of alexandrite I'm working on and grant him a bit of mercy through knowledge.

"This will become Abril," I say. His oldest daughter. The first stone after him was shaped into that of his wife Elena. I pick up the next stone in the line of natural alexandrite. "Your boy Jorge." I rub it in between my fingers for a moment before placing it back in line and tapping the next one. "Your feisty whore Rei." I glance up at him, my eyes hardening. "Elena is first so she doesn't suffer the truth of your infidelity."

Even if we weren't enemies, I would kill him for that

alone. Men should worship their girls. Give them the world they deserve. And the only justice for a cheater is death.

Glancing away from him, I pick up the last gem and hold it close to my face, looking it over. "Pretty little Zita," I murmur. Cid's youngest daughter. The one Maddox, my youngest brother, is obsessed with. But he hasn't claimed her yet, and so she is free to be tortured.

"Don't you fucking touch her."

My eyes find Cid's face again, but his gaze is on the rock. I tsk. "A father shouldn't have favorites," I chastise as I put the stone back down.

"I will find you after death." His soul vibrates with his anger, but I pay the threat little heed. He does not know which gods I worship, which of the three underworlds I will go to when I die: Niflhel ruled by Hel, the Otherworld ruled by Arawn, or the Underworld ruled by Hades. But even if we do end up in the same one, I'm under no illusion that we will be sent to anywhere but the darkest realm of it. We might be tortured side by side, but we will never get to torture each other. No fun is allowed.

Pushing my magic into Abril's stone, I hold his gaze. "Tell me what your father is planning."

He lunges for me again in his rage.

A trapped rage he can't expel or do anything with.

As Cid Garcia continues his pointless rampage, the circle flaring up red around him, I finish crafting his eldest daughter's image and move to pick up Jorge's stone. Then Rei's. His curses intensify. The runes around me flare red as I pull on more and more power. Sweat pours down my back, but he can't smell it in his soul form, his senses reduced to just touch, hearing, and sight.

Knowing I'm getting nowhere, I put Rei's stone down and pick up his wife Elena's. Holding his gaze, I form a ball of fire in my other palm.

He slams against the bindings of his cage, his blows felt

across my body as the magic connects us, punishing me for controlling it. Blood trickles up my throat again with his newest ram, but I swallow it down. The metallic taste fills me, and for a moment, I think of my girl. Her taste on my lips. The start of my claim.

My cock jerks, and Cid glares at it.

"You sick fucking bastard."

I smile as I curl my fingers around Elena's stone and rub the back of my knuckles against my hard-on. "What is your father planning?" I ask, my voice betraying not a single ounce of my pain and exhaustion from keeping his soul caged. It would've been easier to hold him in his physical form, but we need to send a message to the Garcia Family: we will not sit idly by, waiting for our turn to be attacked.

"Fuck you."

"Fuck Elena," I say dismissively as I drop her stone into the fire. Her screams roll around the room, pulled from her body, wherever it is, as it suddenly bursts into flame.

"Elena!" The new voice is loud, very close to her, and I raise a brow as Cid trembles, his fists clenched. Every time she makes a noise, we're able to hear those around her as well.

"What is your father doing so close to your wife?" I ask mockingly.

"Fuck y—" He stops as I pick up his eldest daughter's stone.

"Is he fucking her like you're fucking Rei?"

Cid's soul solidifies as a full werewolf for just a second, sending shivers down my spine. My fingers flex around Abril's stone as I prepare myself for another attack. If he can keep his soul into that of his wolf, he'll be able to rip his way through the magic circle. In less than a second, he'll be on me, a werewolf's speed unmatched.

"If you kill her, they'll come for you." His face twists with agony as her screams falter and his father's shouts of concern and command to others nearby echo stronger.

I shrug. "They will already come after us for killing you."

I lift Abril's stone to above the fire, right above her mother's. The flame is purposefully weak, although Cid can't tell without touching it. Its white hot flames burn bright, but its temperature is controlled by my magic to be relatively cold. Elena and the rest of Cid's loved ones are to suffer, not go out in a burst of flame before they can even scream.

An anguished cry comes from Cid, and his soul flickers rapidly between man and wolf. I drop Abril's stone into the fire.

"Stop!" he shouts, and I still, holding his gaze. "If I tell you what I know," he grits out, "will you release your curse of Elena and Abril?"

"You better talk quickly," I say. "Poor Elena sounds like she's already dying."

Abril's screams overtake her mother's, but hers are alone. No one there to try to put out the flames. No one there to comfort her.

"Mom!" she sobs, her cries muffled under something crashing around her and the roar of the flames. "Dad! Someone...please help me!"

"Abril, baby, just –"

"She can't hear you," I cut in, picking up Jorge's stone. His only son. His heir. But not his favorite. Perhaps I should skip the line and go directly to Zita.

No. There is chaos without order.

And I am a man of my word. Jorge is next, then his whore Rei, then Zita.

"He's trying to make hybrids," Cid spits, dropping to his knees, a proud man forced to beg.

The door opens behind me. "Burn them, Khalid," my mother says as she enters.

I incline my head as I curl my fingers around the ball of

fire. It explodes up, its heat sucking the air from the room as Cid screams with a raw fury. He slams himself against the cage, and it falters for a moment as blood spurts out of my mouth. I grunt as I lash out with my own power, forcing him back as the flames grow ever higher, ever hotter.

"Daddy!" Abril screams.

"Elena!"

"You can't save her!" someone shouts, the sounds of a scuffle bleeding through the flames.

Their voices fade, Cid's wife's whimpers extinguished forever. Now it's only Abril's screams filling the room. Pathetic and desperate, she begs for her father to save her. Does she know she is dying because of him?

I bow forward as a blow ruptures across my stomach. Blood sprays across the black floor, and I wipe it free of my mouth as I straighten. Cid is slamming back and forth against the cage, attacking every part of it, hoping for a weakness somewhere. His form solidifies into that of his wolf, and with a chilling howl, he lunges straight up.

He's found the weakness.

His claws dig into the shield, and for a moment, he hangs as power crackles across his body, a circuit for pure agony. Snarling, he fights through it, his arm and back muscles bunching as he pulls himself up.

Mother walks past me and to the werewolf's cage, her footsteps sure and unafraid – *foolish*. Cursing, I increase the power of the flames, and Abril's screams are snuffed out just as Cid manages to rip through the magic circle.

Chaotic energy rips across the room, the broken magic uncontrollable, and I'm tossed back as I throw up a shield around Mother. My head snaps against the wall. I crush Jorge's stone in my fist, my magic killing him quickly.

Mother stays standing just in front of the werewolf, a billowing vortex of blue energy surrounding her as I use my power so she doesn't have to. Cid lunges for her neck, and the runes around me glow red as I dart forward to intercept him.

Our souls touch. Agony burns through the both of us, like bolts of electricity made of knives dipped in acid and salt. I scream as he howls. My body curls in on itself, but Mom's close presence forces me to fight through the pain.

"Don't!" I shout at her as the air around her crackles.

Holding my arm out to the stones, I call Cid's to me. It flies towards my palm, and I pull a pin out of the hot electrified air. The stone slaps my hand as I shove Cid's soul away from me. All the runes in the room burn red, and I slam the pin into his soul doll. He jerks on a howl, his claws brushing my leg.

Blood ruptures from my lips as I kick him away and pull into existence another pin of energy.

"Areic poland eockin viltovar," I chant, stabbing his stone in the heart and finally releasing his soul from this world. The runes around me and Mother glow bright blue, keeping us safe from the rapid release of energy exploding from where he stood.

Mother stands unmoving, her long black hair billowing around her. My fingers press into the floor as my body shudders against the onslaught of power. Magic does not care who it attacks. If I cannot control it, if I am too weak from pain, it will just as greedily take my life as it will my enemies.

When the room finally settles, I cough up more blood. Dealing directly with souls requires the energy of your own to do it, and exhaustion hits me with all its force. More blood sprays across the floor; pain quakes from my chest, Cid's blows still resonating inside my soul. As I shudder on my hands and knees, Mother kneels in front of me.

"You did well, Khalid," she says. Reaching out, she touches my forehead. "Now rise. We need to discuss how to kill the Garcia line."

Her magic flows through me, warm and soothing, but I move away, knowing the drain it has on her these days. She's been cursed, and the more she uses magic, the more it will consume her until it eventually kills her.

Rising to my feet, I glare at her. "You should not have entered," I say.

She waves away my concerns. "I brought you into this world, son. It's going to take more than a measly curse of your father's to take me out of it."

"Why did you?"

"Give birth to you? It's a woman's responsibility –"

My glare hardens, not in the mood to listen to her jokes. Although a woman's top duty in this family is to breed, to give birth to healthy sons and daughters that can strengthen our footing in our wars against the vampires and werewolves, she knows that was not my question.

Exasperated, Mother says, "You know the dangers of breeding hybrids, Kal. They will cause an imbalance –"

"Catching the attention of the archangels and damning us all," I finish, but the words don't have meaning in this moment. They do not explain why she entered when we could've just talked about this after I finished Cid off myself.

But the door opens before I can push for the truth. Maddox, my youngest brother, strolls in and makes no effort to hide his concern. Walking straight over to Zita's untouched stone, he surrounds it in his magic. The strands of auburn hair I bound inside the alexandrite pulls free between his fingers, making the stone just a stone, no longer connected to her.

He winds the strands around his fingers, then brings them to his lips as he turns to face us.

"Claim her or leave her, Maddox," Mother says sternly, her green eyes on him. "A war is coming, and she must know where her loyalty lies."

He grins as he pockets her hair. "Don't try to change the

subject, bruh. You shouldn't have entered."

"You shouldn't have let me then. Now come," she says, heading for the door, efficiently changing the subject. "We must discuss how to kill Antonio Garcia before he does us."

My eyes find Maddox, the concern for Mother mirrored back at me. Then he shrugs. *What can we do?* And turns to follow her out.

My fist loosens, releasing the dust of the alexandrite. I wipe my palm on my jeans, gritting my teeth as my body aches with the agony of broken bones and stab wounds – phantom pains that will linger for days as my soul heals. Rolling my shoulders, I spit out the blood still pooling in my mouth. Reminded of the blood of my girl again, I smile.

A war is coming.

I make my way for the door.

So I must bring her in before it burns across this city, which means...

Soon.

Soon she will be mine.

FIVE

HIM

As soon as I step out of the room, Mother and Maddox nowhere to be seen, Varius pins me with his glare.

"You shouldn't have let her enter," my oldest brother says, his flat voice hiding his ire. He leans against the wall, his muscular arms crossed. It's a look I see often. Disappointed Varius is going to make a great father.

My teeth flash in a bloody smile. "And how would you propose I did that? I stopped her from using her magic –"

"And yet, you walk easily. I saw how much blood you spat up. How Cid grabbed you. You should be in a ball on the floor."

My smile turns into a sneer. Ever since we were young, Varius has been a stoic pain in the ass. His shoulders bear the weight of responsibility proudly, never sagging. When Father left us, Varius stepped into the role at twelve. I was ten, and overnight, I went from having an annoying older brother to a *super* annoying older brother who kept trying to put me in time out.

Bloody lips and noses filled our every day, and Maddox came up with a great acrostic that describes him perfectly:

Verifiable

Asshole

Reigns

Insufferably

Upon

Shadows

Smirking, I start to walk past him – being the 'better man,' something that is sure to piss him off.

But just as I reach him, I can't help myself.

Clasping him on the shoulder, I turn my head towards his. "You know...not all of us are as weak as you are, Vay-vay."

My grin widens as I take another step, but it's quickly lost as I stagger face-first into a wall. Blood punches up from my lungs and splays across the green paint as agony rips up my spine.

"Not all of us rely solely on magic, dumbass," he mocks as he steps past me. The urge to crumble to the floor is beat back only by the refusal to give him that victory. Biting back a groan from the force of his punch, I glare at his back even as a smile tugs at my lips. My six other brothers and I all constantly take the piss out of his lack of magic, but when it comes to a fight, Varius can hold his own against werewolves and vampires just as well as the rest of us. Granted, he cheats by using spelled items like those damn rings of strength he always wears.

But still, for one whose ascension never came –that time of magical puberty where vampires gain the ability to phase (teleport), werewolves gain control over their shift, witches gain the ability to cast spells, and all our bodies start to heal themselves, albeit at different rates– Varius isn't a total waste of space.

Spitting more blood past my lips, I straighten, then wipe

at my mouth. By the time I take a step forward, my blood is gone, having seeped into the bones of this house, keeping it fed with our power.

I walk down the hall and into the rustic kitchen of Mother's home. Where humans converse and greet guests in the living room, witches prefer to use the 'original spellroom,' where potions were once mixed beside cakes.

My seven brothers are sprawled out around the place as Mother stands in front of the S-shaped counter facing them. Varius, Talon, Leno, and the twins sit around the large table.

Talon is a capo in Shadow Domain, running our legit side of things, our hotels and landscaping businesses, as well as our Floridian network of drugs. He has his 'talons' in everything and got his nickname from Maddox when we were kids.

Sitting beside him is Leno with his pet familiar Krypto. Having lost his eyesight due to a brawl with a werewolf when he was younger, he rarely goes anywhere without his seeing eye dog, a dog that can literally *see* for him. Krypto sits at Leno's feet, getting his head scratched. He's a mutt with beautiful red fur and a curly tail, but it's his ears I love the most. They're massive and point up high.

Across from Talon and Leno are the twins Enoch and Ezriel. The double Es, Batman and Robin, the Shining Burns – all names Maddox has bestowed on them over the years. They're telekinetic, and their magic nearly doubles when they're together.

Maddox and Rudy, the two youngest, perch on the stools at the rich wooden counter. It curves twice, dividing the cooking area from the table, unnatural knots twisted in its grain, power humming from them like a soft lullaby.

Rudy is the cleaner of the Family. Any time we commit a crime, he goes and cleans up the place. He likes to dance while he does it –an all around bucketful of sunshine– but out of everyone here, he's also the darkest given his magic twists one's fears into reality. Thank the gods, he's not as shitty as Maddox, who would definitely terrorize the lot of us.

Settling between my brothers at the counter, I rib Maddox out of my way. He shoves me back, his magic seeking the bruises on my soul. Blood rises in my throat, and Mom leans over to smack him. My youngest brother tries to shy away, but she lands a blow across the back of his head.

"Hey!" he says, raising his hands to fix his 'stylish' mess of black hair. He makes me want to ruffle it up again, but he's quick to lash out. My magic has already given me a beating, and I want to be well enough to go out hunting werewolves tonight.

Mother pins Maddox with her green eyes as she pulls on an apron patterned with black cats riding brooms. "Don't think that just because you're twenty-two now," she says, tying a knot behind her, "that you're too old for a spanking." Then she turns her gaze to Varius as he leans back in his chair at the head of the table. "And you. Stop treating me like I'm frail. I'll be a thousand and still have the strength to shove you back up my womb."

"Ew, Mom!" Talon, son number six, shouts as he covers his ears.

I groan along with the rest of my seven brothers, the images suddenly assaulting me ones I never wished to see.

"Oh please," she says as she grabs seven onions from a bottom drawer. "I've seen the porn you all watch."

"Mom!"

She cackles, taking delight in our pain. Her eyes land on someone behind me, and I turn my head to see it's Talon. Chills rush down my spine as my ears burn and I tense in anticipation of whatever ungodly horrors Mom's about to release.

"I was okay with you watching werewolves fuck each

other in both their forms, T," she says, "but watching them shit in each other's mouths first? That's just –"

"I don't watch that!" he sputters as he jumps to his feet, knocking his chair onto the floor. It skitters across the wooden planks before banging against the light-blue wall.

"I think thee protests too much." Maddox grins as he elbows me, lighter this time.

"And you," Mom says, turning to him as she places the onions on the zebrano counter.

"How are we going to kill the Garcias?" my youngest brother blurts, his voice soldier-like as he leans forward.

She eyes him for a moment longer, and the whole room tenses as we wait to see if Mother accepts the change of subject.

Shit. She's not going to –

When she opens a drawer to pull out a knife, the fear in the air dissipates.

Thank gods.

The last thing I want to know is what my twisted little brother gets off to. I already have shitting werewolves and Varius going back up Mom's –

I slash out at my soul, magic erupting inside me. Pain flares through me like ice shards hit with lightning, but it's a welcome reprieve from the images that were about to toss around my skull.

Mom looks at me dryly as she pulls out a cutting board. "Antonio's death," she says as she starts to peel and cut the onions, "will create a vacuum of power in this city. He has ruled the wolves for decades, long before any of you were born."

"We know," Maddox says, then immediately ducks as one of the onions comes flying at his face. I snap my arm out, catching it before it can go much further past his head, not wanting to risk her retrieving it with her magic. Her stubbornness will be the death of her.

And me.

And Varius given I can sense the lock of his jaw as he stares at her.

"Don't be a little shit." Mother holds up her hand, and I toss the vegetable back to her. Cutting it, she says, "His reign started without a drop of blood, if you can believe it. There was a time when he spoke only of peace between our species. Where he asked us to look past our centuries of hate –"

"The furries sold our grandparents out to the Spanish," Maddox spits. "They dissected us for years. And Antonio thought what, we'd just forget?"

"And we taught the natives how to skin them so they could wear their fur," Talon says.

"We were helping them survive a harsh winter while they fought the Spanish. That practically makes us Jesus." Maddox snorts as he turns to face him. "But of course you would back them. But, bruh, you're not supposed to simp over the porn actors." A yelps leaves his lips without Talon ever having moved.

I catch the onion that bounces off the back of his head and place it down on the counter. Mother smiles at me, but her words are for Maddox. "What did I tell you about being a little shit?"

He waits until the last onion is diced before mumbling, "At least I don't like watching werewolves eating it."

Even Mom snickers while Talon glares at Maddox in silence. He knows if he protests, that'll just set the little shit off more. Maddox is the baby of this family, eleven years younger than me, and four and a half years younger than his closest brother Rudy. He was a last-ditch effort for our parents to rekindle their marriage.

Meaning Maddox was a failure before he was even born.

And so Mother spoils him, making sure she loves him enough for two. Not that Father ever loved us.

Although Varius and Leno, the two oldest, say they remember his warm smiles and crushing hugs, I reckon they lie, their brains twisting memories or making them up entirely just so Father's rejection doesn't hurt so much.

I smother a snort. *Not that it matters now.*

He died putting a curse on Mom – hating her so much he gave his life to the dark magic in order to strengthen it. There is always a way to break a curse, but the curser is the one who decides what that is, and Father died, taking that answer with him.

A blessing of mercy considering what I would've done once I got my hands on him.

Containing her smile, Mom turns to rummage around the kitchen. "Antonio Garcia has been alpha for over a century," she continues. "He has made a lot of alliances in this time, a lot of enemies too. With his death and the death of his Family..." She pulls out a pot and places it on the stove. A dash of oil goes inside. "Wolves will come in from all over the U.S., trying to claim his territory."

"Which is why we haven't already killed him," Varius says, forever the dutiful student. Despite Antonio's anger over Cid's death, it is, in fact, insignificant in the piles of bodies that have washed this city. They kill one of us. We kill one of them. We break bread in a few days. Such is the way of power and alliances. But *his* death...

Mom nods. "And why they have not killed Aleric or us."

Aleric Zadar is the leader of the vampires, and he is so hated, a likeness of him used to stand in Mom's basement, a target dummy that took the full force of her wrath every night. Varius removed it after she was cursed, worried she'd risk death just to desecrate his face over and over again with her magic.

Mother dumps in the onions, and they sizzle as they hit the hot oil. "If we kill Antonio, we also kill the peace of the last thirty-eight years. Death will touch us all."

Maddox scowls and rolls his eyes. "There is not much *peace* left. The suckies keep encroaching on our territory, and the furries keep cutting into our businesses. I say we kill them all and rule St. Augustine on our own."

She smiles at him as she continues to cook, then her gaze sweeps across the room. "It might very well come to that. You must decide if that is a future you wish to see."

"But they're trying to create hybrids," Varius says, and our future is clear as day. We will fight. There is no other option. "If Antonio manages to succeed in good number, he'll catch the attention of the archangels, and they'll kill every sup in this city."

Probably further. The archangels uphold the balance in the universe, and they do not take kindly to anything that threatens that. They allow children to be conceived from two different races as long as they are born with only one set of power. A hybrid, though, is an abomination that takes magical genes from both parents, coming out more powerful than both – and more deranged. Their kind is abhorred across the entire Seven Planes, their mothers hunted down during pregnancy, their wombs ripped open and the babies burned.

Their mere existence doesn't draw the attention of the archangels as they are few and far in between, but if Antonio actually manages to create them *en masse*, then none of us will survive.

The archangels are not known for their mercy.

One of them –Azreal, the Bringer of Death– sucks the souls of his kills into his own body, trapping them forever beneath his skin as grotesque tattoos that helplessly claw over each other in their attempt to find freedom.

A shiver arching through me, I shift on my stool. The archangels will kill my girl, seeing her as one of us sups given I marked her last night, starting the blood ritual that will take her from the human reality and bring her into ours. My pulse kicks up. The urge to kill Antonio Garcia soon consumes me.

"We've already killed his youngest son," I say, turning to Varius, the head of this Family. As much as we all respect Mother and follow her advice, the final decisions come from my oldest brother. "They'll retaliate tonight. Antonio was with Elena, and his concern for her was more than that of a father-in-law."

Varius holds my gaze, leaning back in his chair, his thick arms crossed, his face unreadable despite his earlier support for going to war.

"Cid's body has just been picked up from the morgue," Talon says as he glances at his phone, and the very air in the room holds its breath.

"So?" Maddox cuts in, oblivious in his youth. "They already know we killed him and his bitch."

"And eldest daughter," Rudy, son number seven, signs. He was born unable to talk, Mother having taken a blast of magic while he was in her womb. He is lucky that is the only thing magic took from him. One of our soldiers recently gave birth to a baby so twisted, it felt wrong calling it human. Or maybe that is just what I tell myself since I was given the task of ending its life before it could bite off its umbilical cord.

The wet sounds of chewing mixes with infant laughter in my mind. I push it down.

To leave dark magic to fester is to bring death to all those you love. I did what I had to. As the Family reaper, it is my duty to kill any of those we call friends.

Holding Rudy's green eyes, I sign back, "Don't forget his son."

A grin curls his lips. "I haven't. But Antonio wasn't fucking him."

I raise a brow. "You know this for certain?"

He glances at Varius, no doubt feeling the heat of anger

boring into his skull. Varius doesn't like anyone holding back any information. A control freak through and through, he's desperate to provide structure where life and the hands of Fate do not.

Rudy shrugs nonchalantly. "I did tell you," he signs, his hands moving in front of him, "but you weren't looking at me."

Varius' eyes narrow as the rest of us chuckle.

"Cid might have become an ally with that information," Varius says flatly, killing our humor.

Chucking more food into the pot, making it sizzle loudly, Mother adds, "Cid never would have turned on Antonio. He was too weak to take on the alpha, and he knew it. If he ever became an ally, he would've turned on us to gain favor."

Varius' gaze lifts to hers, and the tension eases a bit from his face. He nods at her to continue.

I swivel back on my stool to face her, as do my two brothers sitting at the counter beside me.

"The significance of Antonio picking up Cid's body," she says, looking at her youngest son, "is it means he's planning on consuming Cid's flesh."

The Garcia Family has always eaten their dead, but they've also always left those killed by magic, not wanting to risk any nasty side effects. Although werewolves have a strong resistance to magic, they still have an aversion to it, like a cat to rotten meat.

"Antonio will gain Cid's power." The aroma of a rich tomato sauce fills the room. "He might even eat Elena, Abril, and Jorge too. If he does, he'll be too strong for any of you to take on individually." Her green eyes land on me. "Even you, love. You are strong, but you are young."

Antonio is pushing two hundred and eleven, nearly a century older than Mother. And with age comes power, faster speed, and faster healing. I nod, letting her know I am not stupid enough to be reckless.

I will not die before getting a lifetime with my girl.

"So you must attack him in pairs at the very least." She reaches into a cupboard and grabs a variety of herbs to chuck into the pot. Heather. Horehound. Thyme.

I glance at Maddox, knowing we will be paired. For all the ribbing that goes on between us, our magic is the most compatible.

"And we will attack tonight," Varius says from behind me. "Before Antonio has a chance to consume the fallen."

Mother looks at him, her face blank of any desires. "Why?" she asks, ever the teacher.

"Because it doesn't matter if there's a chasm of power that is filled with blood and bodies. Anything is better than an archangel's arrival."

A smile of approval graces her lips as her gaze sweeps across the room. "Remember that, boys. When you're knee deep in bodies and cradling the fallen, remember that we cannot stop before Antonio is dead."

"We won't." Maddox's words come out as a growl, a hardening from his earlier flippancy. And I wonder if he's thinking that if Antonio was fucking both Cid's wife and eldest daughter...if he's touching Zita too.

If anyone touched my girl...

Standing abruptly, I nod at Mother, then turn to Varius. "I'm going to go rest," I say before glancing at the hall. He nods at me, dismissing me from this meeting, but I do not head for my room upstairs.

Instead, I head outside to my car, get into the dark-blue Buick, and drive to my own house.

My girl will be getting home soon, and I cannot rest without checking in on her first.

A war is coming.

A small chuckle escapes me as the tarmac runs beneath my tires.

A war is already here.
And now I *must* bring in my girl.

SIX

HER

Sitting alone in the backseat, I am driven through the streets of St. Augustine. Benjamin was left at his car at the city hall, where my driver picks him up every morning. The low hum of the engine is the only sound, interrupted by the vibration of my phone. I glance at it, half expecting to see a text from Benjamin despite both of us having just finished our day.

Derek: *Bring your daughter tonight. It's about time she joins us.*

A frown pools on my face. Although I have tried to talk to Scarlett about the truth of the gangs plaguing these streets, she always ends the conversation with a laugh and a quick, "Good joke, Ma."

My fingers swipe across the phone multiple times, but each sentence I immediately delete.

Hunts are dangerous.

But staying ignorant is even more so... And she is an adult now.

Perhaps Derek is right.

Maybe it's time to throw her into the deep end so she doesn't drown when she goes back to college, away from my and Derek's secret protection.

My fingers start typing again.

But once again, the sentence is deleted.

Rubbing my forehead, I glance out the window.

I have seen two members die right in front of me – both having come back from hunts I wasn't allowed to go on. For all of Derek's hatred of the witches, vampires, and werewolves, he doesn't risk our lives just for the sake of killing one.

He's calculated and smart.

He won't endanger Scarlett. My support offers him too many favors to risk.

Unless you lose this election, a small voice says.

But I crush it.

Even without my power protecting him and his crew from prosecution when they break laws, even without me greasing the hands of judges or getting police officers to 'lose' evidence, I am still of value.

My reach across this city is far from just political. People owe me favors. Powerful people that Derek cannot gain an audience with himself.

Some of my nerves settling, I finally hit send.

Hannah: *I will bring her.*

My street comes into view. I straighten, my body tensing as my gaze fastens back out the window. I sit on the left side of the car, and as we near my house, I look for Khalid. A kegel involuntarily spasms through me at the sight of his car in his drive. *He's home.*

Better yet, he's standing beside it shirtless, a bucket of suds by his feet. His back is to me, and the bulges and valleys of his muscles ripple as he stretches across the roof of his car. His dark-blue jeans hug his tight ass as he works the sponge across the dark-blue metal of his Buick.

I want to tell my driver to stop on this side just so I can watch Khalid, but instead, I simply raise my phone to start a quick video to watch later in the privacy of my bed.

His head turns, and my breath catches as my thumb hovers over the camera. My body tight, I don't move even though he can't see me through the dark tinted windows.

Another kegel pulses through me, and I do a few more, imagining squeezing his cock as it pushes into me. He turns his head, his attention back on his car, and then we're in our drive, and I realize I never pressed start on the video.

Dammit.

Sighing, I put my phone away and grab my cheerful purse, ready to get out of the car once my door is opened. My driver stands beside it, closes it behind me, and then nods as he heads towards his own car parked in my drive.

"Thank you," I say, searching for a name but coming up empty.

If it bothers him, it's not shown in his voice. "My pleasure, ma'am," he says smoothly. He pockets his set of my keys for tomorrow, then digs his own out of his suit.

Turning away from him, I look across my yard to Khalid. He watches me, his brown eyes making me want to strip off my clothes and let him take me against the side of his car.

Smiling, I walk over to him. "It's a hot day, isn't it, Khalid?"

He nods, his arm moving across the windshield of his car, dripping water. My eyes latch onto his strong fingers as they squeeze the sponge, and I can almost feel them moving inside me. My thighs clench, and I clear my throat, trying to work past the heat drying it out.

"Um...uh." I swallow before stretching my smile again. "While you're already out here and all wet..." Another swallow. My eyes on his fingers again. "Would you mind washing my car too? I can pay you with a beer inside..." Heat flushes my cheeks, but I force my eyes to meet his, the image of his head between my legs giving me courage. "Or..."

But before I can suggest something else, he nods. "I'll do it now."

He straightens, then reaches down to grab his bucket.

"Oh, thanks." Wetting my lips, I stammer for air before managing, "Thank you." Wincing at the repeat, I swivel on my heels before he can see my embarrassment. I might be fifty-one and well experienced, but fuck, he makes me feel like a schoolgirl all over again crushing on my history teacher.

But you fucked him, remember?

Confidence seeping back into me at the memory of my teacher eating me out a day after graduation, I turn back around. My eyes widen as Khalid steps out from behind his car.

His erection is thick and hard as it pulses against his thigh, trapped in the constriction of his jeans.

"Do you need help with that?" I breathe, my eyes still low, my lips parted, my breath ragged, and so much fucking hope filling my pussy, another involuntary kegel rips through me.

"Mom?"

His eyes flick over my shoulder, and the urge to ground my daughter even though she's no longer a child makes me clench my teeth. Forcing a smile, I turn to face her.

"Yes, Gen?"

She stands in the doorway of the double glass sliding doors leading into the dining room, letting all the AC out. Her clothes are getting too tight for her again, her waist being the problem rather than her breasts this time. As the faint smell of a burger fills my nose, I breathe out hard. "What did you have for lunch today, Scarlett Jo?"

She blushes as her eyes dart to Khalid.

Not wanting to have this argument in front of him, I switch and say, "You remember to eat?"

She looks at me blankly for a second, then nods.

"Good. Now what is it you want?"

Her mouth opens and closes a few times. "Uh…"

Well, come on.

"Ben…Benjamin called me," she says, shaking her head as she takes a step back into the house, her eyes quickly darting over my shoulder. "He says he tried texting and calling you –"

I pull out my phone and see evidence of such.

Benjamin: *Someone took a picture of you pushing the little girl off your lap. It doesn't look good.*

My blood runs cold with rage. Fucking vultures. "Sorry, Khalid," I say, heading for the door. "I need to deal with this." Scarlett steps out of my way, no doubt to disappear back into her room.

"Gen, wait. Show Khalid where the hose is so he can wash our car."

"Why is he washing –"

"Just do it, please."

She sulks as she nods. Her gaze lowers to the floor. What happened to my outgoing little genius who loved to talk to everyone she saw? "Thanks, Gen. I love you," I say as I step past her.

But then I stop and turn to look at Khalid. His eyes are on me, hot and hungry, and I fucking hate Benjamin in this moment. And the bastard who took the unflattering photo with plans to twist it to their shitty agenda.

"Make sure you remember to come inside after for that beer," I say smoothly, my voice low and sultry.

He smiles. Tilts his head. "I'd never forget."

And fuck, I really want to kill Benjamin now.

Instead, I smile before stepping all the way into the living room and tapping his contact on my phone. Lifting it to my ear, I wait a ring before he answers.

"How bad is bad?" I ask, cutting straight to the point so I can get back to Khalid. Scarlett slides the door behind her, but it doesn't shut all the way, so I turn around to do it for her. *How hard is it for her to just keep her hand on the handle until she feels the click? I've told her so many times...*

"You look like you want to yeet her off your lap."

"I want to what?" *Yeet?*

"Throw," he says. "And the headline they're going with is, 'Mayor Davis Says Sick Children Should Be Left to Die.' Did you *ever* say anything like that?"

"Of course not!" The words are barely out of my mouth before I flinch. "Fuck. Maybe."

His disappointment reaches through the phone and chokes me, so I start to pace across the dining room. The click of my shoes on the light-gray wooden floor is soon silenced by a lush white rug.

"They're twisting my words." Irritation bleeds from my every step as I cross the wenge table, a reflection on the dark tropical African hardwood making me pause. My eyes narrow on the wet ring of water.

I tell her all the time to use a coaster.

"What exactly did you say?" he demands.

Marching into the kitchen, I head for the roll of paper towels. "I was talking to one of the mothers. You know, the one whose girl sat on my lap?"

"Mrs. Keller."

"Yes. About how they decided to stop treatment for her." Tearing off a sheet of paper towel, I head back into the dining room. A quick glance through the double glass doors shows me Scarlett is still outside talking to Khalid. My throat tightens. "She wanted to know if she'd made the right choice."

"And what did you tell her?"

"That I understood her decision. I can't imagine what she's going through, but if Gen was that sick…" I wipe up the water ring. My eyes find her again. She's standing awkwardly by the car, shifting from foot to foot. "I told her sometimes death is the right choice."

Benjamin's silence hangs heavy in my ear, so I shift the phone to my other. It doesn't make him talk.

"So can you fix it?" I ask, walking back to the kitchen.

His sigh comes with a look of disappointment I can see as good as if he were really here. "I'll talk to Mrs. Keller and see if she's willing to be interviewed. Will you be willing to sponsor a day out for them? Maybe to Disney World or –"

"Of course," I say immediately, tossing the wet paper into the kitchen bin. "Anything."

"I'll sort it then. But be careful what you say this close to elec–"

"I know," I cut in. "I'm sorry. Thank you for dealing with this, Benjamin."

Hanging up, I slide my phone into my bag. Fucking vultures, twisting everything I do and say I was just trying to comfort a mother stuck between two hard choices.

Closing my eyes, I push thoughts of work away, then grab two beers from the fridge and force a smile. Scarlett looks over as I slide the door back, then hurriedly comes towards me.

Or rather, the house.

Off to hide upstairs in her room.

As she starts to pass me, I say softly, "Go have a shower. You stink of grease. And we're going out tonight."

She opens her mouth to protest, but I cut her off, not in the mood for her defiance. I gave her one rule when she came home for the summer: no food in this house was for her unless it was a fucking salad.

"Don't backtalk me," I hiss as I smile at Khalid. "You're

coming."

"Fine," she mumbles as she steps past me.

"And shut the door all the way!" I say before she even has the chance to leave it open. Satisfied at the click, I turn my attention to my hot half-naked neighbor. "Thanks for the favor," I purr as I walk towards him, holding out a beer.

"The pleasure is mine." His words are soft, yet loud in their heat. My pussy pulsing, I walk all the way to my car.

He takes the cold bottle from my hand, twists off the lid, and takes a sip, his throat working beautifully in the sun. I want to run my lips across his pulse, carry on down to the hard slab of his abs.

Further.

"Why don't we enjoy these inside?" I breathe.

"Don't you want me to finish your car?" he asks. "If I leave the suds on, you'll have streaks."

I smile as I wave a hand dismissively. "I'll get Paul to arrive earlier tomorrow to finish it," I say, guessing at the name of my driver, assuming he won't know either way.

Khalid stares at me for a second. "Do you mean Phil? The bald guy who drives you?"

I laugh, the heat of a curse burning my cheeks. "Yeah, of course. It's been a long day." I dig out my phone and hold it up. "And it's still going. Some jackass is posting an unflattering photo of me tomorrow in the papers, saying I hate sick kids. It's like they don't know I have a daughter."

"She *is* rarely with you."

Because her image isn't pretty enough for Benjamin's taste, but I don't tell him that. "Yeah. It's a fight getting her to go anywhere these days."

He takes another sip as his eyes flick up to her bedroom.

"She just stays in there all day." I shake my head and finally twist the lid off my bottle. "Do you have any kids?"

Ever married before? Anyone still in the picture?

"No."

I smile. "You're lucky. I love Scarlett, but Lord, does she try my patience sometimes."

He doesn't smile.

Maybe he doesn't like kids...

Though who cares? Scarlett is twenty-two now, and I just want to fuck him, not marry him.

"So you want to come inside?" I take a step closer.

A phone rings from his pants pocket just as he moves forward, and I curse under my breath when he looks down to check it. Placing the beer down on the top of my car, he wipes his wet hands on his jeans and fishes out his mobile. A frown mars his lips.

"Definitely later," he says, texting a response. "I'll leave the bucket and sponge for Phil. Just have him put them beside my back door when he's done with them."

He turns, making his way to his two-story house, his fingers moving rapidly, purpose in his steps.

My eyes linger on his tight ass as a disappointed groan lodges in my throat. When he disappears inside, I wash it down with my beer, then sigh and pull out my phone to text Phil about my car.

No point staying out here, I grab his beer and step into my dining room. I close the glass door behind me. The urge to go upstairs with his bottle, to taste where his lips have been as I touch myself nearly pulls me to the stairs. But then I stop at the kitchen, and my eyes narrow.

Motherhood requires sacrifice.

Entering the kitchen, I put both our beers down on the white marble counter and then head to the fridge. I pull out all the burger meat. Opening the packages, I chuck the beef down the waste disposal unit in the sink. My anger mounts with each whirl of the blades, and the last packet deforms in my fingers.

Thinking of her enjoying a burger at my dining room table, in *my* house, defying my one and only rule, I head upstairs. Hearing the shower on in the bathroom at the top of the landing, I beeline to Scarlett's room and start rummaging around for any hidden snacks, hoping there aren't any. Hoping she wouldn't be so disrespectful as to disobey –

I glower at the pile of candy under her mattress.

The cookies in her underwear drawer.

The chips in her closet.

Disgusted by the quantity of snacks I find, I leave to grab the trash bag out of the kitchen bin.

How is she not worried about herself?

The shower stops just as I finish throwing everything away. Standing in her room with the bag in my hand, I wait for her to enter.

She comes in with the towel twisted atop her head. She jumps a fraction –all that weight not being able to go any higher– as her eyes land first on me, then the bag. "What are you doing in here?" she mumbles, but I know she already knows. Her guilt is painted all over her chubby face.

"What did I tell you about eating this crap?" I lift up the bag.

When she doesn't say anything, I purse my lips. "The doctors have told you you're obese, Gen. Do you have a death wish? Well, answer me."

She stares at the floor as she mumbles something.

"Speak up."

"I get hungry."

"And I get the craving to run people over with my car. That doesn't mean I give in to it." I throw the bag at her. She catches it, fumbling with it in her hands, some of its contents spilling out at her feet before she closes the flaps.

"Go ahead, eat something," I snap. "Eat the fucking trash you love."

Her cheeks flush red. "Ma..."

"Go on. Eat something."

"Please don't –"

"You want to stay here, then you'll do as I say."

Her eyes plead with me as she clutches the black bag in her trembling hands. Perhaps all the shaking will make her lose weight.

At five foot five and two hundred and thirty pounds, she's at a high risk of developing type two diabetes. That's what the doctors say. I watched my ma die from it; I'm not going to lose my daughter to it too.

All the sick children at the hospital assault me. All the parents hopeless to fix them. My voice trembling, I order, "*Eat*, Scarlett Jo."

My patience wearing thin, I take a step towards her.

She flinches back. "I'm not hungry right now," she whispers.

Yanking the bag off her, I reach in and pull something out. It's a paper bag of cookies now stained with some sticky sauce. I thrust it in her face. She tries to step back, but I drop the bag and grab her by the hair. "Eat them, Scarlett Jo. All of them."

Tears burn her eyes as she reluctantly takes the bag of cookies from me. When she just stares at it after opening it, I grab her mouth and pinch apart her lips. A soft cry leaves her as I release her hair to grab a cookie. I shove it into her mouth, and she chokes as she pulls away. Spittle and crumbs fall down her double chin.

"Eat it! Or I swear to God I will make you finish the whole fucking trash bag." Anything to get through to her that she can't keep doing this to herself.

She cries silently as she starts to chew. Her eyes on the floor, she finally swallows. I tremble with disgust and rage and fear, wondering what the fuck happened to my lovely daughter. I don't recognize the woman in front of me anymore. The lack of drive. The quiet. She doesn't get up in the morning. She doesn't come down to eat. And then she sits up here, killing herself in my own home.

Memories of walking in on Ma, of finding her having a heart attack caused by her diabetes when I was nineteen. I dropped to my knees to cradle her as I screamed for our neighbors to call for an ambulance. Someone had come in, telling me help was only ten minutes away.

But it was eight minutes too late as I held her dying in my arms.

I step back, a tornado of emotions hitting me from all directions. Too volatile to be in the same room with her right now, I head for the hallway.

"Take another shower, Gen," I say as I pass her. "You smell like trash."

SEVEN

HER

Stepping out of my ensuite half an hour later, my own shower having calmed me down somewhat, I dry myself, but I can't rub the guilt from my skin. The memory of Scarlett's tears eats at me, her choked sobs. I just want to help her. I want there to be a monster I can slay for her.

I want…

I want my daughter back.

The one who used to laugh.

The one who used to run around, asking a million questions an hour as she tried to understand every piece of the universe. The one who didn't hide upstairs, eating her weight in snacks, passively killing herself as if she doesn't care about living.

My chest tight, I wipe at my cheeks, tears and water coming off onto the towel. I cannot take back what I did, but I can work on fixing it.

Send her to a weight loss boot camp or something.

She needs help I can't give her.

Resolved, I face the mirror to dry my hair.

I jump, a scream erupting as a twisted figure moves beneath the glass. I backpedal quickly, my ass hitting the shower door, my heart stuck in my throat, strangling the thoughts that ducked down to hide there.

That same twisted figure from the hospital shoves an arm through the rippling mirror. My heart thuds wildly as a deformed face pushes against the surface, a black mouth stretched over with taunt charred skin gaping open as it screams in silence. Flecks of flesh fall from its arm, hitting the sink as its fingers claw for me. Its bald, earless head is full of holes filled with maggots. They wiggle around its bleeding eye sockets, curling to go into its cavernous nose.

Pushed by pure adrenaline, I grab a bottle of coconut shampoo – the only 'weapon' around. To hell if I'm going to die without a fight. But just as I take a step forward, the mirror goes back to normal.

The monster gone.

My heartbeat stays at a strong beat, remembering how the creature came back a second time at the hospital. Not wanting to be caught off guard again, I lunge forward and rip open a top drawer beneath the basin. A pair of nail scissors in my hand, I stand back with my ass against the shower, waiting.

But nothing comes.

It stays flat.

Just a mirror.

Reflecting back nothing but my fear.

My wild eyes.

My shaking hands.

"Ma?"

"Don't come in here!" I shout, terror filling my words. If it comes back... My fingers tighten on the nail scissors. *You're not taking my daughter.*

"Are you –"

"I'm fine!" I struggle to keep my voice steadier, not wanting to panic her, not wanting to make her enter in concern. "I just..." I flounder with a reason. "Just wait in the car, Gen," I say, a parent's command strict in my tone. "I'll be out in a second."

"Are you su—"

"Yes. Now go." *Please.*

My ears strain for the sound of her footsteps. I hear nothing over the pounding of my heart.

Sweat pools on my palm, making the scissors slippery.

But the mirror doesn't ripple.

Nothing moves.

My hand shaking, I keep the scissors with me as I shuffle for the door, my eyes on the mirror. I twist the lock on the knob before stepping out and quickly closing the door behind me. It locks shut.

I shudder in short relief even though my brain is quick to point out that if it can come through the mirror, it can come through a measly door.

No, it can't. It's just a hallucination.

Because it doesn't make sense for the witches to have conjured up some monster only to call it back before it even exited the mirror. So it has to be a trick of my imagination. An output of stress. A manifestation of my fear that I can die at any moment.

Shaking out my hands, I finally release the scissors. They drop to the floor, mocking me from the gray carpet, looking so small and useless.

A feeble laugh escapes me.

It's just a hallucination.

Don't go crazy on me.

Striding with surer steps, I head to my closet and pull out clothes for tonight. Comfortable, stretchable pants matched with a skin-tight shirt. Derek says to dress to move even if we can never outrun a werewolf, vampire, or magic. And from the back of the closet, in a safe, I retrieve a gun and ankle holster. Strapping them on, I head for the door.

My eyes drift to the ensuite as my feet root to the gray floor beside my bed. As much as I will myself to move, to go downstairs and meet my daughter, I stop.

Then inch towards the ensuite door and twist the knob. The lock stops it from moving, and so I press an ear against the door, listening even though the creature never made a noise.

It's just a hallucination, I tell myself as I straighten.

I test the lock one more time before heading into the hall, then downstairs and out of the house.

Scarlett sits in the passenger seat of my half-washed car, nerves twisting her face. A small bit of relief fills her eyes before she looks down at her feet.

Swallowing with shame over how I treated her, I stay silent as I get in and buckle up.

The silence stretches as we drive down the street. I want to break it so badly, to soothe her pain, but what does a mother say when she's the one who caused her daughter to cry?

When she did it to try to get through to her?

'I'm sorry' doesn't feel like enough.

My fingers tightening on the wheel, I turn right onto Highway One, heading towards the outskirts of the city, up near Stokes Landing Conservation Area. I glance over at Scarlett.

She keeps hers on her window, gazing out.

The silence starts to hurt.

Clenching the wheel beneath my fingers, I grasp for words. "You know I love you, right?"

"Yeah," she mumbles, easing the chains around my heart a bit.

"I just want you to be healthy."

"I know."

"Insulin costs about seven-and-a-half thousand a year. We can afford that now, but I won't be here forever, Gen, and with you failing college... That's six month's wages working full time on minimum, and the prices are only going to rise. Then there are all the other issues caused by obesity. Mom couldn't afford it, you know, and I watched her –"

"I know," she says softly, finally turning to face me. "I'm sorry I had a burger. I knew it was wrong."

And yet, you still went through the whole process of cooking one.

I don't say that though. Instead, I just reach over and grab her hand, squeezing it with a small smile.

She turns back to look out the window, but she doesn't pull away.

Perhaps what I did got through to her.

Then it was worth it.

The right thing to do.

"So..." I say, grasping for more words to fill the space between us. "How's college going?"

"You already know I'm failing," Scarlett mumbles, her words a mere breath on the glass rather than sounds of substance.

"Other than classes then. College is about connections just as much as grades."

She looks at me, studying my face for a lie. But she eventually takes the out I'm giving her. "It's okay."

"Making any new friends?" *Or any at all?*

"I thought I was, but..." She shrugs and turns to face her reflection again.

"But what?" I overtake a slow driver with a 'Baby on Board' sign. The dad flips me off as I pass, so I cut in a bit closer than necessary. He honks, slamming his brakes, and I throw my hand out the window. The carseat was empty anyway.

He rides up my ass.

"Nothing."

"Come on," I encourage. "You can tell me, and we can go TP their car or whatever it is you youngsters do these days."

A smile cracks her resolve. "There was a guy..." she finally says.

"Oh?" I glance at her, an eyebrow cocked, hoping I look intrigued rather than shocked anyone would give her the time of day. "What's his name?"

"Daniel."

"How'd you meet?"

"He's in my psychology class."

My smile falters a bit, but I don't let it retreat far. There has to be dozens of Daniels taking a psychology class at Flagler College. Derek's son is only one of them. And he never mentioned knowing my daughter.

"So what's the issue?" I ask, glancing in the mirror. The asshole is still riding my bumper. If I wasn't in a hurry, I'd slow down just to piss him off.

"I don't know. He just started ghosting me."

My eyes slide to her rolls. *I can guess why.* "Sorry, Gen."

She shrugs.

"You know what? This weekend, let's go to the spa. We'll get a total makeover. Then go to the park and hire a professional photographer. You post the pictures up on MySpace –"

"MySpace, Ma?"

"What? Facebook?"

She laughs with a small shake of her head.

"People still use MySpace, you know," I tease.

"Old people," she mumbles.

"Benjamin has a page for his music."

"Exactly. *Old* people." It's a rib at me, I know, but I 'fall' for it anyway.

"What are you saying, Gen?" I pull my hand away from

hers to poke her in the side. "He's decades younger than me."

She giggles but doesn't verbalize her insult. Smart girl.

I pull right onto Island Landing Dr., finally losing the asshole with the empty car seat.

"So where are we going?" Scarlett asks.

"To meet up with some friends of mine."

I turn right again, pulling onto Detective Howard's drive, just off a cul-de-sac. No one knows where Derek lives. His car is here though, and I glance at my daughter as we stop beside it, crammed in with six others. No sign of recognition in her eyes. I relax a little. *It's not the same Daniel.*

"Come on," I say, unbuckling. As we approach the door, I wave to the security camera mounted above it. The door swings open with no one there to greet us, Howard liking his toys. The whole place is rigged with gadgets he's made himself. Voices carry from the stairs, and I lead Scarlett up the wooden steps to the second floor.

Sprawled out across the living room are two dozen men and women all geared up for war.

Scarlett freezes beside me as several heads turn in our direction. A few people wave but more nod, their hands occupied with guns and knives. Seeing Daniel off to the side, his back to us as he talks to Detective Howard, I push Scarlett towards the kitchen. "Nicole?" I call out as we maneuver around the stairs and step into the bright lights of the modern kitchen. "This is my daughter. It's her first visit. Can you watch her for a second while I speak to Derek?"

I don't wait for the slim dark-haired woman to pause from watching the oven. Pushing Scarlett at her, ignoring my daughter's protests, I turn back to the living room, making a beeline to Daniel.

Detective Howard stops talking to greet me, but I wave him off. "Sorry, Howard. I need to talk to Daniel. Alone."

Grabbing Derek's son by the arm, I glance over at the kitchen. Not seeing Scarlett watching me, I pull Daniel out onto the screened porch, then close the glass door firmly behind me.

"Want to get started already?" he asks, ducking his head to my neck.

I step back. "Have you been ghosting my daughter?"

He straightens, a sigh leaving his lips. "No. We talked a couple times, but then she started getting weirdly clingy."

"And you didn't think to tell me my daughter thought she was going out with you?"

"I didn't think it mattered," he says, his eyes dipping to my skin-tight shirt stretched across my breasts. "I mean." He takes a step forward, his attention still riveted on my body. His voice lowers as he brings his lips to my ear. "You slept with Nick an hour after he took Scarlett's virginity."

I reach up to smack him across his arrogant face before remembering the doors behind us are glass. Clenching my fist instead, I growl, "If you tell her –"

"I would never hurt you, Hannah." He nudges me out of sight from the door, then cups between my legs. "I love your pussy too much."

I grab his wrist, pinching my nails across his skin. "You won't get *any* of this if she sees you tonight. I don't want her distracted when we're out there hunting. It's too dangerous."

He starts to massage me through my pants, his fingers pushing lightly into me. Heat flares beneath desire and anger, a volatile mixture that is sure to burn. "Fine. But tonight, I want you to tell Dad to finally let me fuck you."

Shoving him away, I shake my head in disdain. "Grow some balls and tell him yourself." Turning, I grab the door handle to wrench it open.

"So you want me to then? Good. Because I'm going to fuck you long and hard, Hannah."

Ignoring the images summoned by that promise, I open the door and step out.

Derek appears beside me just as Daniel exits. A look is shared between them, but I'm not in the mood to be fought over. I need to make sure bringing Scarlett here tonight wasn't a mistake.

"I mean it, Daniel," I say. "Don't let her see you."

"Whatever you wish." He disappears down the stairs, and I turn to Derek.

His five o'clock shadow paints the lower half of his face black, while his long wavy dark hair frames the rest of it in shadows. His hazel eyes pierce me with unspoken questions. A cruel intelligence lingers behind them, and I wonder if he sent Daniel to play with Scarlett just to fuck with me. Despite us sharing a bed – or a wall or a desk, as it may be, I wouldn't put such a thing past him. *Don't forget, I can control you.*

But I don't ask him – some things better left unknown. Instead, I ask, "What are you going to have Scarlett do?"

He stares at me a moment longer. Then gestures over at Detective Howard, who's playing with something on a computer. "You, Scarlett, and Henry will be running recon tonight. It's too risky for you to be seen with us with the election coming up."

I nod, the muscles in my shoulders relaxing a bit. I've never run recon, but Detective Howard is always in the van with his gadgets, never in the line of fire. Scarlett will be safe tonight. "Thanks."

He nods. "Now get geared up. We leave in ten."

He smacks me on the ass, then heads off to talk to some others. There are a few people in here that make me uncomfortable, so I head for the kitchen to stand guard beside my daughter.

"Ma, what's going on?" she asks, hurrying to my side, her voice hushed, her eyes darting as if she's afraid cops will bust through the doors at any moment.

But this is a cop's house. And both my contacts and WALL's will give us ample warning.

"You're going to be shown the truth of the world, Gen." I usher her into the living room, nodding a quick thanks at Nicole. The woman doesn't respond, just continues to watch whatever it is in the oven. Probably the creation of C4. Although Detective Howard told me he'd bought his wife a lab-grade dial-read thermometer for Christmas a couple years ago, Nicole prefers to watch the stuff herself when the timer's almost up.

"What does that mean?" Scarlett asks, her voice soft and trembling. "What have you gotten yourself into, Ma?"

"We're not the only occupants of Earth, Gen. There are werewolves, vampires, and witches."

She stops as I continue into the room. "You're joking."

"No, she's not," Detective Henry Howard says as he joins us, slinging on a jacket, a tablet tucked under one arm. "Just experience everything tonight with an open mind, Scarlett, and then make your own conclusions."

He offers her a bottle of spray. When she doesn't take it, he says, "It's harmless to humans. Nothing worse than pepper spray, but to vampires, it's like getting a face full of acid. You'll want it with you."

"What is it?"

"Werewolf saliva. Their bites are lethal to vampires."

She laughs weakly, but when neither of us do, she stops on a cough. "I don't..."

"Just take it," I say, taking it from Henry and holding it out. "You don't have to use it, but I want you to be safe." When she still doesn't move, I ask, "Or would you rather carry a gun?"

Her eyes widen as she shakes her head.

"Let's roll out!" Derek shouts across the room, and as one, we all move towards the stairs.

I push the spray into Scarlett's hand. "Just put it in your pocket. You won't have to use it tonight because we're on recon, but I want you to have it just in case. Now come on. We'll fill you in on everything in the car."

"But..."

"Move, Scarlett."

Dutifully, silently she follows Detective Howard and I out to his van and then climbs in.

Adrenaline shoots through my veins, buzzing through my limbs as I close the passenger door behind me.

After waiting all day, it's finally time to hunt.

May God guide our bullets.

May He rid the scum from our city.

May He protect my daughter.

Amen.

EIGHT

HER

I turn to glance at Scarlett sitting behind the driver's seat, not wanting to use the mirror. I don't know how big of a surface that monster – *hallucination* needs, but I'm not going to risk freaking out in front of Detective Henry Howard. As friendly as we are, he reports everything back to Derek, and if Derek thinks I'm tagged, being used by the witches to spy on the WALL, he'll kill me as a mercy. If he thinks I'm cursed...I wouldn't put it past him to dissect me. Knowledge is power. It's why we don't always hunt to kill. Sometimes we hunt to capture. What the WALL does with them afterwards, I don't know, but I can guess.

Derek's hatred for them is the only well-known fact about him. He lost his wife and daughter to sups. Daniel was just a baby, so he doesn't remember them outside of flashes of smiles and laughter. But Derek... their memories haunt him every day.

"The goal is to grab a werewolf tonight," I tell Scarlett. "Detective Howard here tagged one –"

"You're a cop?" she asks, her eyes flicking to the back of his head.

"Yes. So you can trust that these monsters are real."

She glances back at me, a bit more fear in her eyes.

Good. She understands the gravity of this situation.

"As I was saying, Detective Howard here tagged one when it came to pick up a body in the morgue. It was killed by a witch."

"*Was being* killed," he cuts in. "Its body was dead, but its soul wasn't." He turns right onto Highway One, the convoy of vehicles splitting off to their own destinations to cover more ground. Vampires are fast. Werewolves are faster. And most of the terrain requires us to travel on foot. We would have no hope of catching them if we didn't split and set up traps.

"What do you mean, his soul wasn't dead? Like he was a ghost?" Scarlett asks.

"Yes. But the witches had him trapped so they could continue to torture him."

Her round cheeks pale, and I wonder if all of this is too much for her blood sugar. Although Scarlett doesn't have diabetes yet, will tonight trigger them? *No. She'll be fine. She's not getting out of the van.*

I continue, "You'll know the werewolves better as the Death Hunt."

"The gang?"

"Yes. And the vampires are the Blood Fang."

"So the witches are what, the Shadow Domain?" she asks, and I can't tell if she believes this or not.

I nod. "Not every member is a sup – a supernatural, but all the higher ups are."

"How do you know this?"

"Because I watched a woman get killed by a vampire in broad daylight."

"Wait? They can walk in the sun?"

"Some can," Detective Henry Howard says as he makes another turn. "There are two types of vampires. You have what we call the regs – those that can't go out in the sun without burning or consume anything other than human blood. Then you have the daywalkers, who can pass for human in every regard."

"So how do you know…"

"There are signs. Most notably, the spray I gave you. To a human, that's just like pepper spray, but to a vampire, any vampire, it burns like acid. One bite from a werewolf will kill a vampire in twenty-four hours unless they can find a healer."

"They don't heal themselves?"

"They do. But werewolf saliva greatly hinders their healing ability for some reason."

"There's also their eyes," I say, taking over the lesson again. "A lot of sups have a unique eye color you won't ever see in a human. Like purple or silver."

"Can't they just be wearing colored contacts?"

"We don't kill people we aren't one hundred percent certain are monsters, Scarlett," Detective Howard says, a bite to his tone.

"Sorry, I didn't mean it like… How do you…kill them?"

I look at her in approval. The first time Howard told me all this, I called him more than just crazy. At fifty, I was too old to be believing in monsters. But believing in them or not didn't change the fact that they were here.

And they were destroying our great nation.

"You don't need to stake them in the chest, if that's what you're wondering," I say. "A bullet to the heart, any damage to the heart, really, will kill them. Regular bullets will slow them down unless they're in a rage. They can regrow limbs, but it takes weeks, so cutting one off is a good way to incapacitate them."

"But you need to cut off their head or rip out their heart

after, just to be certain they don't heal," Detective Henry Howard pipes in as he turns left, towards the Twelve Mile Swamp Conservation Area.

"But we're just on recon, right?" Scarlett asks, her eyes flicking between us. "What does that mean?"

I nod at the electronics all set up beside her. "If we don't have a target already tagged, we send out drones to search for them. Once we find one, a minimum of three teams close in on them."

"And then what?" Her voice is quiet, on the verge of belief.

"And then we send them back to Hell, or we bring them in to learn more about them."

She blanches, and I know she's able to read between the lines. "Are any of them good?" she asks.

Detective Howard snorts. "They're not like criminals with a bad past or rough upbringing, Scarlett. They're the devil's children. That's all they are. Not one of them is capable of love."

He makes a final turn onto a dirt track, then pulls over a short while later. Crawling into the back, he motions for Scarlett to move. She does so without question, trying her best to stay out of the way. But she takes up a fourth of the space, and I have to shove past her when I wriggle through.

For a moment, all that's heard is Scarlett's heavy breathing and the gentle hum of Henry's electronics. On the screen of one of the three monitors he has set up, a small blue dot moves quickly down the streets of St. Augustine. He picks up a radio and gives its coordinates and direction of travel to the teams stationed somewhere out in the woods and swamp.

He hits a few keys, and on the other two monitors, sixteen cameras pinned to the front of shirts and jackets come online.

"Nicole, Nicole, Nicole, this is control base, over," he says into his radio.

"What? Over."

"Angle your camera so it's pointing out. I can only see your feet, over."

Camera six jerks up and down a bit before focusing on a group of three heavily armed men in front of her.

"Is that better, over?"

"Thank you. Out."

I lean forward as the four teams of four move through the woods and swamp surrounding us. "Why are we out here if the mutt's still in St. Augustine?" I ask.

"We don't have the manpower to take them at their compound. We have to wait until they come out for a hunt. They split up then."

"And you're certain he'll come this way?"

"No. That's why teams three and four are south of the city."

"Why couldn't we have watched everything from the house?" Scarlett asks as she hugs her arms, glancing warily out the windows.

"We're also the medic van," he says without looking away from the screen.

"Do people often get hurt?"

"No, but we want to be prepared," I lie. Anytime we don't successfully kill or capture, someone dies. If not that night, then in a couple when the sups hunt us down for knowing about their world, tracking us through our scent or circadian rhythm or some magical voodoo I don't yet understand.

Shifting uncomfortably, I think about the newest thing I don't understand: the monster in the mirror.

"Hey, Henry," I say casually, not wanting to pull his full attention away from the monitors. "Have you ever heard of a charred humanoid monster coming out of a mirror?"

He glances at me. "Have you seen one?"

And there's something in his eyes and tone that makes my skin crawl. Makes me want to jump out of the van and run away screaming.

"No." I shake my head. "No… a child at the hospital mentioned seeing one. She really seemed to think it was real."

He holds my gaze for a moment longer, and I make sure not to waver despite the strengthening of my pulse urging me to run. Sweat glistens on the back of my neck, raising each individual hair with the cold trickles of its touch.

"They're signs of death," he finally says, glancing back at the monitors.

Cold torment lances through me, and I swallow hard as I stare at the side of his face. My pulse intensifies, screams in between my ears as it pounds around my skull in denial. *I'm too young to die.* "Signs of death?" I push out. "What does that mean?"

Praying that it doesn't mean what I think it means.

Already knowing that it does.

"Like reapers." He shrugs. "They don't seem to hurt people themselves, but everyone who sees them dies within twenty-four hours of them coming all the way out of the mirror. It makes sense for them to lurk inside hospitals."

My eyes dart to the handle of the van's side door. But despite my urge to run, I know such an attempt would be futile. You can't outrun a werewolf. You sure as hell can't outrun death.

"Has there ever been a case where it doesn't come out all the way?" I ask, reaching down to find comfort in the hard steel of my Sig P365. Even though I know I can't shoot death either.

Another shrug. "I'll have a look in the books when I get ho– What the?" He jerks forward, his eyes pinned to the screen as he grabs his radio. "Nicole, Nicole, Nicole, this is control base. Turn left. I want to check –"

Scarlett screams as he maximizes the camera just in time to see a man's head go flying across the screen. Nicole falls back as she raises her gun, and the two other men panic with her. Bullets spray into the woods as a massive body of fur blurs through the trees. It darts forwards on two legs, its teeth locking around one of the men's shoulders.

"Nicole, run!" Henry shouts into the radio.

I pull out my gun, my fingers white as they grip it. My eyes wide on the screen, I watch as the werewolf, eight, nine feet of towering muscle, rips the man's arm off before turning to lunge at the other one.

Bullets tear into its hide, but it doesn't seem to feel them. Nicole's gun clicks empty.

"Run!" Henry screams again.

Dropping her gun, she turns.

Another werewolf instantly fills the camera.

I want to shoot it.

I want to not be helpless.

But all I can do is be her helpless witness.

Trapped with one in front of her and one at her back, Nicole pulls out a knife. It barely leaves its sheath before her arm goes flying, and her screams rupture the safety of the van.

"Nicole!" Henry screams, his spittle flying across the screen.

"Babe, I love –"

The camera angle drops. A vicious howl fills the mic. And then the video goes dark.

Breathing heavily, Scarlett grabs my arm. "We need to get out of here."

I don't disagree, but we can't just leave everyone to –

"Shit!" Detective Howard shouts as he jerks back in his chair. A werewolf face fills the screen, its bloody maw spread wide in a smile. Its tongue flicks across the camera, cleaning it of dirt, yet making it blurry with saliva. Then it leans in, putting its eye right up close to the lens.

I see you.

The camera goes black once more as the werewolf drops Nicole's body to the ground.

A chilling bark of laughter echoes through the mic. The sound of bones popping mixes with snarls. Teeth gnashing under pained groans. And then a man's raspy voice comes online.

"We're coming for you. Might I suggest running?" He laughs, deep and deranged, and then he starts to howl. A human's howl, not a wolf's, sending goosebumps along my skin.

Animalistic howls erupt all around us, not from the speaker but ricocheting off the outside of the van. I snap my gun up, facing the windshield. Steel surrounds us on every other side, but it all just feels like glass. Glass I can't see through. Can't aim through.

"Henry, *drive*," I hiss as the detective crumbles against the monitors, chanting his wife's name.

"Nicole is such a pretty woman," the werewolf taunts. "Don't you want to come out and save her?"

Henry's head comes up, tears streaming down his face. "She's alive? Nicole, Nicole, baby, can you hear me?"

"Oh, wait, no, yeah, she's dead. That was my bad." His chuckle cuts like knives. "I forgot how fast you humans bleed out when you lose two limbs and your intestines. Hold on, wait, I'll put her back together."

"You bastard! I'm going to –"

"Die," he cuts in smoothly, a second before an arm punches through the metal of the van, making a hole in the monitor. Its claws snap around Henry's face and pull off his flesh. As he falls back screaming, clutching at the exposed muscle and one dangling eye, I pull the trigger of my gun over and over again. The wolf whimpers in pain, snatching its arm back, but another clawed hand is quick to cut through the metal.

Scarlett jerks forward, grabbing at Henry's pockets. "Where are the keys?" she begs.

The van shudders as a huge weight drops onto the roof. I raise the gun and fire, trying to fill the fucker with holes, but although blood drips in from the ceiling, there aren't any screams accompanying it. Just howls of laughter that sicken my stomach.

"The dashboard!"

She tries to move past me, but she's too fucking fat and knocks into me. The gun drops to my feet as I'm crushed between her and the wall.

And I can *feel* a presence behind me, a werewolf lining up its shot to rip through the side of the van and pull out my heart.

I try to shove Scarlett off me so I can move, but she's too heavy. Too focused on her goal to grab the keys.

A horrible wrenching sound ruptures above us as the roof of the car is peeled back like a mere page being turned in a book. A werewolf's head lunges down, and I instinctively grab Detective Henry, pulling him in front of me as Scarlett manages to wedge herself in the front seat. His screams increase in volume as he's yanked out of the top of the car. Blood splatters around me, a waterfall of red bits that soak my clothes and mat my hair. The wolf on the roof of the van howls before jumping up and down, flinging bits of Henry everywhere. Metallic iron explodes in my mouth and nose until it's all I can focus on.

The car shakes.

Glass shatters.

Scarlett screams.

Fumbling around in the footwell, I search for my Sig.

My fingers brush cold metal.

The monitors play a slasher flick of the other team north of the city, but my focus is drawn to my daughter. A naked man is on the hood of the car, down on his hands and knees, his fingers digging into the black paint. His teeth flash a bloody smile. His laughter rips into my chest and clenches around my heart.

His golden eyes are pinned on Scarlett as she fumbles to put the key in the ignition.

Punching through the windshield, he grabs hold of her hand. "Let's have some fun, shall we?"

I grab the gun and jerk upright, but by the time I'm ready to line up a shot, my little girl is being dragged through the glass. He throws her out behind him, and I scramble forward as he turns. A *thud* vibrates the ground as she cries out in pain and fear.

Bang!

My gun goes off.

The man turns to me in slow motion. The very air, sound itself stills as he swivels his head, one arm out in my direction, blood pouring down his body from bullet wounds already healed. Holding my gaze, he smiles. Then opens his fist and down drops my bullet.

What the – A werewolf shouldn't be that fast. That strong.

I pull the trigger again, aiming for his heart.

He appears a few feet to the left, his speed too fast to track even in his human form. Trembling, I jerk my arm to line up another shot, but before I can get him in my sights, someone grabs me from above.

I'm yanked up on a scream. The ragged jaws of the van's roof cut into my side, and I flinch instinctively from the metal. Pain flaring across my body, I dig my fingers into the arm holding my hair. A teeth-filled face fills my own, but as the werewolf's breath reeks across my cheeks and its jaws open to close around my throat, I shove my gun into its chin and pull the trigger.

Brains splatter across my face as I fall back into the van.

The edge of the seat digs hard into my tortured side, making my eyes roll as a scream leaves me.

From my blurred peripheral, I see a charred monster fully crawl out of the rearview mirror.

Hope of survival abandons me as I struggle to breathe through the pain.

But Scarlett's scream keeps me rooted in the moment. Keeps me fighting despite the lure of a pain-free sleep.

Dragging myself to the front of the van, I look out the open windshield.

And my entire world. My entire reason for fighting, for living, for creating a better future, vanishes as I watch the man rip off the last of his skin as he finishes transforming into his wolf. I raise my gun, but I already know it's too late.

I'm too late to save her.

With a speed I could never hope to match, the monster drops down on my daughter, his jaws opening around her skull.

The creature from the mirror rushes towards me, its maggot-ridden fingers grazing my cheek as I fire bullet after bullet at the werewolf.

A broken scream ruptures from my lips as his teeth close around –

Air?

Flung off her by a force I can't fathom, the werewolf spins, hitting a tree and cracking it in two. The thundering break is like another gunshot. He hits the tree behind it, then drops to the ground with a growl.

His muscles bulging, he climbs to his feet as two unnatural shadows dart across the ground.

Witches.

Scrambling into the front of the van, I throw open the passenger door and scream for my daughter to get in.

No longer focused on us, every werewolf lunges for the two shadows, running past me and jumping over Scarlett.

She whimpers but doesn't freeze, rolling onto her hands and knees as she crawls towards me. I hold open the door, urging her to crawl faster as I raise the gun just in case.

But all the sups are suddenly gone, hidden under a magical veil to keep them out of human sight.

"Move your fat ass and get in!" I shout, terrified she's taking too long. I shift into the driver's seat, thanking the good Lord that the keys are already in the ignition.

Dragging herself to her feet, Scarlett runs the last few paces and jumps into the car. I throw it into drive, and with a whirl of the tires spinning dirt and blood, the van lurches down the road.

NINE

HIM

As I wrap around the legs of a wolf, dragging half of her body into my shadow domain, I'm filled with an anger that drives my magic. Strengthens it. Makes it greedy for blood. *They tried to kill my girl.*

Antonio fucking tracked her scent *through me.*

Because I started the blood ritual, marking her as mine.

The wolf I'm wrapped around starts to scream in pain as the monsters in my shadow domain finally grab hold of her legs. When my brothers and I travel as shadows, we can open ourselves up to the monsters who live there, allowing them to feast on things we touch. It is a massive drain on our body, and something we rarely use, but my anger is volatile in this moment and needs to be sated.

The sound of crunching bones and tearing flesh rises up from the realm of darkness. Digging her nails into the soft earth, the wolf tries to drag herself away from me. To freedom. To safety.

There will be no fucking safety.

I will kill them all for trying to hurt her.

Not trying, I growl to myself. *Succeeding.*

I smelled the blood on her skin. Felt her fear through our budding link. And now Antonio thinks he can run away? That he can leave his six lackeys to die in his place, as if their deaths will appease my rage like their blood does my magic?

Not a fucking chance.

Leaving the half-consumed wolf to cry and howl for a mercy I will never give, I start to shift into my human form, my body still healing from this morning's ordeal. If I use too much magic when I'm weakened, it'll turn on me as the easier target, consuming my organs and making me too weak to fight Antonio.

Four of the wolves don't hesitate to lunge for me now that I'm not protected by being an ethereal form they can't touch. But reapers are not trained in just magic. We are often sent to kill other witches, old friends and family members that know our secrets and how to nullify both our innate and learned magic. We're taught to fight when the gods have forsaken us and the devils have opened their arms to embrace us.

Pulling a double tipped war scythe from the shadows as I fully emerge, I meet the first wolf with a smile. His arm is sliced off on my first swing. Shock parts his lips as I spin and twist the weapon so the flat of the blade on the other end smacks into his detached limb, sending it flying into the face of the wolf beside him, startling her just enough she's distracted from my follow-up blow. With a wet *squelch*, her intestines drop before her knees, and she lands in them with a high-pitched howl.

I dart towards her, kneeing her in the face as my arms twist around my body, spinning the scythe around me. One end cuts across the original wolf, removing his snout as the other tip slices into the shin of a third attacker, who tried to get me from behind.

The blades spin.

My body moves.

And a shower of blood circles around me like a tornado sucking up wayward limbs. The wolves step back, warier now, but one is dead and the other three are mortally wounded – not that they know it yet.

Small cuts they think they will heal from.

But with every second, more blood will pour from their wounds in greater quantity. In twelve minutes, they'll be dead, their innate healing ability useless against cursed tools like this.

Tools that take payment in blood. Either mine or theirs.

But it's always theirs.

And soon, it'll be Antonio's.

Boiling with the need to end this before the alpha has a chance of getting away, I spin the scythe one last time and shove one blade into the ground. It disappears, sinking into my shadow as I fling my arms out, throwing magic with deadly accuracy.

Three hearts explode inside their chests.

I drop to one knee as my soul screams. Blood spurts from my lips. A grinning face appears in front of me, dragging me back upright.

"Getting old, Kali." Maddox smacks me on the back, putting a touch of his magic behind it so I hiss in pain.

You fucker.

But my attention is already off him, narrowing on the nearby trees. I cloaked my girl's scent as soon as we arrived on scene. Antonio won't be able to track her now, but still, not having him in my sights sends bolts of unease through me, urging me to move.

To hunt the fucker before he hunts my girl. *Again.*

"Relax," Maddox says as he nudges me in the side. "Batman and Robin" –his nickname for the twins– "will get him."

"He'll kill them," I state flatly. "He'll kill all of us."

Maddox laughs. "Sure he will. That's why he ran." He shakes his head, licking blood off his lips. "Because he was terrified of ripping us apart."

I glance at him dryly. "You're a fucking idiot," I say.

Antonio tracked my girl on *one fucking drop* of blood. He shouldn't have been able to smell it coursing through her veins, and I know he didn't pick up my scent on her skin because I've been careful to remove it with magic.

Which means he has consumed fallen wolves at a rate we never picked up on. Mother's fears of him becoming too strong for us to take him on one-on-one have already come to pass.

But where in Hel's name is he getting the corpses?

Until four months ago, our gangs were at peace with one another. It was a strained peace that would've made the Cold War seem like a teenager's slumber party with her best mates, but the killing between us was miniscule. But when the wolves finally broke that pact by attacking the vampires, the bloodsuckers failed to deal any solid blows. It's why we got involved. If the two were evenly matched, we would not have stepped in, content to let the idiots kill each other before we slaughtered the survivors.

So is Antonio killing them himself?

Werewolves are pack animals, but make the pack too large and they constantly go to war amongst themselves, juggling for hierarchy. Wolves aren't born as alphas, betas, or omegas. They fight for those positions whenever the opportunity arises. And though the bottom rank of omega is rarely held for long, it *is* a lifelong position, made shorter the bigger the pack.

More wolves equals more bullying.

More bullying equals a higher risk someone takes it too far. And then the cycle to find the new scapegoat starts all over again, triggering a lethal brawl involving the entire pack.

But even if Antonio ate all of the fallen, he would have only consumed the weakest members. They wouldn't have given him power like this. Besides, constant brawls would have been impossible to hide from us, and they would've also caught the attention of the Special Crimes Unit – the only professional agency on Earth that knows about us. The WALL we can basically ignore as they buzz around us like annoying mosquitos, but the SCU are the big game hunters, established thousands of years ago to protect this world from monsters like us. They are our official and only governing body. They know all our weaknesses and run like a well-oiled machine of zombies. You might kill a few, but eventually, they *will* bring you down.

Antonio wouldn't have risked calling them in.

So again, who the fuck is he eating?

And what other surprises have our scouts failed to discover, our spies failed to mention?

My skin crawling, I head off in the direction of my girl, no longer capable of standing still. The budding blood bond between us gives me a trail only I can follow.

Maddox darts in front of me and shoves me back. "You call me an idiot, yet you've started a blood ritual with a fucking WALL member? She ain't ever gonna accept you, bruh."

"Fuck off." I move around him.

He shakes his head. "Your funeral. I'm getting the popcorn for when Varius finds out!"

Raising an arm, I flip him off as my pace picks up until I'm running at full speed. Then I'm slipping into my shadow form, to hell with the drain it'll have on me, with the payment it will suck from my body.

Because although Antonio can't track her, he *can* do a grid search.

And with his speed, he could be on her before my brothers find him.

I will not fail her twice.

TEN

HER

"Holy shit. Holy shit. Holy shit."

As those two words keep tumbling out of Scarlett's mouth, I want to tell her to shut the fuck up. I get that she's scared, but so am I, and I'm not anywhere near as annoying as her.

But my body's shaking too much to handle words, so instead, I just squeeze the steering wheel between my left palm, my gun still in the other, and suck in one deep breath after another. The van rattles over the narrow dirt road, hitting bumps and holes indiscriminately as I hold a high speed, gaining us distance as fast as possible. The wind stings my eyes through the shattered windshield, but I don't dare slow.

We could've died.

I will die.

That thing crawled out of the mirror and touched me. A reaper marking my death in twenty-four hours. *Holy fucking shit.*

My arms tremble as my eyes dart to the rearview mirror. It stays glossy still. Nothing ripples across its surface. Nothing reaches through. Not even a werewolf darts across its reflection chasing us.

Life is normal.

It's just us that's acting crazy.

"Holy shit, holy shit, holy – Those were *werewolves*!" my daughter trembles beside me, blood gushing down her face. I glance at her before my eyes latch back on to the mirror.

Still normal.

My shaking doesn't stop.

"Has anyone ever survived seeing one come out?"

"Not that I'm aware of."

Fuck...

Fuck!

I don't want to die yet. I'm too young, only fifty-one. And Scarlett, this world needs me. Not many people know about the monsters lurking in the dark. And tonight, we lost so many. I can't go yet. I'm too important. I'm the mayor of this fucking town. I'm not some lackey the world just forgets about. I'm not some overweight college student who's failing all her classes.

My hand squeezes the wheel.

My breaths come out short and sharp.

Pain squeezes my lungs as I look back at my daughter.

Maybe it wasn't here for me.

Maybe it was here for her and just got confused...

That makes more sense.

All she does is spend her day in her room sleeping.

She doesn't contribute to society.

She doesn't do anything.

She isn't *important.*

Tears burn my eyes.

Crazy talk.

Shameful talk.

How can I hope for her to be the one marked? My own fucking daughter.

"Holy shit, holy shit, holy shit."

I love her more than anything, but...

That doesn't stop me from wishing in the darkest part of my soul – that place no one likes to admit they have, that it's not *me* the reaper is here for.

It's *her*.

Please, God, save me.

I swap my Sig to my left hand. Reaching over to her, I grab my daughter's hand and squeeze. She flips her palm up and grabs me back, her fingers tight on mine, desperate to hold on to a reality her brain can accept.

Mother is safety.

Am I?

Yes.

We drive for another minute or two before my heart rate starts to calm. The city isn't far even though I took off in the wrong direction, just throwing the van into gear and driving whichever way it was pointing. Convincing myself that the werewolves and witches killed each other, I take another deep breath and release.

We're okay.

"Are you okay?" I ask, my shaky voice belying my new calm.

She nods, then winces before raising her other arm to her head.

She touches it, and her fingers come away with blood.

My grip jerks on the wheel. My world stills even as it rushes past, harsh contradictions pulling me in conflicting directions.

My heart stops, yet beats rapidly.

My senses dull, yet flare to life.

The gun feels cold in my hand, yet hot enough to burn.

My brain scrambles to understand the significance, and

yet, the knowledge of what I need to do is crystal clear as flashes of that wolf on top of her, his mouth around her entire skull slam into me.

Choking me.

Beating me.

Making me want to scream.

My daughter's been bitten.

There is no cure.

She *will* turn.

Slamming on the brakes, I fall against the wheel, my chest pressing into my fingers as I wheeze. Her scream sounds so distant, a quiet beneath the ringing consuming me.

She's.

Been.

Bitten.

"Ma, what's wrong?" she shouts, scrambling to undo her seatbelt. But when she turns to me, her arms reaching, I jerk away, flinching against the door.

She's been bitten.

She will turn.

My death in twenty-four hours makes more sense now.

My own daughter is going to kill me.

Grabbing for the door handle behind me, I pull it free and tumble out of the car. My legs twist as they try to keep me standing, but I stumble around on the dirt track.

"Get out!" I shout, my chest choking on the words, crushed by the weight of their purpose.

"What?"

"Get out!" The words are high-pitched and frantic. The gun heats in my hand, drawing my attention even as a part of me wishes to throw it away. To toss it into the woods and drive off with my daughter.

But I can't.

She's been bitten.

There is no saving her.

Only mercy.

The children from the hospital fill my thoughts. All sick and dying with no monster to slay. All terminal. Already dead, just living on borrowed time.

And then that girl on my knee, she starts to cough, and her mother comes up and smacks my face. *"You're letting her suffer,"* she says.

No. I won't.

I won't let my daughter suffer.

My eyes drop to my gun, and I raise it just as Scarlett steps around the hood of the van to reach me, concern in her watery blue eyes. Blood down half her face.

"Ma?" Confusion and fear overrides the concern as her legs root her in place. "What are you doing? Why are you pointing that at me?" she whimpers, and I nearly drop the gun and run to her.

But a mother must make sacrifices.

I must stay strong for her.

She's been bitten.

There is no cure.

There is no cure!

"There is no cure!" I shout, begging her to understand, begging her to know that I'm doing this out of love. To become a werewolf is to toss away your soul. An afterlife of eternal damnation. I will save her. *I will save her.*

I.

Will.

Save.

Her.

"Step away from the car, Scarlett."

"Ma?"

"Do it!"

I thrust the gun at her, holding back the tears. My side splinters in pain where I was cut by the roof of the van, but that's nothing to the agony ripping apart my soul.

A mother should never have to make this choice.

But she'll turn and kill me just like the reaper was warning me about.

She's already dead, I tell myself, keeping the gun steady.

Infected.

One of them.

Just like a fetus will grow into a baby, she *will* change into a monster.

"Ma!"

"Do it, Scarlett Jo!"

Tears flood down her face as she holds up her hands, begging me with words lost beneath her sobs.

"Move!" I stride towards her, the gun leading, and she steps back with a whimper.

"Ma, please! What are you doing?"

I herd her towards the treeline, off the road.

"Ma!"

I don't let her get to me.

I *can't.*

I won't let the devil take her soul.

"Ma! Please don't do this! Ma! *Ma!*"

As her pleas pound my ears, each one a sledgehammer to my senses, tears erupt from my eyes. My heart shakes, but my arm stays steady. She's bitten.

She's already dead.

She'll kill me if I don't kill her.

This is mercy.

"*Ma! Please!*"

She's sobbing now, her words broken into incoherent pleas that wring my heart and make me –

No.

Stay strong.

She's been bitten.

She's already dead.

She'll kill me if I don't kill her.

This is mercy.

"Ma! Please....please..." She trembles in the darkness of the woods.

She's been bitten.

She's already dead.

She'll kill me if I don't kill her.

This is mercy.

She's been bitten.

She's already dead.

She'll kill me if I don't kill her.

This is mercy.

"Ma! Ma, please!"

We venture deeper into the darkness.

She's been bitten...

She's already dead.

"Ma!" She trips over a loose root, the *thud* of her body hitting the ground.

I shudder, images of her brains scattered all across the earth suddenly filling my mind.

She'll kill me if I don't kill her.

"Ma, put down the gun. I don't understand –"

This is mercy.

Mouthing, "I love you," I aim for her head.

And then I pull the trigger.

ELEVEN

HER

Click!
She screams, throwing up her arms to protect herself.
But no bullet comes out.
No bullet…
Because it's empty.
My eyes drop to the Sig still aimed in my hand.
My vision narrows on it, seeing nothing else.
The cold metal.
My finger on the trigger.
Oh my God.
Scarlett's screams finally reach the haze encircling me.
Oh my *God.*
Dropping my arms, I then drop to my knees, a broken cry exiting my body in a sudden explosion. "Gen!" I sob as I crawl towards her, the harshness of the gun pushing into my palm with every movement forward.

"You tried…to *kill* me," she wheezes, her arms wrapped around herself, her whole body trembling.

"You're bit…" My words trail off as I suddenly recall why I pulled the trigger in the first place.

The gun being empty doesn't change anything.

She is still dead.

She will still turn.

Then kill me.

But as much as Derek would tell me to find a rock and bash her head in, I *can't.*

"I'm not," she says, strained words that have confusing meaning.

And then they make sense, hitting me so hard it hurtles my stomach up into my throat. "What?"

The raspiness of my voice shakes the air between us.

My fingers dig into the soft earth, my nails biting into the ground.

"I wasn't bitten."

"But the blood…his mouth…" My eyes lift to her head as she sits up and moves away from me. *In fear.*

I lurch forward, shivers spasming my body, making my limbs uncontrollable.

"I hit it when I was thrown from the car," she says, her voice soft in its brokenness. "He didn't bite me."

"No…no…that can't be…" I shake my head, unwilling to believe it. That I nearly killed my daughter for nothing. Would have if not for the gun being empty. "No…no," I say, stuck on repeat as my brain struggles to wrap itself around the current change of events, the adrenaline rush making it fuzzy. "No…"

"Yes," she spits out, pushing herself up into a sitting position. The mud clings to her skin, morphs into blood in my mind. I was going to blow her brains out. I pulled the trigger.

I *wanted* to pull the trigger.

Not just to save her soul, but to maybe appease the reaper after mine.

My throat constricting, I look away. "I'm sorry," I rasp.

"Fuck you," Scarlett says just as brokenly, making me flinch.

There's so much I want to say, I'm sure of it, if I could just find the words, but my mouth is too dry and my throat is too parched to speak. So instead, I push myself to my feet, knowing we can't stay here, knowing nothing I say will make up for the fact that I tried to kill my own daughter. That I wanted to offer her life for mine.

"Come on," I say, my eyes darting around the woods. "We need to get back to the safety of the city."

She snorts and looks heavenward, and the irony of my statement isn't lost on me.

"Move it," I snap, my anger at myself bleeding out. "You can yell at me at home, Gen, but right now, we need to –"

The sound of tires steal my words, and Scarlett's eyes widen as they flick over my shoulder, back towards the road. I raise a finger to my lips, the gun slick against my palm. She nods.

The werewolves would've driven here.

And the witches.

Even if it's just the police doing patrols, the vampires have them in their pockets.

Fuck, it could be the vampires themselves wanting to get in on the action.

Sweat trickles down my back, raising each hair in its path, prickling my skin. My ears strain, muscles pulling at the sides of my face, desperate to hear the car over the thundering in my skull.

My pulse runs fast and wild.

My gun is empty.

Keep going.

Keep going...

Don't stop.

The tires crunch over the rough ground, each rotation

twisting my nerves. The trees seem to close in around us, their whispering leaves, ominous crackles in the dark. The feeling of being watched, of something hunting us peels at my skin.

We're not alone.

My eyes dart around the woods. I see nothing, and my attention is pulled back to the car as its engine grows louder. My heartbeat quickens.

I look at my daughter.

"Gen, get up," I hiss, my voice an urgent whisper as I transfer the gun to my other hand so I can wipe my palm on my thigh.

The Sig grows heavy between my fingers, reminding me it's empty.

Shit.

The tires slow down, then stop on the road behind me.

I want to turn, but I don't dare move, knowing a werewolf only needs to hear one crinkle of a leaf to hone in on its prey.

My tongue sticks to the roof of my mouth as I swallow.

My chest vibrates with shallow breaths.

The engine dies, the quietness of the night like the slam of a coffin.

A car door opens.

No.

Heavy pairs of shoes crunch over dirt, coming our way.

Spinning, I raise my gun as Scarlett scrambles to her feet. I don't care if it's empty. I'll –

"Hannah?" a man calls out, his voice unmistakable even though it's a mere hiss on the wind.

My shoulders cave in. The gun drops to my side as I rasp, "Daniel?"

His experience is a light to my terror, and I stumble through the woods towards him.

Heavy footsteps hurry behind me as I bolt out onto the

road.

"Jesus Christ. Are you okay?" he asks as he heads towards me, slinging his assault rifle across his body as a silhouette behind him stands guard. His hands grab my hips, stilling me as he looks me over. "Is this –"

"It's not a bite," I blurt. "We're both okay."

Trembling, I sag against him, and he catches me with a small step back. "They killed Henry," I mutter, the whole thing finally crashing onto my shoulders.

It gets harder to breathe.

Harder to hear as my senses become a pinpoint, my brain desperate to shut off. To sleep. To wake from this nightmare tomorrow. To let someone else take care of it.

The silhouette moves to the side of the van, lugging a jerry can, and I realize it's Derek.

Cold, efficient Derek who's never failed to make me wet. His touch is the one I've always craved, feeding off his strength, but now I cling to the comfort of his son. The warmth.

My fingers dig into his jacket. "They killed everyone."

"I know," he says gently. "We saw the footage. But right now, we need to get you –"

"Daniel?" Scarlett nearly screeches his name, and I jerk away from him, suddenly recalling their history. "*This* is why you haven't been returning my texts? Because you're fucking my *ma?*"

"Shut the fuck up," Derek growls as he steps in front of her, his gun raised. "Any louder, and I'll shoot."

He has a silencer, never takes it off, and I watch my daughter tremble under his warning. I want to tell him to back the fuck off, but no one stands up to Derek. He isn't empty threats and a teddy bear beneath his armor of trauma. He's the real deal. A psycho with a cause.

And he'll kill her if it means living another day to fight this war between the sups.

"Now everyone get in the fucking car."

She doesn't respond, but the hatred in her eyes as she looks at me speaks enough to not need words. Marching past, she heads towards the passenger door of the black SUV, clearly not wanting to have to sit beside either one of us.

I open my mouth to say something, but the energy to comfort her is robbed from me as soon as Daniel pulls me back into a quick hug.

"It's going to be okay," he murmurs before kissing my head and ushering me into the backseat. He stands guard at the door, his gun raised as his dad walks back over to the van. Derek pulls something out of his pocket, and a flicker of light breaks the darkness. Tossing the match into the vehicle, he pauses a moment to watch it catch fire, then turns and strides over.

He glances at his son as he gets behind the wheel, and as he starts the engine, Daniel sweeps the surrounding area with his rifle.

My blood rushing beneath my skin, I look around too.

The feeling of being watched doesn't dissipate, and I jump when I see eyes glaring at me from the darkness. But on second glance, it's just the moonlight glistening through the leaves.

Not that my heart knows the difference.

Perched on needles, it waits for death to come even after Daniel gets in and the car starts to pull away. I don't dare speak, no one does. My thrumming heart rocks me. The only sounds are the crunch of the tires and the roar of the engine, and with each passing second, they seem to grow in volume. *Here we are. Come kill us.*

Swiveling in my seat, holding my gun tight in my hand despite its heavy emptiness, I peer out the window. My pulse vibrates through my body, keeping me on edge. The darkness is impenetrable, but a shadow darts between the trees, keeping up with us.

"Derek!" I blink, and the shadow is gone. Just a trick of my paranoia.

My tight nerves.

"What?" he snaps as I move my lips wordlessly before shaking my head. Grasping for something to say, I blurt, "One of the werewolves caught a bullet with his fucking hand. Is that normal?"

"Fuck no," Daniel says from beside me. "Are you sure you –"

"I know what I saw," I snap.

"But that speed's impossible. A bullet travels eight- nine-hundred miles an hour."

"Hence, my question of, 'Is it fucking normal?'"

"Hey." He grabs my hand, and when he squeezes it, I take a deep breath. Exhale. My nerves are turning me into a bitch. I know that.

"We'll talk about it later," Derek says, turning towards the safe lights of the city. "Right now, you need to get home and some sleep. You have an important meeting with the Commissioner and Deputy Mayor tomorrow you can't fuck up."

My use to the WALL. Most likely the only reason Derek came out to save me. I need to approve the higher budget for the police and get Derek's out-of-town buddies transferred here to join a new gang-focused task force that can go to war with the sups and finally weed the vampires out of the police department.

But any anger I might've felt about being so blatantly used is swamped under my desire to kill every last sup in my city.

That werewolf might be able to catch one bullet, but I'd like to see him try that with a whole fucking SWAT team armed with automatics.

"I'll get it done," I vow, bending down to tuck my gun

away in its holster. "So what are we going to do about the bodies?" I ask as I sit up, my brain grinding through ways I can spin their deaths to my political advantage. "I won't be able to bury all that paperwork."

"Henry died as a hero tracking down a gang lead off duty," Derek says so quickly, I know he's thought of this before. I wonder if he has stories ready for all of our deaths in all the different scenarios. What would he have said if I shot Scarlett?

Shifting with a hard swallow, I look out the window. "I'll make sure to put pressure on the Commissioner to bring in as many Death Hunt members as they can."

"If they pick up the mutt that can catch a bullet, call me," Derek says. "I'll deal with him in jail."

I nod, not bothering to ask how he'll do it. He always finds a way, and he isn't keen on sharing the details. Says it's too risky if we get tortured for the information.

I wonder if anyone I saw get attacked tonight is alive.

Taken somewhere to be tortured.

The car slows as Derek pulls onto a random drive. Far from the road, behind hedges and trees, he stops at a garage. The door opens to show my black Lexus parked inside.

This must be Derek's house.

And he must have had someone move my car before coming out to get us. Wouldn't want anyone seeing me arriving at Detective Henry Howard's house after his time of death, especially if they already saw me leave with him in his van. No one exits until the garage door shuts behind us, granting us privacy.

"What's my alibi?" I ask as I dig out my keys and step out.

Daniel grabs my wrist, his thumb brushing over my skin. "We need to get you patched up first."

Because we can't go to the hospital.

And I can't be seen with any wounds.

"You went to see Henry Howard for a get together," Derek informs me. "You left with him, but he dropped you off here. One of the neighbors will collaborate your story, saying he saw you get out and the van drive off around eight o'clock. You then went inside and stayed for a few hours before sneaking back home."

I purse my lips. Benjamin is going to flip hearing this story, but an affair will stop the police from asking any further questions. With owed favors and greased palms, with luck, it won't even end up in the news.

Daniel guides me to a cabinet along the wall and pulls out a first aid kit. "Where are you hurt?" he asks.

Wincing, I pull up my shirt, the blood caked to my skin hugging the material and irritating the wound as it peels off.

His mouth tightens in a thin line as he bends down for a better look. "Luckily, you don't look like you need any stitches."

Thank God.

As he starts to clean and dress it, I look at Scarlett. Her face is hidden behind Derek's bulk as he tends to her, but I know she's glaring at me. Hating me.

"What's Scarlett's alibi?" I ask.

"She went off with Daniel before you left with Henry. They've been dating for months, so no one will dig further into it."

I flinch. So Derek knew all this time and didn't tell me. "You're *dating*?" I hiss, my voice venom as I tug my shirt back down.

"It wasn't serious," Daniel says, not looking at me. "It was one bad drunken kiss."

"Fuck you."

Stepping away from him, I head for my car. Derek intercepts me. "You need a shower." He inclines his head at a sink. A mirror hangs over it. My face is splattered in blood, my hair matted with it. Bits and clumps stick to me, and my stomach twists at the knowledge that they're part of Henry's brains.

Walking swiftly to the metal sink, I slip my keys back in my pocket and do my best to get clean.

Derek tosses me a towel and a fresh shirt. I pat my skin before drying my hair, though once I get home, I'm going to have another shower. A long hot shower where I can scrub away my skin. Maybe I'll get a haircut too. I don the new shirt.

Scarlett shoulders in behind me, hitting me hard, and I stumble forward, the wound in my side erupting in pain. Spinning around, I slap her across the cheek, my palm stinging, as do my eyes.

"I'm your fucking mother," I hiss, my emotions volatile, my stress exploding down to my hands. I want to hit her again. I want to scream at her that I've been touched by a reaper, and that she doesn't get to spoil my last twenty-four hours with her shit. I'm falling apart, but trying so fucking *hard* to hold it all together. *For her.* So she doesn't panic.

So I can get her home safely.

And she does this?

"Respect me, you little shit."

She stares at me in shock, her blue eyes wide as she clutches her face. My chest aches with her pain, and my lips wobble with words I can't garner.

I'm sorry.

Wordlessly, she turns to the sink. Her hands shaking, she turns on the tap.

I move away from her, not trusting myself to be within reach of her. I dig my keys out of my pocket, twisting them in my fingers, needing to move.

When Scarlett is all cleaned up, she keeps her head down as she shuffles to my car. Derek grabs her arm, his eyes on his son. "Choke her."

"What?" I step forward, but his glare halts me.

"You slapped her across the face. When that bruises, her alibi is going to be weak. Unless Daniel chokes her, and they both tell the police she likes it rough."

"No," Scarlett chokes, but my thoughts are racing too fast to respond.

"Dad –"

"Do it, Daniel. Or I can shoot the both of them and hide their bodies. Fighting this war is more important than any of us." His free hand drops to the gun at his hip, and I know he's serious.

I take a small step back, my eyes skittering around the garage, but there's nowhere I can run fast enough. Even if I could reach my gun in time, it's empty.

"Then shoo–" Scarlett starts, but I blurt, "Daniel!"

Cursing, he walks over to her. Scarlett trembles as her eyes find me, begging me to stop them.

I don't.

I can't.

She needs an alibi.

A shutter closes over her, and her lips trembling, she yanks her arm free of Derek's. Lifting her chin, she waits for Daniel's hands to close around her neck.

He hesitates only a moment.

And then he grips her throat and squeezes.

Her eyes bug wide.

Her face starts to grow red, then blue.

But she doesn't struggle.

Just glares at him until her eyes flutter.

And then her knees buckle.

Daniel lets her drop to the floor, stepping back with a glance at his father.

She gasps for breath. I jolt forward, but as I kneel and reach for her, she shoves my arm away. "Don't...touch..." She struggles for air, her body quaking on the concrete floor. "Me."

"I'm just trying to help."

"Fuck…you."

My hands balling into fists, I fight the urge to grab her hair and yank her to her feet. The ungrateful shit only thinking about herself. Doesn't she know how much I'm hurting?

Twenty-four hours.

That's all I have.

And I'm spending it here, *with her* because she's my fucking daughter.

She's my daughter.

Pushing to my feet, I step away from her. Cross my arms over my chest. "Are you okay?" I ask her softly.

She doesn't answer as she crawls to the Lexus, then uses it to climb to her feet. In heart-stabbing silence, she opens a back door and climbs in.

I swallow hard.

Daniel reaches for me, but I step away from him, no longer yearning for his touch. Continuing to my car, I get into the driver's seat. "I'll text you about the meeting tomorrow," I tell Derek hoarsely.

He nods, opens the garage door, and watches us drive away. The tinted windows hide Scarlett from view, but at this time of night, no one's out anyway.

Silence boils the air between us, prickling my skin and heating the walls of my throat until it all melts together. Verbal fingernails claw for the exit, scratching up in their desperation to be heard. But the rage burning off Scarlett keeps them trapped.

I swallow, flicking my tongue across my mouth, trying to get it to work. It isn't until I turn onto our street that I manage to blurt, "I'm sorry about tonight."

She seethes in silence for a moment. Each word pulled from her, she hisses, "You tried…to kill me."

"I couldn't risk you turning. Your soul would've been

damned for eternity."

She spins towards me, spittle flying along with her arms. "So you, what? Decided to *execute* me without even checking?"

"You were bleeding. And I saw his mouth –"

"He yanked me out of the fucking window!"

I flinch as I pull onto our drive. "I didn't –"

Shoving open her door, she steps out.

I scramble after her, undoing my belt, but she doesn't head for the house. She heads for me, grabbing at my hands. Taken by surprise, I can't hold on to the keys as she rips them from my fingers. Grabbing my shirt, she yanks me out of her way, shoving me to the ground.

My hands scrape across the drive as she climbs in. I push against the ground to turn around.

"Scarlett!" I shout as the door slams shut.

The engine revs, and I scramble out of the way. Maybe she doesn't kill me by turning into a werewolf. Maybe she drives me over.

"How long have you been sleeping with him?" she shouts, her voice raw and cracking.

Bruises are already starting to form on her pale flesh.

The engine revs again.

I step to the side, my heart racing. "I didn't kno–"

"How long?"

"Six weeks!" I shout, terror pushing out the words.

Her face twists as she screams and bangs a hand on the wheel. "I fucking hate you! I hate you! I wish you were dead!"

The urge to grab my gun has me bending down as the engine revs once more.

But before I can yank up my pants leg, she reverses down the drive.

"Scarlett!" I chase after her a few steps before halting.

A movement to my right catches me, freezing my legs

along with the air in my lungs. *Wolves.*

Tears burning my eyes, I scream inside. I'm going to die with my daughter hating me.

But as I turn to face the wolf the reaper foretold, all I see are shadows.

My skin crawling, I swallow hard and pedal back.

When nothing moves, I run for the house, grab the spare key from its hiding spot under a false rock, and rush inside.

The door slams behind me.

I fall against it with a shudder.

My ears straining, I listen.

Nothing but silence.

No scratch of claws.

No terrible howls.

My heart still in my throat, I race up the stairs and to the back of my closet. *I need bigger ammo.*

TWELVE

HIM

I stare at the closed door of my neighbor's house, my hands fisting as I shift out of my shadow. The fight I just witnessed between mom and daughter, between my girl and *her*, fills me with a rage to kill. To seek vengeance for her pain.

No one upsets my girl.

My eyes dart down the street, following the direction the car disappeared in, the smell of burning tires still crisp in the air. My girl loves her family. *She's* all she has in this world.

But I don't care if *she's* fucking family. *She* hurt her. And that is an unforgivable sin.

I take a step forward, rage building in my chest at all the emotions, the pain and panic, I sensed flowing off my girl as that engine revved. My magic burns, yearning for blood.

Her blood.

I'll kill *her*.

Maddox forms beside me and throws an arm across my

chest before I can move again.

He's been holding me back all night.

Convincing me with his fucking psychology degree that killing people in front of my girl will make her fear me too much.

Make her hate me too much to accept our blood bond, allowing the blood magic to drain me, then kill me simply by refusing to finish the ritual.

But my girl is alone now.

She won't see me kill anyone.

"Varius wants us back −" Maddox starts.

I shove him away from me, my magic burning beneath my skin. Hungering for the blood of whoever hurts my girl, and that list grew long tonight. "Then go," I snap, taking a step forward. "I'll follow as soon as the bitch is dead."

"Killing her m−"

Might make my girl hate me. Fear me.

I cut him off, already ahead of him, having had ample time to think of a plan while watching her in that damn garage, getting touched by that man. "She won't know it was me."

My youngest brother sighs, clearly more on his tongue, but without a word, he vanishes back into his shadow, knowing there's no bartering with a reaper.

There's no outrunning one either.

I take another step forward, strong with purpose and cold rage.

Tonight, *she* dies.

Tonight, my girl becomes family-less.

But I will be her new fucking family.

And she will never know pain again.

THIRTEEN

HER

I sit with my back against the wall of my closet, my shotgun aimed at the door, my ears straining to hear any foreign movement. The wolves aren't going to catch me off guard. For the next twenty-odd hours, for all the time I have left in this world, I will be vigilant. I will not make it easy for them to kill me.

But with every minute that passes in silence, my heart rate starts to slow. There's not one sign of the werewolves having found me. Nothing lurking downstairs. Or outside of the house. The only sound is the rush of blood flooding my skull.

And even that starts to quiet.

Surrounded by silence, I wonder where Scarlett is. If she's safe.

I should've done more to get her to stay.

My heart rate spikes at the thought of her alone. What if she's already dead? What if, right now, my little girl's being murdered? Right now being hunted by the sups not hunting me? Screaming for me to save her as wolves tear her to pieces? Their claws digging into her skin as she begs and cries, ripping off flesh, her intestines spilling down her legs.

I shake my head, trembling against the wall of my walk-in closet.

No.

No, she's alive, I try to convince myself even as a bone-deep truth squeezes around my lungs.

She's probably just driving around, letting off steam.

A car will not save her.

Not from a werewolf chasing her.

Or a vampire or a witch. My blood pounds in my skull as that terrible knowledge claws at my chest, making me feel as if I'm the one dying. As if I can actually feel her last moments. *A mother knows...* A mother knows, and I'm just sitting here alone in my house while my daughter is being killed right this moment.

I can *feel* it in my bones.

Her life leaving her.

Her screams of pain.

Tears rolling down my face, I shift my legs, about to climb to my feet. But the noise of the front door opening cuts through my plans and my grief, and I become attuned to everything. Every brush of the still air over the raised hairs on my arms. Every creak of the house. Every bead of salt that fills my nose. The bitter tang of fear creeping across my tongue. The grip of the gun, its trigger slick beneath my finger.

"Hannah?" a man calls up the stairs, breaking the spell of intense awareness.

Scrambling upright, I run to the locked door of my room. My fingers fumble with pulling it open. My heart thunders in screaming relief. I start to run downstairs and into his arms, but a sudden thought freezes me just outside the door.

"Daniel?" I whisper into the darkness, half raising the

gun in case it's some sort of trick. "What are you doing here?"

I don't ask how he got in. Derek has a key to every WALL member's house in case he needs to go in after their death or while they're in jail and clear out any incriminating evidence. And not just about the world of the sups or our involvement in the WALL. Any crime we ever commit, he'll clean. All members are too precious to lose, our fight against the sups too important.

Daniel's head pushes through the lighter shadows as he climbs the stairs, and at the sight of him, I nearly crumble. He's real. Not a trick of a voice. Not a lure to bring me downstairs.

"I wanted to make sure you're okay," he says.

"If anyone sees you –" I start, thinking about our alibis, an instinctive response that pushes me closer to a level-headed calm.

"I'll say I came back with Scarlett."

Scarlett. My heart shatters as he rounds the railing, his hands up at his sides, unthreatening. "She's not here," I whisper. "I think she might be –" The word digs its claws into the sides of my throat, refusing to get pushed into the air. To become real even though I *know* it already is. I shudder as Daniel's arms come around me.

And the feel of danger I've been consumed by all this time doesn't disappear; it merely changes into a different sort.

He's my daughter's ex-boyfriend.

Whose body feels too damn good in the dark.

"You should lea–" I stop as he lifts a hand to brush his thumb across my tears, swallowing the words that would make him go. I know his feelings for me grew past fuck buddies weeks ago. He became more gentle, more...aware of me outside of his father's office at the WALL complex. Going out of his way to do things for me. Searing me with lingering looks and touches I've tried to ignore, not returning the feelings, but now...

With less than twenty-four hours to live, having been marked by that reaper, and with Scarlett, the only family I have – *had* undoubtedly gone...

She would understand our coming together in grief.

So I don't step back when his hand feathers into my hair. I lift my chin when he bends down to kiss me.

I need this.

After everything I've suffered tonight, I need to just be loved. Tears roll down my cheeks.

His touch is soft and gentle, but as soon as the gun drops from my hand, I wrap my fingers in his shirt and yank him against me while backpedaling into my room. I need this.

I need this.

His hands dig into my hair, my ass. One palm comes around my good side and squeezes my breast. I arch my neck, my tongue pushing between his lips, the desperation clawing in my veins urging me on. To get closer. Go deeper. To taste what it's like to be loved before I die.

Scarlett's father never loved me. He was a one-night stand whose name and number I never got, never wanting him in our lives.

No one after him was substantial either, all my love, all my attention given to my daughter.

A woman who wished me dead without even giving me a chance to explain.

I slide a hand between us, cupping the bulge digging into my pelvis. "I need your cock inside me."

Filling me. Chasing away the loneliness of death. The fear. Letting me know what it's like to be loved.

His tongue dances hotly with mine. His cock thickens in my hand. Our breaths mingle in each other's lungs as he lowers me gently onto the bed, careful not to jar my wounds.

I tug at the waistband of my pants as he jerks at his own. His cock springs free, and he grabs the fabric on my legs and pulls it down just past my ass, the bare minimum we need. Wrapping his fingers around himself, he pushes the head into my pussy. I arch against him, sucking him deep inside me as my lips find his, crying out against his tongue.

I shimmy my legs as he begins to move, trying to get my pants completely off. I don't want to feel constricted. I want to move in mindless bliss. To not think anymore. About Scarlett... About the reaper coming for –

I scream.

In fear, not pleasure as Daniel is ripped from my body and flung straight up. He hits the ceiling with a *crack* that resonates inside me, making me flinch, then he drops back on top of me. His knees and elbows bruise my body and jar my wounded side. I scream again as I try to shove him off me.

He groans.

Blood gushes down his pale face and into my eyes. I instinctively close them even as my brain screams at me not to. His body jerks to the side this time.

Horrible thuds echo around the room. The walls shake. One hand wipes frantically at my eyes as the other grasps to pull up my pants. I swing my legs over the bed. His body slams into me again, knocking me to the floor. He groans in a broken plea. More blood stains me. More fear squeezes me.

Shoving him hard, I push to my feet and run for the door. I squint through the darkness, catching a silhouette staring right at me as their arms move, flinging Daniel in another spell.

I dive for the shotgun left in the doorway.

My fingers curl around the metal as I roll onto my back and lift to aim. The gun's knocked from me as Daniel's bulk crushes my chest. It skitters across the hallway out of reach, and I gasp as I struggle to breathe.

Air rushes into my lungs when his weight is lifted, then leaves again as I'm picked up too.

My muscles still with a heaviness I can't break free from. Sweat pours down me as my eyes flick left and right, searching for the witch.

I half expect to see the reaper from the mirror, but all I see is darkness.

And then light floods my retinas, and I close my eyes on reflex.

Daniel's scream has me opening them again, and I match his with one of my own as I watch his intestines hit the floor, his stomach cut open with a long knife.

The witch holding it has his back to me, but his black ponytail beckons recognition.

Khalid!

My neighbor turns to face me, his dark eyes piercing my soul. Grabbing Daniel by his throat, Khalid hauls him forward. Daniel's feet twist in the mess of his intestines. Inhuman screams leave him as he shudders forward, his shoulders caving in.

My eyes can't leave the trail he's leaving behind. It stretches from the bed to me, magic weighing it down so more is pulled from Daniel with every step.

I don't look up from it until Khalid is right in front of me. He grabs the back of Daniel's head, fisting his hair, and lifts.

"No one touches my girl," Khalid says, his voice boiling with a rage that reeks of death.

My body twists in chills that leave me shaking, my feet off the floor, caged in the muscles he holds with magic.

His girl?

"I'm...sorry," Daniel whimpers as his eyes roll back into his head. "I didn't know...she was..."

Khalid laughs, the noise piercing my stomach.

Slamming his knife into the wall beside me, he then

grabs Daniel's chin in his free hand and turns his head to face his. Humor fills my neighbors eyes, but it is far from easy. "Do you think," he says slowly, a vicious draw to his words, "that I would treat my girl like this?"

He nods at me hanging in the air, unable to move. My heart runs too fast to stay in my chest. My fingers twist beside me, but my arms stay still. Locked and caged under his spell.

"That I would hurt her? Just for having a bad taste in… garbage?" He hisses that last word with a derision that slices apart my pounding heart.

"No," he says softly, strongly as his fingers tighten on Daniel's chin. "No, this *bitch* isn't my girl."

My eyes widen as a scream breaks through my lips.

Scarlett. He's talking about fucking Scarlett.

All the little pieces slam together. How every time he smiled at me, my daughter was behind me. How he was washing his car so he could get a better view of her. How he knew where her room was despite never being in the house. How he came over just to see her, leaving when she did…

"If you touch her –" I start, not flinching when his eyes turn to me. "I'll kill you."

He drops Daniel's chin to grab his knife from out of the wall. All humor gone, he plunges the blade into the side of Daniel's neck and jerks it forward, ripping vocal chords, arteries, and bone. A fountain of red sprays across my body.

"You let this piece of shit touch her. You let him *choke* her. And now you will learn what happens when anyone hurts my girl."

Daniel's body drops to the ground, and Khalid runs the knife across my chin.

I glare at him, refusing to give him any satisfaction in killing me.

"Fuck you," I seethe.

A smile curls his lips, as dark as his eyes. Reaching into a pocket, he pulls out a bullet and holds it up to my face.

"Curse me all you want. But you will die for your sins."

My eyes pound with the blood in my veins.

Freezes with it too.

I know that bullet.

I use them in my Sig.

The one I aimed at Scarlett.

"You would have killed her tonight," he says, his words colder than the knowledge suffocating me, "if I had not arrived in time to grab this out of the chamber."

It heats in between his fingers, the metal glowing hot.

I thrash around frantically inside the binds of my prison. But my body doesn't move. My head doesn't twist as he lifts it to my eye.

"You fired your own bullet," he says, then plunges it deep into my socket.

FOURTEEN

HIM

I want to take my time with her. I want to punish her correctly for her sins, but the sun will be rising soon, her driver will arrive soon after, and the things I want to do can't be hidden under a werewolf attack. Wolves can't wield magic, can't keep healing their prey so they can carve into them over and over and over again.

I push the bullet deeper inside her eye as she screams, but I don't pierce her brain.

I want her alive for a while longer.

With the bullet fully embedded, I trail my fingers down her cheek. I wanted to heat the bullet until it melted her eye, leaving it to drip down her face, but a werewolf can't do that either.

And I need to make sure the WALL thinks this is a wolf attack. I need Scarlett to think the same.

Her mother screams as she hangs in front of me, my magic keeping her from thrashing.

"I want you to know I've warded the room," I say as I

grip her jaw, digging in my fingers. "You can scream as loud as you want, but no one will hear you. No one will call the cops on your behalf. You will die here tonight, by my hand. You will not be saved, Hannah. You will not be shown mercy. You touched my girl. You *hurt* my girl, and so I will hurt you in return."

I release her chin as I turn my attention to the wall beside her. Slipping the knife inside the hole already there, I yank down, slicing apart the wall. Three more times, and I've created a false set of claw marks.

"Fuck...you," she spits, her words harsh with pain. They make me smile. Maddox enjoys breaking his targets – the more feisty at the start they are, the more of a thrill he gets. As a reaper, I've killed more than him, more than anyone in our family, but I never embraced the enjoyment of it. Perhaps because I hunt our old friends, our cousins and uncles. All the Family that turns on us, trying to steal our legacies.

But I'm enjoying it now.

The thrill of breaking her, of making her scream in the throes of death...I'm looking forward to it.

My smile stretches.

"I'm going to cut open your chest," I explain to her as I trail the knife over her stomach. "I'm going to slice open your face. Then I'm going to carve out your liver and your heart as it still beats. A werewolf is obsessed with those two, you see, and I need your little boy toy to think what I want him to, to *do* what I want him to."

Her eyes widen, and I laugh.

"Oh yes, we know about the WALL. I know all about Derek and the reason he hunts us."

"Why haven't you killed us then?" she rasps, and it's cute how she tries to grasp at 'logic' to convince herself I don't really know about her friends.

"You don't go out of your way to kill mosquitos," I say

dismissively, angling the blade so the tip digs into her. She grits her teeth so she doesn't scream, but it's only a little knick. She won't be able to stop herself when I go deeper.

"Scarlett is already...dead," she hisses before a forced laugh expels through her lips. "You'll never have her..."

I straighten and take a step back. The knife spins in my hand as I study her.

Her laughter increases, and I let her bask in her hope before shattering it completely.

"She is alive and showering in room 241 of my family's hotel," I say, knowing the pain of that will hurt her just as much as my blade. "I will have her tonight."

She screams and actually manages to lunge forward a bit. Magic feeds off raw emotion, and right now, the rage burning through her nearly matches mine.

Nearly.

But not quite.

Because she's mad her daughter is going to live a life with 'monsters.'

And I'm pissed she tried to kill her.

Our anger is not the same.

Our love for Scarlett is not the fucking same.

Binding her limbs completely again with my magic, I step forward and slice the knife across her body. She screams, her body convulsing, and I work quickly so she has time to feel every punishment before she passes out.

Three more cuts open her up, and then I move to her face, digging into her bloody eye and ripping down. The bullet falls out, and I catch the evidence of my presence here. Pocketing it, I carry on methodically.

She screams.

I smile.

Blood pours around us, but it isn't enough.

I want her healed.

I want her under my blade for months.

I want her chained away, forced to watch as Scarlett becomes what she so desperately tried to stop. I want that knowledge tearing her up inside.

I want her to suffer for her sins.

I want to make her do more than bleed for one night.

But I.

Fucking.

Can't.

Because Maddox got into my head with his fucking psychology degree, telling me how Scarlett can't know I killed her mother. How that would push her away from me to the point she might try to kill me herself. Where she never accepts our bond.

Because my girl is stubborn and strong, and she will make me work for her love.

I'm looking forward to it.

But first I need to kill her mother. Eliminate the threat that would rather see Scarlett dead than with me.

Basking in the choked sobs and whimpers falling from Hannah's lips, I cut out her liver.

Silence descends, and I hate that she's passed out before I can cut out her heart.

She doesn't deserve such mercy.

Pushing out with my magic, I wake her up. I force her to live through every cut of her chest, every tug of her heart as I start to pull it free, snapping arteries and veins.

She doesn't even have the energy to scream anymore. She just sweats in pain, her one eye glossy and unfocused until I finally rip out her heart, giving her *mercy.*

As her last breath leaves her, I call on the magic of my shadows. Dropping both her organs into it, I then dig into my pocket and pull out a sachet of fur.

Releasing my spell, I wait for her body to hit the floor. As she sprawls out at my feet, I crouch over her and shake the evidence of wolves carefully into her wounds. I do the same with Daniel.

Out of the two of them, I'm not sure which one I regret not being able to play with more. Daniel was supposed to be her boyfriend, yet he was fucking her mom all this time. He hurt my girl too. Both with his hands and his actions.

And I let him off so fucking easily.

My jaw tight, I force my thoughts on the future. I can't protect Scarlett from the pain these two inflicted, but I can be there for her now. I can give her a family that really cares.

Sinking into my shadow, I reappear in my shower, turn it on, and scrub myself clean. Freshly dressed, I then head for my family's hotel.

For my girl.

It's time she knows she's mine.

FIFTEEN

HER

Sitting in the shower, my legs sprawled out in front of me, I stare at the white tile walls. The water pelts my skin. The droplets run in random paths.

They split.

They connect.

They split again.

Completely ignorant of how lucky it is to be inanimate, without all the pain and rage and damn emotions of the living world.

I clench my fist with the urge to scream.

My whole body shakes as I sit under the sizzling spray.

My own fucking ma...

I see myself in the woods, down on my knees, with sticks and stones digging into me. Thick tears run down my face, and I can feel the snot that choked me. It doesn't feel real, and yet, it feels entirely *too* real.

More real than anything I can feel now.

She raises the gun.

My throat closes.

Words scream silently from my lips.

She pulls the trigger.

I flinch at the *bang* ringing in my ears. My body flashes cold beneath the spray. The bullet digs into my brain.

I'm dead.

My own fucking ma...

It was only blind luck that the gun was empty.

Pushing an arm against my mouth, I scream.

My own fucking ma...

Someone bangs on the wall in the next room, and I want to ignore them, *need* to ignore them as I expel all my pain, but I don't. I was raised better than that.

A broken snort leaves me at that thought. My scream abruptly ends.

Raised better.

Ma barely raised me.

I raised myself between cowering in the principal's office, wishing she would stop forcing me to wear tight clothes that 'accentuated my body' – a body I didn't want as a fucking child.

Between eating more and more so she'd be disgusted and let me wear what was comfortable.

Between the sneaking downstairs in the middle of the night, terrified she'd catch me. Hiding food in my room to eat in the comfort of privacy.

And between boyfriends. Two fucking boyfriends, both of whom she fucked.

I rub my arm angrily across my cheeks.

I've never told her I know about Nick, the guy I lost my virginity to. How I know she seduced him minutes after he slept with me, minutes after I told him I loved him.

I crept downstairs to find something to eat, having not had anything all day due to her being home, and I caught them in the act. She hadn't even closed her door all the way.

But I was so numb, so desperate to not believe what I saw, I pretended as if it didn't happen. My own ma with my first…

At least Nick didn't come back to my room after to tell me goodbye, that he was going home. He just ghosted me, and I cried myself to sleep for months.

Not that Ma noticed.

Not that she showed one ounce of fucking guilt or regret.

And although I had loved Nick a lot more than I ever cared for Daniel, this betrayal hurts more.

The final straw.

The crack that's splitting me open.

Opening me up to all her bullshit and abuse.

And it *hurts*.

It hurts so fucking much knowing the only person I have in this world, my only family…

Broken sobs, unable to pass my too-tight throat, pour into my tears. I turn the tap up higher, letting the water burn me. Seeking a pain to override the agony inside.

The heat barely registers.

I turn it up higher.

The *bang* of the gun reverberates inside my skull again, and I drop my arm with a sudden flinch.

Fuck. I knew she hated me. I knew she despised having me and wished I was skinny and succeeding in school and active in something she approved of. Be something she could be proud of. But to actually try to kill me?

To march me out into the woods and have me down on my knees like a fucking execution?

Hot angry tears burn my eyes, so fitting with the steam curling around my body.

"How could you *do* that?" I seethe, but the wet cubicle gives no answer to my pain.

I slam a fist into the tiled wall.

Pain shoots up my wrist. It feels so good. The person in

the other room shouts at me, but I don't care.

I hit the wall again.

And again.

And again.

Until my arm shakes from the agony that's blissful to my broken heart.

My own fucking ma...

Bang!

SIXTEEN

HIM

I reach Noir Hotel, my magic coiling in my veins. Pain lances through my shadow form, pulling me towards the front door. My girl is two flights up, and I'm forced to take the fucking stairs. A true shadow can climb walls, but our family cannot, our magic limited to only traveling across horizontal surfaces.

So I slip between the cracks and into the lobby, Xander sits behind the desk, his slicked-back black hair glistening under the warm lights. He lifts his head as I start to shift out of my shadow. Then he scrambles to his feet, his arm shooting forward underneath the desk.

"Khalid –"

"Give me the key to room 241."

He pulls out a resealable bag full of labeled packets of hair. "We've collected –" He stops as I stride towards him, his brows snapping together as he muses over what I said.

But I didn't fucking stutter. A small smile curls my lips as I stop at the counter. "Give me the key, Xander," I say softly, "or it will be your hair we leave at the next crime scene."

His eyes widen briefly. Then he drops his arm holding the bag of hair the cleaning crew here collected for the Family's use. Business owners, visiting CEOs, politicians, and even celebrities that stay in the penthouse at the top – they're all in there. All for us to blackmail or hurt with my magic. Manipulating the soul like I did with Cid's requires a piece of that person's physical body. This is how we collect most of them.

We have hotels all over our territory, which spreads up half the eastern coast, and each one collects hair left in the drains and on the pillows, the nails on the floor, the semen on the sheets.

But I don't care about any of that right now. I just want the fucking key so I don't freak out my girl by suddenly appearing in her room.

Xander spins on his heels, his arm reaching out before he's turned all the way, muscle memory guiding him to the key I want.

He doesn't ask me why I need it or why I'm here before the sun's risen as he hands it over. He's a good little soldier. Loyal and smart enough not to be any nosier than he's paid to be.

"Maddox will collect in the morning," I say over my shoulder on the way to the stairs, meaning for the bag of hair and other bits. I yank open the door and run up them three at a time.

On the second floor, I head left, towards the rooms 231-260. A door opens further down the hall, and my eyes narrow on the angry-faced man stepping out. He stomps over to his neighbor's room and raises a heavy-handed fist. *241.*

"Knock and lose your hand," I say without the slightest rise to my voice. I'm not far from him now, and my power pulses restlessly beneath my skin, latching onto his puny form, poised to take his hand.

"What the fuck did you sa–" He stops abruptly as he swings towards me. His face pales as he meets my gaze. A smile graces my lips.

He cowers against the wall, his bulk hitting it with a *thud*. He reaches behind him, grasping for his door as I stop in front of 241.

"Go check out," I order without looking at him. His lips spew spittle and fear as he mumbles something about having an early appointment anyway. Yanking open his door, he falls inside his room. The door slams shut.

I tap gently on 241. Despite the key in my hand, I don't want to use it unless I have to. She's on edge tonight, and me suddenly appearing in her room will most likely send her over.

"Scarlett?" I call out as silence burrows into the space between us. I know she's awake, the pain and rage rolling off her too strong for her to be asleep.

"Khalid?" My name is muffled but coming closer, and I slip the key into my pocket.

The door parts, and she's standing in front of me with a towel wrapped around her head. Damp patches darken her shirt where it clings to her skin, and in my peripherals I notice the two large circles around her nipples. She isn't wearing a bra, and the urge to fill my palms with the beautiful weight of her has me digging my fingers into my thighs.

"What are you doing here?" she asks, her voice a little broken. She stands to the side of the door, already half inviting me in, a desperate need not to be alone clear in her eyes.

The urge to pull her into my arms makes me take a step forward. "I saw you drive off earlier," I say softly. "I wanted to see if you were okay."

Her eyes are red and raw, and she glances away briefly.

"I'm fine," she mutters.

Cupping her cheek, I tilt her chin up. Wide eyes fly back to mine as she shuffles back. "What are you...what..."

I brush my thumb across her lips. She swallows, and the working of her throat brings my gaze to the angry bruises marking her skin.

My girl.

With another man's fucking mark on her.

The fingers of my other hand dig into my thigh, but the ones on her face stay gentle. I will never hurt her, even in my own rage.

"You don't look fine," I say, my eyes purposely on her neck.

I kick the door shut behind me as I guide her further into the room.

"It's...nothing," she lies, and my gaze finds hers in the low light of the sun just now peeking through the blinds.

"Who did this?" I ask as if I don't already know. As if I haven't already taken him out like the garbage he was.

She swallows, and I can see the stories flickering across her face as she debates which lie to tell me. Not giving her the chance to force such distance and mistrust between us, I push the tip of my thumb into her lips.

A gasp of air feathers across it, followed by the damp heat of her mouth. Her cheeks hollow out just slightly as she sucks me in, and a hiss leaves me as my cock jumps in a desperate bid to feel the same.

"I told you earlier" –while I was washing her mother's car– "that if you ever need me, to call. Why didn't you?"

Her tongue strokes the underside of my thumb as her eyes grow heavy. Her chest rises rapidly as silence spreads between us.

"*Scarlett*, why didn't you call me?"

She pulls her head back, but I follow her, keeping us connected. Her eyes flick to mine as a beautiful pink blush heats her cheeks. I slide my thumb out slowly, leaving in just the tip as I wait for her to speak.

"I just had a fight with my ma," she says, so much pain left unsaid. "It was nothing to trouble you over."

"*Nothing* you ask of me is trouble," I respond, pushing my thumb slowly back into her mouth. "If you need me to reach the top shelf or pick up some tampons at three in the morning, you call me. If I just left, and you remember something else you need, you *call* me. It would be my pleasure to help you however you need."

She stares at me, so many thoughts rushing across her face. Eventually, her tongue moves beneath my thumb as she murmurs, "Why?"

I hold her gaze as I pull my thumb out and push it back in. "Isn't it obvious?"

Her pretty blue eyes widen.

Her nostrils flare as she stares at me in silence.

Withdrawing my thumb completely, I raise it to my own lips and suck it in.

A small, hot moan pierces the air, zinging it with an electricity that wraps around my cock.

My blood pulses with my magic, a feverish hum filling me as I stand still, waiting for her to make the next move. My thumb tastes of her, but it's quickly gone, and I want more.

"But you don't even know me," she whispers.

I pull my thumb out of my mouth. My eyes bore into hers as I smile, thinking of all the little parts of her I've fallen in love with. "I know you roll your lips in when you want to laugh because you're embarrassed of the noises you make."

Her cheeks flare a gorgeous red.

"I live for those noises. Those half-snorts, half-cackles followed by the coughing you try to use to cover them up."

She glances away.

"I know your favorite food is a burger with onions and

pineapple." My chest expands with the memory of her dancing in their kitchen a day when her mom was out of town on a work trip. She smiled as she waved her arms around her, moving her hips as she danced freely. My voice lowers as if sharing a secret. "It's mine now too."

Her gaze flies to mine, a hesitant light inside them. "It's good, right?"

A full grin spreads across my lips. "It's fucking terrible, but every bite makes me smile because it reminds me of you."

She sucks in a breath as she searches me in the silence I allow to linger. "That's so fucking cheesy," she finally says, and I laugh.

It's deep and surprising, but it feels good. As the reaper of my Family, I don't get close to many people. Even my brothers are kept at a distance in case there's a day I am forced to kill them too. That is the role of the third eldest. The first is the heir. The second is his right-hand man. The third is the shadow that protects them.

She looks at me, a softness lighting her face.

Fuck, I love her looking at me like that. "I know you're smart and strong and have so much passion for the things you love."

She wets her lips as sorrow overtakes her. "Ma says I'm unmotivated."

"Your mom's a fucking idiot." And dead. But I don't say that.

"But I don't have any ambi–"

"You write every night in your journal. Like clockwork. Even established writers don't have such commitment."

Her eyes leave mine again. "It's just silly musings."

"Nothing about you is *silly*, Scarlett."

She hesitates with her thoughts, and I shift where I stand, willing her to see her how I do, not like how her bitch of a mother did.

She sucks in a quick breath as her body stills, and I know *that* question has finally weaseled into her brain.

"How do you know all this?" she asks, fear widening her eyes.

I take a step back, trying to give her the distance she needs to feel safe. "I don't sleep very well." The souls of my victims scream in my ears during my dreams when my training can't keep them down. Not all of those I've killed haunt me. Most I don't care about. But there's been a few good friends who got greedy with power. A few relatives who made one damning mistake. And one feral cat – an accident that got in the way. That one hurts the most.

The tabby was so innocent.

So pure.

It didn't deserve to die.

Not like everyone else I've killed.

"It calms me, watching you write," I admit freely. "So many emotions flit across your face."

She blushes hotly, and I know why she does. I've read her entries in the darkness of her room, the fantasies she jotted down about me, the memories of our interactions with a twist of the direction she wished they'd gone in.

I wonder what she'll write about the carwash.

If she'll mention she couldn't take her eyes off my cock as she fumbled with the hose. How she jumped when I brushed my fingers across hers taking it from her. How she nearly fell on her ass, tripping over her own feet. How she clutched at my shoulders when I grabbed her. How she not so subtly pressed herself against my erection.

A grin spreads as I raise the thumb that was in her mouth back to my lips. I run it across the lower one, my eyes heating on her body, remembering the taste of her pussy on my tongue.

Was that only twenty-four hours ago rather than the eternity it feels like?

I wonder if she'll write about the words I murmured against her ear. How she wishes she did something other than just stammer and flee back inside. She's so much more sultry in her journal. So many dirty thoughts.

"If you ever need me, kira, *just call. Any hour of the night. For anything at all." I flick my tongue against her ear, and she whimpers in the back of her throat before stepping back, a gorgeous blush coloring her cheeks.*

She clears her throat as she breathes out slowly. "What does *kira* mean?" she asks, and I like that we were both thinking of the same thing.

I shift to lean against the wall, crossing my arms as I study her. "It doesn't really translate into English."

"Oh. What is it? Italian?"

"Drazic."

Her brows pinch. "Is that an ancient language?"

I nod but don't elaborate, allowing her to believe it's a lost language of Earth rather than a demonic one that's been around longer than humans have existed. All witch texts are partly written in it, the first of our kind having learned language from them "Badly translated, it means 'master.'"

Her eyes widen. "You call me master?"

"It's a bad translation." I pause a moment, finding the right words for her, ones that don't require me to explain the special bond between an enslaved drazic demon and its master – something that also won't translate well.

"One's *kira...*" I say slowly, still thinking it through, "makes up all the things that make life worth living for."

Her lips part, but she doesn't interrupt.

"Your *pain* feeds into mine. Your *happiness* feeds into mine. Your desires, your dreams. So you *control*, for lack of a better word, my life through the existence of yours. Therefore, you master it. You own it." I shake my head, a frown pulling at my lips. The word means so much more than that. "It really doesn't translate well."

Scarlett stares at me, her mouth opening further and further as she grasps for words. "I... That's...that's... Are you saying...you...lo..."

She falters, but I don't look away, not embarrassed by her knowing just how much she means to me. Real men don't make their girls work for their affection, don't make them wonder with any doubt. They love unconditionally.

"Fuck." She falls back on the bed, sitting on the edge of it, her words still lost somewhere inside.

I wait, not caring how long it takes. Whatever my girl needs.

My phone vibrates in the quiet, a text pinging through, but I ignore it.

She looks at me, speculation in her eyes, a want for a distraction as she's not yet ready to deal with everything life has thrown at her tonight.

"It's my brother," I say, not needing to look at the phone to know Varius' patience has run thin. "He wants to discuss business."

"You have a brother?"

"I have seven."

"*Seven?*"

I smile, liking the look of shock on her face.

"Your poor ma," she breathes, and I laugh.

"Any sisters?" she asks.

I shake my head. A hundred years ago, mom had her first batch of children, doing her duty to create soldiers for our gang wars. Seven children –five boys, two girls– all dead before their twentieth birthdays. The next batch of kids didn't live much longer. Mother refused to bear anymore, deciding instead to fight on the front lines. It wasn't until a treaty was called that she had Varius and the rest of us.

"Are you the oldest?"

"Third."

"I wish I had siblings." *A friend, us against the world –* words she doesn't say but are clearly voiced in the light lilt of her tone.

Words only ever uttered by a single child.

My brothers and I all get along for the most part now, but growing up was a bloodbath of testosterone.

"You can have mine," I say without hesitation, and she half snorts, half giggles before she coughs, a hand flying over her mouth.

My eyes narrow on her, not liking that she's hiding herself from me.

She drops her arm, but her laughter is already gone. Stolen from me by her bitch of a mother beyond the grave.

Still, my body relaxes because she gives me a small smile. "You really don't mind it?" she asks.

Straightening off the wall, I walk towards her.

She sucks in a breath as she tilts her head back to hold my gaze. I stop right in front of her, nearly touching her knees. Her eyes become half-hooded. Her throat works beneath the dark purple bruises.

My lips tighten as I'm reminded of that fucker having his hands on her. Of Maddox holding me back as I stood outside that fucking garage and let it happen.

I want to heal her with my magic, but what I know won't take away bruises. I can keep her from the edge of death but can't do anything for her now. Besides, she isn't ready for an introduction into my world, not after all she's been through tonight... And not until after she deals with what is to come when Phil finds her mother's body and Derek convinces her it was wolves.

Lifting a hand, I cup her cheek. My cock jerks with how close her face is to it, and her eyes dart down and linger. A low growl rumbles from my chest as I lean down and slide my hand into her hair, tugging it back with a sharp pull.

The towel falls to the bed.

Her eyes widen before fastening onto my lips. A few more inches and I –

Her phone goes off, lying on the mattress, its ringer making her jump. I still, knowing the significance of this call. The sun is up. Phil would've arrived at their house a few minutes ago, walked in through the open door, and found their bodies.

If that isn't him calling, it will be the police.

Straightening, my fist still in her hair, I grab her phone to give it to her.

SEVENTEEN

HER

"Don't!" Panicking, I lunge sideways to grab Khalid's wrist. It's either the police having found the massacre in the woods or my ma wanting to 'talk.' And fuck, I'm not ready to deal with either.

My hand trembles against his skin as I wait for him to look at me like I'm crazy. I have bruises all over my neck. Little cuts and bruises here and there from being pulled out of a fucking windshield and thrown at the ground. My eyes are red rimmed and now wide like a psychopath's. I drove off in the middle of the night, tires screeching. He must have so many questions. A feeling that something is very, very wrong.

I want to trust that I can tell him anything, that his declaration of lo...of me being his...*kira*...is real and not just an infatuation he built up during his nights of restless sleep. But how the fuck do I tell him about werewolves and the WALL without sounding even more insane than I look? And if I tell him and he doesn't immediately call the men in white, then that would mean *he's* the crazy one because normal people don't just accept the fact that werewolves are real. Jesus fucking Christ, this is all too much.

I just want to be brainless for a while. Deal with it all tomorrow. It's why I opened the door after hearing his voice, desperate for the familiar so I could pretend this was all just a dream.

But the phone keeps ringing, and he's staring at me for an explanation. My throat clogging, I reach for a truth that won't destroy what he's given me – a small hope that I'm not all on my own.

Because after today, regardless of what Ma wants to 'talk' about, I'm cutting her out of my life, and then it'll just be me…

Me alone in a world full of literal wolves.

I shiver as I part my lips to blurt out some lie, but his fingers tighten in my hair, and the words still in my throat. I look into his deep-brown eyes that flicker with a knowledge of understanding.

"Take the call, *kira*," he murmurs. "It'll be okay."

I want to tell him it most definitely won't be because that single call is going to change everything regardless of who it is.

Unless it's spam.

God, please let it be spam.

But I know it isn't, and my breath comes in shaky gasps.

Khalid's thumb still hovers over the accept button. His gaze stays on mine. I want to tell him to ignore the call, but I don't, a horrible urge to rip the Band-Aid off and just deal with it keeping me quiet. I need to know…I just don't want to do it myself. I need him to do it…

His eyes flicker across my face.

I look at him on a silent plea, unable to find the words to ask such a silly favor.

His face softening, Khalid's thumb presses down on the

button, and I suck in a breath as my fingers tighten on his wrist.

Leaning down, he places his ear against my phone. "Hello?"

There's a moment of silence where I pray it's spam. But then a deep sexy voice rumbles, "Khalid?"

"Vlad," he says, his eyes narrowing slightly. "I thought you were on leave." He grabs my phone with his other hand and straightens. My fingers still circle his wrist, and I realize he's letting me hold him. A hot sharp rise of embarrassment in my cheeks, I start to release him, but he twists his forearm and threads his fingers through mine.

The warmth of his touch heats up a bit of the fear consuming me, and I still, watching as he talks to whoever it is on the phone. My thoughts are fuzzy, my brain not quite connecting how whoever this Vlad is knew to call Khalid on *my* phone.

His muffled voice comes through the mobile, but I can't hear what he's saying anymore. Khalid's eyes never leave my face as he responds, "She's here."

My whole face is burning now as I can guess what kind of questions he's asking. *"Just the two of you? This early in the morning? In a hotel?"* I don't know why he would be asking those, and I try to convince myself he isn't, but I'm too aware of the fact that it *is* really early in the morning (like Khalid stayed the entire night...) and I'm not wearing a bra.

Khalid's eyes narrow on me just slightly, then dip to my lips before coming back up again. My heart beats rapidly in my veins, pulsing across my whole body. His fingers are too sensitive on mine, and my hand burns with a need to move.

His thumb brushing back and forth across my skin, Khalid says, "We're at Noir Hotel."

Then he ends the call and tosses my phone back onto the bed.

I want to ask him who Vlad is and why he was calling Khalid on my phone – *how* he knew to do so, but my words falter when he continues to stroke my skin.

"That was the police," Khalid murmurs. His voice is so factual, without any emotion that it takes me a moment to register what he's actually saying.

My eyes shoot open. "The police?"

I pale, knowing what they're going to ask me. The massacre plays in my head. I struggle to breathe under the assault of so much blood, so much chilling laughter. That 'man' on the hood of the van... His eyes bore into mine, and the words he said crash through my ears, "Let's have a little fun, shall we?"

Strong fingers grip my chin, and a blurry face appears close to mine. I flinch away instinctively, my following blink clearing my vision enough I can make out Khalid's strong jaw and straight nose, his beautiful tan skin. My eyes fasten onto his, looking for a focus that'll keep me grounded.

His left hand is in my hair as his right still grips my fingers. I'm squeezing his hand, panic clenching my muscles tight. I try to relax them, worried I'm hurting him, but no flicker of pain or relief crosses his face. Just concern. For me.

No one's ever...

I swallow down the emotions, trying to focus on what to say to Khalid and the police, police he's told to meet us here. *Wait –*

"You're on a first-name basis with the police?" My voice wobbles just a little as all the crime shows I've ever seen, all the recent news articles I've read about the ramping gang life in St. Augustine hit me. Why else would they know each other with such hostility? My fingers suddenly feel like they're in a vice, and I struggle to breathe calmly amidst rising panic.

"Not all of them," he says. Khalid's eyes holding mine, his

grip on me relaxes as he continues an explanation I couldn't find the courage to ask for. "Vlad has a vendetta against my family."

Holy shit, he means a mafia Family, doesn't he?

I try to shut down my overactive imagination and just listen, but after everything I've seen tonight, all I can focus on is violence.

"He used to date one of my brothers, and it didn't end well."

Relief exits on a small gasp, but what follows is a heavy weight that bars the door to my throat as Khalid crouches in front of me. His face is full of concern.

"He called to tell you your mother is dead, and he needs to interview you."

I stare at him as that weight grows. A numbness flows through my limbs and up to my brain. Sensation stops registering. His lips move, but I don't hear any words. His fingers brush my skin, but I don't feel them. Even the visual world starts to fade into a pinprick...

And then like a broken dam, it all slams back.

Sagging forward, I gasp. He's instantly on the bed beside me, a strong hand rubbing my back. I heave on broken thoughts. *Ma is...she's...dead...how...Wolves?...Did they follow us?...Track our scent?...Can they find me too?*

Jerking my head up, I look at Khalid sitting beside me. Is my mere proximity signing his death certificate?

"Breathe, *kira*," he says as he shuffles behind me, his legs parting around me. His arms encircle me as he leans back, pulling me with him to open up my chest a bit. His lungs expand against my back., setting a pace I frantically try to match.

He breathes in.

I follow in a mad dash.

He breathes out.

A ragged breath parts my lips.

He breathes in...

I run after him.

He breathes out...

I pivot and race for the other end.

My pulse thunders in my chest, fighting for dominance with the feel of his breathing. Which to follow? Panic or calm?

My fingers dig into the cushion of my thighs, my nails cutting through the thin fabric of my pants. Then his hands are there, his thumbs rubbing soft strokes against my skin in rhythm to his breaths.

He breathes in...

My thoughts freeze as I focus on his hands and chest moving against me.

He breathes out...

And in...and out...

With a shaky breath, I follow, finally starting to expel the uncontrollable fear.

The panic.

He breathes in...

But holy fuck, what do I tell him? And should I leave if my presence will get him killed? What if the wolves find him, smelling me on him? Can they even do that?

Releasing one of my hands, he cups my chin and guides my head to look at him. Deep-brown eyes pierce through the lingering panic. "I've got you, *kira*," Khalid murmurs. "Everything is going to be fine."

I want to believe him, but what can he possibly do against werewolves? Ma is dead...as are so many others...

"Vlad will be here in a few minutes." He squeezes my hands, getting me to focus. "He's going to have questions about the marks on your neck and all your cuts..." His eyes darken for a brief moment before flattening again into a grounding calm. "Someone might've seen you two arguing as well. And even if not, you left tire marks on the drive."

My tongue sticks to the roof of my mouth. I know he wants answers, but I can't give them to him. Can't tell him about werewolves being real... I'd be charged with insanity at Ma's trial.

"Look at me, *kira*."

My eyes refocus on him and his five o'clock shadow.

"Tell Vlad the marks are mine. That I was here with you for the past couple hours, and your mom argued because you were coming to meet me."

My brain wraps around his words, at how quickly he came up with them. *Like he has experience.*

Thoughts of him being in the mafia rise again, but this time, they're met with an eerie calm. If he's dangerous, maybe he can stand up to wolves... Don't gangs have heavily guarded compounds?

He's not in the mafia, Scarlett. Stop making up stories and focus.

"What are you going to tell them, *kira*?"

I let out a shaky breath. "That I came here to meet you."

"Good." His hand on my chin feathers across my cheek. "But Vlad knows my preferences, *kira*. I need you to mark me."

My eyes widen. "What?"

"I need you to leave hickeys on my neck and scratches on my back."

I gape at him in overwhelming silence.

"Vlad won't buy the alibi otherwise. He knows I don't stop until a woman loses all control."

My eyes dip to his neck. My cheeks erupt into flames over his words. Over him not stopping until I'm a mess in his hands. The sharp arousal pierces through more of my panic, and I grasp at it in order to try to think everything through.

The hotel phone rings once, then stops. I jump from the surprise, but Khalid doesn't even flick his eyes towards it.

He keeps me the focus of his sight as he says, "That'll be the front desk telling us Vlad is here. Mark me, *kira*." He leans his neck to the side as he threads his fingers in my hair.

I twist on the bed to face him, my heart beating rapidly as I wet my lips. I've dreamed of kissing him for months, the scenes haunting my dreams. Scenes that went a hell of a lot further than kissing… But they never started like this.

Like an alibi to explain my whereabouts last night when my ma was being murdered. Tears burn my eyes. For all my hatred of her, I didn't want her dead. Especially not killed by wolves.

I think about her last moments, the panic and wounds she would've suffered.

Khalid's arms come around me as he pulls me against his chest. Not for me to kiss his neck, just to hold me. Comfort me as I cry.

I dig my fingers into his shirt and weep.

His hand strokes soothingly through my hair as he murmurs words too soft for me to hear over my broken sobs. But I feel their meaning coursing through me. *I'm here*, kira. *I've got you. It's going to be okay.*

But how can it ever be okay?

A knock at the door makes me jump, but he keeps me in his arms. My head lifts to search his eyes, and he turns to meet me, his gaze having been on the door.

There's a moment of heavy silence beneath the raps on wood.

Then my lips are on his neck, and his hold on me turns more possessive as he shifts me over his lap. I crawl onto him as my tongue strokes his skin and my mouth marks him as mine. A groan of unchained arousal pours from his lips as he tilts his head back. His fist tightens against my scalp for a brief moment before he guides my hands to the bottom of the back of his shirt.

I quickly shove up and dig my nails into his shoulders.

He hisses on an arch into me. He turns his head towards mine, and certain he's about to kiss me, I lift my chin.

"Another one," he rasps instead though, fisting my hair. Desperately, I move my mouth to the other side of his neck.

"Scarlett Davis, this is the police. Please open the door."

I suck hard, leaving a beautiful red mark on Khalid.

He pulls me up by my hair. His hot eyes meet mine as my lips stay open on ragged pants. He ducks his head to kiss –

Cursing under his breath, he nudges me off his lap.

A clear erection pushes against his pants as he strides across the room.

The door opens to show Detective Vlad with a hand raised to knock again.

My pulse skitters as Khalid stays in the doorway.

And then he steps back, turns, and leads the detective into the room, changing my life forever.

EIGHTEEN

HIM

Vlad stands in the hotel room with his green eyes on me, his jaw locked tight, his fists clenched. If I knew he was on call this morning, I would've set it up so Hannah's body wasn't found until after his shift was over. Vlad's vendetta against my family started when our father killed his sister. It strengthened when my mother slaughtered a hundred of Blood Fang's soldiers in a single night – revenge for them having killed four of her seven children within a month.

It settled into a tight rope of tension due to the signing of the treaty between the three gangs a few years before we were born. But he developed an instant hatred against Rudy – a mutual feeling that often led to bloody brawls.

One night, I found the two of them in an alley, bite marks all over my younger brother's body, burn marks all over Vlad's, both naked and entwined and doing things I never wanted to see. I tore them apart just as they both finished and got hit with something worse than any blade.

Maddox would laugh his ass off if he heard the story, but

no one but the three of us knew – about *that* or Rudy fucking Vlad in the ass. And no one would ever know because that was the one and only time they'd ever get to do *it*.

As much as I wished to stay silent and let my brother enjoy what he enjoyed, I was a reaper. The Death Hunt would not permit any sort of convergence between our two Families. If the wolves found out about the two of them, the treaty keeping peace between our three gangs would burn overnight and we'd all go back to war – a war Aleric and Varius would not fight side by side on just because two of their loved ones wanted to fuck. And if that happened, Rudy would be charged with endangering the Family.

Then I would be forced to kill him.

So that night, I ripped out a chunk of Vlad's hair – a failsafe to protect my brother. If I caught any *hint* that they were fucking, I wouldn't hesitate to kill him. A doll of alexandrite crafted in his image stays inside my shadow domain, always with me, always ready to be used.

Glaring at me as I sit beside Scarlett, the urge to suck me dry flashing in his emerald eyes, Vlad pulls out a notebook and pen. I'm certain he already suspects me of this crime – did as soon as he heard my voice on Scarlett's phone, and it's killing him he can't pin this on me.

Although a human cell clearly cannot hold a Shadow, any sup charged with a crime automatically brings in the Special Crimes Unit – an international organization that claims to aid government agencies in solving 'impossible' crimes. In truth, their sole purpose is to govern sups, only picking cases that are suspected of being caused by one of us. Meaning their cells can damn well hold anything from demons to witches to werewolves lost in the craze of a full blood moon.

The only reason Vlad hasn't already planted evidence is because Aleric has gone to extreme measures to make sure the SCU thinks the vampires in St. Augustine's police department are all law-abiding citizens. If they knew they were part of a gang, they would destroy his entire coven. So if Vlad wants to nail me without destroying his own Family, he's going to have to do it completely by the book.

Poising his pen above paper, Vlad turns his gaze to my girl. "Hello, Scarlett Davis," he says. "I'm Detective Vlad Laska. I'm sorry for your loss, but I'm going to need to ask you a few questions and then have you come down to the station to identify the body."

She's perched on the edge of the bed, her hands twisted in her lap. Her pale cheeks look whiter above the dark bruises on her neck and face. When her chin wobbles, my girl rolls her lips in to bite them still. Releasing a shaky breath, she looks directly at Vlad. "How did she die?"

"They were attacked by home invaders with a knife."

She shudders, bowing in. A hand goes to her mouth. A tear slides down her cheek. "Wh..." Her question trails off as her shoulders suddenly stiffen. Jerking her head up to look at Vlad, she whispers, "They?"

"Yes. Your mother was found with a younger man –"

"*Daniel*," she hisses, and I reach over to grab her hand, squeezing it to signal she needs to rein in her anger.

Vlad catches it anyway, a smirk playing across his lips. But if he thinks he can pin my crime on her, I will kill him before he can file the paperwork.

"How do you know the other victim, Ms. Davis?" Vlad asks.

"He was my boyfriend."

"Was? How long ago did you break up?"

She hesitates before looking at me, then quickly to her lap again. I squeeze her hand, this time giving comfort.

"Uh...it's complicated... He ghosted me about ten days ago." Swallowing, she looks back at Vlad and exhales shakily. "But a couple hours ago, I found out Ma's been fucking him for the last six weeks."

He raises an eyebrow, his pen poised over the paper. "I bet that made you angry, knowing you weren't as good."

She half-snorts, half-sobs as her face twists with pain.

I move the fingers on my free hand, hiding their dance behind my thigh. Beneath my shirt, one of the runes inked across my skin glows red, and the vampire grimaces as pain flares across his shoulders.

He glares at me, and I hold his gaze, daring him to keep hurting her.

His voice tight, he asks, "What time did you two get here?"

Tears clog her throat, and she sucks in harsh breaths in an attempt to answer. Squeezing her hand, I cut in. "About two hours ago. Around...four?"

"Did you two arrive together?"

"Yes."

"I'll want to verify that with the security tapes."

I grin, letting him know he can watch them all he wants, but they'll only show what I want them to. I'm not magically adept when it comes to technology, but my brother, Talon, loves playing with electricity. "Of course," I deadpan. "I'll get Xander to drop them at the station later." Right after Talon removes my image from them.

"Do you know of anyone who would want to hurt your mom or Daniel?" he asks, going through the motions. He already knows what really happened. The human police might accept that this was a brutal knife attack, and the WALL might believe it was wolves hiding their kills, but Vlad isn't stupid enough to think my presence here is a mere coincidence.

Scarlett chokes, then falls into a coughing fit. She leans forward, her elbows on her knees as her chest shakes. By the time she's breathing normally again, her palm's damp and her fingers are clenched around mine. "Do you think the murderer knew her?" she asks, the slightest bit of hope in her voice.

A hope that it wasn't wolves. That it was just some disgruntled voter. A human citizen.

"She was butchered. In my experience, people rarely expend that much energy on a stranger."

Color drains from her face almost completely, and I know she's imagining the horror of the scene. When she shudders, I pull her hand onto my lap.

"Where did you get the marks on your neck and face, Scarlett?" he asks, scribbling on his notepad.

Swallowing, she raises a hand to her throat.

"They're mine," I say as she stutters over her answer. She ducks her head as Vlad takes a step forward. He stops right before I'm about to make him.

"They look a bit narrow for your hands," he says flatly.

"They're mine," I repeat, softer now, daring him to keep pushing this.

"Was it consensual?"

Scarlett's head jerks up at the same time Vlad grits his teeth in pain. His notepad drops to the floor as his fingers spasm. He bends down to pick it up, ducking his head of ginger hair, denying me the satisfaction of watching the twisting of his face.

My fingers flatten again, releasing the magic coiling around his heart.

"Yes," my girl finally answers as he straightens. "It was consensual." Her words aren't strong, a mere breath of air. Her body shakes against my side.

"Well." He flips the notebook shut and slides it into his pocket. His eyes find mine as his jaw twitches, and I can just make out the tips of his fangs before he tucks them away. His knuckles turn white as he grips his pen. "That's all my questions, Ms. Davis. If you can please come with me to the station now, I need you to identify the body."

"Now?" she whispers.

"Yes.

Her tremors intensify until the whole mattress starts vibrating beneath us.

"We'll meet you there," I tell him, a clear dismissal in the harsh warning of my tone.

His lips tighten, but he doesn't argue. Smart man. With a single nod, he sees himself out.

The door clicks, and I give it a few seconds for him to walk away –his kind having better hearing than ours– before turning to Scarlett. I wrap my arms around her and pull her against my side. "It's going to be okay," I murmur into her soft brown hair.

But those words seem to just break her.

Sagging against me, she pushes her head into the crook of my neck and sobs. Tears seep into the collar of my shirt, cooling the flesh beneath. She hiccups as she cries. Her feet kick with a restless energy. Wails stick in her throat, and her fists clench and unclench against my stomach.

I've never felt more helpless.

More guilt than I do in this moment.

My girl is being torn apart by rage, betrayal, terror, and agony –partly because of me– and all I can do is hold her.

NINETEEN

HER

I don't want to move from Khalid's arms. I don't want to collect my things and head down to the police station to identify my ma. I don't want to stand in their hallways after, trying to figure out where to go because I can't go home to a crime scene.

Tears flood down my cheeks and pool on the fabric beneath my chin.

I clutch at him as I cry, as all the horrors of the last few hours scream inside my skull. The protective bubble I put up at the sound of Khalid's voice earlier, when he knocked at the door, the desperate glass house I erected to keep the real world out now shatters.

I can't keep hiding from the truth in his arms.

Can't pretend everything will be okay.

Can't cling to my bubble of normality.

The truth is my ma is dead.

Werewolves are real and probably killed her.

And *Daniel.* As much as I hated the both of them, their

deaths don't feel like karma. Their deaths just make me feel guilty and terrified. How long until the werewolves come after me?

How long until Khalid is killed simply because I'm with him?

That thought pushes me out of his arms, and I rock to my feet as I rub a hand across my face.

He stands, his eyes on me in concern. It's a look I've never seen before – not rushing me so he can carry on about his day, not judging me for 'being emotional,' just full of worry *for me*.

I wish today was yesterday – when Khalid could have confessed to a girl hopelessly crushing on him, who was halfway in love with him after months of watching him from her window. From my bed I could see directly into his gym and often touched myself while he worked up a sweat. That me would have died to hear him call me *kira*. A dream come true. A fantasy made real. Even when I started talking to Daniel, I imagined him as Khalid.

But present me? New me whose world is completely wrenched inside out?

When I look at him, all I want to do is cry. Even in death, Ma robs me of happiness.

That bittersweet thought shoves a choked laugh out of my lips.

Even in death... Even in death... Even in death...

"I hate you! I wish you were dead!" Those were my last words to her. She died thinking I hated her. And maybe I did. Maybe I still do. But right now, I just want her alive and frustrating me to the point I never want to speak to her again.

I shake my head as I struggle to breathe through my clogged nose and throat. Khalid moves towards me, but I jerk back, and he instantly stills.

I can't fall into the comfort of his arms.

Can't hide from the painful truth anymore in a bubble of Khalid.

Can't...can't stay here while my ma lies on a slab in a police station needing me to identify her so she can finally be laid to rest.

Pushing my palms into my eyes, I scream.

"Tell me what you need, *kira*," Khalid says, his voice cracked and raw, as if my pain really is his.

I shake my head harder and scream again. It breaks off into broken sobs. I crumble in on myself, images of Ma being ripped apart by wolves like Nicole and Detective Henry were just hours ago filling my skull. I start to drop to my knees, my legs no longer strong enough to hold me. *I'm no longer strong enough...*

Khalid's arms come around me, and he grunts as he catches my full weight. He takes a small step back before locking his legs and holding me upright. "I've got you," he murmurs against my hair. "I'll deal with the police. Just –"

I fling my head side to side as I struggle to push out the words. "No...I want...I *need*...to...see her."

To say goodbye. *Ma...*

Khalid's hands rub my back as he tenses beneath me. A second later, his lips press into my hair. "Okay. I'll drive you. Where are your keys?"

I point to my bag on the bed. He shifts me in his arms, still holding me, but he must be struggling beneath my weight. I shuffle back, giving him space – giving me some too. I take a deep breath.

As it releases on a shaky sob, Khalid quickly grabs my bag, then comes back to me. I raise a hand to my mouth and bite down. Needed pain slices through me, the bruise from banging on the shower wall earlier blistering under my teeth. I release my hand, and the pain recedes, under my control. The agony inside does not.

Khalid's fingers thread through my other hand and pull

me towards the bed. "Sit down," he says. "I'll get Xander to bring your car to the door."

The mattress sinks beneath me, and it takes everything I have not to lie down, curl up on it, and go to sleep.

Sleeping won't bring my ma back.

It won't make werewolves mere fiction again.

Won't remove the memory of Ma pointing her gun at me.

That image jerks inside me, barricading my throat, not letting another sob break free. It dams my eyes, and I sit like stone, staring at my feet. She would have killed me. Left my body in the woods for the wolves to eat.

Yet here I am, crying over her, wishing she was alive.

Why? So she can degrade me some more? Make me eat more *trash*?

My stomach churns as the smell of ketchup, the stain that was on the bag of cookies, burns my nose. My fists clench on my lap as anger overtakes the pain.

So she can fuck Khalid to make it a beautiful set of three? So she can find another reason to march me out into the woods and execute me down on my knees?

My jaw clenches as rage burns away the last flickers of agony. Just when I decided to cut her out of my life, she goes and dies, getting in the last fucking word, making me care, making me feel guilty over finally standing up to her. Making me cry when she would not have cried over me.

The look in her eyes when she marched me through the woods assaults me. Wild but unwavering and without any regret. She looked into my eyes, my begging wet eyes, and pulled the trigger.

Bang!

My nails dig into my palms as the sound pierces my brain.

Bang!

It's for the best, Gen.

Bang!
You deserve it, Gen.
Bang!
Another fucking excuse instead of an apology, Gen.

"I hate you," I hiss, and I wish so fucking hard she can hear me over the crackling flames of her new home. "I. Hate. You."

Khalid appears in front of me, crouched low, his hands covering my fists. He looks up at me in concern, but as his eyes flicker across mine, a calmness flutters through his. He's no longer worried. He almost looks...proud?

But before I can be sure, a knock at the door draws him away from me. I lift my head, my gaze following him to the hall. He opens it to show the guy from the front desk.

Khalid says something to him, but all I catch is "Talon" and "footage." My brain doesn't care to piece the puzzle together, but when Khalid starts to hand him my keys, saying something about getting the car, I push to my feet.

"Wait," I rasp. I don't want to wait here any longer. I don't want to exist in this bubble that is being controlled by my mother. I wanted to cut her out of my life. It should not matter that she's actually dead.

My heart twists in my throat, but I force it back down on a swallow.

It *doesn't* matter that Mother is actually dead. If she were alive, I would have nothing to do with her. It's only because she's dead that I miss her. Now my dreams of a future reconciliation, of maybe her seeing a therapist and changing...they're gone, never to see reality. And if I'm honest, that's what hurts more. The death of hope rather than Mother herself.

She was dead to me as soon as she pulled the trigger.
Like I was to her.

I rub an arm across my face as I march over to the two men. My feet are heavy across the floor, but my shoulders are light. Ma's no longer here to make me cower. To make me hate everything about myself. *I hate you.*

Stopping in front of Khalid, I rasp, "I'm ready to go."

His eyes pierce me, looking past my facade of strength to see my shattered soul badly taped up.

Or maybe he sees something more.

Something less flimsy.

Because he nods at me without a flicker of worry.

The man in the hallway steps to the side, and Khalid leads me out with his fingers entwined in mine.

The light of the corridor washes over me, and for a moment I hesitate. The bubble is truly gone out here. The real world is all that waits.

Khalid stops and looks over at me. Completely patient, not rushing.

Taking a deep breath, I lift my chin, then carry on.

Ma is dead. I keep walking.

Werewolves are real. I don't stop.

They're probably coming after me too. I move faster, purpose filling my strides as we enter the elevator.

I need to find Derek.

I need him to teach me how to kill the fuckers because I don't want to turn out like my ma in *any* way.

The elevator doors ping shut.

I hate you, Ma.

When we enter the police station, my eyes are red-rimmed but dry, my voice sore but no longer cracking. Khalid's fingers are still wrapped around mine, but I don't need his strength anymore.

I just need to get this over with so I can cut her out of my life for good.

Vlad walks up to us before we can reach the front desk,

his thick body tight beneath his blue button shirt and gray slacks. A scowl mars his masculine face.

"Ms. Davis," Vlad says, his tone bordering on rude. A few hours ago, I would have ducked my head beneath his withering gaze. Now I just stare blankly at him. His eyes narrow. "Nice of you to finally show up. If you will come with me."

He turns without waiting for an answer, then stumbles a step with a small hiss. My feet stay rooted. The woman at the front desk says, "I'm sorry for your loss."

I want to tell her I don't care. Ma abused me all my life, and just because she's dead doesn't mean I should be sad.

But I don't. I simply pull Khalid after Vlad. The chatter of the police station starts to fade as he leads us away from the public side of the building, down to the medical examiner's room. A cold hall stretches in front of us, only a few marks down from clinical.

Near the end of the corridor, Vlad stops beside a door. He pulls it open when we get close, allowing us to enter first. My legs freeze, my anger suddenly fleeing in the face of seeing Ma on a slab. Once I go in, it'll be final.

I'll be completely alone – a terrifying reality I suffered years of abuse just to avoid.

Moving in front of me, Khalid cups my non-bruised cheek as his eyes search mine. "If you need to go –"

"No." I shake my head. "It's not that. I just... She's all I have – *had*."

His gaze softens. His thumb brushes across my skin. "You'll always have me, *kira*."

My pulse skitters when he tilts my head back. His eyes bore into mine with a promised future I can almost see. My breath rushes out of me, and I want so hard to believe him. Dropping my gaze, I focus on the red circles on his neck.

Mine.

They're my marks. He held my head against his throat,

groaning and growing hard beneath me. *Wanting me.*

His words *are* a promise. I feel that deep in my bones. My chest expands with more than air.

When I lift my eyes, his are hot and fastened on my lips. I suck in a breath as he leans in.

"We don't have all day," Vlad snaps. Then grunts.

I start to pull away from Khalid in embarrassment, but his hand holds me there, and my whole body stills, my lungs included. His mouth closes on mine, and *fuck,* I learn the real definition of *mine.*

His lips are firm and possessive, a mark of claim that doesn't hesitate to take. His tongue pushes inside, not softly exploring but boldly staking. Jolts of pleasure skitter down my spine as he takes his time kissing me.

My cheeks burn with the knowledge of where we are, of what I'm about to do, but I don't pull back. Ma has taken so much happiness from me. I won't give her Khalid too. Won't give her the first man who actually looks at me like I'm worthy of being loved.

His breath fills my lungs as he growls a noise that only belongs in the bedroom. I jerk away on a gasp, desire for wicked things flooding me as my eyes fly open to meet his. A cocky smile curls one corner of his lips as he holds my gaze, letting me know it wasn't my imagination.

My cheeks on fire, I clear my throat and drop my gaze to his chest, not daring to look lower. Yesterday, I never would have made out with someone in public. *Who wants to see that, Gen?*

Embarrassment and shame erases the heat.

Khalid ducks his head to get back in my line of sight. "Talk to me, beautiful."

My chest squeezes over the way he's looking at me. As if he really means it, and for a brief second, he erases Ma's voice.

But he can't compete with twenty-two years of lessons.

"I need to see her," I say.

He studies me for a second, then steps to the side so I can go through the door Vlad's still holding open. I glance at the cop, then quickly away, his cold glare giving me chills. If he didn't like me as a suspect before, he definitely does now. Who makes out right before identifying their ma?

My stomach churns as I walk over to the large window looking into the medical examiner's room, Khalid right behind me. Two metal tables on wheels each hold a corpse under a blue sheet. I try to guess which one is my ma. *Probably the one with the woman beside it.*

The medical examiner, wearing a disposable blue gown, hair cap, and gloves waits beside the table on the right.

I tense as Vlad steps in and closes the door behind us. Crossing the small area, he opens the door leading into the coroner's office.

"Ms. Davis," Vlad says as he gestures me in. I swallow and move towards him. The chill of the room seeps into my bones.

Stopping beside the table the medical examiner is at, I look down at the corpse. Ma seems to be relatively whole, no missing lumps beneath the blue sheet. *Maybe it wasn't wolves.*

I breathe out slowly as the medical examiner reaches to reveal my mother's face.

Khalid tenses beside me. Vlad staggers with a hand to his heart, hissing in a sharp breath, and I look up at him. The ME stills, her eyes going to Vlad before darting to Khalid. Her lips twitch, and the fabric bunches in her fists. "Are you okay?" she asks Vlad softly, but there's a growl to her words.

"I'm fine. It's just heartburn. Pull it back." He winces again, his palm still pressed against his chest.

"Are you su–"

"Do it, Moira."

She pulls it back, and for a moment, I don't look down, my eyes now on Moira's face. Her pale skin is flawless and free of makeup. Her soft blue eyes look almost purple. They glance up at me, and I realize I'm supposed to be looking down.

My gaze falls as if in slow motion.

Then I'm staring at my ma – her face torn apart by claws.

Werewolves.

Silence blisters in my ears.

They managed to find her.

By following us or by tracking our scent long after we left the woods?

Does it matter?

They found her. They know where I live. It's only a matter of time before they find me. *I need to find Derek.*

I stare at the open gashes, and the thought that I can finally 'see into her mind' overwhelms me with the want to giggle. This is the closest we'll ever be to understanding each other.

I press a hand to my mouth as I roll my lips in, trying really hard not to laugh. *Don't do it, Gen.*

"Do you know this woman?" Vlad asks, his deep voice echoing around my skull.

I stare into Ma's one remaining eye. She doesn't look so scary now – doesn't look like someone I need to hide my food from, my boyfriends, my passions.

She looks old, and I love that she doesn't look peaceful.

I hope she rots in Hell.

As the anger rises, it destroys my urge to laugh. My hand tightens around Khalid as I drop my other from my lips. "Yes," I say flatly. "It's my ma...Hannah Davis."

"Thank you. Though I have to say, Scarlett, you don't seem surprised to see her in this state."

"She's in shock," Khalid growls.

Am I?

My eyes stay on my mother even as Moira puts the sheet back over her face.

I'm angry, is what I am.

Angry I can't yell at her for being a shit mom.

Angry I can't tell Vlad she tried to kill me.

Angry the whole world is going to think she was this wonderful politician who 'got things done' instead of a horrible person who abused her daughter to get her way.

And I'm tired.

God, I'm so fucking exhausted.

My emotions are whiplashing back and forth, ramming into me, bruising me every time they pivot from anger to depression to every other stage of grief. I didn't sleep at all last night. Haven't eaten in a while either.

Wordlessly, I turn for the door.

Ma is dead.

I don't have to not eat anymore.

I can have a burger without shame. With fries. And an Oreo milkshake after.

A slow smile curls my lips. I bite my cheek to rein it back in before Vlad sees. A half-snort, half-giggle beats at my chest. Oh, the irony of being charged for killing her, of having her wreck my life from beyond the grave.

You have an alibi, I remind myself, pushing down the rising panic. My eyes dart over to Khalid as he passes me to open the door. He dropped my hand to do so, and it feels a bit bare without his there, but I don't reach for him after stepping out into the hall. I don't need his strength anymore.

Ma is dead.

She can't hurt me anymore.

Can't manipulate me into hurting for her.

Tilting my head back to look at the ceiling, I breathe in deep and close my eyes. The door clicks shut, and I feel the two men moving around me. Dropping my chin, I exhale and walk forward as I open my eyes.

Derek.

He is striding towards us behind a uniformed police officer, his hands fisted at his sides, his lips twisted into a scowl. Dark anger fills his eyes, and for a second, I flinch backwards. Khalid moves in front of me, and I shake my head. I shouldn't be afraid of Derek's anger. I should crave it. It's what has kept him alive all this time. It's what's going to keep *me* alive. Though my anger is less from the loss of a loved one and more from spite to not end up like my ma.

"Is it them?" he asks as he stops in front of me.

I nod. "I only saw ma, but..." I trail off, not knowing what to say to a father about to see his dead son. Did the wolves tear about Daniel's face as well?

"You two know each other?" Vlad asks.

My muscles freeze as my eyes widen. Shit. We weren't supposed to know each other, were we? I try to remember what our stories were.

Derek shifts his gaze to Vlad's and holds it like stone. "Hannah and I were in a relationship. She introduced me to her daughter a few weeks ago. I didn't realize" –he nods at me– "she was dating my son."

"Or that Hannah was fucking him," Vlad says.

I flinch on Derek's behalf, but his face doesn't twitch a muscle.

"Or that."

The uniformed officer who guided Derek down here clears his throat. It doesn't do anything to cut through the tension.

"The body is just through here," he says, opening the door the three of us just exited.

My eyes flicker between Derek and Vlad, my breath held in my lungs as I wait for something to happen. For a long moment, nothing does. Then Derek heads for the door, and I exhale hard.

Although I don't know Derek well, the look he gave Vlad has shaken me. He looked at him like he was vermin, a monster not to be trusted.

My stomach drops as I glance at the thick-muscled man whose arms look as big as my head. *Is he a sup?*

Am I in danger even inside a police station? Have I just painted Khalid as a target by bringing him here?

My pulse rises in sharp tempo as I struggle not to give anything away. Is he the one who killed Ma and Daniel? I try to picture the werewolves from last night, but the only one who shifted into a human form was the man on the hood of the car, and Vlad is definitely not him. His nose is too wide, his jaw too square. But maybe he's that big gray wolf who stood behind him?

I shiver, goosebumps breaking out across my arms.

"Let's get you out of here," Khalid says as he takes my hand. "You need to rest."

But I don't want to go home. "Where –"

The door opens and Derek steps out. His face is slightly paler, and I know without a doubt, it is his son on that other slab.

My shitty ex-boyfriend.

Who died probably banging my ma.

Derek looks at me, and there's something in his gaze that makes me step towards him. Before, I was scared of him. Now, I want his darkness, his strength...

"Can I go with you?" I ask, my voice a quiver.

Khalid's fingers tighten on my hand, but I tug my arm away. Thankfully, he doesn't cause a scene, letting me go easily.

But I can feel his desire to grab me again as if it's my own. I shake the imaginary feeling away. I might like him a lot more than Derek, but Derek's house isn't next to Ma's and he can teach me things Khalid can't.

Maybe he can even protect me…

"Scarlett," Khalid says. "Come with me. I'll introduce you to my brothers."

I look at him, wanting to say yes, but all that will do is put everyone in danger. They'll just be more victims for the wolves.

"I can't right now," I say strongly. "But I have your number…" I trail off, not wanting to lie and say I'll call. Even if my mere proximity didn't put him in danger, how can I ever go back to normality?

And any therapist would tell me, jumping into a new relationship this soon after so much trauma… That would not be fair on Khalid.

I look at him, studying his face, wishing like Hell, today was yesterday. He steps closer, completely ignoring the crowded hall of people staring at us.

"You *call*," he says softly, his words a near order. "If you need *anything*, you call."

A phone vibrates somewhere, and I'm vaguely aware of the other people checking their pockets, but Khalid never takes his eyes off me. He cups my cheek, and I'm getting addicted to the feel of his palm on my face.

"Call me, *kira*," he murmurs as he places his forehead on mine.

I look into his eyes, trying to memorize everything about him. Tears burn in my throat as I realize I might not see him again for a long time, if ever. The wolves might kill me. Or it might never be safe for me to be around him.

Rocking forward, I press my lips to his. It was meant to be a quick kiss that can't tempt me to stay, but his fingers weave through my hair, holding me to him. His tongue sweeps inside as he steps close enough I can feel him hard against me.

And then he's gone, having stepped back and lifted his head, as if he knew I did not have the energy to do it myself.

He stands in front of our audience, completely unfazed about his erection. When he turns his head to Derek, nothing crosses his face, but I can sense a whole conversation passing between the two of them. A man's conversation: *I'm trusting you with my girl.*

Derek nods sharply, then starts walking down the hall. "Come on," he says, and I scramble after him, his long strides not waiting for mine.

Right before we disappear through the door to the public side of the police department, I look behind me.

Khalid's standing in the hallway, exactly where I left him, his eyes on me. His mouth moves.

Call me, kira.

I will.

TWENTY

HIM

It takes everything I have not to go after her.

Not to drag her into the nearest empty room and drop to my knees while she rides my face. The taste of her on my lips competes with previous memories of her pussy, and the desire to compare them in real time is making it difficult to stay standing.

My cock strains against my pants as my tongue rubs the roof of my mouth, mimicking the feel of hers.

"Ouch," Vlad mocks as the door finally closes behind my girl. "She really told you."

He laughs viciously, and I'm tempted to twist his heart completely this time with my magic. But I'm weaker than I want him to know, and if I use much more, he'll smell the blood rising up my throat.

This entire place is infested with vamps. We might be at peace, but you can't tempt pet sharks with bleeding bait and expect them not to attack.

"You pin this on her," I say softly, not bothering to look at him, "and I will destroy your stone." I might anyway given the shit he pulled showing her Hannah's full face instead of just the half I'd left intact.

His hand clasps my shoulder, and I know he's trying to get a sense for how weak I am. I would never allow him to touch me in normal circumstances. So with a pulse of my power, I drop him to his knees. My stomach twists with a pain of its own, but I lock my legs to stay standing, my pain tolerance a lot higher than his.

He grunts as his friend hisses behind me. But although two members of Blood Fang are at my back, I don't turn. Isaac, the cop who showed Derek down here, is a sired vampire, and there isn't a single one in St. Augustine that is older than forty thanks to Mother's rampage sixty-odd years ago. They demand a lot of energy from a sire, and with only the head of a coven being able to create them, it took Aleric years before he could make more.

With age comes power and strength; Isaac has neither. He's so weak he's barely higher than a WALL member on the threat scale.

"It won't change..." Vlad rasps as he leans against the wall to pull himself back to his feet. "...that your girl left... with another man."

I still, my entire body relaxing like it does right before a kill. People think it's anger that drives me, a terrible rage I need to expunge – the only way I can be reaper. But the truth is, it is indifference that pours through my veins. A numbness that turns people from living souls into mere *things* that need to be dealt with.

Isaac shifts backwards, unable to hide his cowardice.

Shadows pool around my feet, reaching out as I turn. Vlad jumps back, his fangs bared, shooting down past his lip. The door bangs open behind me as movement flutters through the air.

Moira comes out too, a scalpel in her hands. Another

sired weakling. So discounting her and Isaac, that only leaves six things for me to kill.

Vlad glances around the hall, his nose twitching, and I know he can smell the blood pooling in my mouth. A smirk curls his lips, but he doesn't attack yet. Doesn't break a treaty that will most likely see his Family dead. The wolves have already weakened them greatly; they cannot afford to fight us too.

Knowing I can't make a move in a place so public, he straightens and hides his fangs, retracting them back into his mouth like a snake's. "Everyone get back to work," he says with a smile. "Khalid here is just throwing a tantrum because his girl –"

He falls to his knees, a hand clutching his heart. Gasps tumble out of his lips as I push heat into the doll I just pulled out of the shadows crawling up my arm.

"Say another word," I suggest as I crouch down in front of him. Blood trickles out of my mouth as I talk, and my magic thrashes inside me, sensing my weakness, wanting to consume me just as much as Vlad does. I sacrifice a bit of my left kidney to push more magic into Vlad's stone.

Hisses and growls erupt around me as everyone shifts, but no one moves, knowing damn well I will kill Vlad as soon as they do. His Family needs to keep the peace with ours, but ours does not. We still have the numbers to fight the wolves...for now.

Vlad's eyes flash red with his anger and pain. His fangs start to poke past his bottom lip again. I tsk. "You should have better control than that. No wonder you all are being picked off one by one. Pathetic. Little. Lambs."

The smell of burning flesh seeps from his mouth as his heart heats inside his chest. It's not enough to kill him, but it'll take him a while to recover.

So many words burn inside his eyes, but they fade back to green, and he wisely keeps his mouth shut.

A pity. I was hoping he needed to get in one more word about Scarlett leaving with that fucking WALL member.

Rising to my feet, I send his doll back into my shadow domain. Vlad slumps forward, spewing out black smoke from his nostrils, and Moira rushes to his side. She bares her teeth at me on a growl but doesn't say anything as she helps her friend to his feet.

Turning, not giving a damn that I'm showing them my back, I walk through the sea of parting vamps.

Blood trickles down my chin, and I wipe it away with the back of my hand. With every step, pain lances up from my half-consumed kidney, but I push it back, keep it contained. Pain is nothing new to a reaper.

The door pushes open beneath my hand, and I step into the public area. Noise buzzes around me as cops take calls and interview witnesses. Heads lift in my direction. A few eyes narrow on me – more vamps that didn't run to poor Vlad's aid.

A scintilla of respect rises for them for being smart enough to know not to get involved.

Under their wary gaze, I step out into the sun. An urge pulls me left when I enter the parking lot, and I look in my girl's direction, our bond giving me a trail to follow. I breathe in, almost able to taste her, and my fists clench with a need to drag her back to my side.

But despite my earlier words to her about introducing her to my brothers, if I took her home now, it'd traumatize her more than the last twelve hours have. I need Derek to watch her for a bit while I smooth things over with my older brother...and make sure Maddox knows not to be a little shit.

Antonio Garcia is undoubtedly still trying to find her, but Derek's house is magically protected. Werewolves and vampires can't get in. Nor can most witches.

I can, but then, I'm the one who cast the spell last night

before visiting Hannah.

Derek, the ignorant little fool, is nothing but a puppet in a game he can't understand.

Turning my head from the pull of my girl, I head for Hannah's car. I slide her keys out of my pocket, then settle into the driver's seat. My phone vibrates against my thigh right as I turn the key.

I let it ring as I drive away from the police station. I'm only a few minutes from my house, but as soon as the station is behind me, I pull my mobile out and hit the accept call button.

Maddox has probably been telling them all sorts of lies in my absence. *"He's bonded to a WALL member. Worse, she's their creepy scientist." "She dissects all the bodies." "Cuts off bits for trophies too, which she hangs over her bed..."*

"Where the fuck are you?" Varius spits, his tone not its usual flat control, and I know he's angry over something more than a few missed calls and Scarlett being a 'high' member of the WALL. Something has happened, and I sit up straight as my foot presses on the accelerator.

"Who's hurt?" I ask, overtaking a flashy red Mercedes driving under the speed limit.

"Talon," he says sharply. "Antonio caught him alone, but he's stable. Why haven't you taken any of my calls?"

I glance in the side mirror as I knock the indicator to pull back in. "I had some personal business."

"Maddox told us you started a blood ritual." He doesn't sound happy about it, but Varius rarely does. "Assuming it's the woman?"

He's known about Scarlett –albeit not by name– for over a year. Him being the head of the Shadow Domain Family, me being his security – there can't be any secrets between us. He knows I ran into her two years ago, right before she went off to uni for her sophomore year.

Or rather, she ran into me with her head in a book,

laughing that half-snort, half-laugh over some scene. She mumbled an apology, but by the time she looked up, I was gone.

I tried to ignore her. A reaper with such a weakness is laughable. But every few months, my shadow form ended up in her dorm.

Then every month.

Then every week...

Towards the end of the school year, I started shifting into my human form whenever her roommates were out. I didn't touch her, just stayed on the other side of the room, trying to figure out what in Hel's name was drawing me to her. But every time I did, she seemed more restless. As if she could sense me. And when she first started touching herself in her dreams, moaning and gasping as she rode her fingers...

It drove me mad, making me not myself. Making me want things a man in my position couldn't have.

I told Varius when it started to affect my job as reaper, half expecting my brother to give me the order to kill her for the good of the Family. He didn't – perhaps he knew even then that I wouldn't. Nor did he give me an order to stay away from her, knowing that if I failed to follow, he'd have to carry out my execution.

He simply told me to get a handle on it. He didn't care how I did it, just to make her no longer a problem.

So I followed my girl home for the summer. My visits turned more frequent. Nearly nightly unless I was on a job. Yet, I still convinced myself she meant nothing. That she wasn't mine. Just a puzzle to figure out.

I went through all her belongings, first started reading her journal. But the more I discovered about her, the more I lingered.

Until one day, Varius nearly died because I was there watching her instead of him, instead of protecting him from those who wanted him dead simply because he was an 'abomination' without magic.

As my brother lay recovering in a bed for a week, his body incapable of healing like ours, Mom used her power to save him, and I vowed to stay away from her.

A reaper's control is unmatched.

For over a year, I avoided her.

But then three months ago, *I* nearly died. An uncle who'd taught me how to be reaper had tried to assassinate Varius and put his own son on the throne. After I tracked the two of them down, the fight was long and bloody. I passed out from blood loss, woke up in my bedroom at Mother's, and the only face I was desperate to see was Scarlett's.

I was back in her room that night, burying my head between her thighs for the first time. I nearly came all in my pants, watching her finish herself on her fingers. The next morning, there was a sudden sale of the house next door, its occupants getting paid a handsome sum to move across the country.

"Yes, it's her," I say as I turn right off Highway One.

"Fucking finally."

My lips twitch with a smile. Despite his words, he still doesn't sound happy. But then, he keeps everything close to his chest; too many friends and family have tried to kill him over the years, not liking that the head of the Family is magicless. An abomination.

Many want to support Leno, the second eldest. Many want to support their own sons. I kill them, but Varius has to live with their hatred. With knowing that every word they ever uttered, every smile and laugh they ever shared with him was a lie.

He is an island in a tumultuous ocean.

"Come here for a debriefing," he says, then hangs up the phone before I can answer. It was an order. There's only one answer I could have given anyway.

I pull onto my road. Traffic gets heavier before coming to a standstill. The front of Hannah's house is barricaded by the police and further blocked by news vans. Tapes are already rolling when I step out of the car. An officer in uniform moves towards me as the reporters recognize the car en masse. Cameras swing towards me, but I don't bother ducking my head, which is what I normally did in case Antonio Garcia was watching. But it doesn't matter if he knows where this house is. I bought it to watch over Scarlett, and now it's no longer needed. It'll be put on sale tonight.

Questions are thrown at me about why I'm driving her car, if I can confirm her death, if I heard anything in the night, saw anything. I move silently beneath their gazes, pretending to be too flustered and scared to speak.

The officer leaves me at my door, and I head in to pack my belongings. Everything fits into one bag, most of it clothes. The furniture will all be donated. They were only purchased so those looking in through the windows would see a furnished house.

Slinging the bag over my shoulder, I grab my keys off the table by the door, and head out to my car. The officer parts the crowd of cameras and questions. I get into my blue Buick and drive off, heading to Mother's.

TWENTY-ONE

HIM

I park the car and step out onto the L-shaped paved drive. A four-car garage is full in front of me, and three other cars fill the adjacent stretch of concrete. Mom's and Micha's (Varius' fiance's) are most likely in the garage attached to the house.

Thirty acres of private land surrounds the two-story building, but the biggest stretch one can see is the seven acres across the lake in front of the front porch. The rest of the land is thick with plants Leno uses for his magic.

We all have two innate abilities: the genetic power that binds the family (magic that allows my brothers and I to shift into shadows) and the one magic bestows on us individually after it courses through our system during our ascensions (a sup's puberty), judging us to see how it wishes to fit within our bodies.

Mine allows me to manipulate soul dolls. Leno, the second eldest, controls plants, both their physical shapes and interior properties. He can kill an entire family with a single almond stirred into their dinner. All my childhood, I woke up covered in vines strapping me to the bed as a Venus flytrap tried to consume my toes. It did manage to eat my left pinkie at one stage. Regrowing that had been a bitch.

"Your poor ma." My girl's earlier words come back to me, and I smile.

Perhaps we were a bit of a handful growing up.

I open the door beside the garage and make my way into the kitchen. The family is already inside it, Mother at the stove, this time with Micha. They're chopping up meat and vegetables for a big lunch as my brothers sit around the table, discussing something I don't catch before they all stop and turn to look at me.

Maddox grins wide. "Nice job with Ms. Davis."

Although the WALL are nothing but annoying gnats, the legislation Hannah planned to bring in today would have disrupted our business. Joe Kennedy, the most likely replacement for her in the republican party, and Mark Reynolds, the democrat running, might both understand how the power system in St. Augustine works, but it's only a matter of time before another Hannah comes along and is actually successful in creating a task force that will bring 'order' to our criminal streets.

Settling into the empty chair at the other end of the table from Varius, I look at Rudy sitting on my left. His hands move in front of him as he signs, "Lovely marks on your neck, Kali. Finally break your years of celibacy?"

Not giving him the respect of a response, I turn to Talon on my right. Maddox hoots and hollers as he signs something back to Rudy.

The table erupts into laughter. Talon's green eyes flash with humor as he half-wheezes, half-winces along with them. Ugly red wounds stretch across his shoulders under his black tank top. Varius clearly only allowed Mother to heal him 'well enough.'

"Ow!" Maddox rubs the back of his head as an onion bounces onto the floor behind him.

"No rude talk while we're cooking." Micha's stern voice only gets him to laugh harder as he turns to face her.

"Don't take your frustration over Varius being unable to please you out on us. Maybe if you two tried –"

He properly yelps this time as one of Varius' knives slices across his ear. The idiot should have known turning his back on Varius while he goaded him was a bad idea.

"Your poor ma..."

I grin, lifting a hand to one of the marks on my neck. I can feel her lips on my skin, and her bond pulls me left. I look in her direction and catch Rudy's eyes.

He signs. "You look happy."

My smile drops. He laughs with his hands.

"Between you and Varius, the next generation is going to be all stern faced and no joy to play with. If I leave snakes in their beds, they'll probably stab me."

I shake my head with a small curl of my lips as Mother chastises Maddox for harming her chances of grandkids.

"How is Varius going to perform well now with that hanging over him?"

The table roars as Varius sits in irritable silence. Micha ducks her head as her cheeks blush red.

She has only recently moved into our family home, her body having been traded for the support of Varius backing her father's claim of territory up north. Despite the year, most marriages in the three gangs are still business deals. He needs an heir, and although Mother will never say it, she recommended Micha Black because she's one of the few strong enough to still have a good chance of making offspring with him who are capable of wielding magic.

The stronger a parent is, the more likely their ability to control it passes down. Magic consumes the weak full stop;

it does not care about age. The hope is that Micha's magic is strong enough to overcome Varius' curse.

If not, she will be passed over to Leno, and his heirs will become the next generation. It's a silent deal Varius backed; his loyalty is to the Family, not just his own grasp of power.

It's why I will die for him.

Why I kill for him.

He has earned my respect a thousand times over with the sacrifices he has made for this Family, starting at the age of twelve when our father walked out the first time.

"Khalid," he says softly, and the table quiets, only a few snickers from Maddox still heard. "You have spoken with Vlad. Tell us what happened."

Rudy tenses beside me, all his humor frozen fake on his lips. He might pretend to support the deal I forced him to make with me, but anytime he learns I was near Vlad, he shuts down. I wonder if they're still fucking behind my back. The obsession Rudy has with him is clearly growing.

Really hoping they aren't –for my brother's sake, not Vlad's– I turn to look at Varius. I fill him in on how I killed Hannah and Daniel, then pinned it on the wolves to keep the WALL occupied, how I am clearly suspected by the vamps, but I left no evidence.

The aroma of spicy meat fills the kitchen, along with the sound of sizzling. Micha and Mother discuss cooking in low tones as my brothers and I continue to talk about Antonio and how he's clearly consumed the fallen. Rudy burned all the bodies we slaughtered last night to make sure he couldn't grow more in power, but I doubt it will matter.

"He has a stash of food somewhere," I say. And as long as he has that, we can't predict how strong he'll be the next time we see him.

"You think he's captured a rival pack?" Rudy signs.

It is not uncommon for one of the three Families to attack outsiders. We did it ourselves after I culled nearly a third of our coven for turning on Varius a few years ago. The werewolves and vampires thought us weak, prime for the pickings, so we attacked another coven, a powerful one up north past our territory, and brought the survivors into our Family. It stretched us too thin, but it kept the Blood Fang and Death Hunt off our backs.

Talon shakes his head. "We would've heard something if he had."

"He could be eating his own?" Maddox throws out as he glances at Varius.

But it's Leno, the second son and underboss, who says, "He would have been challenged."

An alpha is not a born position. It's fought for, and if Antonio started attacking his own pack, they would have turned on him.

"So if it can't be outsiders because we haven't heard of any attacks, and it can't be his own pack because they would have killed him, then who the fuck does that even leave?" Maddox says, kicking back in his chair until it balances on its back legs.

My stomach growls as the spicy aroma of Schezwan beef fills my nose. The sound of plates being collected and cutlery being taken from drawers fills the background as our meeting continues.

"Regardless of who he's eating, Antonio must be killed before he manages to make a hybrid," Varius says. "That gives us only a few months max." His gaze circles around the table as Micha puts a plate in front of him.

He doesn't look at her, his eyes on me. "Which is why you and I are going to visit Aleric today to make a deal."

"What?" Maddox drops his chair down on all fours.

A plate shatters beside Leno, and we all turn to see Mother standing in a mess of stir fry. "Varius," she starts, but he cuts her off.

"We cannot allow hybrids to be made whatever the cost.

I understand your disliking of him with everything you two have been through, but this is not a discussion. We will eliminate the Death Hunt together, then divide their territory and business."

"Why not kill them too?" Talon sneers as Mom bends down to clean up the mess, her jaw clenched. "What they have done to this Family demands retribution."

Despite being born after the treaty was signed, Talon's hatred of the vampires is personal. When he was in high school, he fell in love with one of their 'bloodbanks' – the name of those they feed on. On their first date, he took her to a picnic under the stars. When he went back to the car to get more drinks –a two minute job– the vampires bled her dry and painted 'witch whore' on her forehead with her own blood. Talon returned just in time to see the last flicker of life leave her eyes.

As a capo in this Family, my brother's private feud has caused a lot of deaths between our two gangs.

Rudy tenses beside me, no doubt worrying about Vlad, but he doesn't protest as Varius studies our brother. Micha continues to move back and forth between the table and kitchen, bringing food to each one of us in order of age. Leno. Me. The twins – Enoch and Ezriel. Mother joins her, the floor pristine, and sets down a plate in front of Talon as Micha serves Rudy. Maddox gets his last, and only then does Varius break the silence.

"The Blood Fang hasn't broken any terms of the treaty." The bloodbanks are their property, and they have every right to do whatever they want to them. "And they make up almost half of the police department and a good chunk of the local court system. Weeding them all out will open positions for WALL to fill. A drawn out war will have more chances of bringing in the SCU."

"They haven't visited this city in decades."

"Thanks to the treaty Mother got everyone to sign. That

is now gone, and they *will* return if we drag out another war. Our business doesn't clash with the bloodbanks and sex trafficking the vampires do. They will avoid hunting and dealing in our territory after this meeting. So until they become a threat, we will leave them be. There will be no more attacking them, nothing to break the deal I make with Aleric today. Do I make myself clear?" His eyes pierce into Talon's.

Jerking his head, Talon seethes in silence, and Varius' gaze roams around the table.

We all nod. Rudy's head is more of a jerk of energy he can't contain. He sneaks a glance at me, and I know the question he doesn't ask. As much as I hate Vlad, Varius has already declared war on the wolves. Their *reunion* won't change anything. I nod subtly before returning my attention to Varius.

Leaning back, he waits for Mother and Micha to take their seats. Then he picks up his fork, ending the meeting and finally allowing us to eat.

With the table cleared, my brothers disperse. Mother and Micha do the washing up, and Varius nods for me to join him on the porch. I step out into the bright sunlight, my gaze focusing on the hundreds of plants flickering in the wind. The bond connecting me to my girl lures me to the east, the direction behind me. I want to go to her, my cock twitching with the memories of her taste on my lips. I stay looking at the flowers.

"How soon will she be joining us?" my eldest brother asks, drawing my attention.

"A few days."

My girl is smart and compassionate. She won't buy into the WALL's speciesism once she calms down enough to think. But she needs time to process things on her own. Despite Maddox's advice earlier about how I can quicken her love for me by killing everyone she can turn to for protection and emotional connectivity, I don't want to bond with her through manipulated trauma.

Bonding is for life, and I want it to be as real for her as it is for me.

My fists clench around the wooden railing as I lean out. Low bushes and flowers cover the entire lawn from here to the lake. As I watch, a few blossom. Leno spelled those near the front porch to open under gaze – calls it therapy. A dose of serotonin trickles through my system.

"What is her relationship with the WALL?" Varius asks as he leans out beside me.

I glance at him, wondering what the fuck Maddox told him. Varius' face gives nothing away. "Her mother was a member for the last ten months. Scarlett went on her first hunt last night. As far as I know, that was the first time she learned about them."

"As far as you know?" his voice is flat, but the question warns of something more. "You've been stalking her for two years, and you don't know for sure?"

I still, not sure if he just cracked a joke. A reaper is trained to know how to handle every dangerous situation, but trying to decide if Varius is joking or not is making me nervous. Skinwalkers exist – creatures that steal the flesh of a person so they can slip into their life; they're extremely rare though, but he could also be another witch who's changed their appearance to match his. Both seem more plausible than Varius having actually cracked a joke.

He glances at me, his face as expressionless as always.

"What finger did Leno cut off me when I was six?" I ask. Neither skinwalkers nor a witch spelled to look like Varius will know that.

His expression turns dry, but he humors me. "It was your

left pinkie toe. He didn't cut it. A Venus fly trap ate it, and you were sixteen at the time."

Hmmm. Figuring he wasn't joking and is expecting an actual answer, I say, "She didn't know about them before last night."

No sign of that having been a joke lightens his eyes. He just jumps straight into the next question. *Yep. That's Varius.* "Where is she now?"

I turn to face him fully. "With Derek."

"How far along are you in the blood bond?"

It isn't reversible, so I know that's not why he's asking. "I started it two nights ago."

"And you're certain she'll accept?"

"Yes."

"If she doesn't –"

"She will," I cut in, and he holds my gaze in silence. If she doesn't, I will weaken to the point of vulnerability. Eventually, the bond will kill me, it demanding blood one way or another.

He turns for the door. "We have another hour before the meeting. Get some rest." He pulls it open. "And wash the blood off your face. I don't want to tempt Aleric into eating you after the shit you pulled at the station."

The door shuts, and I turn towards the pull of my girl.

TWENTY-TWO

HER

I sit on the brown leather sofa in Derek's living room, watching him clean an assault rifle (the third gun out of a line of four) on the coffee table in front of me. Silence lingers heavily in the air, thick with guilt and pain for those we've lost.

Not just Ma and Daniel, a mother and son, but also for Detective Henry Howard, his wife Nicole, and the other seven members killed by wolves. Their bodies don't seem to have been found yet. The television plays the news in the background, mentioning Ma's death and how much good she's done for this city.

"...taken too soon. It's a true tragedy not just for her boyfriend Aaron Golden, the CEO and founder of Golden Realty, but for everyone in St. Augustine..."

I try to ignore it.

"Tell me about the guy you were with at the station," Derek says as he puts the assault rifle down and picks up the shotgun to clean.

"Uh..." I blink, trying to figure out where the question came from. It's the first thing he's said to me since we left the station. Maybe he's just paranoid? He seems the sort. Or maybe he thinks I was cheating on Daniel too?

My stomach twists. "Khalid? He's...my..." *Concerned friend? Boyfriend?* My pulse quickens, but I chicken out of saying it out loud. "...neighbor. He moved in a few months ago. He heard Ma and I arguing when we got back and followed me to make sure I was okay."

I expect him to ask why my 'neighbor' had his tongue down my throat or to demand if I did wrong by his son, but instead, he asks, "Is he always up that early?" Intense eyes drill into me.

I frown, confused about where this line of questioning is going. "He's a light sleeper. He probably woke up when I revved the engine." *Or when we started screaming at each other.* I wince.

"He followed you immediately?"

"I guess?" My frown deepens. "Well, he didn't show up at the hotel until maybe an hour or so after, but..." I trail off, my brain trying to put the pieces together when it can't even see what puzzle it's trying to do. An uneasy feeling settles in the pit of my stomach, and I fidget as heat rises up my cheeks.

"How did he know where you were?" His eyes are still so intense. The gun looks dangerous in his hands despite the chamber being empty.

My mouth opens, then closes, the answer alluding me. I shake my head as I dig my nails into my thighs, trying to keep my hands from shaking. My blood pounds in my ears as my eyes stay trained on the shotgun.

"Scarlett." My name is clipped, demanding an answer.

I focus on his face, ignoring the gun in his hands. His face looks no less dangerous. *You want his dangerousness, remember?* I swallow as I wrestle with my pulse. "It...it would've taken him a few minutes to get into his car," I say, my words becoming stronger. "He probably drove around until he saw Ma's car in the parking lot."

The lingering silence is heavy with words he doesn't say, making me fidget more. *Does he think Khalid is a werewolf?* The question clogs my throat, but I force a hard swallow, needing to know that answer.

My pulse thunders as I rasp, "Do you know him?"

"No."

My whole body feels hot as I force out the words, "He isn't..." I trail off, unable to picture warm Khalid with the crazy coldness I saw in that wolf's eyes. He was so kind to me, and the way he kissed me...

My lungs burn with air as I suck in a deep breath. *He can't be.*

"Do you think he is?" Derek demands.

I shake my head. I don't for one second think all sups are evil just like all humans aren't, but Khalid *can't* be a werewolf. I barely know him outside of a girl's fantasies, but being around him feels *right*. Like the world stops in all its crazy. He lets me breathe, holds me up when I'm about to drown. And the way he looks at me, as if I'm *worth* something...as if I'm beautiful and desirable... He really sees *me*. He doesn't see a plaything like a werewolf would or a meal. He sees me.

"You were just asking questions," I say, "and after all that's happened..."

"It's good to be wary. Sups can be anybody. They can look exactly like us. Act like us. *Pretend* to be capable of feeling. Don't trust anyone until you get to know them. And even then, keep watching them for signs."

A frown pulls at my lips. "They can't feel?"

"Wolves don't care for sheep." He stands and slings the assault rifle over his shoulder. "It is in their nature to kill us. Letting one live is willingly stepping around a mine instead of detonating it so no one can get hurt." Picking up the shotgun, he heads down the hall. I stay where I am, chewing his words over.

Are all sups wolves?

Wolves evolved into dogs, man's greatest companion…

"…a scorched van was found abandoned in the woods near Saltwaters Shooting Club…"

The television interrupts my thoughts, and I pick up the remote to turn up the volume.

"…by a dog walker's German shepherd, which then ran off into the surrounding trees. Its owner followed it and claims to have seen blood on the ground. The police have not issued an official statement as of yet, but reports have come in saying numerous unidentified bodies have been found. The entire stretch of woods has been cordoned of."

The anchor woman is replaced by photos of Henry's van in the area where Mother tried to kill me. I swallow hard as the woods close in on me, as loose twigs press into my knees. *"Ma! Please! What are you doing? Ma! –"*

Bang!

I jerk, dropping the remote just as Derek comes in. It tumbles to the floor.

"Get ahold of yourself, Scarlett," he says. "The wolves won't wait for you to come to terms with your grief."

My grief? I want to tell him I'm not grieving, but the words lie trapped in my throat. He won't care, and I don't want to scream that Ma tried to kill me. Don't want him to make me strip to see if I really was bitten or not.

Clenching my fists on my lap, I force a deep breath in. Even though I'm not grieving, he is still right. The wolves won't wait for me to come to terms with everything I've seen and experienced.

Looking up at him, I ask, "Do werewolves have any weaknesses?"

"If you mean something like silver, no. Think of them like

animals." He taps his head. "You fight them up here. You can't win a fistfight against a tiger, so you trap them. You poison them. You lure them into a pit of spikes. You know how to shoot?"

"He caught a bullet," I say, not liking my chances with a gun.

"Then shoot him in the back." He picks up the last of his guns and slings them over his shoulder. "Come with me."

He doesn't wait for me to stand. Bending down to pick up the remote, I turn off the TV, then climb to my feet and hurry after him. He leads me down the hall to a closed door. Opening it, he gestures me inside.

As soon as I step past him to enter, my jaw drops. The four guns he cleaned are nothing in the ocean of his stash. Assault rifles, pistols, and shotguns all hang from the walls. As do knives, crossbows, and –

"Fuck? Are those grenades?"

He moves past me to put the guns he's carrying onto the empty spaces on the wall. "Yes."

Turning to a small safe in the corner, he crouches in front of it and spins the dial. I stare at him, wondering what lethal monstrosity he's going to pull out of it. I inch backwards towards the door, my eyes flicking from one wall to the next, my throat closing, my pulse roaring. The woods flicker in my skull. My ma's crazy eyes bore into mine.

Clenching my fists, I force my feet to stop. Ma *isn't* going to keep ruining my life from beyond the grave. I *need* to know what Derek knows. Train how he does. I won't survive otherwise, and to hell if I'm going to end up like her in any way.

Preparing myself for him wanting to teach me how to control drones for an airstrike or something of that severe magnitude, I blink in confusion when he stands with a mere stack of notebooks in his hands.

"Read these," he says, shoving the pile into my arms.

I look down at the one on top. *Werewolves* is scrawled across its cover. I flip it open and am met with an image of a wolf halfway through its transformation, its face twisted in pain as it rips human flesh off a chest of fur.

Best time to strike – a shift is painful, and their new senses overwhelm them for the first few minutes. They are stronger than humans in their human form, and once they change, you are dead. Kill now when they are unable to defend themselves. Granted, you are unlikely to ever witness a change.

I look up. "How long have you known about all this?"

There are over a dozen notebooks in my arms.

He doesn't answer my question as he turns for the hall. "If you think of anything to add to them after what you saw last night, tell me."

He waits at the door, clearly expecting me to vacate the room, and I hurry out. I breathe better in the hall. He shuts and locks the door.

"There's a partly filled notebook at the bottom of the stack. Rip out a piece of paper and write down a list to discuss with me in the morning. We're up at six."

Walking off, he disappears through another door and shuts it firmly behind him.

Clearly, he's not the talking type.

Despite it being barely past lunch time, I head towards the spare bedroom he showed me upon arrival. I was not comfortable with sitting in the living room in Ma's house when she was home; in Derek's, the thought of doing so makes me nauseous. I pass Daniel's room to get to mine, and my eyes linger on the closed door with a mixture of anger and guilt for hating him in his own father's home.

Tearing my eyes away, I enter my new room, kick the door shut, and put the books down on the bedside table. Rearranging the pillows, I lean against the headboard and go through the stack, picking out the ones about wolves, as well as the half-filled one to make my notes. Flipping to a blank page, I realize I don't have anything to write with. I pull open the drawer in the table. No pen.

My eyes go to the closed door.

I chew my lip.

Ma is dead, but years of hiding keeps me contained where I am.

I'll just remember all my questions and the things I need to tell him.

Removing the blank page from my lap, I pick up the notebook I opened earlier.

My brain floods with the sight of the man on the hood of Henry's van. *"Let's have a little fun, shall we?"*

My fingers tighten on the notebook. I raise a hand to the wound he gave me. The smell of rancid breath mixed with the copper tang of blood makes me shiver. I can feel his breath across my face, the damp wetness and flecks of red spray.

My pulse screams inside my ears.

And then there's a sudden calm pushing through me.

It's almost as if Khalid is here with me, helping me breathe, helping me weather the storm of my trauma. I can feel his hands on me, closing over my fists.

"You'll never be alone, kira. I'm here."

I hold on to the image of him, of the promise in his eyes, letting him wash away the fear of the wolf.

When my breathing settles, I close my eyes briefly, then force my hands to open the book. The picture of the wolf tearing off his skin mocks me for my cowardice. My hands shake, but the fear stays containable, and I flip the page.

A werewolf is fucking fast. Don't bother outrunning. Stand and shoot. Aim for head and chest. Will bleed out like a human or any other animal. Has innate healing, and can regrow limbs, but it takes time. Shoot it enough times, and it will die.

As the passage goes into more specifics about the time it takes for them to heal from various types of wounds, a horrible knot twists my stomach. My blood drains from my face with every new word, and I know they have captured and tested. *Dissected or vivisected?*

The question makes me shudder, and I flip to a new section.

Wolves might not care about us. They might think we are just food to eat or toys to play with, but I know they still feel pain. Even plants give off a chemical when they are being eaten to warn others nearby. Pain is a universal feeling that connects us all – sup or plant or human, and I can't help but be uncomfortable with torturing anything, even if it is a 'monster.' Death is one thing; pain stops. But to deliberately draw it out, to be the cause of it, to be deaf to one's screams and signs of agony...

"Ma, please! Ma! Don't do this."

I snap the book shut, tears falling down my cheeks as I relive that moment over and over.

Khalid's face appears in my mind again, his warmth trying to get through my pain, but he can't help me this time.

Nothing can.

I fucking hate you, Ma. I'm glad you're dead.

TWENTY-THREE

HIM

I swing my legs out of bed and stand a moment before the door to my bedroom opens. Mother enters with a tray of tea.

"I'm heading out," I say.

She blocks my way, a look in her eyes that tells me she will use her magic, her precious lifeforce at the moment thanks to Dad's dying curse, to keep me here. "Varius gave you an order to rest, son. Now sit."

"She's hurting," I growl, the bond to my girl vibrating with her pain.

"Is she in danger?"

My jaw clenches, but I don't need to verbally respond for her to know the answer.

"She needs time to deal with everything, and she can't do that if you're constantly fixing things for her. Now sit."

My hands fist. I glance over her shoulder at the open door.

Magic electrifies the air, radiating from Mother, and I

snap my gaze back to her. "I'm fucking sitting," I snap as I plonk my ass back down on the bed. A whole childhood has taught me it's futile to try to run.

She shuts the door for privacy, then places the tray on the dresser. She doesn't bother asking me if I want any tea. She simply pours a cup and hands it to me.

Suspecting it's laced with whatever she got Leno to put in it, I eye it warily.

"Take it, Kal. Varius needs you well rested."

Exhaling strongly, I take it and throw the whole thing back. An instant warmth fills me, making my eyes heavy. I shake my head, wanting to stay awake, wanting to keep pushing comfort down the bond to Scarlett even though I've already used up one full kidney.

"Don't fight it," she says as she picks up the tray. "You kill yourself soothing her, and you know Maddox will kill her for it."

"If he even thinks..." The magic of the drink takes root like a weed, and my thoughts scatter in deep sleep.

I jerk awake with a growl as someone raps hard on my door. Ignoring them, I focus on the bond. It's weak, the drop of blood of mine in her system mostly gone, eaten away by the magic keeping us tied. A trace amount will stay, but it won't be enough for me to feel her any longer. I need to continue the ritual, trade more blood for me to use.

But right now, I just focus on coaxing the small tether into something I can decipher. She's not panicking any longer, but a pain lingers in her heart. I ache to soothe it, but doing so will hurt her – the magic requiring her blood as much as mine, and what blood of hers is left in me is not enough for me to use.

"Get up," Talon says. "We're leaving,"

Swinging my legs over the bed, I roll my shoulders, then stand. As much as I don't like how far she is from me, she is safe, and Varius requires my full attention.

Striding across my room, I open the door.

"You're coming with?" I ask, wondering what in Hel's name Varius is thinking. Talon's presence at this meeting will be like if we all walked in with bomb vests on.

His jaw tightens as he sneers. "He thinks it'll be a show of good faith."

If Talon doesn't attack Aleric, then yeah, it would be, but I don't have as much faith in that as Varius clearly does. Still, it's not my call, so I simply follow Talon's back as we head downstairs to the kitchen. Varius and Mother are discussing in low voices around the sink but stop as soon as we enter.

After drying her hands on a towel, Mother pats Varius on the shoulder, then heads over to me. "You look a lot better," she says. "How're you feeling?"

The pain in my kidney is completely gone. "That better be due to Leno," I say.

"My life is mine. I can spend it how I wish." When I scowl, she smiles. "But yes, you can thank Leno for that." Lowering her voice, she adds, "You keep an eye on these two. Make sure you all come back."

Make sure Talon doesn't do anything stupid.

Worry coats her tone. I don't lie by saying we will be fine; we're heading into the lion's den, Varius wanting to meet Aleric on his turf so he can feel more at ease.

Although we are at peace, the temptation for him to take us all out at once will be strong. He won't be able to do it on his own, and his coven's numbers have been greatly reduced, but he has an unknown amount of sired vampires. They might be gnats individually, but a horde of them can overwhelm us by sheer number.

"He won't kill us," Talon growls.

No, he won't. He'll kidnap us and torture us, bartering our lives for territory and business. He knows how much Mother loves her children, knows she will offer anything and everything to get us back even though she is not the head of this Family.

Leno will rule in Varius' absence, being the second son, and he is a mama's boy through and through.

"Let's go," Varius says in the monotone he always talks in. Fear lingers inside him, but he never shows it. Never gives his enemies a weakness to manipulate or any insight to use against him.

Family. Enemies. To him, we're all the same, a lesson taught harshly many times over.

I lean in to kiss Mom on the cheek, then pivot on my heels and follow my brother out. Maddox leans on Varius' car, a black Mercedes, his ankles crossed, a dumb driver's cap on his head.

As we near, he takes the hat off and bows, then opens the back door with a flourish. "Hot and sexy chauffeur at your service."

We both ignore him as we climb into the backseat. Talon joins us soon after, sitting in the passenger. Leno and the twins will most likely follow in their shadows. Rudy will stay with Mom and Micha – not that they need his protection. Micha is more than capable of doing that herself. Rudy just actually listens to Varius even when he doesn't give an official order.

The car reverses down the drive, goes around the L-shape, then pulls forward off the paved track and onto the private dirt road that connects us to our neighbors. As we drive to Vilano Beach, St. Augustine, Maddox sings along with the radio. Thank the gods, we only have to suffer it for twenty minutes. Screaming metal might be enjoyable when it's not being howled by an idiot who tries to go as high-pitched as possible, but I wouldn't know.

When we get within a block of our destination on the waterfront, Maddox switches off the radio. For all of his annoyance, he knows when to shut up.

Vampires step out of their million-dollar-plus houses as we pass the 1ˢᵗ street-Myrtle street intersection. They're all wearing sunglasses, their eyes more sensitive than ours to the bright sunlight. Vampires, as well as werewolves, originally come from a world called Blódyrió, which never sees a sun. Its massive moon only offers as much light as a sunset on Earth, and the species born there have yet to evolve to tolerate the high sun. Long sleeves and pants are the staple every day of the year, though sunlight won't kill them like they've let the humans believe, whispering long tales to authors and other societal members of influence.

What's the best way to tell if someone's a vampire? Put them in the sun or in front of a mirror or tell them to enter a house without an invitation. Oh, look at that, I'm clearly not a vampire, says the vampire.

Sired vampires are a different story though. Created by dark magic, they must give a price to balance out their rebirth. The sun at high noon will burn them into ash, but on cloudy days or when the sun's at a lower angle, they'll only suffer a bit of sunburn. They're also never as strong as born vampires, can't consume anything except blood, are infertile both sexually and magically so they can't sire, and they never develop the ability to phase.

Rolling down his window, letting in the ocean breeze, Maddox puts his arm out, but before he can raise a certain finger, Varius orders him to be on better behavior. *Best* is not something Maddox can do.

He mumbles about sticks and asses, but wisely keeps his hand down, just letting it ride in the wind.

Turning off at the end of the road, he pulls onto a large brick driveway lined by trees. The door to the house opens as soon as he parks.

"Stay inside the car and don't pick any fights," Varius orders our youngest brother as he steps out of the black Mercedes.

Talon and I follow as Maddox sighs, "Yes, Father."

He turns the car radio back on and starts blaring it as he whacks the wheel with his fingers and howls like an idiot.

Varius gives him one look, his face unchanged, and Maddox switches off the radio. Slumping in his seat, he waits for us to return.

My eyes scan constantly as we head for the open door. My magic pulses in my veins, coiling in readiness to strike. Aleric himself stands in the doorway, dressed in red surfer shorts and a white cotton T-shirt. His dark-gray eyes linger on Varius before shifting to Talon, then me. Then back to Varius.

I don't like the focus in them, the lurking of something secret hiding within their depths.

But Aleric is over three hundred years old –the oldest soul I've ever met, though far from the oldest alive– and with age comes a look that is always unsettling. As if they already know what you're going to do.

He steps back, leading us into a wide entrance hall that merges into an open plan living room. Sunlight fills the place through floor-to-ceiling windows. My eyes scan the room as my magic seeps through the house, noting the number of vampires inside. *One.*

My gaze snaps back to Aleric. He smiles at me, then turns his full attention to my brother.

"It is a new era when the head of the Shadow Domain visits my home." He inclines his head, his eyes not leaving Varius' face. "And without any guards either."

He looks pointedly at me and Talon, his eyes light with a mockery that bounces off me. Talon's aura strengthens with magic, then quickly quiets again as his eyes flick to Varius. Orders have been given. No fighting. We're here for peace.

"It became a new era when the Death Hunt started massacring your people," Varius says.

"Yes, quite." Aleric moves through the living room and kitchen, then continues on through the house to a study on the upper floor. Books line the walls on both sides from floor to ceiling, and a wide double window with an alcove stretches between them, opposite the door. A large dark-red tambootie-wood desk fills nearly a third of the room. A black leather swivel chair rests behind it. Only one other chair, positioned in front of it, is available. Talon and I are to stay standing.

Pulling the door shut behind me, I raise a hand and swivel my fingers. Magic flows around the room, sealing us in so no one can eavesdrop.

Aleric kicks back in his chair, not a hair seemingly risen in worry about being in a room where no one can hear him scream. "I want Anastasia Island, his territory in Miami, and his stretch from Georgia to North Carolina. That basically gives you all of Florida."

"But leaves us surrounded by your territory."

He smiles.

"I'll give you" –his smile drops at my brother's phrase claiming he's in a position to *give* rather than to barter– "Anastasia Island and his streets in Miami, as well as his stretch from Tallahassee to Atlanta, which will strengthen your hold in Alabama. You can have the coast of South Carolina and the range of mountains all around Asheville, but the rest of Antonio's territory is ours."

Aleric's gray eyes flash with a hint of mahogany as they narrow on my brother. "You drive a hard bargain."

"We can always help the wolves wipe you out."

"You think Antonio will stop with our extinction now that he's made hybrids?"

The room chills. *Why have we not heard of this?* The idea of a mole weasels its way into my mind. Too often, we've had issues within our Family, Varius' lack of magic a great catalyst for causing plays for power.

"How many has he made?" Varius demands.

"Four."

"We'll kill them tonight," Talon cuts in, disgust twisting his face. Hybrids are seen as lessers to too many people.

"No need," Aleric says, his words a blizzard across my skin. "He consumes them soon after birth." A lazy smile mocks us. "I'm surprised Sau hasn't felt the imbalance. She was always so sensitive to such things..."

At the mention of our mother, Talon's aura blares with energy. Shadows move beneath my heels, out of sight but undoubtedly felt by my brother. I rein them back in before Talon feeds off my emotions and does something brash. He isn't as stupid as Maddox, but his hatred for the vamps makes him volatile.

"Is she sick?" Aleric asks, looking at my brother, either unaware or completely uncaring that Talon is a second away from blasting him with magic.

"No." Short and clipped, an end to the conversation.

"Is she grieving for that turdstain she called a mate?"

Talon shifts, and Varius turns his head to look at him. "Do you need to step out?"

A locked jaw and a shake of his head. Talon exhales, his magic quieting like a phone on vibrate.

Varius turns around. "I'm not here to talk about her."

"So she is." His lips tighten. "Maybe she should have run away with him when he begged her to."

"Father was not a coward," Talon says, taking a step forward. He halts immediately when I shift, a warning in my eyes.

"Being a coward was your father's defining trait," the vampire says. "Why do you think Sau had to take her own revenge for her dead children? If she had been allowed to lead, we would be living in a very different world."

There is almost a hint of respect in his eyes, but when he turns to look back at my brother, it is gone, flattened by the talk of business. "I will accept the dividing of his territory you proposed."

It wasn't a proposal, but Varius doesn't correct him.

"However, there is one thing I need to discuss with you first – in private."

Talon and I tense. Varius can handle himself against most Death Hunt and Blood Fang members, but he is magicless and Aleric is over three hundred years old. He will kill him before we can get back into the room.

"Out," Varius says without hesitation. Talon takes a step forward, but I move in front of him and gesture to the door. His eyes narrow over my shoulder, undoubtedly at the vampire. Magic hums off him, but he turns without trying to kill Aleric. We linger outside in the hall. I search the house again with my power. Still no other vampires.

"He shouldn't fucking be in there alone. *We* shouldn't fucking be here. We should just kill him while he's alone." Talon paces across the hall, rubbing his head in his rage. "What do you think they're saying?" he asks, stopping to glare at the door. Electricity flickers between his fingers, and my gaze settles on them.

Exhaling sharply, he forces his magic down.

I shrug. "Varius will tell us if we need to know."

Barely a minute passes before the door is yanked open. Our brother steps out with a dark energy boiling off him. Talon and I both look past him. Aleric stares at Varius' back, his lips tight but no urge to attack in his eyes.

Varius doesn't pause in the hall, heading for the stairs that'll take him outside. We follow in silence. Maddox jumps out of the car and opens the door with a flourish. Once we're all inside, he spins the Mercedes around and heads home, singing at the top of his lungs.

Blocking him out, I look at Varius expectedly. Secrets are

rarely kept between us, but he keeps his eyes on the window. It isn't until we're back home and Maddox and Talon have disappeared inside that he finally turns to me. He gestures towards the lake, and we walk down to its lapping shore.

Insects buzz around us in the balmy heat. A few land on my skin, only to immediately die, their mouths and proboscises activating the minor *protection* rune tattooed on my skin.

"Are you going to her tonight?"

I glance at him, but his gaze is on the lake. "If I'm able."

He nods. "Do it. The ritual needs to be completed as soon as possible. I need you at full power."

An uneasiness fills me. A war, I expected. Antonio will not go quietly into the night, and he already declared us as enemies by attacking my girl. But the cloak of energy around my brother speaks of something worse. "What did Aleric say to you?"

"He has ninety-six sired vampires, half under twenty years old. Antonio hasn't bothered killing them."

Why would he? They were infertile, useless in making hybrids.

"Everyone we saw today driving in, that's about all he has of born males, minus those at work."

Less than fifty or so males... It made sense. A wolf's fluids were toxic to vampires. After being forced to fuck a female wolf, they would die – if they even managed to finish. A female vampire could not survive the following pregnancy, the child's blood killing her long before the second trimester. "How many women?" I ask.

"Three hundred and seven. He's already ordered men from other parts of his territory to come here. They arrive tomorrow."

"And the condition he put on our alliance?" I ask, knowing there is one. Aleric's hold on this city might be greatly weakened, but he has connections with powerful vampires all over the world. The Kacic brothers, pirates from Croatia in the twelfth century, are hundreds of years old and capable of phasing across continents. But the biggest ace he has in his pocket is a born vampire called Sebastian the Ancient Destroyer. He's the whole reason the portals between Earth and the rest of the Seven Planes were closed by decree of the archangels four thousand years ago.

Over five thousand years old, Sebastian has the power to phase from plane to plane. Although he is being hunted by the Elv've'Norc, an interplanal force that was created solely to kill him, he rewards his allies with unspeakable power, and Aleric helped him find a special woman a few months ago. If he calls, Sebastian will come, and hyped up on hybrid babies or not, Antonio will be nothing but a stain on the floor.

But it is a one-use card, and with Sebastian's activity heating up after a three-and-a-half-thousand-year hiatus, Aleric fears what is to come.

The last time Sebastian moved with this much flourish, he caused a war that reached to six of the seven planes. One was entirely destroyed, now nothing but a wasteland where space and time constantly folds in on itself. Another is rapidly dying, Sebastian having killed off all but one of the primordial elementals keeping the plane alive. Lakes and rivers there are drying up. Forests are withering. Grasslands are turning into arid deserts where nothing can survive. Earth lost Atlantis and its connection to the rest of the Seven Planes in a bold attempt to save it from utter annihilation, humans being mere toothpicks to Sebastian's army.

He is a true trump card, but Aleric won't use it unless the alternative is known death.

Still, he has many other connections that will allow him to dismiss Varius' alliance.

My brother stays staring out at the lake. "I will tell you later. Right now, I need you focused on resting so you're at full power. We take out the Death Hunt in two weeks."

The dismissal is silent but brokers no argument. I pat his shoulder as I pass him, trusting he will tell me when I need to know. Inside the house, Mother greets me at the door, her eyes scanning me for wounds. "We are all fine," I tell her, but the worry doesn't leave her face.

"Where's Varius?" she asks.

I point towards the lake, and she heads out while I head up to my bedroom on the second floor. The pain from my missing kidney is starting to come back, the numbing agent from Leno's tea fading with time. It's going to be a bitch to regrow.

Opening my door, then kicking it shut, I strip off my clothes and crawl into bed. Although it's only a few hours past midday, I have plans to be up all night.

Closing my eyes, I focus on the bond, falling asleep to the lure of my girl.

TWENTY-FOUR

HIM

The moon shines overhead as the whispers of the night permeate the heavy humid air. Derek's house, a tiny one-story, sits before me, behind a shimmer of magic I erected to keep out all sups.

Raising my hands, I work my magic, my runes lighting up softly beneath the dark material of my shirt. I step past the barrier, my hairs rising with electricity. My cock jerks, thickening with every step that leads me to her.

Her room is down the hall, across from his, and I push out with my power, making sure he's not still awake. I smile. He's in bed, his heart rate slow.

He's undoubtedly a light sleeper, and the urge to kill him with a heart attack before going to her calls to me. I don't want to be interrupted for the next few hours, but I leave him alive as I slip into my shadow and under the door of his house.

Darkness greets me, hiding my movements, not that anyone is awake to see them. Slipping under my girl's door,

I find her asleep atop the covers, the summer heat too much for even a sheet.

She's wearing the same clothes, but her bra is on the floor, and my cock hardens to the point of pain. I shift into my human form, cloak the room in a spell of silence, and then pick up the simple white bra. I bring it to my lips as my eyes crawl up her legs, wishing her pants were off her. When she's in my room, she'll sleep nude so I can see every beautiful part of her.

Dropping her bra, I step towards her. The bed is a mere single, leaving little room for me, but there's enough for me to bury my head between her legs. I lick my lips as I let my magic flow around her, keeping her under so she does not wake up and panic. Now that her ex-boyfriend is dealt with, the urge to claim her isn't as violent. It's content for me to take my time.

And fuck, I'm going to take my time.

Fucking hours of it.

Stripping off my shirt, I drop it into my shadow, not wanting to leave it on the floor in case I need to leave quickly. If Derek learns a witch is obsessed with her, he'll torture her to get to me.

The urge to kill him flairs again, but I smother it. My girl has seen too much death already. She needs time to heal from it so she doesn't fracture beneath the weight.

Dropping my hands to my waist, I undo the button on my jeans and pull down the zipper. She moves in her sleep, rubbing her thighs together as if she can sense me beside her. A small moan parts her lips, and I drop my pants, a hiss escaping at the feel of freedom, at the close proximity of her pussy, one less barrier between us. I step out of them, and the shadow takes them away. Standing in just my boxers, not having bothered to put on socks or shoes before coming over here, I trail my eyes over her face. The bruise on her cheek isn't as prominent in the dark nor are those around her neck. But I know they're there, and my blood boils with the need to heal them. To clean her of the touch of those assholes.

But Derek is too paranoid, and he does not need hard evidence to torture someone. The mere potential of being able to draw out a sup will make him hard.

So I force my gaze away from the bruises and focus instead on the soft V of her thighs. I'm going to mark her tonight with my teeth, breaking the skin enough to trade blood right where her legs curve into her ass.

My boxers come off swiftly.

My cock jerks at the image of her spread out before me, her mouth pushed into her fist as she rides my tongue on a scream. Harsh breaths leave my lips as I lift a leg and put my knee on the mattress. It sinks beneath my weight. She rolls towards me, and our bodies touch in an innocent brush that has me throwing my head back on a groan.

My palm fills with her breast as I lean down and kiss her neck. She arches her head, baring her throat, and I finish climbing onto the bed, my weight pressing onto her. My cock leaks precum onto her belly. Her hands flutter at her sides as I kneed her flesh beneath the thin fabric of her shirt. I brush the material across her nipple. My lips trail soft kisses up to her ear.

She moans, then whimpers, my name fluttering free. "*Khalid.*"

Desire punching me hard, I wrap my teeth around her earlobe and lick across the bottom of it. She moans again, her hands lifting as she rubs her thighs together.

"Khalid…"

My tongue traces down her neck as my fingers find her nipple. Awareness lingers on the edge of her dreams, and I push out with my magic, keeping her asleep.

"*Kira,*" I murmur against her neck as I nuzzle aside the collar of her shirt. "I'm going to fuck your breasts while your mouth swallows the tip of my cock."

Her clothes are gone in an instant, stripped by magic and tossed messily on the floor – a simple case of getting too hot in the night.

My palms cup her breasts as I shift my hips, pushing my cock in between her thick thighs. Her pussy lips rub the top length of me, and I groan as I rock up and down them.

She moans as she moves against me, and I cover her mouth with mine. She parts for me instantly, her tongue sleepily seeking the pleasure I can give her. I pinch her nipples as I kiss her. My cock slides between her pussy lips. A primal growl rises from my throat as our tongues dance under the cover of darkness.

"I need to fuck you, *kira,*" I rasp against her lips even though I know I can't tonight. I still want her awake for our first time. I want to watch her emotions in her eyes and listen to her screams as she begs me to fill her with my cum.

"I need to taste you." I kiss my way down her neck to one large breast. I lick the bottom of it, swirling my tongue around her ample flesh as my other hand plucks at the tight bud of her other nipple.

She cries out, and I shudder on top of her, my orgasm rushing blood between my skull. Forcing it down, I lick her nipple then suck on it hard, flicking my tongue across it rapidly as I push the length of my cock against her pussy. The bed creaks beneath us as my hips move faster, my lips suck harder, and my teeth scrape against her.

She whimpers loudly, her hips pushing up as I keep her asleep. Her body thrashes beneath mine as she lingers on the edge. Her hands come up, her fingers through my hair, pinning me to her. I growl out around her nipple as I push her other breast towards my mouth. Angling both nipples together, I suck them in at the same time, swirling my tongue around them. I shudder on the verge of coming all over her sheets.

"*Khalid...*" Her hands tighten in my hair, her fingers pulling at my scalp.

I let her hold me to her for a moment longer before releasing her breasts and kissing my way down her belly. She sucks in harsh breaths, aware in her dreams what's about to happen.

"My beautiful *kira*," I murmur against her skin as I reach the soft curls of her pussy. Shifting down the bed, nestled between her legs, I spread her open. She glistens in the moonlight, damp and begging me to fuck her with my tongue. I brush my thumb across her lips. A delicious moan stirs my blood, making my cock pulse against the cotton sheets.

"I'm going to lick you slowly, *kira*. Until your taste is all over my chin and dominating every tastebud on my tongue. Then when you're begging me to go deeper, I'm going to fill your pussy with my fingers as I suck on your clit until you're screaming for mercy."

I place the softest kiss on the crease of her thigh, and she shudders on a whimper. Her legs part more, giving me whatever I want. My beautiful girl.

Dipping my head, I lick from her ass to her clit.

One long slow lick that has her thighs pressing against my face in a silent plea for more.

I lick her again. Slowly. Taking my time. Swirling over every inch of her as I move up between her lips. My girl shudders. Her hips buck. Her fingers tighten in my hair, nearly burning with the force of her pull.

"*Khalid...*" she whimpers, and the sound of my name is killing my control.

Wrestling with my need to slide my cock inside her, to wake her up and let her know she's mine, my muscles tremble as I lower my head and lick her again.

One.

Long.

Slow.

Delicious.

Lick.

That covers my tongue in the full taste of her. I lick the inside of my mouth, spreading the scent of her sex so it fills me, so every time I breathe, I'm breathing in the beauty of my girl, the gripping taste of her moans, the clutch of my hair, the brush of her thighs against my cheeks. It's a memory of smell that's going to leave me with a hard-on all fucking day, and I'm looking forward to the torture of her taste when I can't be beside her.

Diving my tongue back through her lips, I continue to take her to the edge of insanity, her thrashing become wilder as her pleas morph into near cries of mercy. My fingers wrap around my cock, and I hiss against her skin as the sensitivity of a mere touch nearly drives me over the edge. Cum coats my hand as I jerk it once, then let go. It throbs in relation to her pleas, begging me as she does.

But I will not cum unless it's inside her.

My eyes lift to her mouth. It's parted in her sleep, and the urge to use it as I wish begs me to crawl up her body and fuck my cock between her breasts and into her warm lips.

Focusing on her pussy, my body shakes as I lick her slowly.

Her nails dig into my scalp, drawing blood. "*Khalid!*" she nearly screams, a whimper of pure desperation as her thighs shake around my lips.

Lifting my head, I push three fingers inside her and suck on her clit hard. She jerks off the bed, her orgasm squeezing around my digits in vibrations that make my cock jerk in longing to feel her truly. My teeth gently scrape her as my tongue teases the hard bud that has my precum leaking down my balls.

Releasing her, I kiss her curls and thighs softly, giving

her time to come down, away from the edge of waking up. My breaths feather hot against her skin. My body burns with a flush that breaks sweat across my shoulders. My lips tease hers as I curl my fingers and pump them inside her. They're soaked to the knuckle, and I lick the sweet taste of her off the back of them.

She shuffles with little moans, and I nuzzle her legs further apart. As she rides my fingers, I kiss the crease of her thigh right below her ass. "I'm going to bite you now, *kira*. I'm going to strengthen our bond so you can feel how crazy you're making me."

She sighs a subconscious *please,* and I can't resist such a request from my girl.

Fingerfucking her slowly, I bite her with a building pressure until it breaks the skin. She jerks beneath me on a long moan, and my magic swirls around her, keeping her in a dream. I wish I had the power to dreamwalk, to worship her on a plane of existence where I can already leave her pregnant with my children.

Instead of having to wait until I bring her home. Until she's ready to face being married to a sup.

The taste of copper mixes with the sweetness of her, and I bite my tongue to draw my own blood. Swirling it over the bite on her thigh, I strengthen the bond between us. Magic flows with an ancient power, connecting us in a way that can never be severed. We are one until death. She's *mine*.

I'm *hers*.

Fuck, I need to push my cock inside her and claim her in another ancient way.

Withdrawing my fingers, I suck them into my mouth as I crawl up her body. My lips feather across her breasts, and I suck a nipple in. I take my time, licking and nipping the full area rather than just focusing on the tip, wanting to taste every inch of her.

I can feel her desire through our link, building beneath

my caresses. Sitting up, I stretch my knees carefully on either side of her, beneath her arms. Then push her breasts together. My cock jumps in anticipation, and I have to take a moment to regain control of it before I come all over her chest.

Hissing in a breath, I knead her tits as I push my cock in between them. A groan drops my head back as my nerves fire in an explosive light, ricocheting up my spine and down my legs. My toes curl as I slide into the weight of her breasts. Moving back and forth, I pump slowly, then move faster and faster as I fuck her beautiful body. The bed knocks against the wall, the magic flaring with each beat to keep the noise in.

She places a hand on my thigh, another on my ass as she balances on the edge of waking up. I force myself to slow, my pulse beating heavily, my cock screaming at me to finish all over her face.

Releasing her breasts, I lift her head forward, prop it with a pillow, then push my thumb into her mouth. She parts instantly for me, and I stroke her tongue, groaning when she starts to suck on me.

Her hot wet sounds clench around my balls, and I lean over her to rest one forearm on the wall above her head. Pushing my cock between her lips, I rock my hips until she's taking me halfway. A heavy groan rips from me as pleasure explodes down to my balls.

Sweat beads across my brow and shoulders as magic hums in tune to my arousal. It ripples across my skin, my runes flaring as it fights for a way to please itself along with me. It wants to be inside her, to become part of her as it is me, and I allow a bit more to pulse between our bond.

She jerks on a spasm, her orgasm triggered by what I'm experiencing with my cock inside her mouth. She cries out around it, and I press her boobs together around the base of me as I slam further in. She gags, her throat squeezing my tip, and stars explode in my vision.

My body vibrates.

My balls clench.

My cum shoots down her throat.

Groaning, I drop my head against the wall as my cock pulses in hot bursts.

Heavy breaths are ripped from me, uncontainable as my body flushes with the heat of my magic rolling around in pleasure. It seemingly purrs as it languidly stretches inside me.

Shuddering, I look down to pull out of her mouth. As my tip leaves her lips, her eyes flutter.

My entire body freezes, kneeling in an awkward half position that forces my thigh muscles to tense on the verge of pain. I know I should push out with my magic to keep her asleep, but I don't. I want to see her looking at me with those sex-filled eyes.

I don't dare breathe as she flickers on the edge.

Seconds pass...

Long moments that feel like hell.

And then her eyes open half-lidded.

A slow hot smile curls her lips. My name breathes out of her on a purr, grabbing hold of my heart like a vice.

In another second, my girl's yawning and falling back asleep, but that look she gave me, not just of utter content, but of knowing she is loved...

It cuts through everything, even my desire to bury my tongue back between her legs.

Kneeling over her half-crouched, I stare at her for a long moment. Tears burn at the back of my eyes, and my throat closes. She is so fucking beautiful. So perfect.

I stroke her face with my fingertip as a single tear falls down my chin and splatters on her pillow, seeping into the cotton. My chest expands so much it fucking hurts.

My lungs burn with the need to wake her, to have her

look at me like that again.

Instead, I move to stretch out beside her, lying down on my side, half hanging off the single bed. My girl snuggles against me even in this summer heat. My heart squeezes hard. I thought I loved her as much as was possible, but the emotions I'm feeling now tell me I was a fucking idiot.

"I'm going to give you the world, *kira*," I promise in the darkness of her room. She'll never want for anything – love, safety, food, jewelry. I'll give it all to her.

I kiss the top of her head as I stroke her hair. The hot Florida heat pushes between us, but I use my magic to keep us cool just so I can keep holding her.

All through the night, I stay in a precarious balance on the edge of her bed. It's uncomfortable in a dozen places, but the gods themselves will have to pry me from this position. Ignoring the pain in my side, I breathe in utter contentment.

TWENTY-FIVE

HIM

My subconscious wakes me at five-thirty – a full hour and a half before Derek rises like clockwork to get ready for work at John High School. Squeezing my girl's breast, I groan at the feel of her nipple erect in the palm of my hand. All night, I've just held her, and my cock is now desperately hard to the point of pain. Rocking my hips so it rubs against her thigh, I trail my fingers down to her pussy.

I have a bit of time before I need to go.

And I know just how I'm going to spend it.

Shifting over her, I kiss my way down her belly to between her thighs. I can't get enough of her taste on my lips, of her hot sleepy moans, and the feel of her hands on my hair as she pulls at my scalp and rides my tongue.

My magic seeks her out in the budding light of her room, the sun peeking through the thin curtains. A soft glow paints her beautiful body, and my fingers spread her pussy lips as I kneel before it. It glistens already, and I wonder if she's still locked in a wet dream.

Licking my lips, I just stare at her for a long moment.

So pretty.

So delicious.

All mine.

Leaning in, I press a kiss to her clit, then swirl around it with my tongue. She doesn't stir, too deep inside her dreams.

My blood quickens at the thought of how much I can do to her before I need to use my magic to keep her under. She's so innocently unaware. So beautifully asleep. *Fully at my mercy.*

That thought resonates inside me on a groan, and I press my lips against hers as my eyes watch her face over the mound of her stomach. Her mouth opens on a sigh, but she doesn't move.

My pulse increasing with the building rush, I kiss her slowly. No tongue. Just gentle passes of my lips against her sexy pussy.

Holding her open with my fingers, I run my tongue from right above the entrance of her ass to her clit. I swirl around the tiny bud once before diving back down to lick her pussy.

Her only movement is another sigh.

My cock throbs painfully, wanting to be inside her, and I wonder if that's what it'll take to wake her up. She's so utterly content in her dreams.

Licking her again, I rub her taste all over the inside of my mouth, needing it to last me all day while I'm away from her. Then I slide a finger along the path my tongue just took. The warmth of her pussy sucks in my tip, and my breath leaves on a little hiss.

Fuck. I need to fuck her.

I need to empty my cum inside her.

Need to fill her womb with my child. *A son.*

Groaning, I push my finger in slowly to the knuckle. My cock weeps in open frustration and jealousy, precum sliding down to wet my balls. The memory of her mouth sucking on me earlier makes the blood pound in my hard-on. My cock jerks, and I wrap a hand around it. I pump it in rhythm to the fucking of my finger.

With a sexy little moan, she spreads her thighs wider. Opening herself for me. Desperate to have me all, my pretty, pretty girl.

"I'm going to fuck you soon, *kira*. I'm going to fill your belly with my children while you sleep. I'm going to fuck you every night you're in my bed."

I push another finger inside her as I stretch out above her. My other hand tightens on my cock. Fastening my lips onto her left nipple, I suck on it as I pleasure the both of us. She moans, her head moving as if to look at me.

Excitement courses through my veins as I wait to see if she wakes. I want her to look at me like she did last night. That small smile. With the knowledge that she is loved.

But she stays asleep this time, and the split second of disappointment is quickly overridden by the prospect of going further. Licking her breast, I take my time enjoying the underside, giving it little bites and hickeys she won't see unless she deliberately goes looking. With every new red claim, more precum wets my hand.

Pulling my finger out of her, I wipe it across her nipple. My other hand takes up its vacated position, rubbing my cum against her pussy lips before my thumb pushes it inside.

"I'm going to make you pregnant, *kira*. I'm going to fuck you while you're swollen with our child."

The images crashing through me have my head falling against her breast on a groan. I rub my cheek against her, licking the taste of her off her nipple. My body shudders.

She doesn't move, and I take that as an opportunity to push more precum inside her. I won't slam in balls deep until she's awake, but each drop of my cum is already hers.

It's only right that I gift it to her as she gifts me with her body.

Wrapping her fingers around my cock, I close a fist over them. Grunts rise from my chest as I position the tip right between the wet lips of her pussy. Jerking myself off, I kiss her breasts, imagining her swollen with my seed.

"You're so fucking beautiful. So perfect, *kira*." And I'm so fucking close, another few beats of her fist will have me spewing my cum against the lips of her pussy. They suck my tip, wanting to pull me deeper. She finally moves, her hips rocking as she dances from the edge of sleep.

Despite my absolute *need* to see her looking at me as I orgasm, I keep her down with my magic. I can't risk her panicking and interrupting me from filling her with my cum.

I groan as I suck on her nipple and play with her clit with my other hand. She cries out, her hips bucking hard now, her body desperate for my cock. I kiss my way up her breasts to her throat. Her hand squeezes me through mine. Her pussy beckons me to slide inside.

I push a fraction past the tip.

My teeth clench. My spine heats, an intense ball of hot pleasure building in my lower back.

"I'm going to cum inside you, *kira*. I'm going to –"

I jerk on an uncontrollable groan, my head falling back as I arch. My cock pulses against her sweet hand. Cum shoots from me, and I pray to the gods that it takes root inside her womb. I want everyone to know she's mine. I want *her* to know. I want her body to accept my seed and make children from the both of us.

I kiss her neck as she whimpers in her sleep. She wants more, and I'm more than willing to give it to her.

But first I need to taste her with my claim inside her.

Leaning over to give her a quick kiss on the mouth, I release my hold on her hand. She opens for me instantly, her tongue seeking mine, and I let her take her fill before kissing my way down her delicious body to her full pussy.

It glistens and smells of me. The muscles in my back and shoulders spasm as I drink her in. A bit of my cum escapes her as I watch.

"Take it deep into your wet pussy," I murmur as I wipe it up with my finger and push it back in. "That's a good girl. That's a good girl who I'm going to reward by licking you to orgasm."

Her pussy eats me greedily, and I lower my head to return the favor. But just as my lips are graced with the claimed taste of my girl, I'm aware of a horrible noise.

It's soft but deafening – running ice through my veins.

The door creaks as it opens behind me.

A split second of heavy silence slams into the room as Derek and I both still.

Then I'm moving, barreling backwards into him with a push of magic. We fly into the hall, and before we hit the adjacent wall, I shut the door to Scarlett's room with a flick of my hand. The silence spell I placed on it upon my arrival works both ways. It'll keep her from hearing me as I kill Derek. It's why I didn't hear him getting up before his normal schedule.

Cursing myself for letting my guard down around her, I slam my elbow into his stomach as we hit the wall.

He grunts, then sinks his teeth into the base of my neck.

Blood spurts.

My heart pounds.

Death beckons, but I twist away, just barely escaping having my artery ripped out from my throat.

The fucker fights dirty.

He slinks down the wall, then leaps forward, not giving me any time to use my magic. Raising my hands to block his punch, I take a knee to my side. Pain explodes from my half-healed kidney, and I let my legs buckle, ducking under his next swing as I fall back. He pushes me quickly, having clocked me as a witch rather than a vampire or a werewolf. If I had been either, fighting this close would have meant certain death for him.

But a witch needs their hands (or another conduit) to cast a spell. Magic can be spoken into existence, but the outcome is twisted and unfocused, and it's more likely to kill you rather than your target.

Blocking another blow, I step backwards down the hall, trying to put distance between us as well as lure him away from Scarlett's room. Although he doesn't have the time to try to grab her –I only need a second to kill him– I don't want her waking up, stepping out hearing the house is quiet (the spell of silence tricking her), and walking in between the two of us.

He matches me step for step with constant blows, a military background clear in each fist and knee. I do not retaliate, letting him feel encouraged to keep coming.

And then we make it to the living room, far enough away from my girl.

On the next block, I wrap my arm around his to anchor him down, but instead of trying to pull away, he reaches behind him.

For a knife or a gun, it doesn't matter. This close and with his training, I'm about to bleed.

Scraping my nails into his arm, I dig past skin just as a blade rips out around his hip.

"Valek ke zef," I murmur, not a rise of infliction in my tone. Even still, the magic splits in the air, twisted and deranged from how I meant to use it.

The uncontrollable energy ruptures between us, tossing us back like change to a rude customer. I slam into the edge of a table and flip over it. The wound on my neck boils hot, the blood frothing with angry magic, and I slam a hand over it, drawing the magic out and shooting it into the room with my other hand. A bubble forms around me, keeping the energy from seeking my wound out again.

Derek hits the wall opposite, screaming as his arm melts, the blood I drew attracting the wayward magic. It burns through his body, causing blisters to bubble on his skin as it arcs towards his heart.

Blood pours out of his mouth, followed by whispers of smoke. The blisters pop, exploding magic. Pieces of him fly free, painting the ceiling and furniture.

Half of his face lands in front of me, an eye melting into the carpet.

His other eye rolls back into his half-collapsed skull as he slinks against the wall. Lifeless.

The magic sated, it disappears in the air, and I climb to my feet, only to fall sideways, flipping over the arm of the couch and then tumbling to the floor.

A hiss ruptures the air as I lie on my back, agony shooting through both sides of my body. My half-healed kidney is one of the culprits. The other is a six-inch knife embedded in my stomach. The fucker must have stabbed me just before we were ripped apart. Adrenaline kept the pain down until now, but with the fight over and me staring at the fucking thing embedded to the hilt, my nerves catch up on a scream.

Gritting my teeth, I place a hand on my stomach, the blade between my thumb and forefinger. Then with my other hand, I pull the knife straight up. Pain flares deep, but it is quickly soothed by the warmth of magic flowing through my fingers.

Although I'm not a healer like Mother, she's taught me a few spells to keep me from dying. I can't heal the wound completely, but I can stop it bleeding, and that's all I need for now.

Dropping my head back against the floor, I breathe out with a curse. I fucked up. I fell asleep with her in my arms instead of heading back home because I convinced myself one night would be fine. Derek was a man of habit. I'd leave before he woke up.

"Fuck."

I could have got her killed, and if I had died, she would have been tortured for information, her cries of knowing nothing not believed.

I need to hide his body and clean the place before she –

"Derek? It's six…"

Her voice freezes me on the floor, and I am intensely aware of just how bad the living room looks. A drop of blood falls from the ceiling and lands on my face. My hands moving, I start to conjure a spell that will get her to walk in the opposite direction.

Tension tugs at every muscle and every bead of sweat as I work as fast as I can…

"Derek? It's six," I call out as I rub the sleep from my eyes. My phone is gripped in my other hand, the list of questions and extra information I have for him written on an app.

I half-hope he's not up yet so I can go back to sleep, a delicious dream still lingering on the edges of my mind. I could've sworn I could actually feel Khalid's arms around me a few minutes before my alarm went off. And before that, his tongue, his fingers, the tip of his hard cock…

My pussy clenches, a wetness slides down my thighs, and I turn to look longingly at my bedroom door.

But I need to learn quickly about this new world if I'm going to have any hope of survival.

Forcing down my arousal, I take another step towards the living room. A chill runs down my spine when I drop my hand from my eyes.

There aren't any lights on, but the soft rays of coming dawn peek through the blinds and curtains. It's enough for me to see the flipped over table.

Why didn't I hear anything?

My chest squeezing, I don't dare breathe as my feet root to the floor. The smell of blood suddenly permeates the fog of sleep, and my eyes widen as they dart around the part of the living room I can see from the hall. There's so many stains and new bits I can't make out – but the place was cleaned immaculately when I last saw it.

The gun room is just a few doors behind me, and it screams like a beacon for me to run towards it. I start to turn, but as I do, I catch sight of a mirror on the living room wall, and in its reflection, I see Derek.

Half of Derek.

Throwing a hand over my mouth, I bite back a scream as his one eye bores into me, imploring me to run.

A noise behind the sofa has my feet jerking beneath me, and I stumble as I run for the gun room. I place a hand on the wall, catching myself, still moving quickly. Can't stop.

The sound of movement whispers behind me.

Don't look.

I can't waste a precious second; a werewolf's speed is unmatched. Throwing myself at the door, I yank it open.

A modern bathroom stares back at me, and I realize I've miscounted doors.

My blood draining from my face, knowing I don't have the time to try another one, I jump inside and slam the door behind me.

My hands fumble with the lock. My phone clutters to the ground, and I wince at the hard clatter of it on the tiles.

My pulse slams inside my skull, making it hard to hear anything else. But I *know* someone is still in the house.

Snatching my phone up off the ground, I back away from the door, my breaths shallow, my thoughts in too many directions and not one of them is calm.

Trembling fingers punch at the damp glass screen in my hands. I start to call nine-one-one, only to stop on the first one.

The way Derek looked at Vlad assaults me. Is he a sup? Is he the one who killed Derek?

I can't risk it.

My pulse in my throat, I tremble.

"*Call me*, kira."

Can I?

Can I really call Khalid? Tears burn my eyes. What will he even do?

Nothing.

He can't do anything.

But at least I won't die alone.

Pushing the button on the number he put in for me, I raise the phone to my ear. It rings, but I'm focusing on anything I can hear outside. Footsteps. Breathing. Are they about to knock the door in and rip me apart like they did Derek?

I hear nothing.

Only silence.

And then...

A phone vibrates.

It's faint behind the closed door but not much further.

My blood chills, my fingers running cold as my brain tries to tell me something I don't want to believe.

The phone rings in my ear.

My pulse skips a beat.

A second never felt so long.

Straining, my ears search for the answering vibration, praying it doesn't –

Bzzzz.

My phone drops from my sweaty palm.

"Oh, *kira*. I wish you didn't hear that."

TWENTY-SIX

HIM

Despite the mess her calling me has caused, my heart squeezes over the fact that she did. I place a hand on the flat of the door, debating if I should go in all bloody or make her fall asleep, then talk to her at home after I have a shower.

"I'm not going to hurt you, *kira*," I murmur.

"What are you?" she hisses.

A weight settles on top of me, and my fingers press into the wood, wanting to comfort her even though I know she needs the door between us. "A witch."

"And you killed Derek?" Her voice is biting and angry, and I wonder if she is painting me like he did – all sups to be hunted.

"Yes. He was going to kill you."

The sound of soft ceramic clanking draws my brows together as I try to make out what she is doing. She won't fit through the small window above the toilet, so it can't be her climbing on top of it.

My brows relax as pride fills me.

She took off the toilet's tank lid. It's a solid weight, and the only good weapon in most bathrooms.

A corner of my lips curl upwards.

My girl's a fighter.

I like that.

My hand drops to the doorknob. "May I come in?"

"You're asking me?" Shock laces her words, and I frown.

"Why wouldn't I?"

"You're not going to kill me?"

"*Kira...*I would never hurt you." Pain has me sagging against the door, pressing my forehead against the wood as I close my eyes. I relax my grip on the knob, making sure not to turn it as I move, not wanting to freak her out anymore.

"Um...okay."

Happiness jolts through me, straightening me on a smile. *She trusts me.*

I twist the handle, using magic to break the lock easily.

My grin widens as I step inside the bathroom, then falters when I don't see her.

Fury shoots down our bond a second before the shower curtain attacks me. She jumped out of the bath, taking the railing down with her, hiding her bulk behind the dark-blue fabric. I stumble back beneath her weight, hitting the opposite wall in only a couple steps, the bathroom tiny. A heavy weight slams into my chest –*crack!*– knocking the wind out of me and breaking at least one rib.

She swings again as I slip down the wall, the toilet tank lid connecting with where my head just was. Plaster and chipped paint rains down into my hair, and I close my eyes to keep them clean. Yanking at the shower curtain, I look up at her.

Gods, she's beautiful.

My smile stills in a split second when her eyes widen and she falls back, the fabric tripping up her feet.

Her arms flail.

My hands move.

Magic catches her before she can crack her head open on the bathtub, and not liking the close call, I cast another spell, pulling her into sleep.

Her eyes close. The lid drops to the floor with a loud thud.

Climbing to my feet, I look down at her half-floating in the air. I wanted to bring her home in a state of happiness. I wanted to gift her with the family she never had and watch the smile light up her eyes, knowing she was loved by all of them, not just me.

She deserves the world.

And instead, she's going to wake up in a new place.

Terrified and uncertain about why she's there.

Running a hand through my hair, I try to think of a better solution.

But there isn't one.

Derek is dead.

The WALL will suspect her if she's left alive.

Antonio is hunting her, knowing we've bonded.

Dropping my hand, I lean down and scoop her up into my arms. My muscles strain even with the aid of my magic. Pain rips across my body, begging me to drop her, but I don't. I need to hold her.

My vision narrows as the agony is almost too much, and I stand still for a long moment as I wrestle with the broken ribs and open wounds that have started bleeding again beneath the strain. Thank the gods, the magic aimed for my neck. If I had to pull out the knife before dealing with it, I would be dead just like Derek.

Gritting my teeth, I take a step forward. A wet heat slides down my side from where Derek stabbed me.

Clenching my jaw tighter, I keep going.

Once our blood bond is complete, I can put her in my

shadow, but as it stands now, doing so will kill her. There are *things* lurking inside that place, twisted disfigures of magic that attack anything with a heat signature. Even cars that are put inside right after running will be pulled out with claw and teeth marks in the metal, the windows shattered, the frame distorted and crumpled. My and my brothers' genetic magic allows us to travel the pitch-black domain, keeping us safe from such things. But anything we put inside it isn't given the same protection.

She needs more of my blood running through her veins first.

So I take another step as sweat beads down my naked body. Growing pains explode with every foot gained. Ragged breaths are sucked in between broken ribs as I make my way to the front door.

The sun is up, but the street is quiet, so I open the door with a push of magic, then pull out a car from my shadow.

After putting her in the passenger seat, I turn back to the house. My hands rotate as magic builds between my fingers. The rune beside the knife wound glows red, then fades again.

The spell cast, I settle into the driver's seat, shimmy into the clothes I pull out of my shadow, and drive off. I make it to the end of the road, then glance in my rearview mirror. Orange flames are just starting to flicker out of the windows. It'll act like a normal fire and be put out the same, but it will consume Derek's body within minutes. The cops will assume he wasn't home when it caught fire. They'll list him as a missing person on official reports.

Glancing at my girl as she fidgets in her sleep, I reach over and grab her hand.

"I'm sorry it happened like this, *kira*," I say, kissing the back of it. "But we can be together now, no obstacles in our way."

Settling her hand on my lap, I drive my girl home.

"Khalid's gone and kidnapped her!" Maddox shouts, his head poking out of an upstairs window as I get out of the car. It's not even six-thirty, and the little shit is already being a nuisance.

Ignoring him, I open the passenger door and unbuckle her seat belt.

"Yo, Rudy wants to know if she passed out after seeing your ugly dick!"

A thump sounds from the upstairs window.

"Sorry, mistranslated!" Maddox continues brightly, not needing any fucking encouragement. "He wants to know if she passed out after you told her his dick was –"

He yelps this time, Rudy most likely having hit him.

I swirl my shadows around another car, the one I drove needing to cool down before it can enter that domain, and head for the house with my girl in my arms. As I near the door, Maddox topples onto the pavement in front of me.

He wheezes as he stares up at the sky, a shit-eating grin still on his face. Stepping over him, I call out to Rudy, "Thanks."

He raps on the window. "My pleasure."

Maddox laughs in between winces of pain as the door opens to show Mother.

Her eyes narrow on my face, no doubt noticing the pale coloring of my cheeks and the sweat on my brow.

"I'll get Leno to make a tea," she says, stepping back to allow me entry. I turn sideways so I don't knock Scarlett into the frame, then follow her through the house. She splits off towards the kitchen as I head for the stairs, my body screaming with every step. My palms grow damp, and I shift her to try to relieve some of the pain from my wounds.

They flare stronger. I grit my teeth.

Standing on the landing, Krypto wags his tail as he noses my girl. Leno pulls on a black shirt, stifling a yawn. "Next time, kidnap her in the middle of the fucking day," he says as I pass.

With a wave of my fingers, I open my bedroom door. It's bare of everything but a bed and a small bedside table, me not being one for material things. After removing the covers, I place her down on the bed. Pain rips through my body as I straighten, and I want to drop on top of the blue sheets beside her.

But first I need a shower.

I look down at the wound in my side. It's still bleeding, which explains the dizziness rushing through my skull. My vision blurs for a moment when I press a hand firmly on top of it. The smell of burning flesh accompanies the spell I use to 'heal' myself.

Rolling my shoulders, my muscles protesting, I pick up the blanket and place it over Scarlett. She will sleep for another hour or so. The magic needs to come out of her system on its own; forcing her to wake will hurt her.

Tucking the blanket up to her chin, I lean down and kiss her forehead.

Straightening, I grab one of the five sets of clothes out of my closet, then head for a shower. Varius steps out of his bedroom further down the hall, and the look in his eyes has me bypassing the bathroom and entering his room.

It's just the two of us inside. Micha sleeps downstairs, not trusted to be beside him when he's vulnerable. Even I don't get that honor.

"What is it?" I ask, neither one of us keen on small talk.

Glancing at me, he shuts the door, then seals us in a ward of silence by activating the rune I carved into his door years ago. The hairs on my neck rise.

"There's another traitor," he says, his voice flat, his eyes empty.

The pain inside me fades as adrenaline kicks through my system. "How do you know?" It isn't an accusation, a display of disbelief. It's a simple need to know the facts so I can do my job as reaper.

"Aleric told me yesterday. He won't accept the deal to be allies unless we deal with it." For any deal they make will be instantly broken if Varius got killed.

"Does he know who?" I ask.

"No. Someone just reported an anonymous tip about a witness seeing you arrive at the hotel after Hannah Davis' murder."

The fucking coward who tried to bang on her door.

"Was there anyone else in the hall?" he asks.

I study him, knowing he would've checked the security tapes before bringing this up. "No."

"You didn't sense anyone watching?"

"No."

"So only Xander saw you enter and knew the witness checked out soon after you arrived?"

My jaw locks as I nod sharply. Xander has been loyal to this Family since he joined it seven years ago. He keeps his head down, doesn't make waves. He isn't interested in climbing the ranks. He just wants our protection, and for that, he does his job well, collecting and cataloging DNA evidence for us to plant at crime scenes. I can't see him as a traitor.

Then again, I didn't notice our uncle was planning to kill Varius until the day he struck.

"I'll deal with him," I say, heading for the door.

He steps out of the way. "Do it now. Antonio will grow in power rapidly if he's consuming hybrids, and we don't know how many women he has pregnant."

My fingers tighten on the doorknob, not wanting to be away from Scarlett.

But an order is an order.

Opening the door, I nod.

TWENTY-SEVEN

HIM

Scarlett's still asleep in my bed when I'm preparing to leave. I finished with my shower, and Leno made me a tea to heal my wounds, having pulled the regenerative power from his plants, thus allowing me to use my magic again without sacrificing my organs. Mother stood beside him, wanting to heal me herself but under orders not to from Varius.

The bite mark on my neck is completely gone, as is the knife wound Derek gave me. My broken ribs are healed too. Only my kidney is still half missing.

When magic demands a price, only a fool tries to find a way not to pay.

My eyes linger on my girl's sleeping form. I want to crawl into bed with her and hold her until she wakes. I need to explain what's happened to her so she doesn't panic in a new place. My brothers can be a handful, as can Mother, and I don't want to leave her in their care.§

But as much as they might annoy her, she will be safe with them and they will not scare her. I've marked her as mine; the blood ritual completed or not, we've bonded and she's part of the family. They will treat her as one of us.

Placing a kiss on her forehead, I then open the drawer on the bedside table. On a black cushion indented to cup it is a black mask with two sets of gold horns curving out of its forehead, two going out, two going up. Nestled above them is a painted rune, gold in color and meaning: *Death claims all.* The face is expressionless.

Picking it up, I turn from the room. "I'll be back soon," I promise as I slip the reaper mask onto my face and melt into my shadow.

TWENTY-EIGHT

HER

Awareness comes to me slowly, having to fight through a thick layer of grogginess to pierce my brain.

But then my eyes snap open as memories assault me.

Khalid killed Derek.

I attacked him in the bathroom.

And then –

My mind blanks, but with it comes a heavy dose of anger.

Why can't I remember?

What did he do to me?

Where am I?

The walls in Derek's room were eggshell. This one's a dusky gray, and the bed isn't a bag of springs digging into my back.

Turning away from the wall I'm facing, I tense, half-expecting to see Khalid watching me. But the room is empty – of both him and seemingly anything else.

Is this a luxury prison?

The thought blisters rage across my heart as I sit up and swing my legs over the edge of the bed. The fucker kidnapped me.

He *lied* to me.

He used me as bait to get to Derek, and now he thinks he can play with me like that werewolf wanted to?

The fuck he can.

I'm going to kill him.

Standing up, I look around for something to use as a weapon, but there's nothing. Just the bed and a small table beside it. No lamp on top of it. No pictures on the wall. There's a window covered with plain black curtains, and that's it. It might not be barred, but I don't care to check.

I'm not running; he'd just catch me. And there was a truth in his voice when he said he wouldn't hurt me when I was in the bathroom that I believe.

The sucker.

I'm going to use that against him when I beat him to death.

Moving to stand beside the door, preparing to pounce on him when he comes in to check on me, I take five steps before it opens.

A young man steps inside, holding a tray of food. "You ain't a veggie are ya?"

I stare at him as he stares at me. My stomach growls, but I ignore it.

The door closes behind him without any brush of his foot, and fear slams into me, shoving aside my anger as it pedals me back. "You're a witch."

Khalid being one isn't scary. It's heartbreaking and cruel and fills me with the urge to punch him in the face, but I don't know this man, and I have seen what they can do.

Derek's destroyed corpse attacks my mind, his one eyeball imploring me to run. My lips tremble as I realize I have nowhere else to retreat and nothing with which to hit him with.

"No!" The man gasps sarcastically. "Really?" Laughing at his own joke, he walks towards me. "Khalid not tell you anything, huh? Just like the ass."

With every footfall, my pulse spikes until I'm certain it's going to punch its way out of my ribcage.

"Relax. You die of a heart attack, and Khalid's going to blame me."

"Who are you?" I demand as my brain struggles to make sense of his joking manner. Although I've never been kidnapped before, I'm pretty certain this isn't how it normally works.

With breakfast in bed carried by a cocky male who looks young enough to still be in high school.

"Just the best looking one of the bunch." His grin lights his hazel eyes, looking so genuine, I want to smile back. "Name's Maddox, but you can call me Sexy."

"You're one of his brothers," I whisper, finally piecing everything together, relaxing with the knowledge that he's close to Khalid. "You live with him?"

He snorts. "He never moved out." Then laughs. "None of us has."

"Your poor ma..." The words slip out before I can stop them. Witch or not, raising eight sons that won't leave must be hell.

"Trust me." He cracks his neck on a wince. "There's nothing poor about her. Now eat before Khalid gets back and yells at me for starving you."

The crispy smell of bacon mixed with the tomato smell of beans makes my stomach growl, but I don't want to eat with him here.

God, Gen, you're disgusting. You make everyone else lose their appetite.

"Going to try to starve yourself to get to him, huh? Not a bad idea, but personally, I'd go with pretending you're into this whole captured kink shit, wait for Khalid to put his guard down, and then stab him with this knife."

My eyes widen when he pulls a twelve-inch blade out of an unnatural shadow in the palm of his other hand.

"Here." He offers it to me, hilt-first.

"You're *helping* me? Why?"

He chuckles. "You're clearly an only child." The knife vanishes as quickly as it appeared. "Sorry," he says. "Just realized Khalid will probably actually let you stab him and then Varius will throw a huge hissy fit, then he won't fuck Micha properly and then Ma will get on to me about not getting grandkids, and well... that's more than I can be bothered with.

"So yeah, you're going to have to find your own knife. May I suggest asking for steak for dinner?" He cocks his head to the side. "You ain't a veggie, right?"

I shake my head mutely, no fucking idea what else I can do. None of his words make sense in the context of being kidnapped.

"Good. Eat breakfast, gather your strength, go through my brother's belongings to see if you can make a shiv, and I'll check back in a couple of hours."

My mouth gapes, but he doesn't seem to understand how weird he is. He just heads for the door.

Just as it opens, I call out, "Wait."

He stops, looking over his shoulder.

"Where is Khalid?" *How long do I have to wait to yell at him?*

He shrugs. "Don't know, but considering he left all hush hush and right after bringing you here..." His face loses a hint of his smile. "I'd say he's on a job."

"A job?" I highly doubt he means the landscaping business I believed Khalid ran.

"Mmm." Without further explanation, he nods at the tray of food behind me. "Now eat. You need fuel if you're going to escape."

The door shuts firmly behind him, and I'm left staring at it in utter confusion. *What the ever loving fuck?*

When I'm finally able to get a bit of sense back into my brain, I turn slowly to rescan the room. This is Khalid's? It's so...empty. An uncomfortable feeling settles in my chest at the sight of how little comfort his life has.

Shaking my head, I walk over to the closet door and pull it open. It's as empty as the rest of the place. Four shirts on hangers. Three pants. A stack of underwear sits on the shelf below. The urge to pick one up and see if he wears boxers or briefs is quickly followed by the image of him in both.

My pussy kegels involuntarily, and I jerk my eyes away from them. Bending my knees, I check out the other shelves. A pair of four socks sit in a row.

That's it.

That's all he owns.

A tightness fills my lungs again, and I straighten in an attempt to ignore it.

Walking back to the bed, I sit down and stare at the tray of food.

It could be drugged...

My stomach growls.

Why would they need to drug me?

They are witches who can just lift me with a wave of their hand.

Picking up the food, I stab a piece of bacon and raise it to my lips.

TWENTY-NINE

HIM

Xander's house is empty. His belongings packed. His bed still made. He didn't stay here last night, and I'm certain he'll never step foot in here again. Removing my reaper mask, not liking to wear it if I'm not about to enact justice, I turn towards his bathroom.

I don't expect to find anything given what he used to do at the hotel. The shower drain is clear of hair. There's no flecks of toothpaste-filled spittle on the mirror. No shitstain in the toilet. There's no reason for me to be here.

The pull of my girl urges me back home, but instead I pull out my phone and call Maddox. "I need you to shift into Xander," I say as soon as he answers.

"Hello to you too. Xander, huh? Pity, I liked him."

"I'll be back in half an hour after I pack Scarlett's stuff. Get a stone from the vault."

"Varius sign off on that?"

My jaw clenches. The alexandrite is fucking precious, and Varius would have given me a stone if I was allowed to use one. But I'll argue my case with him later. "I want this done today."

"Ah…so you can come home and fuck your girl, right?"

My eyes narrow.

"You gonna ask me how she is?"

I hang up on him before he can say anything, a cold jealousy eating its way into my chest. *Needing* to ask my brothers or *anyone* else how *my* girl is, is making my knuckles turn white.

Magic bunching inside my muscles, feeding on my frustration, I head for the door. A few minutes later, I arrive at Hannah's house and grab everything of Scarlett's to chuck into my shadow. My hand lingers on her diary instead of tossing it in.

Opening it to the last entry, I read about the car wash.

How she wishes she could have done more than just feel my cock through our clothes.

A smile curls my lips.

My girl has a dirty imagination.

Thirty minutes later, I'm back at the house. Maddox meets me at the door with Varius behind him. Of course the fucker ratted me out.

"You wanted this done quickly," I say to Varius.

"I wanted you to interrogate him. He's been with us a long time."

"Not as long as Uncle Myers." For twenty-three years, he was like a father to me. He helped raise us even when Father walked out – not as much as Varius did, but his presence was always there. And now it was snuffed out, never to be felt again except for in the dreams that didn't let me sleep.

His lips tighten. "I still want to know why he's turned

traitor before we kill him."

"Before *I* kill him," I say, my desire to have this over and done with bleeding into my words.

Maddox steps back, moving out from between the two of us on a low whistle.

"He is the only one who knows about that witness," I push, my tone a bit more respectful, knowing it's the fastest way to convince him.

He doesn't say anything, but he does step aside. "Carve a message into his flesh. Tell him to come in, and he'll be shown mercy."

I nod, not caring if he lives or dies. As long as my role is done, I'll get to see my girl.

Maddox heads upstairs, then continues past my room to the newer extension of the house, built a few decades ago when the twins were born. My eyes linger on my door, and the bond connecting me to my girl hums with a need to detour inside.

Rolling my shoulders, I walk past it.

Maddox's room is a shrine to various metal bands, the walls painted a dark maroon to highlight the numerous black posters he has taped to the walls. As I start to shut the door behind me, he strips off his pants. Xander is six inches taller than him, and to quote my brother, "I don't like my pants riding up my ass and squishing my balls."

I wait as he cracks his neck from side to side, rolls his shoulders, and exhales. Magic hums in the air, electrifying it in a cloud around him.

His body shudders as his muscles rip and his bones break beneath tearing flesh. A black vortex opens beneath him, his magic feeding on the slices of meat he's left in a locker in his shadow. We might be witches, but we can't create things from nothing. Magic requires payment, and Maddox's extra six inches and extra bulk requires human flesh to make.

A pained groan breathes through a pair of new lips as an

exact image of Xander stands in front of me. "One of these days, I really need to learn how to change just a part of me. Just like, a hair or something…"

It's not outside of the realm of possibility, but he has centuries of study before he gets there.

"The stone's in my jeans," he says as he reaches up and rips out a few strands of hair. After retrieving the green alexandrite, I take the DNA from him. With it entwined in the stone, I start to mold.

He shifts back into his original self, grinding his teeth hard enough to hear as his magic flays the six inches off his back. It doesn't get deposited back into his locker – the payment owed.

As he stretches his arms above his head, I finish off the final few touches of the stone doll.

Conjuring a scalpel from my shadow, I carve a message into its stomach.

Return tonight, and we will grant mercy.

I don't bother writing what will happen if he doesn't. He knows us well enough to know.

Dropping the stone into my shadow, I head for my girl. I've waited fucking long enough.

THIRTY

HER

I can't explain it, but I can *feel* when Khalid enters the house, my chest becoming tighter with frustration and lighter with a giddiness I don't want to feel. Breaths linger in my throat, held with the tension of a pin poised to be dropped onto an avalanche of destruction.

My eyes flick to the door, and I take a step towards it, pulled by a force I don't understand. My tongue sticks to the roof of my mouth, and I move it around as I try to rid myself of the nerves gripping me. Reaching for the door knob, I let my fingers graze the cold metal before jerking my hand back as if it's burned.

I shuffle back, my pulse a mad beat as I can see that pin teetering so clearly on the edge...

My lungs burn with the anxiety of watching it in the depths of my mind.

Left...right...left... the angle increasing with every rock it does back and forth.

And then the door opens, toppling it completely.

I watch in utter stillness as it tumbles end over end as Khalid fills the doorway.

Thick silence stretches between us, a moment where the pin hits the mountain of heavy snow.

And then the avalanche roars in a blast of rage as Khalid walks into the room.

"You fucking bastard," I seethe. "All this time, you were just playing me." When I wasn't. When I was falling for his charms and believing him when he said he would always be there for me. *Fucking lies.* "Just so you could what, find Derek and the WALL? Have you killed all of them yet? Does it make you feel like a man to rip us *playthings* to pieces?"

Tears burn my eyes, and I wipe them angrily away, hating just how much I'm feeling betrayed rather than scared.

I *trusted* him.

I believed I was finally going to get something *good* in life, something worth living for.

And he's just a fucking sup, and I was just bait.

"I wasn't playing you, *kira*," Khalid says as he prowls towards me, his eyes intense with an honesty that makes my pulse feral.

"You used me to find Derek's house," I spit, but it's not as strong, trembling under the heat in his eyes. My lips stay parted on strong breaths.

"I already knew where he lived."

"Bullshit."

He stops in front of me, his gaze sharp as broken glass, and I'm forced to lift my head to hold it.

"Then why didn't you kill him earlier?"

"He was of no importance then."

"So why kill him now?"

His eyes linger on my throat, on the bruises Derek's son left on me. When they rise back to mine, rage darkens them considerably. "He was going to kill you."

I snort. Such fucking bullshit. "He took me in. He was teaching me –"

"He wasn't planning on killing you then."

"That doesn't make any sense. Why would he go to bed not wanting to kill me and then before I even wake up –" I stop abruptly as it barrels into me even though Khalid's face doesn't change, doesn't twitch one damn muscle. I *know* why, my brain slamming pieces together to a puzzle I can finally see.

"You..." I growl, an inferno across my nerves as I stare into his dark-brown unflinching eyes. "He was going to kill me because of you."

Because he knew Khalid was a witch.

Not at the station – not when Derek gave him a nod between men, but at the house.

My dreams from last night, fucking delicious dreams that had me so wet this morning, rush into my skull. "You were in my room."

My pulse spikes as I imagine those dreams being real. Of him touching me with his hands and tongue, his cock sliding into me as he groans above me, his hands full of my breasts.

But it's not from the rage I want. The rage I should be feeling like any *normal* person would when learning a man's been fucking them while they sleep. Slapping at his chest, I try to shove him back as I dig for the rage I *should* be feeling. "You sick pervert! You had no right –"

"I have every right, *kira*," he says, grabbing my hands and pinning them to his chest as he steps closer. His head dips as one hand grabs my chin, forcing me to stare at him when I would have looked away. "You're mine. This body is mine. Your pussy is mine, and every time I want to make love to it, you'll spread it for me as you beg me to fill it."

"Like hell I –"

His lips crush my words with an undeniable mockery as his tongue sweeps inside my mouth. I struggle against him, trying to yank my arms free of his clasp so I can smack the smugness off his face. But his muscles bulge as he holds me tight.

His fingers, strong but not bruising, force my head to tilt to the perfect angle for him to slide his tongue deeper into my mouth. He sucks on my bottom lip as a groan escapes him. "Let me show you how much I own your body, *kira*. How it begs me to be its master."

My pussy clenches, already begging and crying for him to fill it. Wet heat stains my underwear. Gasping under the onslaught of his tongue, I kiss him back, and the groan of approval he gives me turns the last tendrils of my anger into a need to be fucked hard and fast.

He might be a sup, but I've been crushing on him for the last three months. And the way he looks at me makes it impossible for me to hold on to the lies of him using me. Grabbing his shirt, I slide my tongue around his and moan.

Jerking my head to the side, he licks his way up the full of my neck, then sucks my earlobe into his teeth. His hot breath caresses me. "I've waited so long to fill you with my children. I'm going to take my time fucking your wet, begging pussy."

A spasm rips through me as I involuntarily kegel. He releases my wrists and slips both hands beneath my shirt to cup my breasts. "You're going to squeeze these around my cock and open your pretty little mouth to catch my cum."

His lips cover mine again, hard and rough as he spits into my mouth, mimicking the burst of his seed. I swallow greedily as my body shakes with the force of his promises.

Pushing up my bra, he pinches my nipples in between both fingers, rolling them until I cry out against his lips.

"Good girl," he murmurs, his tongue lapping around mine. "You know what you want, don't you?" He thrusts his hips against me, and my pussy spasms from the hard feel of his cock on my stomach.

Yes!

I reach for him, lost in the madness he's making me feel. "I want your cock," I whisper, my cheeks blushing profusely as I still. *Did those words really come from me?*

A low rumble vibrates in his chest as he kisses me deeply. "Where do you want it?" he rasps, and I want so badly to answer, but my mind blanks.

"You want my cock sliding down your throat," he says, each word spanking my core, "as I lick your sexy pussy. You'll hold it open for me, won't you? Freeing my hands, so I can squeeze your ass and tits and slide my fist deep inside your hole."

Fist? I tense as that image shoots through me.

He pulls back with one last kiss of my lips, then holds my gaze, his eyes hot, his mouth smug. "I'm going to cum inside you, *kira*, then push it all up with my fist, and you are going to come again around my forearm while I'm sucking on your clit."

I gasp as he tugs on both my nipples and his mouth finds my neck. My hand flutters up to the back of his head and tugs at the ponytail holding his hair. Once it's free, I thread my fingers through his black strands, and hold on for dear life.

"Oh *god*!" I moan as his right hand drops to my jeans and opens them on its own.

"God has nothing to do with how I'm going to make you feel, *kira*." His tone bites with jealousy, popping my eyes open as I realize the depth of his obsession with me. A whispering voice tells me that's dangerous.

A louder one cries out his name.

"Good girl," he murmurs in approval as he slides down my zipper, and those two words stoke the heat inside me, making me a melting mess of need.

Bucking my hips, I chase his teasing fingers. A chuckle breathes across my neck as he kneads my breast.

"So greedy...so desperate." His fingers dip between my lips, making me arch. "So." He pushes one digit inside me. I clutch around him on a whimper.

"Deliciously."

Another finger stretches me. I squeeze my eyes shut as electricity zings my spine, making my muscles spasm on a switch he surely controls.

"*Wet.*"

Pushing up my shirt, he leans down and takes my left breast in his mouth. I cry out, both hands in his hair as he fucks my pussy with one set of fingers and pinches my right nipple with the other.

My hips buck uncontrollably as I ride him to oblivion.

He curls to hit just the right spot. He pumps at just the right speed. He palms my clit with just the right pressure.

Gasping, I chase the edge of ecstasy, but right as I'm about to reach it, Khalid pulls back, wringing a desperate whimper from my lungs.

His hand rises to the hem of my shirt and lifts. I help him undress me, and my bra falls away before it hits me that I'm half naked in front of him.

In good light.

My eyes pop open in horror.

Jerking just as his mouth reaches for me again, I cover as much of me as I can, ducking my head to try to find my shirt. "Can we turn off the lights?" I ask, my cheeks on fire as he stares at me.

You're disgusting, Gen.

"Open your arms, *kira*. I told you I own those breasts. I want to see them."

"But..."

"Look at me." I glance up nervously as twenty-two years of abuse assaults my ears. His eyes steal the air from my lips, their intense obsession making me feel beautiful. "Do I look like I'm disgusted by your body?"

I shake my head slightly as nothing but love and sheer desire fills his face.

His hands drop to his waistband, drawing my eyes like a heavy weight. He undoes the button of his pants. Then the zipper before dropping them to the floor. His boxers slide down his legs, and his cock, hard and long, springs free. "Do you see how hard I am thinking about sliding between those perfect breasts of yours?"

I swallow as I focus on his throbbing erection, my pussy begging me to drop my hands so I can feel him against me already.

Cupping my cheek, he lifts my gaze to his. His eyes are soft and so fucking honest it hurts. "So how can you not think you're beautiful?

My throat works hard as I slowly drop my hands. His gaze holds mine for a second longer before dipping to my breasts.

"So fucking perfect. Now keep your eyes on my face."

When I do, he steps back to see me fully. Hunger fills his brown eyes as they slide down every inch of me. They linger on my breasts, a vision of heat and desire that has me squeezing my thighs together on a shudder. He is a man obsessed, looking at me as if I'm some great treasure to cherish and worship. His gaze slowly trails up to mine, and when our eyes meet, I suck in a sharp breath, finally understanding what he means when he calls me *kira*.

Like I am the sun he revolves around.

The reason he breathes.

The sole holder of his obsession.

"Do you see, *kira*?" he murmurs, his body poised on the edge of moving, waiting until he knows I can see me how he sees me.

Tears burning my eyes, I nod.

He steps back in and kisses me reverently, lovingly. His arms go around me, squeezing my ass as his cock presses against my stomach. I push up his black shirt, and he strips quickly, allowing me to see him fully.

My eyes growing hooded, I bask in the knowledge that every inch of his perfection is mine. I run my hand down his chest, across the light sprinkling of hair, and shiver as he groans in pleasure. When I reach the V of his hips, he shudders against me.

Wrapping my fingers around his cock, I suck in a hot breath. He jerks in my grip as I slide my fingers up and down his length.

He lets me pump him only twice before pressing down on my shoulders, guiding me down with a roughness that has me quaking. On my knees, I push my breasts together frantically, barely in time to cup his cock as he slides it against my chest. Groaning, he drops his head back. His tip peeks out of the top of my breasts and rests there for an electrifying moment.

Then he's pulling back and thrusting forward at a pace that shakes my entire body. Threading his hand through my hair, he squeezes my scalp and guides my lips to his length. He pushes into my mouth before I can suck in a breath and fucks it hard as he groans in utter pleasure.

My hands grab his ass, feeling the beautiful flexing of his muscles as he rams his cock down my throat. I choke around him, and Khalid moans loudly, his thighs shaking. Knowing he'll come if I keep squeezing him, I suck my cheeks in and bob up and down quickly, taking him as deep as I can. Even though that barely means half-way, he's soon bucking into me as if he's about to come. I suck him harder, but he starts to pull away.

"Stop, *kira*. I want to –"

I don't let him finish, pulling back his foreskin so his head is completely free, the sensitive tip completely open to my onslaught.

He groans as I flick my tongue rapidly across his head, swirling around it and sucking hard.

His fingers tighten on my scalp, a sharp pain as he tries to pull me off him. My hands dig into his ass, holding him there, needing him to come on an uncontrollable wave.

His nails dig into my skin as he finally gives up and holds me to him rather than away. Thrusting hard, he groans as he works himself over the edge. Crying out as hot cum shoots down my throat, he holds me still, his eyes squeezed shut as he loses himself in the sensation of *me.*

"Don't swallow it, *kira,*" he rasps, his head still thrown back, his words hoarse and raw.

My cheeks expand as I try to obey, but there's too much to keep it all.

Groaning, he looks down at me, piercing me with eyes that have me shivering in anticipation. Pulling out slowly, he hisses in a breath, then cups my chin as a bit of his cum dribbles out of my mouth.

"You're going to pass this to me," he says as his thumb wipes up his seed. My eyes widen from the hot, intense pressure building inside me. "Then you're going to lie on your back and spread your pussy for me so I can put it where it belongs."

Leaning down, he kisses me, his lips swiping across mine for a second before covering them completely. His tongue dives inside, and I frantically give him everything he wants, driven by a need to have his head between my legs as he fills me. The contraceptive implant in my arm keeps me from worrying about children.

With my mouth empty, he pulls back. The command in his eyes has me weeping as I hurry to lie down and tear off my pants. He slides down my body, kissing me every few inches, and the knowledge that he has his own cum in his mouth, that he isn't afraid to give me anything has me on the verge before he even gets to my underwear. Pulling them down my legs, he looks up at me.

I stare at him, my breath held in my lungs. Waiting.

And then it clicks *why* he's waiting.

"Spread it for me, kira.*"*

My arms shaking, I reach my hands down between my legs and spread my pussy open wide.

A rumble of approval mixes with a growl of desire as he dips his head and kisses me.

I arch against the floor, the cold wood against my back turning hot from the fire burning inside me. His tongue pushes into my pussy as he feeds his cum-mixed-spit into me bit by bit. When it dribbles down my thighs, making everything wet, his fingers meet his mouth as he scoops it back in.

Pleasure builds in my core as I squeeze my eyes shut. I want to grab his head and hold him to me as I ride his face to orgasm, but I keep them on my pussy like a good girl.

His fingers push inside me and curl as he kisses my lips. Bucking, I cry out, my hips lifting off the floor. He takes his time, building me slowly, adding to the inferno one small lick at a time until my entire body is alight with the need to come.

"Not yet, *kira*," he says around the mound of my pussy in his mouth. "You're not to come until I tell you."

I thrash beneath him on desperate whispers. "I need to come. Please let me come."

He chuckles as he pushes another finger inside me and lifts his body to look at me. "I told you not to make me come, but you disobeyed that, didn't you?"

I gasp as he curls his fingers to hit that special spot. My thighs tremble. My need is killing me.

"Why did you do it?" he asks, sliding another finger inside. The pain from him stretching me flickers for a second before rushing into pleasure, and my pussy eats him greedily as it begs for more, consumed by his promise to fist me.

My hips buck. My orgasm stands on the edge and whimpers, but he doesn't call it forth. Doesn't give it permission to rush through me, so I squeeze my thighs and beg. "*Please.*"

"Tell me why you did it, and I'll let you come."

"I wanted..." I falter, heat filling my cheeks as he ducks his head and his breath feathers across his fingers.

"You wanted what, *kira*?"

"I wanted you to fuck my face..." I gasp when he kisses me, my breaths wild. "To see you lose control with your cock in my mouth."

Lifting his head, he stretches above my body. The look in his eyes tell me he's about to fuck me hard, and I quiver with a matching need.

He grabs my hands, removing them from my pussy as he lifts them above my head. The heat in his gaze flickers for just a moment as his attention is diverted to my arms. His eyes narrow as his lips cut into a flat line. He trails a finger across my contraception, spiking my pulse until my whole body is shaking from it. Obsession darkening his face, he leans down and sucks my arm into his mouth.

His utter feralness drives my fingers into his hair as every nerve is ablaze with his need to claim every inch of me. He kisses me passionately, stroking his tongue across my implant as he leaves a giant hickey.

Lifting his head off my arm, he comes down to kiss me. I part my lips instinctively, but at the metallic taste on his tongue, I freeze. He rubs a small cylinder tube against my bottom lip, and my eyes snap open as I stare at him in utter stillness.

He bit out my contraception.

His eyes flash with conquest and warning, daring me to argue against its removal.

A smirk curling his lips when I don't, unable to find any words under the screaming of my pulse, he lifts his head, spits the implant free of his mouth, then comes back to kiss me.

My arm doesn't hurt, magic surely numbing it, and I use it to reach down to grab his cock. He groans against my lips as I rub him up and down my pussy. He angles down between my thighs and rubs his full length against me. I arch on a shudder, needing it inside.

Palming my breasts, he pushes in just the tip. I cry out, a coppery taste filling my mouth as the blood on his chin rubs onto me.

"Don't come yet," he breathes as he pushes in another inch. He rubs my nipple in between his fingers as he rocks his hips. Another few inches.

The pleasure builds alongside pain as he stretches me too much. He's big, and it's been years for me, Daniel having only kissed me once before ghosting me. "Stop," I rasp as another buck of his hips blinds me with pleasure and pain.

"Not until I'm all the way in, *kira*. Relax for me."

He groans against my neck as he stills, his muscles clenching in tight control as he waits for me to obey.

Grabbing my hand, he places it between our bodies, resting it a handspan above my pussy. He jerks his cock inside me, and I can feel it beneath my palm.

"This belongs here," he says, applying pressure to my hand. "This pussy is mine, and my cock is yours." His lips gently rub against mine. "And I'm going to fuck you until you're too hoarse to scream." He rubs my hand against my clit as he rocks deeper into me.

I squeeze my eyes shut as tremors rip through me, my sensitive bud so overwhelmed, it forces me to loosen.

"That's it. Good girl," he growls as he pumps his cock another few inches. "Good girl. Keep relaxing for me."

He slides in slowly, and by the time his pelvis is pressed

against mine, another movement will send me over the edge, the blissful pleasure of his cock and my clit warring for the right to topple me.

"Such a good girl," he murmurs as he kisses my neck and palms both my breasts. "You feel so fucking good wrapped around my cock. Your pussy is so greedy for me, so desperate... Are you ready to come for me?"

I nod frantically, a heat rooted in all my limbs. My lips parting, I breathe heavily as the anticipation makes me whimper.

Kissing my neck, he stays still inside me.

The anticipation builds as his lips caress the base of my throat.

"*Please*," I beg when he still doesn't move inside me.

"Please what?"

My mind blanks with inexperience, but that doesn't stop my mouth from blurting out words I'm certain don't make complete sentences. "Cock...fuck me...please...move your...I can't...hard...*Khalid*!"

He laughs against my throat, a rumble vibrating in his chest. My fingers grip his ass as I try to get him to move. He doesn't.

Struggling to find the words that will help me, I moan. Then start to cry, not caring about how I sound anymore, just utter desperation driving me. "I need to feel your cock slamming into me. I want to come when you're sucking on my nipples."

The memory of the contraception in between his lips slams into me, alongside the darkness in his eyes when he noticed it in my arm.

"Please fill me with your cum. Make me pregnant. I need to –"

He groans, and the buck of his hips thrust into me. I cry out, my arms wrapping around his shoulders as his biceps flex, holding his weight as he fucks me hard. My nails dig into his skin, drawing blood. My back pounds against the wooden floor, slick with sweat. Spreading my thighs, I take him deeper, and his balls slap against my pussy and ass.

"Yes... Yes... Oh!" I moan loudly, wild and desperate as his lips suck on my neck, leaving marks to show the world I'm his. "You feel so good, baby," I cry, my orgasm cresting to the point of blindness.

Throwing my head back as his cock continues to beat inside me, I open my mouth and scream. Thrown into a world of ecstasy where my nerves are sensitive to every raised hair, every brush of the air as it circulates our bodies.

Khalid grunts and groans as my pussy grips his cock, vibrating on waves of pleasure. He fills me hard, takes me rough, not giving me any reprieve to come down off my high.

Kissing my lips, he pushes his tongue inside, sweeping in greedily as his thighs bunch. His cock slams deep one last time, and he holds it there as he shudders against me. His body jerks on top of me, and he throws his head back, the veins in his neck bulging as he groans.

My heart thuds loudly as I stare at his face, a weight squeezing it that makes tears burn my eyes. He drops his head and covers my face in kisses.

"You feel so good, *kira*. Your pussy took my cock so well." His lips find mine as another tremor ripples across his back. "Your ass is going to take it too one day. But first I'm going to get you pregnant."

My pulse crescendos inside my skull at the thought of swelling with his seed. I said that just to get him to fuck me, desperate to be able to come, but now... The thought of him running around after little squealing children that look like him...of him holding a newborn in the palm of his hands, looking at them like he does me...

My throat closes as I kiss him back.

Utter terror over being a mom, of being like my mom,

slams into the need to be loved, to be enough for him *to love*. He wants kids, and I want him, but...

"I love you, *kira*," he murmurs as his mouth covers mine, and I close my eyes, letting those words wash away my fears. He loves me, so I should give him this...

Sliding down my body, he rests his head in between my legs again. His fingers trail up my inner thigh, then his whole hand pushes inside me, the slickness of my orgasm sucking it in. Arching my back, I cry out as he fucks me, my hips moving in gentle lifts as he pushes his cum deep into my body.

"I love you, *kira*. I'm going to spend the rest of my life fucking and eating this sexy hole."

Lowering his head, he sucks on my clit, making me jerk beneath him. My hands grip his hair. His forearm fills me, and I clench around him as my breaths turn ragged.

"Make me cum again," I beg, whimpers hoarse in my throat as I push myself up on my arms to watch his mouth claim my pussy.

He lifts his eyes, holding mine as his tongue dives between my lips.

I breathe out harshly as I watch him.

He's so fucking beautiful.

So beautiful and all mine...

Struggling not to throw my head back as I crest the edge of another orgasm, I hold his gaze and scream.

He sucks and licks me mercilessly. His hand moves out, then pushes against my ass. I tense at the intrusion of the wet tip of a finger into my tight hole.

"Relax," he murmurs against my pussy as he continues to eat me out. "I'm only going in to the knuckle. Play with your breasts while I do. I want to see your nipples rolling between your fingers."

My hands move instantly to obey; I put all my weight on one elbow. He pushes into my ass in one quick motion, and

I jerk and squeeze my eyes shut.

Blissful pain consumes me as he starts to pump in and out of my hole, ramming to his knuckles every time. His tongue runs from his hand to my clit. "So beautiful," he murmurs. "So sexy. That's it. Good girl. Suck my finger into your greedy little hole."

Moaning, I fall back, my muscles too exhausted to hold me up. My fingers stroke my breasts as he strokes me. His tongue moves faster around my clit, and soon I'm flying through the stars again...

My arms dropping away, utter exhaustion wraps its fingers around me. My eyes droop even though he doesn't stop. But I'm too tired to move any longer, and sleep drags me under its blissful hold...

I drift into awareness for just a second as I'm lifted into the air. My brain struggles to understand how he's doing it, carrying me as if I'm nothing, but then I'm placed on the bed and the only thing I can focus on is the feel of his cock as it slides into me.

Moaning, I give in to the pure sensation of being loved and fall back asleep as he fucks me.

The next time I wake, Khalid's head is in between my thighs. I sigh as I thread my fingers through his black hair. An orgasm pushes me back into sleep...

He finally stretches out beside me, breathing heavily as he kisses my shoulder. I snuggle deep into his arms.

"I love you, *kira.*"

I mumble in drowsy response. "*Mmmm.*"

THIRTY-ONE

HIM

The hum of magic in the air wakes me – Mom's signal that dinner is ready so she doesn't have to raise her voice. Now, it's Micha who gives it given Mother's curse, but it is hers all the same.

Opening my eyes, I smile at the sight of my girl in my arms. She sleeps soundly, brown tendrils of hair curling over her face. I brush them back, then lean in and kiss her. She sighs dreamily, her lips parting for my tongue.

Diving inside, I wake her gently, and when her eyes open to find me, a slow light fills them in relation to the curling of her lips.

"Hello, beautiful," I murmur. "You hungry?"

She tenses, a blast of anxiety shooting down our bond. The urge to kill her mother all over again sits heavily in my stomach.

"I'm going to get us a plate and a box of strawberries for you to hold in your pussy. Then I'm going to eat them for dessert."

Her eyes widen on little pants. "That sounds like it'll cause a yea–"

"I'll never let anything hurt you." Raising a hand, I wiggle my fingers. "I can make sure it's safe with magic."

She squirms as she looks at my hand, and I know she's thinking about how it was inside her. My cock hardening, I kiss her again. Her rumbling stomach has me pulling back, and I hop out of bed to serve her.

I kiss her one last time after I pull on a pair of pants, then hustle downstairs to grab us dinner.

As soon as I step into the kitchen, the fucking table erupts in applause, the loudest clapper being Maddox. He hollers as he bangs the table. The twins, Enoch and Ezriel, sitting opposite him whistle. Micha giggles as she places a hand over her mouth. Varius glances at her before he digs into his plate, not partaking in the idiocy of our brothers.

"Where's Scarlett?" Mother asks before taking a bite of her burger.

"Probably dead from all that screaming," Rudy signs.

They couldn't hear shit. I cast a silence spell as soon as we started. Flipping them off, I head over to the counter to make two plates. Homemade fries and two beef patties with cheese, onions, tomatoes, ketchup, and one thin slice of pineapple. Happiness flits in, doing a gentle dance in my chest at the sight of the fruit.

"What the fuck is that monstrosity?" Maddox says as he pushes in beside me. "Yo, ya'll, come look at this."

When I place the burger bun on top of it, Maddox tries to take it back off. My other hand grabs his, and he yelps as I squeeze his fingers, but that doesn't stop the little shit from using his other hand.

I grab that one too as I glare at him.

Only for Rudy to unlid the patty. He drops the bread upside down, making sure not to get the ketchup on the counter, then points at it with a smile. "That's not right. You sure she's human?"

"Fuck off, you two," I say as I release my brother and reach for the bun lid to put it back on. Talon, Leno, and the twins have joined by this point, and they start ribbing me too. Ignoring the lot of them, I grab a box of half-open strawberries from the fridge and head for the door.

"You're on call tonight," Varius says right as I'm about to pass the threshold. "Xander has been in touch, but I don't trust him not to run."

I turn to face him.

"Xander?" Talon asks, freezing with a fry to his lips. "What's he done?"

"He betrayed us to the vampires."

"Are you sure?" Rudy signs, disbelief clear in his eyes. "He's never been anything but loyal."

"Xander's the only one who knows there's a witness contradicting Khalid's alibi for Hannah's murder," our Boss signs. "And, unfortunately, he knows of Scarlett. He must be dealt with."

A plate hovers in the air, and Xander's stone appears in a swirl of shadows in my palm.

"Don't kill him," my brother says, and despite my every desire to refuse this order, I don't. He has earned my trust a thousand times over. They all have.

"Does anyone know why Xander waited seven years to move against us?" he asks, his gaze sweeping around the table.

A moment of silence rings loudly between us before my brother, Talon, shifts uncomfortably in his chair. "He's Antonio's godson."

"What?" Leno demands as Krypto growls softly at his feet. "How long have you known?"

Talon looks at Varius. "Seven years ago, you told me to find out what he was hiding from and if it was worth helping him."

He doesn't say anything, just holds our brother's gaze in utter silence.

"And you didn't think that was worth sharing, bruh?" Maddox shakes his head.

"Xander didn't want anything to do with him. He has recessive genes. He can't shift, and Antonio only wants him to breed a line of omegas." Meaning he won't lose a 'real' pack member every few months when that position is reopened. In the coming days of war, that'll give Death Hunt a massive edge.

"Why would he stay in the city?" I demand, my magic unsettled in my still limbs.

"I gave him a new face and scent."

Disguise magic is fucking dangerous. Maddox using it is one thing; magic has bonded to him and given him that gift. But to try it on another often leaves them braindead and disfigured.

"Xander wanted to keep an eye on the pack so he'd know if Antonio got any leads on him. He was willing to risk death to get away. And if he was a mole, then I was planning on using him to feed false information to Death Hunt. But he never told them anything."

"He is now, though, isn't he?" Maddox says with a snort. "The fucker thinks we'll lose in the coming war and picked his side."

"That doesn't make sense," Rudy signs. "He told Aleric, not Antonio, and why would he run back to the Death Hunt if he's to live as a breeder, watching his kids get killed?"

"If we're fighting with the vampires, we'd be too weak to fend off the wolves effectively. Maybe he thinks that by pitting us against each other, he can gain favor before his return," Talon counters.

I don't care what Xander's reason is. If he's a risk to my girl's life, he's dead. Simple as that. My eyes go to Varius, a silent conversation passing between us.

He nods, dismissing me. "He is to arrive in three hours. I will let you know if you are required."

When he goes back to eating, I head out.

Scarlett is sitting up in bed when I enter the room, the blanket held up to her chest as if she needs to hide. My eyes narrowing, I stop in front of the door after I close it.

"Come here," I say, wanting her to walk naked across the room to grow confidence in her beauty.

Anxious shame flutters down our bond. I combat it with my desire, and her nostrils flare as she looks at me.

"Let me see what's mine," I say, my cock growing hard as I anticipate her rising.

She wets her lips, then drops the blanket, and my eyes zero in on her chest as a groan rumbles from mine. "So beautiful," I murmur. "So perfect."

Rosy cheeks sit under blue eyes of disbelief, making me want to torture whoever's made her think so little of herself.

She tentatively swings her legs over the edge of the bed, then stands, leaving the blanket behind. A smile curls my lips as I drink her in. She walks towards me, each step stronger than the last, and by the time she's standing in front of me, my cock is straining against my pants and she's panting heavily.

"You actually brought strawberries?" she murmurs, her eyes on the box balanced on top of my fries.

"I am a man of my word."

She glances away, her throat working as she deals with some intrusive thought I don't like. "So you really knew where Derek lived before..." She trails off on a shudder, and I leave the plates to hover in the air as I turn her face to mine.

"I know where every single member of the WALL lives. They are not a threat to us." I shrug by tilting my head. "Well, not to those of us with any power. It's the SCU we need to watch out for."

"The SCU?" Her blue eyes widen. "You don't mean the Special Crimes Unit? The one that's often on TV solving cases around the world?"

I smile dryly. "Mmm. They're a fucking pain."

Dropping a quick kiss on her lips, I step back and pull a table and two chairs out from my shadow. They're not the most comfortable as they're used for when I am staking out targets, but I am not planning on us sitting on them for long.

Her eyes latch onto the shadows as she freezes, wary trepidation flowing from her. "You know..." I say. "I could teach you to wield magic. Not a lot as it hasn't bound itself to you, but you can learn to do a few things."

Her head jerks to me. "Really?"

"Yes. But tomorrow. Tonight, we eat."

The plates settle on the table, and I take a seat. My girl stays standing, hesitation in her anxious blue eyes.

"I've licked your ass, *kira.* There's nothing about you that isn't beautiful. Now sit."

She obeys with a bright blush, but there's less tension flowing through our bond. I nod in approval as she picks up a fry. When she doesn't eat it, my jaw tics, but I don't pressure her. Her mother was a bitch, and twenty-two years of abuse isn't going to be overridden by one long hard fuck.

Luckily, I'll have a lifetime to show her how beautiful she is.

"So is the SCU like your government or something?"

I snort as I take a bite of a homemade fry. "They like to think so. They were created three thousand years ago when a vampire called Sebastian the Ancient Destroyer tried to destroy the Seven Planes."

"The Seven Planes?"

I nod. "Earth is one of them. It used to be connected to the others, but its portals were closed by the archangels two millennium ago."

She drops her fry. "What? There are archangels? I was only told about your kind, werewolves, and vampires."

"The WALL knows very little of what they claim to be specialists on." I glance at her plate pointedly, and she picks her fry back up. This time, she ducks her head and shyly eats it.

"I'm going to get you to eat off my cock one day."

Her head snaps up as her mouth parts. Arousal darkens her eyes, and I smirk at her, imagining her pretty little tongue licking things off my body.

Holding her gaze, I take a bite of my burger. The sweet taste of pineapple makes me pull a face, and she giggles. "It's delicious, isn't it?"

"Mmm." When I put it down for a fry, she reaches over and takes off my bun. "If you don't like it, I can take it."

She plucks the pineapple off the patty, and then an intense heat blasts down our bond, and I know my girl's thinking about my cock inside it.

My free hand fists as my eyes fasten onto her lips. "Eat it, *kira*. Eat it as if it's on my cock."

Rough exhales heat the air between us, and she slowly brings it to her lips, her eyes on mine. Flicking her tongue out, she runs it around the outside of the circle, causing me to groan and my cock to jerk in need. She sucks part of it into her mouth, her eyes growing half-hooded before she nibbles a bit off.

By the time she's licked and eaten all of it, I'm on the verge of coming in my fucking pants. Clenching my fist, I struggle to keep my seat, wanting to go to her and fuck her senseless.

But my girl needs her energy.

Holding her gaze, I pick up a fry. "Eat quickly, Scarlett. I need to fuck you again before I come in my pants."

Her gaze drops to my crotch beneath the table, and I groan as I can feel her looking at me despite the plastic between us. "Eat, *kira*," I beg, and she picks up her burger and takes a massive bite.

"Good girl."

A moment of silence passes as we both wrestle to get our arousal under control. Then her head pops up, worry in her eyes and she raises a hand to her throat. "Derek bit you, didn't he? Did he...hurt you anywhere else?"

"He stabbed me in the side."

She sucks in a sharp breath, and I both like that she worries about me and hate that it's causing her anxiety. "I didn't see anything earlier," she whispers with a tinge of guilt.

"We don't heal as fast as werewolves or vampires, but we know healing spells. I only know the bare basics." I can cauterize a wound rather than bleed out. "But Mother is a full healer, and Leno can fix most things with his plants, so it's completely healed now."

I smile. "They can teach you how to make healing potions if you'd like."

"Why do you need potions? I thought you healed?"

"Not until after our ascensions." At Scarlett's look of confusion, I clarify, "It's when magic properly bonds with us and usually happens during puberty." I pause as I eat a fry. "Unless you're cursed like my brother, Varius."

"Cursed?"

"Mmm. He has magic inside him, but he can't access it, so he ages like a human and scars like one too. You'll be able to tell which one is him as soon as you see him. He looks old."

She studies me as she plays with a fry. "How old are you? You look maybe only a few years older than me, so are you like, a thousand or something?"

I laugh. "No. I just turned thirty-three last month."

"That's it?"

"We have one of the shortest lifespans –two hundred and

fifty being the average– but we can extend it with magic." Dark magic that requires the life of another.

"Oh. Who's the oldest person you know of?"

"Sebastian. He's over five thousand, give or take a few years. They start to blur at that point, but he's millennia above the average. To hit a thousand is equivalent to your hundred."

She eats silently as she mulls everything over. Her eyes on her food, she asks, "So will you live long after I die? Am I just a…blip to you?"

"I've bonded with you, *kira*. That's for life, and you'll live as long as I do because of it."

She gasps as she looks at me. "What?"

"It's a ritual as old as time for us witches. When we find someone we want to bond with, we enter a magical contract through blood. We share a lifeforce, meaning part of me is inside of you, allowing you to age like me and wield magic. You won't ever be a strong witch, but you'll be stronger than any human who learns."

She raises an arm to where her implant used to be. "Is that why you bit me?"

My eyes narrow. "I took that out because I want you swollen with my children. I started the blood bond a few days ago."

Her lips stay parted as she stares at me. "So that's it?" she whispers. "You decided for me, and now it's done?"

I shift as I finish off the last of my burger, then the last few fries. "No. It will take weeks to complete. If I give you the amount of blood you needed at once, my magic would kill you. And if you gave me it, I'd be weakened to the point that the magic inside me would kill me. Magic is not a friendly beast."

She pales, and I shift again.

"What you saw with Derek," I say slowly, "is what happens when magic isn't controlled. That could've been me just as easily as it was him. It was only pure luck that I was able to protect myself."

"And if you die, I do?"

"No. You'll live the rest of your human lifespan. So you won't age rapidly or anything. You'll just start back at twenty-two."

She stares at her plate as she finishes off the last few bites. So much new information is swarming around her skull, and I sit back, letting her come to terms with it all. As much as I want to eat dessert, I want her comfortable in my world.

"How is the blood bond completed?" she finally asks.

"We share enough blood."

"That's it?"

"No." My jaw locks as the thought of my brothers touching her clenches my fists. "It is finalized through sex magic...that will require all of my brothers to come inside you."

She laughs hesitantly for a few seconds before it fades off on an awkward cough. "You're serious?"

"Yes."

"What if they don't..." Clearing her throat, she looks down at her plate.

"Know what they're doing?" I say, knowing damn well she's thinking about how she's not good enough for them. If any one of my brothers makes her feel inadequate, I'll cut off their dick myself. It doesn't need to be attached to them for the completion of the ritual. Probably.

She shakes her head.

"They'll love you, *kira*," I murmur softly. "They'll love your fire and spirit and those sexy little noises you make. They'll love the face you pull when you're driven mad, and they'll love how you beg them to come inside you."

"They have to finish?" she asks, lifting her gaze under a curtain of brown hair.

"In your ass or mouth. Your pussy is mine."

She swallows as I reach for the box of strawberries sitting between our plates. All this talk about my brothers touching her is making me tense.

"Now scoot your chair back, *kira*. I want dessert."

THIRTY-TWO

HIM

Her cheeks pinken as I stand. Her mouth falls open. Her eyes grow half-lidded. She looks the definition of sex, and my cock hardens fully by the time I take off my pants.

Her beautiful throat works as she breathes unevenly, her chest rising and falling in a rhythm my cock matches, jerking up and down as her eyes fall to it.

Her little pink tongue comes out to wet her lips, and I pick up the box of strawberries as I stride to her. Her gaze lands on mine when I crouch in front of her, her nostrils flaring as need darkens her pretty blue eyes.

Lifting a strawberry, I trail it across her parted lips, then push in. She sucks on it, her cheeks puckering, and my cock jerks with envy.

"You're going to sit on my face while I eat these out of you," I say as I pop the strawberry out of her mouth.

"But I'm too bi–"

"You're going to sit down all the way, and you're going to ride my face until you come."

"But –"

She stops as I grab the back of her head and pull her mouth towards my cock. She parts her lips, but I hold back, just running the tip against her mouth. "No buts, *kira*," I say, looking down into her eyes. "I have dreamed of you grinding your pussy and ass against my mouth for months. I'm not going to wait any longer to have what's mine, so you are going to sit like a good little girl for me, aren't you?"

My hand tightens in her hair as her nostrils flare and little puffs of arousal kiss my cock. She licks my head, and putting down the box of strawberries on the table, I thread my other hand in her hair. "Aren't you?" I breathe, my ass tight as I hold my position just out of her wet willing mouth.

"Yes."

Groaning, I rock gently forward, allowing her to focus on the sensitive tip, her sexy tongue swirling around the fullness of it, her cheeks sucking around the ridge. "That's a good girl," I rasp, still holding her gaze as I hold her head still between my hands.

She whimpers around me, and I push forward, seeking the tight clench of her throat. My eyes growing half-hooded as I pull back out, I reach over to grab one of the little red fruits. Crushing it in my fist, I drizzle its juices over the length of my cock.

Pulling out of her, I cup my balls as the liquid slides down them, then jerk my hand up my cock, covering it everywhere. "Have your dessert, *kira*."

I hold my dick upright so she can lick my balls, and she leans forward with her greedy little tongue. She laps at the juices covering them, then sucks one in, and my head rocks back as I cup her face. "Your mouth feels so good on me, baby."

I groan as she transfers her lips to my other ball. The wet

heat of her mouth consumes me, driving my orgasm to the tip of my cock. My thumb strokes her cheek as I force it back down, letting myself ride on the edge of her blissfulness.

Licking her way up me, she cleans it of strawberry, so I squeeze more onto it. She licks me again and again, moving her head to get every inch clean.

The fruit in my hand nothing but a pulp, I hand it to her. "Rub this over your breasts. I want to taste them on your nipples when I suck on them while filling your pussy with more."

She whimpers as she reaches, her desperation making her arm shake. Her fingers graze mine as she takes the crushed fruit, both our breaths catching on such innocent contact.

I need to be inside her, so as she starts to lavish her breasts, rubbing it everywhere she wants me to kiss, I guide my cock back to her mouth. Scarlett takes me in, blessing me with a burst of pleasure that builds swiftly. Her hand cups my balls, fondling them as she sucks me deep.

My tip leaves the beautiful pressure of her lips as I push in further, giving me a bit of reprieve from the sheer intensity so I don't blow my load like a fucking school boy. I'm always fighting the urge to come with her. "You are so fucking beautiful with your mouth around my cock," I murmur right as the tightness at the start of her throat grips me.

Her hand massaging my balls, she slides a finger along the stretch to my ass. I grunt as I widen my legs. I have never been penetrated before, but whatever she wants, I'll do. As much as I own her body, she owns mine, and if she likes using a strap-on, then I'll get on my knees willingly.

She touches my hole tentatively, then more firmly when I don't stop her. Her head bobs up and down my length. The palm of that same hand massages my balls. Her other wraps around my cock as she focuses her lips on my tip and pushes her finger in.

I jerk on a hiss before locking my legs for her, staying still for her to explore wherever she wants. "My body is yours, *kira*," I rasp. "Use me however you want."

She pushes in further, and I buck my hips, seeking the pleasure of her throat to override the sharp pinch of pain. She whimpers as she penetrates me, and knowing having the tip of her finger in my ass is making her wild, I groan on the verge of coming.

"That's it. Good girl. You take what you want."

Scarlett sucks me deep as her finger withdraws, then pushes back in. I know it's just the tip given her palm is still cupped around my balls, but it's stretching me for the first time and feels too fucking big.

Focusing on her mouth, I dig my hands into her hair and fuck her faster as she fucks me.

Her hand moves from my balls. Her finger goes further inside. It curls in various directions a bit uncomfortably, but then it hits something that causes my legs to jerk on a spasm.

Holy. Fucking. Shit.

She pulls back as I freeze, and a wave of frustration slams into me. Releasing my hold on her face, I grab her wrist, keeping it still.

She looks up at me as my cock pops out of her mouth. "Sorry. I thought –"

"Don't stop, *kira*," I plea, leading her hand back to my ass. "You feel so fucking good inside me. Find that spot you just touched."

Her eyes flare with a reflective heat. Her finger presses against my hole. There's that pinch of pain and discomfort from before, but it's overwhelmed by the anticipation of pleasure like I've never felt. My cock throbs in the air, and I press her face back to my balls. She kisses them gently as she curls her finger and hits my prostate again.

I jerk forward, shuddering as my hands tighten in her hair and my eyes squeeze shut from the million sparks of electricity zapping through my body.

"Holy shit, *kira*," I rasp. "That's it. Touch me there." I widen my legs, breathing heavily as lights go off behind my eyelids.

Normally, it's just my cock that feels good, a building of pressure that's heightened by the fact that I am having sex, but *this*. This is a fucking full body experience that rushes blood through every part of me. My back can feel it. My toes can feel it. Even my fucking face is awash with the buzzing of fireworks as they all arc towards an orgasm that's going to drop me to my knees.

They say a woman's release is more intense than a man's, and I've never questioned that, especially after watching Scarlett come. Her whole body shudders. Her mouth slackens uncontrollably as she arches off the bed with her eyes closed on a scream. I feel like she looks right before that moment, and dropping down to the floor, I hit my knees to kiss her.

My tongue pushes into her mouth as her finger keeps igniting those fuses inside of me. I grope both her breasts, not skilled teasings of my fingers but desperate cups of pure need. Her tongue dances with mine as she pants, and I know she's on the verge herself. I planned on making her come first on my face and on her own so she could just focus on taking pleasure rather than giving it, but I don't have the strength to pull away from her hand. The things it's doing to me are mental, so I lower my head to her breasts as I reach up for the box of strawberries.

I lick the sweet stickiness off her boobs, swirling my tongue around her ample flesh. The sweet flavor of the fruit fills my mouth as she digs her hand into my hair, pulling at my scalp as she squeezes. Her finger fucks me, each push against my P-spot shaking my body.

I cup between her thighs with one hand and push three fingers inside of her. Her pussy eats me like a good girl, and I collapse against her chest as I push another finger in, spearing my hand until it's all the way inside her. She's so wet, I go in without much resistance. I move my hand as I suck on her tits, still finding trails of strawberry.

"You're going to come on my hand with your finger inside me, baby. Then I'm going to eat this box from your pussy."

Her nails run down the back of my neck to dig into my right shoulder, drawing blood.

"I...I want..." She trails off, riding my hand on little moans.

"What, *kira*?" I ask, desperate to please her, to listen to every little fantasy and make them come true.

"I want to eat your ass." She jerks on a moan, five pinpricks of pain seeping through my back. "As I...finish you" –she thrusts her finger faster inside me, letting me know damn well how she wants me– "and jerk you off."

Groaning, I shudder against her, too much pleasure overwhelming me. "I'm not going to last that long, baby." I lift my head to find her lips, needing to kiss her as I come.

I spread her pussy lips with my free hand as my other thrusts in and out of her. I rub her hard clit. She jerks against me, little pants hitting my mouth as she draws close.

"After we come together and you sit on my face..." I promise, "then I'll bend over the bed for you."

But I can't do it now when my legs don't work and the fireworks are hissing in their proximity of being set free.

She moans as we finger each other, and I kiss her neck so I don't interrupt those sexy little noises. Five thin lines burn down my back before she reaches between us to cup my balls. I slide my tongue against her skin and close my eyes as I shudder on the verge of –

My eyes snap open as she withdraws her hand. "Baby, please don't stop."

Heat burning in her gaze, she smiles as her eyes dip between us. "Lie on your back," she says. "I want to eat your ass as I jerk you off."

"But –"

"I'll sit on your face after." Her words are breathless as she licks her lips. "But you make me feel so beautiful and sexy... I want to do this first."

Unable to resist, I lie down on my back and stare at her as she nestles between my legs. Her greedy eyes latch onto my cock as she presses little kisses down its length, taking her time, trying to get me to come down off the edge, but my whole body throbs under her caresses. My hands fist at my sides as the anticipation of her tongue keeps me high.

Her eyes hold mine for a moment before dipping to my ass. She sucks in a breath as raw desire sweetens her face. "I've milked your tight ass," she says as she trails a finger against me. I arch on a groan, tiny sparks lighting up everywhere.

"I'm going to keep milking it as I milk your cock," she murmurs, pressing her lips to my balls. Then she lifts them with one hand while the other grips tight around my shaft. She licks between my balls and ass, making me jerk again as my head falls back and an uncomfortable groan parts my lips.

"Shit. *Kira*, I'm not going to last if you –"

She buries her tongue in me as she jerks the length of my cock. Heat prickles across every nerve as sweat beads down my brow and back. I gasp in tune to every lick. She fondles my sack, one finger reaching back to circle my aching hole. When she thrusts in and out, I arch up.

Twisting against the ground, I struggle to breathe as my cock leaks so much precum it's coating her hand and still leaking more. My nails dig into the floor, then her hair as I keep her pressed tight against my ass

Moaning raggedly, I wrap my legs around her head and arch high off the floor as an intense heat rips through me. My entire body floats from the high. I'm so fucking lost on the ecstasy that I barely register the cum hitting my face in hot bursts that leave me shaking.

She keeps pumping me as I keep going, her tongue still in my ass. I hold her tight against me, my eyes squeezed hard as I struggle to breathe coherently through my head of dizzy heat.

Cum still shooting from me in a fountain of pleasure, she lifts her head, my muscles too weak to hold her down, and takes my cock into her mouth. I groan as I fall back to the ground, the sensitivity of my cock making me spasm with every suck of her cheeks.

My breaths circulate the salt-fixed air around my face, filling my nostrils and nose. I reach for her, wanting to return the feelings she's blessed me with, but my hand drops before I can touch her.

Utterly drained, I fall asleep...

"Khalid?" I lift my head up when his arm falls free and his legs become heavy weights on my shoulders. A soft snore greets me, and I stare at him in shock, taking in all the jets of white on his face before giggling quietly.

I made Khalid come so hard he fell asleep. My chest expands with so many new feelings of confidence and arousal.

Ma always made me feel self-conscious and ashamed over how I looked, but Khalid...

He makes me feel not just beautiful but desirable. His obsession with me, with wanting to see all of me, explore all of me...it built such a strong desire in me to do the same.

Another giggle of pure happiness bleeds free. I had my finger in his ass. And my tongue.

Heat burns my cheeks as I slowly extract myself from his legs and sit up fully. I think about trying to lift him onto the bed, but I'm not exactly strong and he's not exactly small. Perhaps I should just grab some pillows and a blanket and join him on the floor.

My body still buzzing with the need to come, I try to ignore it on my way to the bed. He's asleep and –

My feet root to the floor.

"I have every right to your body, kira."

My toes digging into the floor, I turn slowly in place. He's asleep, cum all over his face and snoring peacefully, but his cock is still erect...

"That's it. Good girl. Take what you want."

I lick my lips as I stare at it, tasting the load of saltiness I was able to catch. He came for so long...he's probably going to be out for a while, and I want to know how it felt when he fucked me while I was asleep.

Making my way back to him, my pulse quickening with every step, I kneel over him, my pussy sliding against his tip. My breaths come short and hot as I grip him with my clean hand and push him into me. Unlike the last time he filled me, he goes in without pain. I'm so drenched I can barely feel him, so I rub my clit as I fuck him with soft lifts of my hips.

He moans, and I squeeze around him. My finger circles faster, building up that outside pressure that never fails to make me orgasm. My eyes on his cum-stained face, I marvel over how far it shot, then lick my lips as I lean down. My breasts rubbing against his chest, I lick up the white salty streaks. Shuddering as his taste fills me, I turn my lips to his. I push my tongue inside his mouth, but he stays still in his slumber.

Little pants breathe into him as I kiss him. Although I

love kissing him while he's awake, there's something about having full control, exploring at my own pace that adds to the heat of the moment. When his cock jerks inside me, I sit up and grab both his hands. Pinning them to my breasts, I ride him faster.

He moans as he gives an unconscious squeeze, and heat blossoms in my belly. I rise up and down on him a few more times, but on one upward stroke, I accidentally come off. And when I drop back down, he pushes against my puckered hole. My cheeks clench instinctively as he slides between my lips. My breath stops as my heart hammers.

I pause for a moment as I think about what it'll feel like. He looked so fucking hot as I fingered his hole, and he's so wet with me now, we don't need lube... My lips parting, I reach down and grab his cock as I hover over him. Placing his head against my tight hole, I slowly sink down.

It pushes a groan out of me, turning it into a harsh whimper as I take in inch after inch of his massive cock. It's hard as a rock now, and I look up at his face to see his eyes open and on me. Half-lidded and full of heat, they focus on his cock disappearing up my ass.

"Fuck me hard, *kira*," he murmurs as he grabs my hips but allowing me to set the pace. I slide down him another inch.

"Good girl." His fingers dig into me on a ragged exhale. "You feel so fucking good on my cock, *kira*."

His head falls back as I take him in further. "Tell me how I feel," he pants as he looks back at me, his eyes hot and hooded.

My lips work wordlessly before I breathe, "It hurts a little, but..." I swallow, heat flaming my cheeks. "I like it."

Sitting up, he wraps his fingers around my neck and hauls me to him for a kiss. No tongue. Just a brushing of lips and heavy breathing as he looks into my eyes. "You want me to get some lube?"

I shake my head, not wanting him to leave me, not wanting to start the assault on my ass all over again. I close my eyes as I exhale hard. Another inch goes in, and then all of a sudden, pleasure overtakes the pain as it feels as if he's rubbing against my G-spot. Dropping down *hard,* I crush my mouth to his, excitement controlling my limbs as I go crazy with arousal.

He chuckles against my lips as he cups my breasts. "I love seeing you like this," he says, bending his head to lick them.

My nails digging into his shoulders, I ride him slowly, then faster and faster until my breaths are nonexistent and the only thing I can smell is that mix of sweat and cum.

Falling back, he reaches for the box of strawberries and plucks one free. My eyes sharpen on it as I press both hands on his chest and take pleasure from his cock inside my ass.

"I'm going to eat this whole box out of you, *kira,*" he rasps as he pushes the red fruit between my pussy lips. I shudder at the cold feel of it as he rubs it back and forth. Pulling it to his mouth, he holds my gaze as he sucks it into his lips.

A moan of pleasure rumbles from him as he throws away the stem and grabs another. Plucking the green off, he pushes the whole strawberry inside me. My nails dig into his chest as my pulse vibrates my entire body. I keep my eyes on my pussy as he continues to fill me.

Blood seeps beneath my nails as his cock pushes me to the edge of ecstasy. Throwing my head back, I drop down onto him one last time, and as his hands squeeze my tits, breaking red fruit across them, I come *hard.*

He leans up to lick my breasts. Grabbing my hips, he lifts me slightly off him and holds me there. "Look at me, *kira.*"

I shudder as I obey.

His eyes on mine, he pounds into me, a jack hammer of pleasure that makes me scream. He pushes my mouth to his shoulder, and I bite down as my limbs jerk and twist, my orgasm building again instead of settling. Heat burns across my back, and I exhale it in hard pants that leave my head dizzy.

He groans as he holds me down, his neck arching back, his cum shooting deep inside me.

I squeeze my ass over his cock as I suck on the base of his neck, marking him as fully as he's marked me. Biting through the tip of my tongue, I press my blood into the mark on his shoulder.

Groaning, he holds me to him, then rolls me onto the floor as he stretches out above me. Ducking his head, he looks at my pussy.

"You're so fucking beautiful. You came so hard you squeezed the strawberries out."

Dropping a hand between us, he runs a finger against my thigh, then brings a strawberry up to my face.

My nostrils flare as he pushes it against my mouth. Salty sweetness explodes on my tongue, and I bite into it. Leaning down, he pushes his tongue into me, sharing in the flavor as he slides his cock out of my ass.

With a last kiss to my lips, he makes his way down. I spread my legs and lift my knees up, no longer concerned over having to move the fat out of his way.

Nestled between my legs, he licks my thighs, cleaning up my cum and the sweet juice of the berries, taking his time to explore every fold. Tears glisten my eyes as my fingers dig into his hair. He makes me feel so beautiful.

His lips caress mine as a groan rumbles across my pussy. "I love the taste of you, *kira*. I fucking can't get enough of it."

Rolling over, he guides me on top of him. My pulse jerks as I hover over him, pretty certain he can't take my weight. I start to suggest I lie back down, but he bites my thigh, stopping the words from escaping me.

"I said you were going to *sit* on me, *kira*, not hover."

A palm slaps my ass, and I jerk from the sting of it. My pussy spasms, and I can feel his cum dripping out of my ass. My cheeks heating, I open my mouth again to protest.

And again he spanks me.

"*Sit* down, *kira*."

Wrapping his arms around my thighs, he pulls my full weight onto his face, and I am too far gone to resist. My muscles are buzzing from too much exercise, lax putty for him to shift.

As his head disappears beneath the roll of my stomach, I tense.

"Relax for me, baby." He kisses my pussy. "I love the feel of your full weight on me, knowing there's not one part of you that you're holding back from me."

His tongue causes me to shiver.

"I love how your body wraps around me." He turns his head to kiss both my thighs, then cranes his neck to reach the bottom of my belly. With soft licks and kisses, he gets me to relax. "What a good girl. Just concentrate on the feel of my tongue inside your pussy."

I kegel, and he chuckles. "Your pussy knows what it wants, doesn't it? It wants me fucking it with my tongue."

He pushes in on a moan of pleasure, pulling one from me too. My heart rate starts to settle as I concentrate on the feel of him, on the *desire* pouring off him in palpable waves.

Tears mist my eyes as I tell myself he wants to be with *me*. All of me. Not some perfectly shaped runway model Ma always tried to get me to be.

Just me.

Reaching behind me, I grab his cock. It's half-down, and for a split second, doubt slices through me. Maybe he isn't as into this as he claims? Maybe he's sickened by –

"You're so fucking beautiful," he murmurs as he kisses me softly. "So pretty. So perfect." His tongue slips between my lips. He goes slowly, taking his time, in no rush to get out from under me. His hands come around to grab my ass. He squeezes me as he sighs. "So delicious." His tongue dips inside me, dispelling the loudest of my doubts.

"You *smell* so good."

He buries his nose against me as he inhales deeply, a groan of pure *need* releasing on the exhale.

"You *taste* so good." He licks me long and slow, his fingers tightening as he shudders. "Like strawberries and me."

His tongue lapping against me, making me quiver, he asks, "Have you ever tried strawberry on a burger?"

The sudden question, the ease at which it came from his mouth drags tears down my cheeks. He isn't just lost in the beauty of my body. He's imagining a future with me and placing himself in it.

My throat clogs as I imagine it. Us trying new foods together even though I'm not comfortable eating around anyone else. Him pulling faces as he forces himself to swallow. Me laughing, finding joy around food for the first time in years...

My chest grips tight as he sighs lovingly beneath me, and I know he's thinking of the same.

Like he can't wait to make those memories with me.

Taking the final weight off my knees, I sit down on a shudder. His cock jerks in my hand, hardening as I exhale sharply.

He pushes his hips into me and strokes me with his tongue. He goes slowly, languidly, building me up like a tidal wave waiting behind a dam.

My breaths catch in my chest as I close my eyes and bask in the feel of his lips.

Slow strokes.

Soft kisses.

Cherishing me.

Loving me.
Turned on by every part of me.
Squeezing his cock, I come all over his face.

THIRTY-THREE

HIM

In the darkness of night, a knock at the door pulls me from my slumber. I kiss Scarlett's lips before rolling out of bed and grabbing my pants off the floor. Slipping into them, I head over to the door and open it to find Varius.

His face is the same blank mask as always, but his eyes are harsh with suspicion. Adrenaline pushing aside sleep, I quickly step back into the room to allow him to enter.

Scarlett is naked on top of the covers, but Varius' gaze doesn't flick over to her.

Nothing but focus for brother dearest.

"Xander got in touch before dinner," he says, his voice clipped. "He told me he'd come in if we housed him here to protect him from Antonio, but he hasn't arrived yet."

"He could have lied to buy himself some time."

He shakes his head. "When I mentioned the witness, he was confused, not afraid. I think he's being framed."

"Or he's a good actor. He was with us for seven years and no one even knew he was Antonio's godson."

When he stays silent, an uneasy feeling twists around my stomach as the significance of his presence finally hits. Varius would have waited until the morning to tell me this. It's well past midnight. The rest of the house is deep asleep. And he has that look in his eyes...the one he gets after a failed assassination attempt from someone in the Family. A guarding of his heart. An 'I told you not to get close.'

"Who?" I ask softly, a tightness in my chest strangling me.

His jaw tics, the only sign he has suspicions. "I want to see his stone first."

Holding his gaze, I pray this is just the paranoia of a man who can't sleep. With only one way to find out, I pull Xander's alexandrite out of my shadow.

My gut twists like a viper around a mouse at the sight of it being black, not green.

"He's dead." I look up at my brother. "Whoever framed him knew you wanted to talk to him."

"And everyone who knew that," he says softly, "is in this house."

THIRTY-FOUR

HIM

I still, the urge to scream building in my chest as the rage and pain threatens to bring me to my knees.

A brother.

A fucking brother.

Killing a beloved uncle, a father figure of mine, wasn't enough.

Now I'm going to be asked to kill someone closer.

Someone I trust – *trusted* to keep my girl safe.

Maddox...

Leno...

Rudy...

Talon...

Enoch...

Ezriel...

Which one will it be?

"Who do you suspect?" I ask, trying to keep my voice from cracking.

A flicker of pain crosses my brother's face, but it's

quickly gone, hidden under a mask he's been forced to wear since he was a child. "Micha," he says softly, his fiance's name a sudden balm on my pain.

A woman does not hold power in this Family, but she is an outsider, a Black – a strong Family up north that lets their women fight on the front lines and hold rank. If she kills Varius correctly, without suspicion, her kids will be the next generation of Shadows, and through them, she can rule, just as Mother did until Varius was of age.

Clasping my brother's shoulder, I squeeze it gently. "I'm sorry," I say. Although their arranged marriage is not a love match, it has to hurt like hel knowing even his fiance wants to kill him.

He shrugs me off. "Her life does not matter. But if her dad planted her, then this will mean war with the Blacks."

My jaw tightens grimly as I look over at my girl. She sleeps peacefully now, but that peace will not last with us fighting on multiple fronts.

"Get some rest," Varius says as he turns for the door. "I will look further into Micha and let you know when I need you."

As the door shuts behind him, my heart aches for my oldest brother, who will never know what it's like to be loved.

THIRTY-FIVE

HER

Khalid is on edge today. As he stands at the counter, his back to me, talking to a woman in a low voice, I can *feel* his unease as if it were my own. I linger in the arch doorway of the kitchen, wiping my damp palms on my thighs as I try to pretend like I'm not dying of anxiety being out of his room.

It's been three days since he brought me here, and in that time I have only been out to use the bathroom and shower. I could blame it on him keeping me too exhausted to leave his bed, but in truth, I've been deliberately hiding from his family.

Not just because they are witches all with the power to kill me where I stand either, but because I've simply never been big on families, let alone *big* ones. Ma was all I've ever known, and she wasn't pleasant company.

Eat a salad, Gen.

You look like a watermelon in that dress, Gen.

Stand at the back of the photoshoot, Gen.

Nodding at her, their conversation over, Khalid turns to

me, and the two of them cross the bamboo flooring.

Feline in her grace, the woman is lithe and well toned, like how I would envision a ballerina to be if they also liked to rock climb. Black hair hangs to her waist. With high cheekbones and a long nose, it's clear Khalid's sharp features run in the family. She smiles warmly as they stop in front of me.

"Scarlett, this is my mother Sau," Khalid says.

My eyes widen. I know witches don't age like humans, but she just looks so young – maybe only a decade or two older than me.

"Hi," I squeak as she says, "It's nice to see you out of Khalid's room."

My cheeks flush hot. "Sorry I haven't –"

She waves away my apology. "I just meant it's nice to see you're getting comfortable here. You've been through a lot recently. It's understandable that you need some time to come to terms with everything."

I smile at her but don't mention that hiding upstairs was what I did long before I learned about sups.

"I have to go," Khalid says as he leans forward to kiss me. He woke me up with his head between my legs, and I can smell me on his breath. My pussy spasms. My cheeks burst into flame, and I want to disappear into the ground, wondering if his ma could tell when he was talking to her.

"I'll be back later," he says, and I want to ask to go with him even though I know he won't take me. We already had this conversation when he mentioned he would have to leave me for the day after making me scream his name three times. He's going to work, and it's definitely *not* as a landscaper.

He didn't go into the specifics, but he's leaving with his brothers to a meeting with the Boss of the Blood Fang.

Worry for him spikes in my pulse as he straightens. I didn't get the chance to read anything about vampires at

Derek's —there being a lot of information to get through, and my focus being on wolves— but the Blood Fang are in the news a lot for assaults, violent crime, and human trafficking.

And I know the Shadow Domain isn't peaceful, and Derek's corpse haunts me, but... Khalid isn't *immortal*. He can still get hurt. Can still die...

He tilts my chin up with the side of his forefinger and looks into my eyes. "It's a peace meeting, *kira*. I promise. We're going to be fine. I'll see you soon."

He kisses my head, then walks past me. I turn to watch him disappear down the hall. Left behind, I don't know what to do with myself. The safety of his room beckons...

"I could use some help in the kitchen, Scarlett." She moves up beside me, and her voice softens. "It helps doing something when they are out."

"Do they go...out a lot?" I ask, my chest tightening with the realization of what a life with Khalid will really mean now that I'm not in the bubble of his room.

I won't ever be strong enough to go with him. I'll just be stuck behind, waiting for him to come home.

And what if one day he doesn't?

Like when I'm pregnant with the child he wants?

My lungs tighten as I think about motherhood. In the safety of his bedroom, it feels like a dream. A white picket fence. Two kids who love each other and behave well and who I can love back.

But out here?

In the kitchen with his ma, when he's gone and the world is spinning fast, no longer still like up in his room?

Then it's *real*.

And reality isn't a daydream. It's harsh and horrible, and it *hurts*.

What if I hurt Khalid's kid like ma hurt me?

Tears burning my eyes, I flinch when a hand squeezes

my shoulder.

"They're going to be fine," his ma murmurs, a hardness in her voice, a factual honesty that makes me want to believe her.

"How do you know?" I whisper, wanting, *needing* to know what she does.

Her face tenses, and she studies me for a long moment. She and Khalid have the same eyes, not in color but in the intensity of their stare. "Aleric," she says at length, "the vampire they're going to meet...he and I go a long way back. There is a lot of pain between our families, triggered by the two of us, but he needs our alliance." She pauses as she stirs the pot, a coppery red soup that froths with a hint of chili and smoked paprika.

"If he harms any one of my boys, he will be left to fight the Death Hunt himself, and he cannot win against them alone. He is vengeful but not stupid."

I want to relax from her words, but there is a stillness in her that makes me tense in horrible expectancy.

"But although they are safe today, Scarlett, I will not lie to you and say Khalid always will be. He is the reaper of this Family. His job is dangerous, and even if it wasn't, we are about to head to war." Her lips tighten as my heart pounds in my ears. I reach out for the counter, steadying myself with one hand.

"What's a reaper?" I rasp, wondering just how many bodies Khalid has left in his wake. How many Derek's... Does he kill like that werewolf did? Does he enjoy it? Take pleasure in the blood and pain he spills?

Shuddering, my knuckles turn white.

Tapping the ladle on the edge of the pot, shaking off drops of soup, she then places it down on the counter. Turning to me, she looks me in the eyes. "He kills the members of Shadow Domain who betray this Family."

My legs don't want to hold my weight anymore, but I

force my knees to lock, knowing by the look in her eyes, it's worse than that. There's so much sorrow for her son, so much worry for me. As if she thinks I won't be strong enough to handle it.

But I'll walk through Hell for Khalid. He is all I have, and I know he would do the same for me.

"He's killed cousins and uncles, people he once called dear friends."

My nails dig into the wood of the counter, spasming in an onslaught of horror. All those deaths on his shoulders. All that guilt and pain. That's why he doesn't sleep well. Why he watched me through his window all those restless nights. He is the sacrificial lamb in this family, doing the dirty work so the rest can stay clean, whole, not haunted by the deeds they've done.

I suddenly hate the woman in front of me. Hate all of his brothers who I have yet to meet. Hate this house and everything about this fucking family. They treat him like ma treated me – a thing to destroy all happiness in.

They might have gone about it a different way. They might laugh with him like I hear when I'm hiding upstairs and he's down here getting food. They might all willingly share this big house, thinking they're this close family.

But they strip him of happiness just the same. They take everything good and taint it with the demands they make on him.

Is that why I've been drawn to him so quickly? I saw his pain the moment he moved in next door, but I never thought it was the same lonely experience as mine.

"How could you ask that of him?" I demand, my words raw and uncontrollable in pitch as my heart breaks for Khalid.

"He is the third oldest," she says as if that explains it all, and I want to fly at her and gauge her eyes out.

"But he's your son!"

"*They are all,*" she snaps before grabbing my hand too tight for me to pull away and squeezing on an exhale. "This life is not easy, Scarlett. It's not some glorious movie where the gray heroes have lines they will not cross. You will suffer cruelly at the hands of fate and enemies of your own creation. You will lose more than you ever knew you had and still more will be ripped from you. Sometimes..." She takes a deep breath as she glances away, her eyes shining with a pain that's quickly buried. "Sometimes you will just want to run and never look back, but these men, *my boys*, don't have the luxury of running. Territories are claimed all across the world, and if we try to move elsewhere, we'll just be going to war in a place whose terrain and people we don't know. This is our home, and to protect it, we *all* have to do things we don't wish to do."

She squeezes my hand as I continue to look at her in horror.

"Trust me, if I could take Khalid's job, I would. But I can't. No one can."

I want to believe her. I want to believe that his family did not *choose* to sacrifice his soul for the sake of theirs, that some magic or fate bound to him, and no one can take his place.

But I know that isn't true. Otherwise, she would have said it.

Pulling my hand away from her, I shake my head. "He deserves better."

"I know," she murmurs. "They all do. And I wish I could give them that life." A short laugh of pain is pulled from her lips as she glances away. "You know, I tried so hard not to lose another child. I overlooked two thousand years of family feuds between us, Blood Fang, and Death Hunt just so we could sign a treaty that would bring peace to our territories.

"They had taken twelve children from me, many of

whom were butchered and left on this very doorstep. I had been tortured by members of Death Hunt and nearly raped by their Boss. I carried so much rage for the two other gangs, but I put that all aside for *my boys*. So they could live in peace, never knowing the horrors I grew up with. That my parents grew up with. That two thousand years of ancestors grew up with.

"So don't look at me as if I do not care for my children because you will never understand just how much I have given up for them." The rawness in her words cuts across my heart, and I look away from her in shame. I jumped in and judged her without knowing anything.

"I'm sorry," I murmur, but she just shakes her head.

"Never apologize for defending my son, Scarlett. He needs someone who will always stand with him, and I am so very happy he's found that in you."

My throat working hard, I blush under her words.

Before I can find anything to say, she picks up the ladle again. "Now, would you like to learn how to make an ifrit potion?" she asks.

Taking the truce for what it is, I nod and step closer.

Despite this being the sixth batch (of different potions) I've helped her make, I am still surprised at how similar this is to cooking. The ingredients are added. The pot is stirred. The recipe is tested and then 'salt and pepper' is added, with salt and pepper being a list of ingredients I would never put in cooking – ground glass, shredded hair, drops of blood...

As Sau, Khalid's mother, stands over the newest batch of potion, this one a lime green that smells of sewage that's been eaten and vomited up again, I try not to gag with one hand over my mouth and nose.

"It needs more rotten meat," she says after pipetting a

drop onto a special strip of paper.

Walking over to the slab on the chopping board, trying not to think about what animal it is (and not having the courage), I grab the potato peeler and slice off a strip from the most rancid part, scooping up some of the puss oozing from it.

My gag reflex kicks in, and I turn quickly away as I struggle to keep my breakfast down. Carrying the peeler over to the stove, the piece of meat dangling from it and dripping puss, I shake it over the pot.

The liquid hisses, spurting boiling spray into the air, and I jerk back, dropping the peeler. Although Sau didn't say not to get this one on me, the sheer smell of it makes me more nervous around it than I was around the ifrit potion, which causes a burn from one side of an organism to the other.

As we were making that one, Sau told me it used to be used as a torture method. Hang someone upside down. Squirt one drop on the bottom of their foot, and wait for it to come out their shoulder.

The SCU made it illegal (and regardless of what Khalid had told me, Sau made it seem like the Special Crimes Unit really was their government), so this batch was for defense only. Although the house was protected to keep out other sups, she wanted to be prepared in case that spell was broken. *In war, rely on nothing.*

Testing another drop of the green potion on the strip of paper, she waits a second, then nods. "Make a note of this color, Scarlett. This is what you want it to look like. If it's too light, add more spoiled meat. If it's too dark, add more banana. You can't go from black to green or white to green, but if you're that far off, you'll need to start over."

After picking up the dropped peeler, I place it on the counter and lean over her shoulder to look at the forest-green drop in amongst a variety of colors.

"Here," she says, picking up the paper. "Tear this into bits so each one has one spot of color while I go get you a notebook to put them in. It'll be your grimoire, and we can go over all the steps you just learned."

Nodding, I take it from her and move over to the table, away from the pot of 'shit.' Although she put the lid on it, it absolutely reeks.

As she heads out of the kitchen, I start to tear up the color dots, trying to remember which one was what.

The greens are for the pestilence potion we just made, and I lay them out on the table in a row of increasing shades.

The reds are the ifrit potion we started with. The color to aim for is a dark maroon.

The blues are from the healing potion, and that was the biggest batch we made. Her boys are 'boys' and haven't learned much healing magic, preferring instead to study those that can kill. Leno, her second eldest, is the only one with much healing magic, but his magic comes from his plants and requires him to have access to them. So we made a lot of potions for them to carry.

My stomach twists as I envision just how many we made, and my mind drifts to Khalid. Both him and his mother assured me he was safe, but there's a feeling I just can't shake that he's going to get hurt.

"Gods, that's an awful smell."

The sound of a deep feminine voice causes me to jump, and the chair I'm on creaks beneath my weight. Pushing to my feet, I blush as I turn to face the newcomer.

Her muscles are just as toned as Sau's, but her stance is less graceful. She walks with her shoulders leading like a man rather than with her hips. More masculine, which is highlighted by her shaved head and lack of make up. Her eyes are pierced, as is her nose and ears. Tattoos crawl down her neck, and if I saw her on the street, I would have assumed she was in a biker gang.

She moves both hands around intricately. A tattoo of abstract lines glows lightly on her neck, and the sewage smell instantly disappears. I take a deep, much needed breath, drawing her attention to me.

She turns, and when her eyes catch mine, I have an instinctive urge to shout for Sau, my heart beating fast and my hands growing clammy.

She smiles at me, but that doesn't make her look any more approachable.

"You must be Khalid's girl. Scarlett, right?"

I nod jerkingly, wondering how long Sau will be. I have no idea what the rest of the house looks like, so can't picture how long it'll take her to go wherever there are notebooks and fetch me one.

"I hear he's bonded with you already," she says as she takes a seat and gestures for me to join her where I was.

I stay standing for a moment before settling back in my chair. I trust Khalid not to have left me with anyone that will hurt me.

"Aren't you worried you'll lose yourself?"

"Um..." I look at her in confusion.

"He hasn't told you, has he?" She snorts. "Just typical of the men here. Do what we say. Don't ask questions. They're so boneheaded and old fashioned. In my family, women are treated equally."

"Khalid treats me like an equal," I say defensively, only to immediately recall him biting out my implant. I'm still not sure how he managed that, must've used magic, but he didn't ask me. I didn't even know he was doing it, and then he came inside me with the sole purpose of getting me pregnant. Although I agreed to it, I wasn't... A frown pulls at my lips as I struggle to truly assess my feelings about it now that I'm outside of the bubble that is Khalid.

"So he's told you all about the blood bond then, has he?" she asks, reaching over to touch my arm. "About how his feelings will mix with yours, so you lose all sight of who *you* actually are? If he wants you pregnant, bam, you're suddenly willing to be pregnant. If he wants you docile, poof. 'What can I make you for lunch, honey?' If he loves you..." She looks at me in a way that curls my stomach more than the pestilence potion did. A heat crawls up my arm where she's touching me, and I pull it away, resisting the urge to rub her essence off me.

"That's not true," I say, but my words are weak with uncertainty, and like a shark smelling blood, she leans in.

"Your relationship is with Khalid, and if he finds out I'm talking to you like this, he'll probably kill me."

Her eyes say she isn't joking, and my breath catches in my throat.

"But I won't be able to live with myself if you don't know what you're getting into."

Her gaze dips to the bite marks on my neck that have broken skin, mementos of the last three days. "Get him to slow down with the blood bond is all I'm suggesting. It'll give you time to figure out if you really want to be with him or if it's his blood tricking you."

I stare at her, wanting to call her a liar but knowing I can't. Her words stick in my chest as I think back on how I asked Khalid to make me pregnant even though I never wanted kids. My ma was shit. I never knew my father. How can I possibly raise a child of my own with no good experience to pull from? My heart racing, I try to think of why Khalid wouldn't have told me this when we talked about blood bonds.

Is he playing me? Is he *making* me fall in love with him? I barely know him. It's only been a few days that we've been together, and yeah, they have been a *fucking intense* few days where emotions have been extreme all around and I might have been half-way in love from him due to me crushing on him for the last three months, but...is it not too soon to be feeling this obsessed with him?

My heart a frantic dance of madness, I force my eyes back to the pieces of paper in front of me. I need to finish organizing them to put in my book of shadows. My hands shake as I rip off a yellow dot.

"Hey," she says, dipping her shaved head to regain my attention. "Khalid really cares about you. I know that, and I don't doubt for a second that he will do anything for you. But the men in this family can be really callous and selfish sometimes, so just keep that in mind. I know it can be overwhelming when they focus on you." There's a hitch in her words that causes me to look at her and really see her for the first time.

She isn't much different than me...

"Which one's yours?" I ask softly.

She laughs briskly. "No one is *mine*. But I'm engaged to Varius fucking Shadow." Her head tilts. "You haven't met him yet, have you?" She nods before I can answer. "Of course you haven't. Otherwise, you'd understand."

"You like him though, don't you?"

She stills, making me confident I hit the nail on the head. Before either of us can speak, Sau comes in with a black leather notebook in her hands.

"Here's a – *Micha*, you're back," she says as she walks towards us with a smile. "I thought you were out until tomorrow."

"Yeah, I got back early. With the boys gone, I didn't want to leave you and Scarlett here alone, what with your curse and all."

"You're cursed?" I ask Sau.

She doesn't look at me, her eyes focused on Micha. "Yes. I can't use magic without it draining my life, but that doesn't mean I *won't* use it."

Micha stills, and as the air burns with words unspoken, I shift uneasily in my chair, my earlier fear over Khalid's absence spiking again. Her gaze locked on Sau, Micha starts to stand. "I know you will die protecting her –"

I don't want that!

"– but if I'm here, you don't have to. The wolves –"

"*Don't?*" Sau cuts in, the air electrifying like a coming storm.

Micha pauses and cocks her head to the side as her eyes fly to me. "Did I say that?"

I nod, a ball of knots pulling tight in my stomach.

When Micha straightens suddenly, her face losing her joking manner, Sau moves between the two of us with inhuman speed. I jump to my feet, not liking the feeling in the air. The tightness. The electricity.

Micha turns to us, her brow furrowed a second before she's launched off her feet by a ball of magic Sau threw at her. Grabbing my hand, Khalid's ma pulls me from the room as howls chorus a scream of pain.

My heart slams into my ribs. "What's going on?" I cry. "Why did you –"

"Micha broke the protection spell keeping the wolves away, and with the boys gone, they're going to come for you."

"Oh...Scarlettttt!" a familiar voice coos outside, making my body jerk in terror. My mind flashes with the wolf on the van who teased Detective Henry with his dying wife. "Let's finish our game, shall we?"

He laughs as his face slams against a window in the hall we're running past, pressing his cheek against the glass. His wild eyes fly to me, pinning me in place, and I scream as the wall behind us rains plaster and wooden splinters as a werewolf smashes a hand through it.

"Don't stop!" Sau hisses as she drags me down the stairs. "We need to get to the basement before –"

Her fingers fly free of mine when she suddenly twists and jumps back the way we just came.

The air electrifies as she grunts, holding back a blast of magic that ripples with dark energy. "Keep going!" she snaps. "The stairs are just there. I'll hold Micha off."

"But –"

"Go! And after you shut the door, call Khalid."

Hating that the only way I can be of help is to get out of her way so she doesn't have to protect me *and* fight, I spin on my heels and rush through blurry tears.

My hand slipping into my pocket, I hurry down the stairs leading to the basement. The door is already open, and I barrel inside before turning quickly to lock it.

My heart hammering as the house shakes, werewolves howl, and that maniac laughs, I tap the screen and dial Khalid.

Ring!...

Ring!...

Ring!...

The call goes to voicemail.

THIRTY-SIX

HIM

Aleric sits across his desk, leaning back in his chair as he reads the terms of the alliance we just spent the last few hours finalizing. Varius does the same, both of them taking their sweet time to make sure they've thought everything through, closed every loophole concerning the division of Antonio's network and territory.

My skin itches with the desire to get back home, and my magic hums beneath it in an equal need. This time, it isn't just Talon who is with us. Aleric wants us all to sign the contract so if Varius dies in the coming war, the terms will still be upheld.

Although our house and the surrounding acres are protected against unwanted entry, Micha is away, having gone up north to deal with an issue Varius created to get her out of the house while we're here, and Leno's plants have been spelled to be another terrifying defense, I don't like being away from her this long.

My phone vibrates in my pocket, and I pull it out, but

when I check the screen, there's no notification. Must be a phantom desire for her to call me. A want for her to be as twisted up about my absence as I am over hers.

Slipping my phone back into my pocket, I wait for this damn meeting to be over.

The urge to throw my phone when Khalid doesn't answer makes my fingers tighten around the rubber case. My body needs to do something, to lash out, to help Sau fight the wolves and Micha upstairs.

But I'm just a fucking human. An overweight human who can't even climb the stairs without getting out of breath.

What did I tell you, Gen? You shouldn't be so fat.

Squeezing my eyes shut, I shake my head, ridding it of that awful woman's voice. Ma is dead, and I'm not going to end up like her.

There has to be something down here that'll help me defend myself. This is a witch's basement, and the kitchen was stocked with magical items to go into cooking and potions.

Opening my eyes, I look around frantically as the howl of the wolves increase. A shelf of glass vials lures me over to them, and I pick two up gingerly.

Out of the six I helped Sau make today, three of them needed to be handled carefully.

I hold them both up to my face to read the labels, but they're in a language I don't understand.

Wanting to scream, I put them back down and take a deep breath. I stare at them, trying to figure out how I can decipher which ones will help me and Sau. Deciding to just go by color and hope for the best, I grab a handful of the red ones.

Sau didn't get the chance to tell me how to use them, but I figure launching them into the face of a wolf will work well enough.

As heavy footsteps pound down the stairs, I jerk towards the door, my heart matching every beat that vibrates through the wood.

Clutching the vials of potions, praying they're ifrit or something similar, I wait for the wolf to tear through the door.

A loud thud shakes it, but the wood holds, and I slowly inch forward, my hands shaking.

The sound of claws rake across its surface, followed by snarls and growls.

By the time the door finally splinters, I'm standing right in front of it. A hand comes through, then pulls back as a wolf's yellow eyes fill the hole. Popping open one of the vials, I toss the contents at the werewolf's face.

It jerks back on a high-pitched howl, its fur smoldering as the liquid burns deep into its skin. Dropping to the ground, it howls in so much twisted pain, tears burn my eyes.

Wolf or not. Trying to kill me or not. The sound of that much agony should never be experienced. My stomach retching up my throat, I shakily uncork another vial and pour it through the hole in the door, hoping to kill it quicker.

A human hand grabs me, and I scream as it twists my arm, forcing me to drop the potion. I yank my arm back through the door just in time for Micha to shove it open.

Covered in blood and heaving, she lunges for me, her hands going for my throat. I stumble back as I throw the whole handful of potions at her face.

A shimmer of light-blue magic shoots up between us, a force field that protects her and damns me.

As I fall onto my back, the potions shatter on the floor, droplets hitting my legs. I scream in utter agony as acidic fire burns through skin, muscle, and bone. My stomach twisting, I jerk on the floor, my body going into shock as Micha stands glaring over me.

We all pile into two separate vehicles. Varius, Maddox, Talon, and I in one. The twins, Rudy, Leno, and Leno's eye-seeing dog Krypto in another. It'll take us only twenty minutes to drive back, but it feels like twenty minutes too long as I pull out my phone and check again for messages.

Nothing.

Mother will undoubtedly be keeping her occupied in the kitchen. I asked her to teach Scarlett how to make potions to help settle my girl's anxiety. I also warned Mother about Micha in case she suddenly returned.

No word has been passed to Varius saying she has, but there's an uneasiness in my stomach that won't go away.

Deciding to call her, I type in Scarlett's number, not having any contacts pre-programed, and raise my phone to my ear.

With every ring that goes unanswered, my pulse beats accelerando until a macabre symphony fills my skull.

Ring…thump-thump…ring…thump-thump-thump…. *ring!*

My fingers tensing, I tell myself she can't be in danger. I would have sensed it through our –

My phone drops.

My pulse skips a beat.

Realization hits me in the solar plexus, caving in my chest. *I can't feel the bond at all.*

Catching Talon's eyes on me in the rearview mirror, I freeze. A flicker of unease is reflected back at me. "What's wrong?" he asks.

Varius turns to face me, his eyes narrowing as one word

flows out of his lips. "Go."

It is an order I do not hesitate to obey.

Shifting into my shadow, I exit through the bottom of the car and race across the city in a straight line, my speed a burst of magic that will have me home in only a few minutes. Anyone who sees me will just assume I was a trick of the light, gone too fast before they can get a good look.

Only two other shadows join me, the others staying back to protect Varius should the wolves attack. Although the Death Hunt won't risk turning in full daylight with a packed city of witnesses, they're more than willing to do a drive-by. Guns will kill us just as quickly as a slash of their claws.

As the first tree on our thirty acres appears in front of me, my heart jerks on a silent scream. The protection spell has been broken, the shield down, my girl and Mother left to defend against an army, which means Micha is back and she's somehow blocked my bond to Scarlett.

Rage for Varius burns through me, fueling my magic as I sprint towards home. I wasn't allowed to kill Micha until he had solid evidence, and now it is too late. She has betrayed us and left us weak.

Corpses of werewolves lie under crawling plants whose stalks and limbs sprout through flesh, rooting them to the ground. But there are more on the roof and porch of the house, slashing their claws through the wood, terrorizing those inside rather than hunting.

They're playing with my girl as if she's theirs.

My magic bursts free, seeking vengeance outside of my control as I shift into human, and a large wave of heat boils the werewolves on the roof. I drop to my knees, spitting up blood, my left lung burning away as my rage traded perfection for power, leaving me open to the dark payment of magic.

Growls wring the air as the other wolves jerk towards us,

leaving their posts to attack. Maddox and Talon appear beside me. The twins would have controlled Varius' car until one of them shifted into the driver's seat.

A black wolf with a white patch on her left eye growls low and dangerous as she approaches cautiously behind three others that run in gung ho. Maddox dances with one, two-stepping its swipes as he keeps his hands behind his back, pleasure in his eyes. He isn't toying with it; he's studying it. Every hair, every bead of sweat, every freckle beneath its fur, his magic seeking to copy its exact form.

It'll take him time I can't buy him as I wheeze for air through one working lung. Digging my nails into the dirt, I bite off one of the red-and-black flowers Leno created with his magic. As soon as I swallow, the pain recedes under a numbness, and I struggle to my feet just as a wolf lunges for me, arms leading. A bolt of electricity, thrown by Talon, slams into it before its claws can sink into my skin and arcs into the wolf beside it.

The wolf rolls to its feet with a growl, the only mark on its smoldering fur. They're strong fuckers, much more so than the ones who attacked the WALL a few nights ago.

My shadows swirling at my feet, I pull out my cursed double scythe. I spin it as I spit out more blood. Knowing I don't have long before my internal injury takes me out, I jump forward, my weapon twirling around me to keep the wolves at a distance.

I don't need to cut them; I just need to buy Maddox a minute or two to study them all. I try not to think about what Antonio is doing to Scarlett and Mother during this time, but the usual calm I'm able to sink into when in a fight is being drowned out by my fear. I want to shift into my shadow and bypass the wolves entirely, but we will just have to fight them on the way out. I haven't shared enough of my blood with her for her to travel my domain safely.

Maddox whistles, snagging my attention, and I swing my

scythe at the werewolf he's dancing with, taking his place as we trade blows, our limbs a blur. His claws rip into my side as I graze his shoulder.

Maddox drops into a pool of shadows beside me on a scream before starting to shift.

Electricity colors the air in blue cracks, keeping the other wolves occupied. But then Talon screams as one drags him to the ground.

Maddox jerks his head to our brother and with a feral growl, he shifts into the wolf I was fighting. Biting his shoulder, he rips out a chunk of flesh and drops it before leaping at the wolf on top of Talon.

I leap to where he was, tucking my shoulder as I roll and come back up on my feet, my scythe spinning in one hand while my other grasps the DNA Maddox left me.

Throwing my weapon at the third wolf trying to jump onto Maddox's back, I pull a pin of green etherial energy from the air. Although a soul doll allows me to target my enemies from a great distance, as long as I have line of sight and DNA, I can still hurt them the same with a soul pin.

Glancing over at my brothers, making sure Maddox has begun his transformation back into himself, I then slam the pin into the strip of flesh.

A ball of fire appearing in the palm holding the DNA, I burn it to a crisp, and the wolf in front of me burns too, his limbs coated in flames that can't be put out and won't transfer to anything else. Dropping the strip of flesh into my shadow, I leave him to be bitten and clawed apart by the twisted monsters in that dark domain.

I turn back towards my brothers and see Maddox and Talon back on their feet, bloody and looking like shit but not dead. Maddox holds his hand across his stomach, a bit of intestines dangling between his fingers. One of his eyes hangs free of his skull. He can heal it if he shifts again, but he'll need time we can't yet buy him.

There are two more wolves to deal with, plus the black wolf with the white spot hanging back – Zita, Maddox's obsession waiting for her moment to rip his head off his shoulders once we've been weakened.

More blood gurgles up my throat, and the numbness in my lungs is wearing off, the flower's properties too raw and undefined to linger for long.

Both the wolves lunge for Maddox, seeing him as the weakest link, as well as the most dangerous given he can give me pieces of them to destroy. Talon and I both try to defend him, but I'm too weak, and with their natural resistance to magic, Talon's electricity is doing little more than pissing them off. He's strong against vampires and great in handling our business, but he's not of much help when it comes to wolves. He can throw them around; he can't kill them.

Ignoring the pain of my lung and still unhealed kidney, I draw on my magic to search for the hearts of the two wolves in front of me. Using this spell might make it impossible for me to go after Scarlett if Antonio grabs her, but at the moment I can't even get to her when she's still inside our house.

Focusing on keeping it contained this time, I swivel my hands around each other, and fling my power into the hearts of the two wolves, my soul magic allowing me to bypass their innate resistance.

I drop to my knees at the same time they do. More blood spurts up like a fountain, and the flower's properties completely fade, leaving me open to the agony of the payment I gave for my spell.

My vision blurs, and my head drops to the damp earth that smells of dirt and blood and burning flesh. Of dark magic lingering in the air, searching for something to kill.

Focusing on my girl, who still needs me, I try not to think about why I haven't been able to feel our bond.

Digging my nails into the ground, I push myself to my feet just as Zita lunges for Maddox. He drops into his shadow, and I go to defend him from her, but Talon grabs my arm.

"He'll be fine. She's young, and he'll come out healed." Maddox is able to shift inside his shadow, but it costs him a great deal of energy, and he only uses it as a last resort and if he thinks the fight won't last long. Talon's fingers dig deep. "We need to find Mom and Scarlett."

When Maddox reappears healthy and with no wounds beneath the blood, I race into the house. Wreckage is strewn about the place from two witches having fought, and claw marks have destroyed all else. Darting for the basement, knowing that's where Mother would've hidden her given it's our safe room, I take the stairs two at a time.

A werewolf with her face burned off lies in front of the door.

My heart in my throat, I jump over her and barrel into the room. Scarlett's in the middle of it, tied and gagged with tears running down her face. Micha stands beside her, at the righthand of Antonio. A sneer curves his lips as he nods, and a swirl of shadows open on the floor in front of them.

My brain scrambles to understand how Micha is able to control what only our family ever has, but the puzzle is forgotten as Antonio shoves my girl inside, to the realm of monsters lurking below.

Diving in after her, I just manage to catch sight of the answer to the puzzle before the darkness closes in on me.

Micha's legs are limp. She isn't holding her weight, and if I had the time to look up, I know I would see her face is slack with unconsciousness or death.

Which means she isn't the traitor.

She isn't the one who opened up the shadow.

She isn't the one I'm going to have to kill...

THIRTY-SEVEN

HIM

A feminine scream breaks my heart in both joy and terror that my girl's alive. Running towards the sound of her, the feel of her as our bond reconnects, I search with my magic in the pitch-black darkness. I find her not far from me, on her knees, struggling to get the gag off her face. Crouching down behind her, I quickly untie it, then work on her hands.

Twisted creatures skitter at the edges of my vision, the black like a fog even my magic can't penetrate. My pulse like a hummingbird's wings, I drag her to my feet.

"Don't leave my side," I say, wanting to grab her hand but needing both of them to protect us in this nightmarish plane.

"Where are we?" she whimpers, but her voice isn't that of a broken mind. She's strong, a fighter, and my chest expands with that knowledge.

The gods won't take me before I get a lifetime with her.

I won't fucking let them.

"We're in the Shadow Domain."

The sound of clicking wet mandibles and gut-churning slurps start to echo around us, lured by the blood of my girl. There's a lot of them, a thick density I can't fight off. One or two minor beings, I might have had a chance, but there is a reason no one else but my family walks through the Shadow Domain. The average person won't last a minute here.

I can't use my shadow magic inside it either, can't conjure any weapons to protect us. Turning to *kira*, I cup her cheeks.

"I need you to bite me, *kira*," I say, grabbing the back of her head and pushing her mouth against the side of my throat. "Bite deep."

"What?" She tries to lift her head, but I hold it down, covering her in my blood the only thing that will protect her. Maybe...

"Do it!"

"It'll kill you!"

"I'll heal; do it!" A lie, but I don't have time to guide her on just where to bite me or how deep or at what angle to pull away so she doesn't rip out my artery. Screaming hisses rush towards us as the clatter of hooves and insect-like legs echo in the dark. We're out of time.

"*Kira, please!*"

Crying, she digs her teeth into my neck and rips away. *Too deep.* Blood spurts free in a jet stream, covering her in a repellent that will hopefully keep her alive.

Using magic to stay conscious for just a few seconds longer, I draw a rune on her skin with my blood. Placing my palm over it, I push my magic into her. When she's pulled out of here, taken to wherever it is Antonio wants her, the rune will protect her from being raped.

The creatures stop only a few feet from us, hissing in rage as they gnash deformed teeth in deformed faces.

"Khalid!" Scarlett cries as I drop to the ground, my

strength disappearing with the high volume of blood loss.

"Heal yourself!" she screams as she places one hand over the wound she gave me. I cover it with my own and squeeze. It seems I cannot defy the gods after all…

"Khalid!" Fumbling with her other hand, Scarlett digs something out of a pocket, and there's a slight *pop* as a cork is freed.

"Do you drink this, or do I pour it over the wound?" she demands as she shoves a blue vial in front of my face. Laughter pours out of me in soft wheezes as I guide her hand to my mouth.

Dipping the whole thing into me, she saves me from the verge of death with a healing potion.

My girl.

My clever, clever girl…

Holding Khalid's head in my lap, I clutch him tightly as tears fall down my cheeks. My palm is pressed against his neck, trying to tell if the bleeding has stopped. I can't see anything in this place, and he's not moving.

"Khalid?" I whisper, praying that he answers. When Micha found me, she made me drink one to counter the red potion eating through my legs, but those hadn't been life-threatening wounds.

She then explained that there was a misunderstanding, that she was being set up, and given she just saved me, I was inclined to believe her.

Then Antonio burst through the door and attacked her from behind. He slammed his whole arm through her back and out her stomach, causing her to pass out in an instant.

He didn't kill her though. She was his scapegoat or rather, Talon's scapegoat and needed to be left alive to take the heat off him. He told me with great delight that Varius, paranoid fuck that he was, would torture her for our whereabouts. Sau believed her to be a traitor, so it would not matter what truths Micha told.

Khalid's hand tightens on mine, and he breathes out softly. "You saved me, *kira.*"

"I almost *killed* you, you stupid dumbass! What the fuck was that plan! You said you would heal. I *believed* you, and you went and... You were going to..." I clutch at him, not sure if I want to pull him to me for a kiss or slam his head onto the ground to knock some sense into him.

"Don't you *ever* do that again!"

"*Kira...*"

"Don't *kira* me! I'm not going to be some...some...some sixteenth-century woman who *knows her place.* I'm not going to just sit back and watch you die to protect me."

I shake his shoulders. "You can't *leave* me. You can't..."

"*Kira...*"

I drop his head on the floor, hoping it hurts when it hits. There isn't a following *thump.* The bastard used his neck muscles, muscles *I* just put back together, not him. *Fucking traitors.*

Tears burning my eyes, I grab him again, groping in the dark to what I think is his head. His hair twists in my fingers, and I shake him.

"*Promise* me, Khalid. Promise me, or I swear to God I will walk and never look back."

A sudden lethalness cuts through the darkness. "Don't joke about that, *kira.*"

"I'm not joking! I can't handle being the cause of your death. I can't... It's cruel... You can't..." Tears trapping my words, I struggle to breathe as I shake him again. "*Please* promise me, Khalid."

"*Kira...*" The word is a soft sigh of defeat, and I clutch him tight as I wait for him to say the words. "I promise as long as you never bring up leaving again."

About to blurt out, 'Okay,' I stop myself, remembering Micha's warning about how the blood bond makes me placid. "That's not reasonable. I can't not tell you what my boundaries are. You don't get to make them for me."

He growls, the show of frustration making me laugh, making me realize he really is okay. The potion worked. *He's okay. He's okay. He's okay.*

Sitting up, removing my hands from their death grip on his hair, he then pulls me into a hug. His lips find mine as he kisses me gently, a thousand promises in the caress of his lips.

"Can we discuss this later? I need you to tell me what happened while we were gone before we're pulled out of this place."

"Okay." *Goddammit.* "But we're not exchanging blood again until we do."

Another growl from him. Another laugh from me.

"Micha fucking talked to you, didn't she?"

I try to push out of his hug, but he doesn't let me, his arms tightening around me. "Don't be angry at her," I say. "You should have told me yourself."

"You're right. I'm sorry. Now will you tell me what happened?"

Shuddering, I press my face against his neck, kissing where I almost killed him. Then I take a deep breath and fill him in on the attack and Micha's innocence, trying my best not to freak out over the monsters watching us.

My heart pounding, I twist my hands in his shirt after all is done. But it's not done because I left out the worst part – the part where his brother is the traitor, not Micha.

Khalid is a reaper, and I know this is going to hurt him. I don't want to say the words. I don't want to damn his soul even more than it is, but I can't keep this from him.

Tears burning my eyes, I take a deep breath, preparing myself to tell him something that is going to crush him.

"There's something else," I say softly, then kiss his neck, letting him know he is loved. That despite what I'm going to say, he is not alone. "I know who the real traitor is." My throat closes, but I push out the words. "I'm so, so sorry, Khalid, but it's your brother, Talon."

He holds me in the dark.

The hissing of movement and mandibles still surrounds us, but they're not as awful as the silence coming from the man in my arms.

I squeeze him tight, tears falling down my cheeks as I worry about the state of his mind, the breaking of his heart, the knowledge of what he is going to be asked to do.

Pressing my lips against his neck, I wait for him to come to terms with my reveal, hoping he doesn't hate me for being the carrier of bad news.

His chest shudders as he finally exhales. Kissing the top of my head, he holds me close and says, "I know."

THIRTY-EIGHT

HER

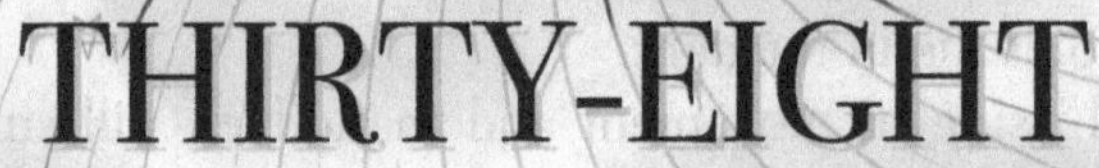

"You know?" I ask, my voice cracking under the pain, wondering how long he's carried this secret on his fragile shoulders. Khalid might be a strong and powerful witch. He might be a man who's never let himself get close to people in fear of having to kill them, but he is still... *human.*

He still hurts and feels loneliness like the rest of us.

"Micha can't control shadows," he says so flatly I can hear the pain under his mask of factual evidence.

"Your ma told me about what you do for this Family," I say, hating how he tenses against me, how the worry that I will see him as a monster flows through our bond. "We can run," I whisper, the words falling from my lips as fast as the tears fall from my eyes. "After we escape from here, we can change our names and just pretend to be dead. We can –"

"I won't leave them."

"But what they're forcing you to do –"

His fingers brush my lips, quieting my words but not the pain in my heart. "They're not forcing me, *kira.* I do it because I don't want any of them to have to."

"Why not?" I ask selfishly. Ma wouldn't have cared for my sacrifice, and I cannot fathom how his brothers can truly appreciate what he is doing for them.

"Because it'll break them."

"And what?" I cry. "You deserve to be broken?" How can he think so little of himself? How can he not see they are using him like Ma used me? To unload all of their shit and to make themselves feel better.

"*Kira...*"

"No! Just because they're your family doesn't mean they get to treat you like shit. It took me a long time to realize this, but we don't need toxic family just because they're all we have. And you have me. We can pretend we died. We can escape and run far enough and settle down with new lives. We can start a family." I choke on the last word, my need to keep him safe clashing with promises I don't know if I can keep. I want to be enough for him. I want to be the woman he needs, but the thought of being a mother terrifies me.

But I can do it if he's there.

We can figure out how to raise his child together.

"*Kira...*" he murmurs as he touches his lips to mine and his thumbs brush away my tears. "Thank you for loving me."

My heart both thuds hard and stops on a locked breath as I shake in his arms, realizing the truth of his words. It might be his bond influencing me. It might be the trauma of the situation tying me to him. But I know it's neither.

It's three months of watching him through my window, of waiting for his smile, for the intensity of his eyes to find mine. It was the moments of breathless anticipation as I did the shopping around town, hoping I would run into him. It's seeing how he looks at me, how he listens to the words I don't say. How he makes me feel beautiful and cherished. It's knowing I can rely on him regardless of the situation, that no matter what happens, he will be there.

It's the feeling in my chest, the overwhelming feeling that exploded when I thought I lost him.

My *kira*.

My sun.

My moon.

My stars.

Gone.

His pain is mine, and I don't know how to save him from it. Threading my hands through his hair, I kiss him hard. "I do love you," I rasp, my words breathless against his lips. "I love you."

"I love you too, *kira*." His tongue sweeps inside my mouth, harsh breaths wheezing from his lungs. I reach between us to grab his cock, needing to show him, to let the overwhelming emotions flowing around me out in some way, but his fingers encircle my wrist, stopping me.

"It's why I am going to kill Talon regardless of my job as reaper. He hurt you and that is an unforgivable sin."

Before I can respond, harsh light pours from above. I squeeze my eyes shut as it burns through my skull. Angry hisses scramble away as whatever monsters circled us retreat from the light of our world. I'm pulled up, Khalid's arms still around me, and experience a moment of utter weightlessness.

Then we're pulled from the nightmarish realm and into one of Hell.

THIRTY-NINE

HIM

I know Talon is going to be waiting for us on the other side, no one else in Antonio's pocket capable of bringing us out of the shadows, and I know how the fucker fights.

As much as it killed me to think of any of my brothers as traitors, I studied each and every one of them. A reaper does not have the luxury of playing favorites.

Talon relies heavily on his magic. He is young, so he has not yet started pulling apart atoms with his electricity, but he still relies on it too much. It's why he was useless fighting the wolves –

My jaw tightens.

Or was he holding back, our every interaction a lie? Has he been playing me from the start, knowing that one day I would come for him? Has he been keeping secret aces up his sleeves, making himself look more fragile than he is?

A screaming pain erupts in my chest over his betrayal, but I lock it down. I can't hesitate to kill him, can't give him one opening to get away, to play on my love for him.

I love him, but he hurt my girl.

He betrayed our Family.

Mother and Micha are severely wounded – not dead. Although Scarlett did not say this in her retelling and I did not see the full states of either of them, I know it's true. In Antonio's shoes, it's what I would do to throw the scent off Talon.

As Scarlett's hand tightens on mine and the light pulls us into the world, I lock down all my love for him and see him for the traitor he is.

The only pain inside me now is from my burned lung and half-healed kidney. He knows the severity of neither, though he will suspect I am weakened due to how much blood I spat up earlier.

He isn't in front of me when the shadows deposit us on carpeted floor facing a wooden door with a glass window in the upper half, so I turn to find him standing behind Antonio, who's sitting behind a large ornate desk, now dressed in a white button-down shirt. He changed but didn't wash, so there is still blood caked on his hands and mouth and matted in his shoulder-length dirty-blond hair. He looks pleased with himself and confident I'm not about to cut his fucking head off.

He's right.

I won't be giving him as much mercy as a decapitated head. He will live slowly and painfully for the rest of his life. I will dissect him, removing parts of him piece by piece with a cursed tool whose cuts can only heal as a human's would. Every arm and leg will eventually be shaved off him, and he'll be placed in a box with breathing holes and one window for him to look out onto a world he can never partake in again.

He will suffer for centuries, his isolation driving him mad.

Only then will I open his box and leave him there to

scream with the taste of freedom. A freedom he cannot have as he is forgotten, with no more goons to save him, with no more limbs to save himself.

"Remember our deal," Talon says as he refuses to meet my cold gaze. He is bloody from our previous fight at the house, along with a few fresh wounds, and I know their plan as if it were my own.

Talon will go back to our family, claiming he tried to chase after us, and they will believe him because he's their brother. Micha will be tortured for information on our whereabouts and Antonio's plans. Her cries of innocence and ignorance won't be believed given Mother fought her herself. Antonio most likely knocked her out, coming up from behind while they were engaged. She would have killed herself otherwise, spending all of her precious life force to save Scarlett, and he could not allow that; he needs her alive to take suspicion off his precious puppet.

"Yes, yes," Antonio says as he waves my brother off. "Now go do your thing while I talk to these two."

Talon has the courtesy to look uncertain, but then he steels himself and slinks away in his shadow. I watch him as he leaves, letting him feel the coldness of my gaze, the promise in my eyes.

He will live today because I need to save my energy to protect my girl from whatever Antonio has planned.

But he will die.

Hurting my girl is an unforgivable sin.

When we're alone, Antonio leans forward, his cold gold eyes on my girl, a smirk on his lips. "Tell me, is your pussy as ugly as your face? My boys don't mind a cow if it's got a nice pussy." His eyes run down her body as she tenses beside me. Her nails dig into my hand as fury, disgust, and fear shoot down our bond.

"If your boys touch her, they'll die." My words are soft and factual, and he turns to look at me, his eyes flattening but his smile staying pinned in place.

"You're in no position to defend her," he sneers.

"You think I will let anyone touch what's mine?" I ask, holding his gaze unflinchingly. He is too strong for me to kill outright, especially in my current condition, so I'm going to have to wait. Bide my time. Play his fucking games until I get an opening. "She is already protected."

If anyone tries to have sex with her, myself included, while that ward is activated, they will die instantly. They won't even have to enter her, the magic triggering off the flair of hormones from the person touching her.

"Mmm. Forgot how *monogamous*," he says mockingly, "all you witches are. It's such a boring way to live." His gaze slinks back to Scarlett. "Don't you want to get fucked by more people with better...*experience*?"

"Is that what your girls tell you?" she sneers with a lift of her chin, her biting nails the only sign of her fear. "Let me fuck someone else, sir, so I can actually come?"

His narrowing eyes tense the muscles in my back. He is not known for his sense of humor...just his psychotic games. His smile doesn't relax the knots any, a baring of teeth beneath a cold stare.

"You have quite a mouth on you, young lady. I'm going to enjoy watching that get beat out of you."

My body stills at his deliberate choice of words as if I can feel an anaconda slithering up behind me. My hairs rising. Senses heightening. Urging me to stand and fight.

"Hit her," he says turning to me, the snake lunging at my back. I bite the inside of my cheek, drawing blood to control the sudden flair of magic boiling beneath my skin.

"No."

"Hit her, or I'll kill her now, then rape her corpse while you watch." For the first time, his sneer is one of genuine pleasure. "Your little anti-rape spell won't work then, now will it?"

She grabs the arm of the hand she's holding, squeezing my fingers tight. "Don't," she whispers on a plea, able to feel I'm on the verge of losing control. Or maybe she can see it. My jaw is locked. My hands are fisted. There's so much magic boiling through me that my skin is red and blistering. If I don't force it to settle, it'll cook me from the inside out.

"*Kira*," she murmurs, stopping my heart with one little fucking word, and I turn to her as if pulled on a string. *Kira* is more than a devotion of love, more than three common words. It transcends the bonds of the humans' soulmate (one you connect with on every level) and the gods' lifemate (the literal other half of one's soul, ripped from them during their creation and flung out into the worlds). It is the giving of one's very soul. All of her. In this lifetime and the next.

I wonder if she's realized that.

If she's managed to translate it through my actions.

Shuddering, I force the magic down, knowing that to let it loose won't just kill me and Antonio but her as well.

"Hit me," she says, her eyes showing no fear or panic. Just an encompassing calm that flows down our bond, giving me strength.

Her strength.

As well as her levelheadedness.

She saw him catch a bullet and how fast he can change into his wolf; she saw how close to death's door I was when I jumped into Talon's shadow. She doesn't need to know the specifics to know that attacking him is certain death.

But I can't hit her.

Hurting my girl is an unforgivable sin.

"No." I wanted it to come out strong and final, but the word is raw and twisted, fumbling hoarsely out of my throat. It lands on its face in front of her, nothing about it capable of protecting my girl.

Pushing back his chair, Antonio starts unbuttoning his shirt, a feral smile darkening his eyes. The magic blisters the veins inside me as I watch him, but *kira* grabs my chin and yanks me to her.

I try to keep my eyes on the enemy, but she digs her fingers into my chin, demanding me. "You promised you wouldn't do anything stupid to save me. You *promised* you wouldn't leave me," she whispers, her words as heated as the magic slowly killing me. "You attack him, and you will hurt me more than any fist, more than anything he can fucking do. Because even if we survive, I will *never* be able to trust a word you say. Don't do that to me, *kira*, please."

Lifting the hand she's holding, she presses it against her heart as she feathers her other hand from my chin into my hair, pulling my head to hers. Looking into my eyes, our foreheads touching, she urges, "Hit me. I want to survive, *kira*. I want to survive and spend a lifetime with you." Her fingers tighten in my hair. "I can suffer anything knowing you are waiting for me at the end of it."

Her eyes flash with words she doesn't say, angry vows of vengeance she doesn't dare utter, knowing how good a werewolf's hearing is. *"Promise me we will survive and kill this bastard together."*

Clutching her fingers, I scream inside, my mouth not moving despite the agonizing need to release the pain. I close my eyes, blocking out the sound of Antonio undoing his belt.

Without part of his DNA, I can't attack him in a way that will actually hurt him. My magic is just a tickle on his nose with his current strength. He's never lingered around Maddox long enough for my brother to be able to study him either, so I can't hurt him if we ever get back home.

My only chance to kill him is in his presence, but doing so will kill Scarlett too and probably everyone else in this building. Maybe even the block. Magic is hard to control at the best of times; now I'm barely standing from the payment it's already taken and my emotions are making it even more volatile.

As much as I hate to admit it to myself, I can't deny that the only chance I have is purely in my head.

Antonio can shift in less than a second thanks to the hybrids he's consumed. He can kill me by the time that second is up. Then Scarlett will be defenseless, her anti-rape ward dying with me – something Antonio knows.

Which means...

I have to hit her.

Sobs clawing up my throat in silent agony, I kiss her on the forehead. "I'm sorry, *kira*."

When I step back, my face is expressionless, the reaper mask a part of me.

"Make it a good punch," Antonio coos. "I want to see her bleed."

Locking down my rage and pain, I step into the calm she needs me to enter.

She looks at me, her chin raised, her lips not wobbling at all. Her eyes are strong and defiant. She's a survivor.

Pride and respect fill my chest, but with them comes the opening dam of the other emotions. The crippling pain that freezes me. The unfathomable sorrow that makes me tremble. *I can't do this.*

I need to at least try to kill Antonio before he changes. Maybe when he bends down to take off his pants, I will get a second to attack.

If I already had a weapon in my hands, I might be able to use that second to make a killing blow. But instead, I'll spend it on drawing one out of my shadow. I am fast, but a werewolf's speed is unmatched, and this particular wolf is hyped up on baby juice.

Tears burning my eyes, I know the only chance I have of protecting Scarlett is by playing the fucker's game.

"I love you," she says. "Now hit me so we can live long enough to kill this fucker."

Holding her gaze, taking the strength she's giving me, I rear back with my left hand and hit her on a scream.

FORTY

HER

Pain explodes in my jaw, snapping my head sideways. Blood seeps from a busted lip, spraying across the wall in little specks as I instinctively close my eyes. My teeth throb, but a quick check with my tongue tells me none have come loose.

"Good," Antonio says, a breathiness to his voice that makes me want to vomit.

Opening my eyes, I turn to face Khalid. His eyes are wild and raw, his skin flushing red as he struggles to control the magic killing him. I can feel its jagged teeth through our bond, feel the darkness of its flames.

"I'm okay," I say, holding his gaze, letting him search the truth in mine. *I'm okay.* As long as we survive and kill this bastard later, I'll be okay. As long as Khalid is with me. I can't lose him.

I *won't* lose him to this fucking bastard.

"Again," Antonio demands, the word followed by the sound of his zipper.

I shudder but lift my chin, my focus only on Khalid, on keeping him from doing something stupid. "Eyes on me," I murmur.

So much pain and conflict wet his eyes, his muscles tense with a need to lash out. He's nearly vibrating as he's standing there, staring at me, trying so hard to do what I want him to.

As our gazes hold with a strength that's stronger than the both of us currently are, I finally understand the full meaning of *kira.*

He will suffer through this much paralyzing agony for *me.*

Because I asked him to.

Tears burning my eyes, I fight them down so he does not see them. "Hit me," I command, and I can hear his heart cracking as he pulls back his fist and swings.

My head jerks to the side again, and I close my eyes to fight back the tears.

A broken sound comes from him.

A moan comes from Antonio.

Opening my eyes, I look at my love. "I'm okay," I assure him, still the honest truth.

"Take off your shirt, Scarlett," Antonio orders as his hand moves beneath the desk. I don't look at him, but I don't need to to know he's got his cock gripped tight. I can hear the sick pleasure in his voice. "I want to see your tits jiggle when he hits you in the stomach."

Lunging forward, I grab Khalid as the temperature in the room jumps high. "*Control it,*" I demand, not showing an inch of pain or disgust, knowing that if I do, he'll snap.

His face begs me to let him go, to let him die in an attempt to kill Antonio with no chance of success. I shake my head. "You're surviving with me," I order. "Don't let him take you from me."

His jaw clenches tight as he closes his eyes, the vein at

his neck throbbing fast as the temperature in the room settles back down. Sweat beads on his brow, and he sways. My pulse spikes, wondering how much longer he can last.

Letting his shirt go, I quickly peel mine over my head. The thought to throw it at Antonio, blinding him for a moment, long enough for Khalid to kill him burns through me.

My eyes flick to him as I hold the material in my hands. His narrow as his entire body stills, and I know that he will be on Khalid before I can even lift my arm.

Gritting my teeth, I drop my shirt. He smiles at me. I jerk my gaze back to Khalid. "Hit me."

He doesn't hesitate this time.

Perhaps he too has realized it's better to hit me here, where I have more fat to protect myself.

Pain throbs across my stomach, and I shuffle back a step as if he hit me that hard, but he pulled his punch at the last second.

Groaning, Antonio starts jerking himself off again. He makes Khalid hit me two more times before he stands and walks to lean back against the wall. "Look at me, Scarlett."

Helpless but to obey, I glare at him. His arm quickens in my peripheral.

"Don't pretend you're not a whore and look at my cock," he bites out. "See how hard I am for you?"

Steeling myself, I look down. I unfocus my eyes so I can't really see him, but the blur of his fist is enough to make me want to scrub my eyes with sandpaper.

He groans, then sighs, releasing his cock. I look back at Khalid, but his eyes are on Antonio. I can't feel his rage-filled agony anymore. He erected a wall, not to keep me out, but to keep himself together on that last punch, and I know I'm looking at the reaper that kills his own friends and family with a deadly calm.

My heart breaks for him even as it soars, knowing he

will survive.

We will survive.

"Unfortunately, I can't cover you in my cum because Khalid over here will just use it to kill me. It's a fucking annoying gift you got," he says, turning to the reaper.

Not a single muscle twitches as Khalid stares at him.

I shiver, goosebumps breaking from the eerie promise he's alluding. Even Antonio looks a bit put off, shoving his cock back in his pants.

"Well, as fun as that was, I really need to be going. I have people to kill, evil plans to begin, yada, yada."

He walks around the desk, cutting right past Khalid as if he isn't worried, but there's a tension in his walk that belies his confidence.

"I'd kill you before I go," he says as he smiles at my chest, passing me on his way to the door, "but I gave Talon my word" –he pulls the door open– "I wouldn't touch either of you."

He darts down the hall a split second before Khalid lunges for him.

FORTY-ONE

HIM

Pulling a cursed sword from my shadows, the same one I'm going to use before I put him in that box I'm going to make with my bare hands, I fling magic at his retreating back.

He spins to the side, avoiding the invisible hand that would have stopped him where he stood. Laughter rings out as he turns to face me, sixty-ish feet away. Raising a hand, he beckons me to him. "Come on. Show me what you've got, kid. I won't even change."

Locking his arms behind his back, he grins at me.

Scarlett screams behind me, urging me to stop, but I ignore her, my focus narrowed on my prey. I dart forward, knowing I'm not a match for his speed. Magic hums in my limbs, coiled and waiting for the moment he gets used to my movements, my slower pace. Then it'll give me that one second advantage to slide across his flesh.

I only need one hit, it doesn't matter where. As long as I can get his blood to spray, I can kill him with my soul magic.

Keeping his hands behind his back, he slips to the side and ducks under the first blow of my blade. I pivot to follow him, and we dance back and forth down the large hall, a business complex full of cubicles, all empty for the day. He laughs as he moves, no hint of breathlessness, no sign of worry as he slides left and right, dodging with a grace that's mocking.

I don't let my anger control me, keeping a steady pace, getting him used to my speed. He's moving before I even think to strike, anticipating where I'll go, but he's getting complacent as he toys with me. He's staying just a split second ahead, lingering to match my abilities.

And in return, I'm learning his.

I shift the focus of my attacks, pushing him away from the center of the open space. When he dances past a door, his hands still behind his back, I jump at the wall and push off it with one leg, using it to gain height. I swing my sword down, my magic grabbing hold of his heart at the same time as it gives me more speed.

The spell doesn't kill him like it would've done any other wolf in the Death Hunt. It simply makes him falter, but that's all I need.

My blade arcs in a perfect line to cut open his chest.

He's suddenly an arm's length away, the smile on his face blooming. Darting back forward as my sword swings down with its momentum, he rakes a clawed hand across my arm, severing the tendon allowing me to hold it. The blade clatters onto the lush carpet, then is kicked away by his foot. Grabbing me by the neck, he slams me into the wall.

I start to pull another blade from my shadow, but he grabs my hand, crushing my fingers. My pulse spikes as I glance at Scarlett, praying she has the good sense to run.

She runs towards us, anger in her eyes. I try to scream at

her to stop, but my vocal chords are being squeezed as I'm lifted off my feet. He turns his head to look at my girl, a smirk of disbelief and enjoyment lighting his face.

Even though he has both his hands on me, he can still hurt her.

I kick at him, but he doesn't even flinch, just twists his lower body so he can kick her as soon as she gets within range. I try desperately to move the fingers on my right hand in a cohesive manner, but the cuts he gave me make the movements sloppy. I can't straighten my thumb or index finger, and if I try to work magic as is, I'll kill all three of us.

Desperate, I open my mouth, but no words come out. No pleas for her to run. No screams to express my agony.

My eyes latch on her, deploring her to turn away, but her gaze is fastened on Antonio.

She gets within kicking distance.

Then drops to her knees as he plants a foot in her solar plexus.

My one working lung is squeezed of its oxygen, and my vision blurs and darkens.

Then it's coming back in a mad rush as I'm dropped to the ground, screams echoing in my ears. I lift my head, trying to figure out what's going on as Antonio pedals away from me, his left shin smoldering from a vial of ifrit potion Scarlett must have hidden on her.

Pride swelling in my chest, I start to crawl to her as she lies on the ground, one arm stretched out and burning with the same magic. Bits of glass stick to her, telling me she slapped him with it rather than threw it, wanting to make sure she made contact.

"*Kira*," I rasp, knowing this is the end for us. My magic is unusable with my broken hands, and I have no DNA with which to actually hurt him with.

"Kali!" Maddox's voice hits me like a bolt of lightning, and I finally realize there are sounds of chaos creeping up from the floors below. Screaming howls of agony followed by shaking walls of magic. Antonio must have smelled my brothers' arrival when we were in the office.

Lunging for him, I try to grab his leg, uncaring if the ifrit potion transfers to me. I just need to keep him here until Maddox can study him enough for his magic.

My three working fingers grab the bottom of his pants, but they're not strong enough to hold him as he kicks me in the face and jerks away.

The sound of snapping bones and ripping cloth pops in my ears for just a second. Then he's running away as his wolf, leaping over cubicles and jumping straight out of a window.

The shatter of glass is a precedent to my screams. I struggle to my feet just as Maddox reaches me, a heavy door saying 'Stairs' closing as he does.

"Drink this," Maddox says, shoving a healing potion in my face. "The rest are downstairs. They'll get him."

"Her first," I say, turning my head. He looks at me long enough for annoyance to flash in his eyes, then turns. "Scarlett, this will heal you. Drink it."

My girl pushes to her knees and grabs the vial with a shaky hand, raising it to her lips. Her eyes find me. "You fucking idiot," she hisses before drinking the potion in full.

Maddox turns back to me, another blue vial uncorked and ready. I tilt my head back, a shudder running through me as the potion does its magic.

"How did you find us?" Screams ricochet around my skull, telling me he is in Antonio's pocket. A false savior whose actions will get me to trust him. Antonio likes to drag deaths out, causing as much pain as he can before granting mercy. I wouldn't put it past him to let Scarlett and I live now just to watch us suffer.

Maddox's jaw tightens. "Micha broke," he murmurs. "I knew then she knew nothing, so we asked Aleric if any of his spies had spotted Talon."

My hairs rising, I stand. Varius torturing Micha himself would've been one thing, but to let Maddox have a go at her... She'll never heal from whatever he did to her. Even I'm not proud enough to think that I wouldn't crack in the end. Maddox's methods are excruciating just to watch.

He normally enjoys it, a twisted little psycho, but there are times when he is forced to endure it just like I am with my role as reaper.

"She broke?" Scarlett asks, her voice trembling. "She survived what Antonio did to her, and then you..." Her face turns white as she looks away, knowing the answer without us needing to voice it. Moving towards her, I cup her face with my left hand. She flinches against me on a ragged exhale but doesn't press for more answers, coming to terms with our fucked up world in her own way.

I study her, so fucking proud over how strong she is. Her bruises and busted lip are free of her skin, but they're stuck in my mind, right at the forefront with every blink. *I hit her.*

I hit her over and over again, breaking with every crack of my knuckles while she stayed strong.

I rest my head against hers. The desire to jump out of the window my-fucking-self makes my muscles tight with the need to move. "I'm sorry, *kira,*" I murmur as my eyes fall to the hand touching her face.

A few minutes ago, it busted her lip. Left ugly bruises across her chest and face.

She says something, but I don't hear her. I don't hear anything even though she shoves at my chest, trying to get my eyes back on her.

I hurt her.

My body shudders.

Noise is nothing but a high-pitched shriek of pain.

I hurt her with my own damn hand.

Hers dig into my shirt and shake me. My eyes snap up,

looking over to where Antonio kicked my sword.

Maddox is gone, undoubtedly having run downstairs to help my brothers.

I should be down there, killing any fucking Death Hunt members still lingering around.

But all I can think about is what her face looked like when I beat it. How the blood welled on her lips. How the bruises darkened her skin. How she closed her eyes after every hit so I couldn't see her pain. How I wasn't strong enough to not need her strength, forcing her to comfort me – the man who was fucking beating her.

My mouth opens, but I don't hear my scream. I want to drop to my knees as agony slices through every tendon and every muscle, as my heart cuts like broken glass with every beat of my fucking pulse.

Tears blurring my eyes, I jerk away when she grabs my left hand, her touch a burn of guilt and shame. This hand beat her.

It'll never touch her again.

Pulling my sword to me through my shadows, I hack off the traitor.

Hurting my girl...
... is an unforgivable sin.

FORTY-TWO

HER

"Khalid!" I jerk forward to grab the sword from him, but it disappears into his shadows. His hand spurts blood into a growing pool that reminds me of the bite I gave him. He almost died then.

He's not going to die now.

Tearing off my shirt, I reach for his arm, but he jerks back from me, his eyes cold and triumphant. "Let it bleed," he hisses.

"You *promised me!*" I scream at him, wanting to slap some fucking sense into him like Ma always did to me.

Balling my fists, *refusing* to continue that cycle, I plea at him with my eyes. "Please let me wrap it."

"It'll just bleed through, and I don't want –" His words twist with so much agony, my heart stops along with his. Adrenaline is the only thing that keeps it pumping. He's turning white, and I fucking know he's too in shock and too damn stubborn that he'll let this go too far.

"Khalid...what you did...it's okay. I'm –"

"It's not." His fingers move in an intricate pattern as he stares at his severed hand. It bursts into flames, and I drop to my knees with my shirt to put it out. *We can reattach it. We can –*

"Leave it," he says, then pulls me to my feet, his fingers strong with a stubbornness that's going to kill him.

"But we can –"

His lips close on mine, and I want to ask him what the fuck he's doing at a time like this, but his tongue is in my mouth, and there is so much desperation flowing down our link, I open for him as tears burn my eyes.

"I'm sorry," he murmurs against my lips. "I'm so sorry."

"It's okay. I'm okay." While he's distracted, I ball up my shirt and press it against his open wrist.

He hisses in pain, then pushes harder against me, still punishing himself for what he did. For what I asked him to do.

His mother's words push tears out of my eyes.

"You will lose more than you ever knew you had and still more will be ripped from you."

"Please let me do this," I beg of him, unable to bear more being ripped from me today. He can be dumb again tomorrow, but right now... "Please, *kira.*"

His lips still against mine, and my pulse skips a beat as I worry he's about to pass out from blood loss. But instead he touches my forehead with his and sighs. "I'm sorry for you still having to take care of me, *kira.*"

"It's what we do. We both take care of each other." I wrap the shirt tight around him. "You saved me from the shadows. I saved you from your dumbass idea." A broken cry rips from me. "You saved me in that office. Antonio giving his word to Talon means shit, and you know it. He just said that to piss you off."

His jaw clenches, and I lean forward to kiss him, my shudder reflecting back in his touch. "I need to make a tourniquet," I say. "I just need a couple of pens to twist the fabric around, and –"

He kisses me more firmly, then steps back, pulling off my shirt. "I'm going to cauterize it," he says before I can beg him to keep it on.

Placing his hand over his wound, he grits his teeth, and it surprises me that he can feel the pain from that when he didn't flinch at all when he cut it off. Maybe the shock is wearing away.

Maybe he's coming back to me. His teeth grind as his nostrils flare, and the smell of a Sunday BBQ wisps in the air between us.

My stomach churns, then growls, and my mouth drops open in horror.

A small chuckle leaves him, pained and short. "Let's get you home," he says, dropping his hand to reach for me, only to immediately sway. I duck under his arm and take his weight.

He tries to pull away, but I rope an arm around him. "You're my *kira* too," I murmur as I turn us and head for the elevator.

Kissing my head, Khalid squeezes my shoulders. "I love you, *kira*."

"I love you too, you crazy ass idiot."

FORTY-THREE

HER

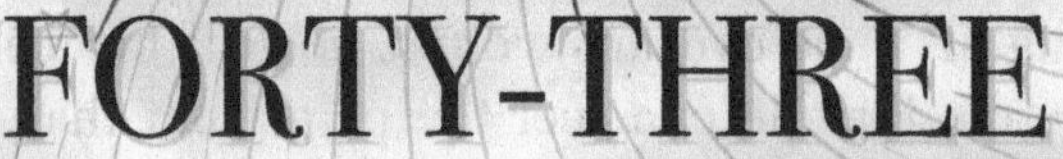

When we step into the elevator, he leans against the wall and I press the button for the bottom floor. I shuffle back to him, my eyes on his cauterized wrist. I hope it hurts like a bitch so he doesn't do it ever again, but his face is a mask of utter indifference and his eyes are on me, seeing how *I* am.

The fucking psycho is going to be the death of me.

My voice cracks as I demand, "Promise me you won't hack off any more pieces of yourself."

"I couldn't live with it attached to me." So flippant. So final.

Emotions slam into me, working my bottom lip. I grab the back of his head and haul his lips down to mine. "Then we'll learn to make it beautiful again together. Promise me. I can't do this if I'm worried about people hurting you all the time and then have to worry about you hurting yourself."

He stares into my eyes as we share breaths of pain for different things. "You're very demanding," he finally says, pulling a twisted chuckle from me even though I don't feel like laughing.

I can still feel Antonio's eyes on me, still see the blur of his fist as he made me look at him. I feel disgusting and dirty and far too naked without my shirt, so I press my chest against Khalid's, seeking his warmth. He wraps his arm around me, and in the bubble of the elevator, we exist for just a moment.

Life as a sup fucking *sucks.*

Sniffing, I rub my face against him, telling myself it's over now. We're alive, and we have all of tomorrow and the rest of our lives to create better days.

My throat tightens as the elevator doors ding open and all the other shit we have to deal with shatters our perfect bubble.

Shit like Antonio still being alive and the impending war with the Death Hunt.

How Khalid still has Talon to kill...

He kisses the top of my head, and I dig my fingers into his shirt, wishing we can carry on existing just in here with no outside forces ripping us to shreds, but life isn't a fairytale.

It's broken and cruel.

"You okay?" he murmurs as he tilts my chin up to look at him.

I nod, my eyes on his.

I will be.

Because he is there, and I am here.

Taking a deep breath, I turn to step out of the elevator, only to immediately stop, my eyes widening at the men standing in the parking lot looking at me.

Six men, their power a palpable crawl across my skin, their judgment a slighter version of Ma's old voice. His brothers. His family.

I hate families.

My heart jumping in my chest, I don't care to stop the

doors as they slide shut.

"*Kira*?" Khalid murmurs as he moves to look at me. "What's wrong?"

"Those are your brothers," I whisper.

"Yeah."

"I've not met them…"

"No."

"This is a hell of a time to meet your family."

He grins. "You could've met them a couple days ago instead of –"

The doors ping open.

"– sucking my cock."

My eyes widen as the air freezes. I pray for the doors to shut again, but ringing laughter shatters frozen time and the faith that it will happen.

Maddox steps into the elevator, invading our bubble.

"Given all the noise you were making," he says looking right at me, "Kali must have one fucking small cock. You need a proper one to fill –"

He laughs as Khalid places a whole hand over his face and shoves him away. Swatting his big brother off him, Maddox grins at me. "Welcome to the family, beautiful."

My cheeks blush, and I am intensely aware that I'm half-naked among these gods.

"Khalid," one says, his voice sharp and chilling, but as we turn, the doors slide back shut.

Maddox bursts out laughing as Khalid grins and I am left in a nervous ball of energy.

"Oh my gods. I love this elevator," Maddox wheezes.

When the doors open again, an older man, mid-thirties stands in front of us, glaring at Khalid. He must be Varius given how 'old' he is.

"Where's your hand?" he asks, and Maddox turns to look at his brother before jumping back.

"He totally had it when I saw him earlier."

The other men step forward, blocking the doors, and the elevator is instantly crowded and claustrophobic. My heart stops as Khalid stills beside me.

"Antonio made me hit her with it," he says softly, still so much pain and hatred burning through him.

Varius' jaw tics as his eyes flatten. "Let's get you two home. Mother is worried sick." He turns, not waiting for an answer.

Threading his fingers through mine, Khalid leads me out of the elevator. "How is she?" he asks.

I squeeze his hand, trying to give him comfort. She is alive and witches heal. Surely...

"Pissed."

One of the red-haired men enters the elevator after we all get out, and I glance at him as he smiles at me. I turn away, ducking my head and focusing back on Khalid.

"Floor eight, Rudy," Khalid says as he turns around to look at the man in the elevator. "There's a cubicle that needs cleaning, as well as a back office."

My fingers grip his hard as Antonio's face haunts me. I shudder, closing my eyes as I shake his vileness away. To hell if I'll let him torture me in his absence.

Rudy gives a two-fingered wave as the doors ping shut for the final time.

We make our way over to two cars parked together. At the sight of a dog bounding over to us, I stop, terrified some innocent bystander is about to catch us. Do witches kill witnesses?

Khalid turns his head to look at me, then directs it down my line of sight. "That's Krypto; he's Leno's eyes," he says as the dog runs up to me and sniffs my hand. I start to pet him, but Khalid pulls me back. "He can also feel through him." He looks at one of his brothers. "Piss off, Leno."

The man laughs, beautiful and serene. His eyes are directed at me, but they're unfocused. *He's blind.* "Aw, just let her pet Krypto once. He loves a good scratch right above his tail."

"Fuck off."

"She's going to scratch it soon anyway," he mutters before opening the passenger door on one of the cars. The dog jumps straight in, sitting on the seat with his tongue hanging out. Walking over to the driver's side, Leno gets in.

I stare at him with an open jaw. *Didn't Khalid just hint that he's blind?*

Maybe he's not fully blind?

It's a spectrum and –

My thoughts brake hard. *He's a witch.* "Krypto's not an eye-seeing dog, is he?"

"He is the most eye-seeing dog out there," Maddox jokes as he slides into the driver seat of the car beside Leno's. Varius opens the door behind him and slides into the backseat. After kissing me with a small grin, Khalid climbs in on the other side. It's going to be a tight fit with me in there with them, so I start to head for the passenger seat, but Khalid grabs my hand and shifts over to the middle..

Smiling at him, I climb in. As he rests his hand on my leg, I close the door. The engine sounds, and Maddox pulls out of the garage. When we exit the underground parking, streetlights glow through the window. Night has come, but the city is far from quiet. It buzzes with a lot more energy and people than St. Augustine.

Jacksonville or Orlando, perhaps?

I don't recognize it, wherever we are.

Turning from the window, I rest my head on Khalid's shoulder. He squeezes my thigh as he talks to his brother.

"Where's Talon?"

"He ran before...we believed Micha."

"Before you tortured her," the words fall out of my lips as I turn to him. "At least have the fucking guts to say it." Tears burning my eyes, I glare at him. I don't want to think of Khalid's family as the same as Antonio, but how can I not when Varius acts like this?

His gaze softens as he looks at me, a flicker of shame that hits me in the stomach. "You're right. We tortured her."

A shudder cuts through me at how easily he says those words.

"Talon planted a lot of evidence against her, and when he came back saying you and Khalid had been taken… I made a decision, and because of that, you're in this car. Alive."

"She saved my life," I whisper. "How could you think she was the traitor when Antonio nearly killed her?"

"He hurt Talon just as bad a few days ago."

Unable to hold his gaze any longer, I look at Khalid. His lips are tight as he studies me, waiting to see if I'll reject his family. *Reject him* given he is a reaper and has done things just as bad.

The bond between us hurts as he waits, and I grab his hand on my leg. I don't want to think about him torturing anyone, hurting people for the sake of doing so rather than as a necessity.

But in the end, there is one simple truth guiding me.

I will follow wherever he goes, learn to accept what needs to be done in order to keep him alive. Micha was hurt in an attempt to save Khalid, and although that does not sit well in my stomach, it sits with a heaviness that mocks my hypocrisy.

Had I also believed she had been the traitor, would I really have tried to protect her? Or would I have stepped aside, deafening myself to her screams?

The truth stares back at me in Varius' eyes. He doesn't force me to speak my discoveries aloud, turning his focus back to Khalid. "I've let everyone know there's a reward if it leads to his capture."

Five points of pressure increase on my thigh, the only sign he gives of the pain of his brother's betrayal. "Have you told Aleric?" Khalid asks. "If Talon puts his weight behind a rebellion –"

"He won't," Maddox cuts in from the front. "Whatever his issue is with Khalid... He loves the rest of us." There is raw desperation in those last few words. "He wouldn't do that to us."

"He made Antonio promise not to hurt us," I say, unable to stop the words from pouring out of my heart. Maddox sounds so broken, and if I can argue Talon's case, then maybe Khalid won't have to kill him either... "What if he was forced to hand us over?"

The utter silence isn't one of relief, and my fingers dig into Khalid's hand. I don't understand how what I said has made matters worse.

Turning his hand upright to hold mine, Khalid exhales softly. "You cannot save him, *kira*. His crimes have been committed."

"But why does that mean he has to die?" *Why does that mean you have to do it?*

He's already been through so much, and I can feel the agony he's trying to hide, it seeping down our bond with a crippling pain despite the small volume.

"If Varius shows weakness by letting him live, another rebellion will rise regardless of whether he's behind it or not. Varius is not accepted by everyone in this Family due to his curse." He pauses, letting his words seep into me. Or maybe it's so they can seep into him, convincing him that he has to do this. "And I'm certain he told Antonio about you that night you were with the WALL. There's no other way for him to have found you."

That night in the woods slams back into me. All those deaths. The gun in my face. The discovery of Daniel and Ma. Shuddering, I swallow my defense of Talon. There is nothing I can say to save Khalid from killing him. He put me in harm's way. Regardless of why, that is unforgivable in my love's eyes.

Leaning over, he kisses me, and I open for him despite the audience in the car.

"Thank you for loving me," he whispers so softly I'd be certain I imagined it if not for the flow of emotions riding hard through our bond.

Sliding my tongue against his, I break for what he is about to go through. I can't do anything to stop it. I can only wait for him to come back to me after and try to help him bear his pain.

That isn't good enough.

I don't want him to do this alone like he's done it every time.

"Is there a way we can complete our blood bond before you go?" I ask against his lips, my cheeks heating over his two brothers being able to hear me. They'll partake in the final ritual, both coming inside me, along with the others. But I need to somehow be there for Khalid, and given how much we can feel of each other now, perhaps when we're fully bonded, I can be there for him in a way that is good enough.

He tenses on a shudder. "*Kira*...I don't want you to feel it when I kill him."

"And I don't want you to do it alone. You always do it alone, but you're not alone now. You have me." Lifting his hand to my chest, I place it against my thundering pulse. "You're my *kira* too, remember? Please let me be there for you."

He holds my gaze for a long moment, trapping the air in my lungs as I'm terrified he'll refuse me. I need to do this. He cut off his hand for me. I can't not do this. *Please.*

My stomach twists as the seconds drag on.

Then he's kissing me, his fingers digging into my chest. "I love you," he murmurs, his tongue sweeping back into my mouth before I can respond. His hand dips down my breast and under my bra. I tense with the awareness of his brothers, then force myself to relax. They're about to do a lot more than watch...

"So we can do it?" I ask, turning my head, needing to hear his answer as hope waits with bated breath.

He pulls back, trailing his hand down to my thigh. "If Varius lets me borrow his dormant magic, then yes, we can potentially do it without killing you and draining me." My eyes flick to Varius.

He nods subtly. "Someone will need to be the conduit, but you have my blessing to drain all of it if you so need."

"Tomorrow then?" I push, not wanting to give him the chance to change his mind or come up with a reason to say no.

A smile tugging at his lips, he says, "I would love to be fully bonded to you, *kira*."

Dragging him back to me, I kiss him hard.

FORTY-FOUR

HER

As soon as we arrive at the house, Sau comes out to greet us using a cane. "I told you to stay in bed," Varius says as he steps out of the car.

I hurry out so Khalid can go to his mother, not wanting to get into the middle of a family reunion when I'm not really a part of it.

Rolling her eyes, she jabs the cane at him. "And I told you, I'll be a thousand and still have the power to shove you back up my vagina."

My eyes widen as the boys groan.

"Now move out of my way so I can see Scarlett."

Khalid drags me forward, and I shift uncomfortably under her gaze, not knowing how to react to a mother who actually cares. Her eyes flash with sorrow as she takes in my shirtless chest.

"I'm so sorry I didn't protect you, Scarlett."

"He didn't rape me," I blurt, not wanting her to blame herself and cut off some body part like Khalid did.

Relief softens her face as she pulls me into a hug. "You know, when I said being a woman in this family wouldn't be easy, I didn't expect you to learn that this quickly."

"You totally jinxed it, bruh," Maddox says as he comes up beside her, not at all sensitive to the guilt clear on her shoulders.

Releasing me, she turns to whack him in the side with her cane, tears in her eyes. But there's a smile on her lips that confuses me. "If you didn't come out of my own vagina, I'd swear you were adopted. Such a disrespectful little shit."

Laughing, he envelopes her and lifts her into the air. "Glad to see you're okay, ma," he says softly, his voice cracking.

She sags against him as she places her arms around him.

"You too." She clears her throat. "Now let me go so I can see Khalid."

When he puts her down, she turns to him, her eyes on his missing hand. Then they lift to his face and she studies him for a long moment. Stepping forward, she cups his cheek. "We will kill him for this," she whispers.

"*I* will kill him," he corrects, and I squeeze his hand.

"No...*we* will." Antonio might be a werewolf where I'm just a mere human. He might be faster and stronger than most, but he hurt Khalid, and I *will* find a way to make him pay for that.

My love looks at me, but he must see the steel in my eyes, or perhaps he can feel my refusal to let this go. Either way, he nods, then pulls me to his side.

"I'm glad he has you, Scarlett," his mother says with a smile that preludes tears. Grabbing me in another hug, she whispers, "Welcome to the family."

FORTY-FIVE

HER

Holding a plate of hot breakfast, I knock on Micha's door. I wanted to check in on her last night and thank her for saving me, but Sau told me she was still healing over what Maddox had done to her.

My fingers grip the warm glass as I remember the look in Sau's eyes when those words passed her lips. Whatever Maddox had done to her couldn't be healed with magic.

"Micha?" I murmur. "It's me – Scarlett. I brought you breakfast."

I wait, but there's no answer. Shifting on my feet, I wait a bit longer.

Still nothing.

"I just wanted to thank you for protecting me," I say through the wooden door. "What Antonio did... I thought he killed you, and I'm really happy you're alive."

Nothing but silence answers me, and my heart twists as I dig my toes into the lush carpet of the hall. "Um..." I move the plate to one hand as I squat down in front of the door.

"This is my number." I push the scrap of paper I wrote on earlier through the crack. "If you want to talk or for me to get you something so you don't have to come out, just text me, okay?" I hated going through the house when I didn't feel wanted at home; I can't imagine how she feels about potentially running into the man who tortured her and the one –her *fiance*– who gave the order.

The fact that he is still her fiance is something I can't wrap my head around. I know she likes him, but fuck.

"Okay, well, I'll just leave this plate here for you if you want to grab it after I'm gone." Placing it down on the floor, I stand, and with one last lingering look at the door, I head down the hall and into the kitchen.

The boys and their mother are still sitting around the table, and I take my place beside Khalid. Nerves eat away at my stomach, so I just push my food around. Although I'm excited to complete the bond today, the fact that it'll end with all of his brothers coming inside me is making me low-key panic. I barely know them, and I haven't even talked to half of them. I'm not entirely sure if that makes it better or worse. Given I'm going to live with them after, perhaps worse.

Oh God, what if I make a fool of myself?

Placing his fork on his plate, Khalid squeezes my thigh. "You okay?" he asks as he looks at me.

I nod, but I know he can tell I'm lying. We shared more blood last night and more again this morning. I can feel his excitement mixed with jealous possessiveness, and he can undoubtedly feel my fear that they will be so turned off when I'm naked that they won't be able to finish.

And then what will happen?

My face feels hot and cold all at once, and my knuckles turn white on my fork.

"If you want to wait –"

I shake my head. "No, I want to do this today." Not just

because I want to be there for him in some way when he goes to kill Talon, but because *I* want it. A bond is forever, and I want to wake up every day hearing him laugh and seeing those intense eyes of his drilling into me. I want a future not tainted by Antonio, which means living as long as a witch does because the fucker is going to be a bitch to kill, I just know it.

A shudder rips through me as I face the final reason. The real reason that's making me want to do this now rather than in a few weeks' time, which wouldn't require him siphoning off Varius' dormant magic.

He could die at any moment. They might have recast the spell protecting this house, but the werewolves broke it once. Even if Talon is actually on the run and not just hiding at Antonio's like Varius suspects...there are more witches he could be using. People have turned on their own people all throughout history, and Khalid has filled me in on all the attempts made inside this very Family.

It's why the tension in the car didn't ease after I tried to defend Talon for Khalid's sake. Their brother wanting us to be unharmed meant he had turned on Varius like all the others. Varius' face never once changed during that car ride —or even in all the time after— but that must hurt him, knowing he is the sole reason for Talon's betrayal.

So I want to be connected to Khalid before it's too late. I don't want to wait a few weeks when in only a few days, I have seen so much death.

Smiling at him, I kiss his cheek, then pick up a forkful of eggs so he truly knows I'm okay. He watches me eat a few bites before continuing his own meal.

As conversation flows around us, I sweep my eyes around the table. Sau sits to the right of me, talking to one of the twins across the table about the girl he's recently entered an arranged marriage with. Though they've been 'just friends' since they were children, it's clear he has a thing for her, his cheeks blushing every time his mother mentions her name.

"And how is Stormie? I haven't seen Stormie since she caught you with that girl? What was her name?"

His twin jumps in. "Adeline."

"I wasn't *with* Adeline," he mutters as he stabs a piece of toast. "We were going over her grandma's grimoire and summoned a demon that shoved me onto her."

"With your pants down." His twin grins.

"It was a fucking demon. They're not exactly nice."

"Uh huh."

He shoves him. "She had her clothes on."

His twin laughs. "Because your game is shit."

"Oh fuck off."

Sau smiles at them before looking at me. "Stormie is the daughter of an old friend long gone, bless her. She'll be moving in in a few weeks, perhaps sooner." She doesn't say it's because of the coming war, how alliances must be made quickly, but it's in her eyes.

Ducking my head, I concentrate on my breakfast, still not yet comfortable being a mother's focus. A few seconds later, after her attention returns to the twins, I continue down the table. Maddox sits beside her, talking to Rudy in sign language. I follow his hands for a bit, but the only phrase I know is 'fuck you' because who hasn't seen that performance on Youtube? The 'fuck you' is signed with wide grins, and I'm slowly getting what it means to have a family that truly cares about each other.

Lots of cursing and laughter.

Making a note to get Khalid to teach me sign language (or maybe even Rudy himself), I skip over the twins and rest on Krypto. He's sitting in Talon's chair so it doesn't sit empty, wolfing down a plate of bacon. His ears are big and pointy, and a smile curls my lips just looking at him. Khalid still hasn't let me pet him yet, but one of these days I'm going to give him a head pat or ear scratch. He is simply way too cute not to. And those ears!

My smile widens as my gaze is pulled back to them.

He finishes his plate, then hops down to help himself to his bowl of water. While his 'eyes' aren't on me, I look at Leno. He is terrifyingly handsome with a bit of scruff on his face. His strong jaw and nose are split by three pink slashes running from top left to bottom right. Whatever wolf cut him open had been right handed.

I wonder if that wolf was at the office building last night. I didn't see any in the garage, but when Maddox had run up the stairs, I'd heard commotion on his tail. I wonder where all the bodies went. My eyes flick back to Rudy. He is the cleaner. Maybe he just dropped them into his shadow for all those monsters to eat?

My stomach twists, and I reach for Khalid's leg as I recall biting his throat. I can't believe I'd been so naive to think he could heal from that.

Granted, I saw Antonio heal from what seemed like a hundred bullets that night in the woods... Or maybe they had never hit him, his speed so fucking fast.

My pulse spikes at the thought of Khalid fighting him again. Antonio wasn't even trying in that office, keeping his hands behind his back.

But I have to trust that together these brothers will win. Otherwise...

My throat closes, and my fork clatters on the table. Khalid places his hand on my thigh as the table stops to look at me.

"Thinking of how big my cock is, aren't cha?" Maddox asks, cutting through my pain and making me blush like mad.

Khalid throws him a look, but I laugh as I shake my head. They're all crazy. His whole family is fucking crazy.

"I was thinking about what I would do when I couldn't

find it." The words blurt out of me, and I freeze in utter horror. *I did not just say that.*

The table erupts into laughter, and Khalid squeezes my thigh. I look at him beneath a curtain of hair, lighting up at the look on his face.

This was what I wanted.

A million mornings like this.

Holding his hand, I gain the courage to sneak a peek at Maddox.

He's laughing with the rest of them. His eyes on mine, he promises, "I'm going to enjoy making you pay for that." My cheeks burn madly as he flicks out his tongue.

"Don't flirt with my girl," Khalid hisses.

"Oh, so I can put my dick in her, but I can't –" He yelps as he hugs his side, and I know Khalid has hit him with his magic.

His grin doesn't fade though. If anything, it grows, and unable to help myself, I giggle.

Khalid turns to me, but before he can say anything, the others at the table start up with their own vulgar offers. My giggle turns into full on laughter even as the heat in my cheeks spreads all the way down my neck.

A snort comes out of me, and I throw a hand over my mouth. Khalid yanks it down; no one else seems to even notice.

My smile spreads as I look at him, my body relaxing.

His eyes are dry as he curses his brothers, but there's a grin on his lips, and I know he loves them all.

Perhaps, one day, they can all love me like this too.

FORTY-SIX

HER

My belly is full of butterflies as I step into our room. His brothers all wait outside in the hall, blindfolded, as he closes the door. Even Leno is wearing a black mask per Khalid's orders – him not wanting any of them to see me. Another one dangles from his fingers, but I won't wear it until he's finished with me.

My lips parting, I shuffle back towards the bed as he walks towards me. His cock is hard and prominent under his pants, and I'm growing wet with every step we take together. I can feel his desire as if it's my own, building me up as I fall back onto the mattress. My hands go to my pants as I shirk them off me, then to my shirt.

"Spread yourself for me, *kira*," he says as he drops to his knees beside the bed.

Heart pounding with the anticipation of what's going to happen –both his head between my legs and the train of his brothers after he's done– I spread my legs on a hot exhale.

I palm my breasts after throwing away my shirt and bra.

He dips his head between my thighs, and I quiver as he picks up one leg and puts it over his shoulder. When the other one is lifted, forcing me to lean back, my pussy clenches.

"Now *spread yourself*, love. Let me see how beautiful you are."

Reaching beneath my belly, I pinch both lips and open them to his gaze. He groans as he looks his fill. Then he leans forward and kisses my thighs, working up from my knees as he alternates between one and the other.

A kiss on the left.

A long lick up the right.

Another kiss on the left a bit higher...

Chills race down my back as Khalid goes slowly, the anticipation killing me by the time he reaches the V of my thighs. Passing my lips, he kisses my stomach, and I twist on a whimper, trying to control where his next kiss goes.

A low rumble vibrates from his chest as he moves his lips back down my leg. Crying out in frustration, I push a finger inside myself, and his head snaps up in an instant, his wet tongue pushing me aside as he takes what's his. My head twists as I shudder on a wave of ecstasy.

I hold myself open wide for him. His shoulder bumps against my leg as he jerks himself off. I whimper with the need to see him, to feel the stroke of it, and I close my eyes to concentrate on our bond.

My cock jumps in my hand. Pleasure builds tight and focused as my lips work against my girl's pussy.

Opening my eyes, I gasp, the feeling overwhelming, and an orgasm rips through me as he sucks on my clit. I roll my hips against him, knowing the quick release was just the foreplay.

My pulse pounds as I sit up. He lifts his head, kissing his way up to my breasts, where he lingers for a moment before claiming my lips. As we share breath in rapid pants, he asks,

"Are you ready to begin?"

I nod, not quite sure how this will go but knowing he will tell me. I have come to anticipate his dirty words, my body heating just from the wicked curl of his lips that precedes him telling me what he's going to do to me.

Dipping his head to my neck, he trails his lips across my skin. His tongue swirls at the base of it, and he sucks a mark onto me. "I will fuck your pussy deep and hard, *kira,* until we rise to the edge three times. You must hold it back until I tell you."

He kisses the other side of my neck as his hand goes between my legs. He pushes a long finger inside me while raising his other hand to my breast before remembering he doesn't have one. His arm hangs on threads of pain between us, and I thread my fingers into his hair as I close my eyes and kiss the top of his head. "Oh, *kira...*" I cry as the memory of him hacking it off is overwhelmed only by the scream that ripped through him at the time.

So animalistic.

So raw.

So *broken...*

He lifts his head to kiss me, and I feel it through our bond. There is no regret over losing it, only that it hurt me. I kiss him softly as he strokes me slowly, rebuilding our pleasure through the lingering pain.

"Focus on how good you feel," he says as he curls his finger, hitting that special spot. "We have a whole lifetime together. Antonio won't take that away from us."

Captured tears in my throat, I nod. I will not break from what he did to us. I will learn everything I can about werewolves. I will learn how to make potions and fight alongside his family. I will protect my *kira* as he protects me.

We will have our bright future if I have to paint it with the bright red colors of Antonio's corpse.

Kissing Khalid hard, I rock my hips against his hand.

"That's it. Good girl, ride me like you own me."

My breaths come faster as I grab hold of his shoulders, my heart pounding, my body slick with sweat. His tongue plays with mine before moving over to my ear.

"After we come together, I will scoop my cum out of your pussy and use it to draw a shadow rune on your skin."

His teeth latch down on my lobe as he withdraws his fingers and wipes my wetness across my breasts. He flicks his tongue against me before releasing my ear to lick the cum he spread on my nipples.

I arch against him, my pussy clenching in a need to be filled.

"Then I will blindfold you and open the door so one of my brothers can enter."

He sucks a nipple into his mouth as he pushes me back onto the mattress, then crawls on top of me. Taking off his clothes, he looks down at me with hot eyes. His teeth find my left breast as he guides his cock to my aching hole.

"They will take turns fucking your mouth and ass" –he slams in, making me scream as he grunts– "one at a time, the door closing between each."

My pussy clenches around him, loving the feel of his cock filling me in hard thrusts that take me to the edge. I clutch his ass as he hammers into me, his lips on my neck.

"You will play with yourself while they fuck you." He flicks my clit, and I jerk on a low moan. "You will come with them." He pinches it, then rolls it between his fingers, and I'm on the edge of exploding with one more thrust.

He pauses, leaving me whimpering desperately as my whole body shakes and my head thrashes from side to side.

"Don't come yet, *kira*. Focus on our bond. You want it, don't you, baby?"

I nod as tears seep out of my eyes, my orgasm so fucking close, if he breathes on me, I'll shatter. Clenching my teeth,

I tremble as I wait for it to subside. My body is slick with sweat, my head fuzzy. I open my eyes to see him smiling at me a second before he leans down to kiss me.

His hand cups my breast, toying with its nipple as he stays still inside me. With just a few flicks, I'm back on the verge, crying as I struggle not to come.

But his cock is jerking inside me with his own control, and each flex is enough to make me a mess of putty in his arms.

Khalid presses his palm over my nipple, stopping his caresses as I come back down. Heavy breaths feather across my skin as his muscles bunch and his jaw clenches.

"Fuck, baby, you're going to make me come if you keep looking at me like that."

He groans as he rocks his hips, and the second of downtime I just managed to gain shatters on a cry.

"*Khalid, please*," I beg. "Let me come already. I want to feel your cock ramming into me and your balls slapping against my pussy. Please –"

He covers my mouth with his hand. "Stop talking, *kira*. I need to deny you one more time."

"Why?" I mumble against his palm, tears falling down my face.

He grunts something about magic and sacrifice and the price to pay, but all I hear is the blood rushing around in my skull begging me to rub myself on his cock.

I rock my hips, and he sucks in a pained hiss. His hand leaves my mouth to twist its fingers in the air, and magic binds me completely still.

Crying in frustration, I will my body to move, but it stays locked in place. He leaves me suspended on the cusp for a long moment, and then when I finally start to step back from the edge, he starts up again, moving with fast jerks that have my lungs emptying on screams.

"That's it, sweet girl. Scream so they can hear you. Can

you imagine them gripping their cocks as they wait?"

He slams into me, possessive and raw, and I'm forced to just take it all. My body trembles beneath the magic, heating with the touch of an orgasm.

"They're going to slide into your ass and fuck your pretty little mouth."

He groans as he shoves two fingers between my lips.

Stars blind my vision as electricity shoots up my spine.

But just as I'm about to topple over the edge, he stops and collapses against me, his chest rapidly moving against mine.

"Last one, baby, hold it back."

Wet streaks of frustration fall down the sides of my face, dampening the pillow beneath my head. He pushes bits of his control through our budding bond, and I latch onto them, needing him to help me.

His lips press gently all across my face as he releases the magic binding me.

Rolling me on top of him, he sits me up, then leans up to lick my breasts. "Push them together for me so I can suck on both your nipples."

I do as he asks, crying out as he does what he said he would.

"Ride me until we come," he rasps as his hand grips my ass and lifts.

Holding his head to me, I lift my hips and slam back down, going as fast as the ragged breaths leaving me. He groans as he holds my nipples between his teeth.

"Tell me when you're going to come." His words are broken gasps that tell me he's close. My nails dig into his back, scratching marks of ownership into what's mine.

As my pussy lifts up and down his cock, I rub my clit with one hand. Stars explode down my back. "I'm going to come," I moan, squeezing my eyes shut as the feeling of it overwhelms me.

He jerks up into me as I fall down onto him, and with a shared cry, we shatter with a blinding heat that touches our very souls, the bond strengthening as he shoots his cum into me.

His back arched, his head back, he holds me to him as he groans.

I pepper kisses across his face. His arms finally relax around me, and then he flips me over so I'm beneath him. My eyes widen at how easily he moves me, and he lies above me with a wicked grin.

"You're so fucking beautiful when you come." He kisses my nose, then both cheeks, then my lips. "I love it when you scream for me."

His tongue dances with mine as I sigh against him. "I love it when you make me."

A rumble of content envelopes me, and I close my eyes, just basking in the feel of him.

The lifetime we have might be cut short in war. Talon's death might destroy him, taking him from me as he still lives. His obsession with Antonio might do the same. But for now, I have all of him, and I cling to that with tight arms. "I love you," I whisper as he lies on top of me, his heavy weight a beautiful thing to experience.

"I love you too, *kira*." He kisses me gently as he slides out of me. Lowering his head, he makes his way down to my filled pussy and pushes his fingers inside. Scooping out his cum, he trails it down my thighs, wetting them with his mark. Then he trails some across the mound of my pussy, drawing the shape of a circle with a line through it. After that, I lose track without being able to see it.

Kissing the lips of my pussy, he then stands and grabs the blindfold off the floor where he dropped it. His gaze on mine, he smiles. "When I see your pretty blue eyes again, we'll be nearly bonded."

Pure joy explodes in my chest, leaking out through a

smile I can't stop. We grin at each other like lovesick idiots, feeding off the happiness spreading through every inch off us.

"And then we'll have a lifetime together."

He nods. "Us and our dozen children."

"*Dozen?*"

"Mmm. I won't be able to help myself from fucking you every day when you're swollen with my seed."

My breath shudders out of me, and although I can feel his desire pushing through me, making me want what he does, Micha's words curb it just enough for me to say, "Um...can we hold off on that for a moment? So it can be just us for a while?"

I hold my breath, but the terror from earlier, that he would reject me and I would be alone if I expressed my different desires isn't there anymore. I know he loves me, *me,* not an illusion of some obsession.

He frowns, then sighs, but his smile comes back as he leans over me. "For a year. But then I'm filling you with my children, *kira.*" He places his hand on my belly, and the raw need in his eyes has me almost going back on my own words.

Swallowing hard, I nod. "One year," I breathe. I'll figure out how to be a good mom by then.

His face softening, he kisses me, and I know he can feel my nerves. "You're nothing like your mother, *kira.* She never loved anyone, and you have so much love to give."

He cups my breast, pushing his fingers against the beat of my heart. Staring into my eyes, he smiles, then rises as he lifts the blindfold to my eyes. "Now put this on for me so we can complete the bond."

Sinking down between my legs as I tie it around my head, he presses his lips against my inner thigh. He kisses it, then bites down hard, breaking skin. Blood flows from me, and a rush of adrenaline pumps down my spine. I lie back, my eyes in darkness as he presses his cock against the wound. I know he's cut his tip, but he didn't want me to see the blood, knowing I am nowhere near over the amount that poured from him when I bit his neck.

My hands clench into fists at my sides, and I breathe deep to get myself to relax them. Another rune is drawn onto my pussy, this time with blood. Then he stands and kisses my lips, his tongue stroking mine.

"I'm going to let one in now," he murmurs. His warmth leaves me.

Then the sound of the door opens.

My ears strain as I listen for any noise.

But whoever it is moves in utter silence.

The door closes, leaving just the two of us.

My heart pounding, I wet my lips, and a cock pushes against them. It's not as thick as Khalid's, but it's just as demanding. Diving into me, a groan sounds above. Rough hands dig into my hair, twisting me to face him better as he stands beside the bed.

He shoves in deep and fast, nearly choking me as he fucks me. My nostrils flare as I grab at his hands, trying to breathe. He doesn't let go, doesn't ease up, and despite the slight rise of panic, heat blossoms in my belly over his rough demeanor. Khalid would never treat me like this, with no thought to my pleasure, but there is something about being used like some *thing* that makes my thighs clench tight. Releasing his hand, I slide a finger into my pussy as I press my palm against my clit. My hips buck against my hand as he fucks my mouth like I'm some dirty little whore.

Heat builds in my cheeks as shame and excitement slam through me with every thrust of his cock down my throat. My eyes watering beneath my blindfold, I listen to his grunts of pleasure as I make my own.

My toes curling, I cup my breast with my other hand, the agreed upon signal that I am close to coming so we can come together. Khalid doesn't want us talking to each other, doesn't want me knowing who is doing what as he knows I would then be too embarrassed to face them in the morning.

But there is a hot allure to not knowing, and as his hands tighten in my hair and he holds my nose to his stomach, just the knowledge that he is going to come without once trying to please me makes me erupt all over my fingers.

A salty fountain cascades down my throat, forcing me to swallow so I don't choke, but a lot of it dribbles down my chin regardless, his cock filling much of my mouth. He pulls out on a grunt, and then his fingers are on my skin, tracing that same rune.

When he steps back, power sweeps through me, tying me to Khalid with a pulse of electricity that has me wet. I can feel his jealousy as his brother steps from the room, but I can also feel his surprised arousal over listening to us on the other side of the door.

This was always going to be a one time thing, a needed train ride that would allow us to bond for life, but as the door opens again, I wonder if this is just the beginning of a voyage we'll both explore together.

My thoughts spasming as the door clicks shut, I listen to the sound of footsteps coming closer. They're slow and uncertain, their owner not used to being blind or in this room. My breath quickens as my mind races with which one of his brothers it is, but I quickly kill that mystery. I don't want to know, and Khalid doesn't want me to either.

He gropes his way around my body, trailing his hands up to my face. His cock is wet with precum already, and it rubs across my lips. When he pushes in, the cold feel of metal on the top of my mouth and tongue makes me jerk back in shock. He doesn't push into me like his brother did, content to wait for me to trace my tongue across his cock and explore his apadravya piercing.

A metal ball sits on the top and another hangs on the

underside – a barbell vertically through his head. Licking my lips, I take him in slowly, and his grip tightens on my hair but doesn't command.

He seeks to give pleasure as much as to take, and I take my time getting used to the metal inside my mouth.

He groans as I suck him deep, and my hand feathers to my pussy. Two fingers go inside me as his cock starts to move, and together we ride to a slow-building orgasm.

When he leaves, the rune drawn, I press my tongue to the roof of my mouth, still imagining the feel of his barbell. I want to feel one inside me, and I start rubbing my clit before the door opens for a third time.

The smell of lube mixes with the sex lingering in the air, and my thighs clench as anticipation hits me. Hands grab my ankles and guide me onto my stomach, my legs over the side of the bed, my knees hanging. Heavy breaths move the sheet against my face, and my fingers twist in the material as the man pushes lube into my ass.

His cock soon follows, stretching me to the point of pain before fading into pleasure. Gasping, I push back against him as he rides me gently, then faster and faster until the slaps of our hips bang like explosions. My pussy rubs against the edge of the bed as he takes me over, and I reach back to grab his hip, letting him know I'm close.

Heat rips through me as we come, and my legs collapse beneath my weight. He sags on top of me, his lips against my shoulder as he breathes heavily. Straightening, he slides out and draws the rune on me with his cum.

The door shuts.

I shudder, not moving from my position, my body hot and sweaty and needing a bit of reprieve.

But the door opens again, and my ass is used before I can catch a breath. My eyes stay closed as he rams hard from the start, and the bed slams against the wall. I reach out for Khalid, wanting to fall asleep with his presence around me, but he pushes arousal down our bond, and I remember I'm supposed to come with each one of them.

But fuck, my body is drained. Although Khalid and I have gone longer than this, the fact is that it isn't Khalid in here with me. The connection is missing.

A smirk of pride fills me, chasing away some of his jealousy, and I can almost feel the puff of his chest as he stands outside the door, knowing I'm about to fall asleep on his brother.

Rolling my lips in, I try to concentrate on what I'm feeling. His cock moves with a rhythm of pleasure, and I shift my hips to get my pussy to rub against the mattress again. Picturing Khalid up my ass, I sigh dreamily against the sheets, my arousal rising.

"That's it. Good girl. You're going to come for me three more times, aren't you?"

I moan in answer as his words coax me into obeying. His name slips from my lips, and his brother stills for a second before taking one hand off my hip and ramming back into me.

My eyes pop open as my cheeks heat. *He did not just do that...*

His cock pushes balls deep before sliding back out, and he grunts as his right hand tightens. He's going to come, and I slip a hand between my legs as I work myself fast. The orgasm isn't strong in any sense of the word, but it is enough to pay the price of magic.

I wonder how this ritual came about as he draws the rune on my ass cheek. Khalid mentioned something about the shadow magic being split amongst his brothers when I asked earlier, but I wasn't paying much attention.

Whistling, the man behind me leaves, and though I've never heard Maddox whistle, I know without a doubt that was him. I bury my face in the sheets as the door opens.

The next brother enters, and he pulls me off the bed to

guide me onto my hands and knees. Kneeling behind me, he pushes into me. It's nothing special...until it fucking vibrates, and I jerk with a small scream.

He laughs as he fucks me, a soft noise he's trying to hold in so I can't tell who he is. But although I don't know which twin is riding me right now, I know it's one of them because one, Khalid told me they have telekinesis, and two, another set of hands are digging into my hair and pulling my mouth onto his cock.

As I'm spit-roasted between them, my fingers curl into the floor. Heat blossoms in my belly, flowing out to every limb. My body tenses, trying to milk another orgasm out of me so soon after the last. Six back to back has been utterly draining, but with their cocks spearing me at both ends, the pleasure builds until I'm a mess in their hands.

Reaching a hand up, I squeeze my breast quickly. My arm falls to the floor as I push backwards, my eyes closing beneath the blindfold.

The twin shoves deep into my ass and holds, and his brother does the same in my mouth a second later. As cum flows into me, I shudder on my own release, then drop to the floor as they slide out of me. Panting heavily, I stay in that position as they leave.

The door shuts, and then the mask is being pulled off me, and hot, intense eyes drill into me. They roam around my body, taking in all the cum covering me, and I suck in a breath as my arousal stretches with a lazy purr. Despite the seven orgasms I just experienced, as soon as I touch him, I want more.

"Are you ready for the final part?" he asks as he lies down beside me. Hot cum dribbles out of my ass as I shiver. My heart beating wildly, I look into his eyes. This is the part where we exchange enough blood to nearly drain us. It can't be avoided, and one of his brothers plus Varius will be with us, Khalid needing his power to not die from being weakened with my non-magic blood inside him.

Cupping his cheek, I nod, trying to ignore the images flashing through my eyes of him bleeding out in front of me.

He leans into my palm, his eyes softening. "Magic can be beautiful, *kira*. I want to show you that."

I nod, this time stronger, wanting to take that final step with him. To me, we're already bonded. Through trauma. Through love. Through an obsession that I refuse to give up or let that asshole Antonio take.

He is mine.

My *kira*.

My everything.

And I will not leave him alone when he goes to kill Talon.

He's never going to be alone again.

Tears clogging my throat, I lean in to kiss him just as he does the same to me. His tongue sweeps inside my mouth, a little growl coming from him as he tastes a touch that isn't his on me.

Placing my hand against his chest, I smile shyly. "I said your name at one point."

He stills before a slow grin spreads across his face.

"I think it might've been with Maddox."

"Serves the little shit right. Cocky fucking bastard."

I roll my lips in, shaking my head and hiding behind my curtain of hair. "How am I ever going to face him?"

"With a fair amount of desire to stab him, I imagine. It's a common feeling shared in this household."

I giggle even as I groan with the thought of seeing him.

"You're so fucking beautiful when you laugh."

A blush crimsons my cheeks, heated from the warmth spreading inside me. "You make me feel beautiful."

"You *are* beautiful, Scarlett. Say it."

My tongue feels heavy in my mouth as all of Ma's words come back to me.

Eat a salad, Gen.
You're fucking disgusting, Gen.
You make people want to stop eating, Gen.
Fuck you, Ma.

"I'm beautiful," I whisper, and those two words grab a part of me that was broken inside. "I'm beautiful," I say stronger as those two halves go back together. They're still cracked and only held on by weak glue, but the glue will bind with time, strengthening as Khalid and I grow old together.

Tears shimmer in his eyes as he kisses me, not stopping this time when his tongue sweeps inside my mouth. He rolls on top of me, and I instinctively spread my legs. He builds us up slowly as he makes love to me, his thrusts long and languid, his lips soft and slow.

I sigh against his mouth as I wrap my arms around him. The pleasure builds into a beautiful heat before it sweeps us over the edge like the lapping of the ocean at the beach.

We hold each other for a few minutes before he stands and helps me up alongside him. Pulling a robe out of the closet, he wraps it around me, then opens the bedroom door to show Varius and Maddox.

My cheeks burst into flames as their youngest brother grins at me and hides his left hand behind his back, letting me know for certain it was him.

"You picked Maddox?" I ask Khalid, wondering why the hell he didn't tell me before opening the door.

"I did," Varius says. "Given he can shift into me, he has the best chance of being the conduit."

"Given he can what?" I ask blankly.

"Watch this." Maddox cracks his neck side to side, then shakes out his arms as he hops from foot to foot. Shadows swirl around him, and I take a step back, the darkness assaulting my memories.

Khalid's hand finds mine, and he squeezes it in silent

comfort. I root my legs, knowing he won't let them hurt me. But then they nearly give out as Maddox's body tears apart, skin ripping and bones breaking. When it's over, he looks exactly like Varius though, and I blink rapidly, my brain screaming and pointing at him as it hops up and down.

"Can you do that with anyone?"

He cracks his neck. "If I've studied them enough, yeah. I can change into Khalid if you'd li– Ow!"

"Stop wasting magic," Varius says, his words directed at Khalid, who's glaring at his younger brother.

Maddox grins, but he holds his hands up in a sign of peace. Then he claps and rubs them together. "All right, let's get this baby started."

The air electrifies, raising the hairs on my arms and neck as he places one hand on Varius and the other on Khalid.

"You ready?" Khalid asks, his voice soft with worry.

I think about the blood pouring out of his neck and arm, and how much more I'm about to see. My eyes search his face as he waits patiently for me to decide.

Taking a deep breath, I nod.

When he pulls a knife out of his shadow, I tense. After a quick slice across his chest, it's gone again, but my pulse still pounds in memory of his screams.

But after this, he'll never doubt my love for him. He'll never be consumed by his own grief. I will help him love all parts of himself just like he does me.

I step close so he can reopen the wound he made on my thigh. As our blood flows into the air, it circulates between us, and I am hit with a burst of power that shocks my every nerve. I fall against him, gasping, and two strong hands hold me up as Khalid weakens from my human blood inside of him.

Fire erupts like a volcano. My body shakes like the splitting of Pangea – monumental tremors that change my world. Raw primal magic flows through my veins, beading sweat along my body.

A blue veil shimmers in the air surrounding us, and my breaths come out hard and fast.

I've never felt so alive, so full of emotions that it makes me want to fall to my knees and cry, overwhelmed by the beauty being shared between us.

Khalid kisses my neck as the magic dissipates, the air losing its blue sheen. I hold him close, tears pooling in my eyes over just how beautiful magic can be.

I feel like I've just watched nature itself blossom back into life after being bombed with radiation.

As the door shuts, Maddox and Varius leaving us to be alone, I thread my fingers through Khalid's hair.

"I can feel your love for me," I rasp, trembling against his chest. Such intensity pours through me, wrapping me in a comfort that's all consuming.

His lips meet mine, wet from tears as he kisses me. "I can feel yours too, *kira*. I can feel it all..."

We cling to each other, happiness pouring down our cheeks as we pepper each other with kisses.

Our blood bond is complete.

We're tied together forever.

And whatever happens with Antonio or his brother – we will face it all side by side.

He is my *kira*.

And I am his.

EPILOGUE

HIM

She's sitting with Mother and Maddox beside the pool, laughing that half-snort, half-giggle she's gotten used to not hiding. Her hand still cups her mouth, and her cheeks still blush red in embarrassment, but she doesn't roll her lips in trying to stop it. She splashes Maddox with water, then he throws her into the pool with his magic.

She comes up sputtering, her face light with laughter, and my chest eases as I watch them from inside the living room. I want to be outside with them –*with her*– but my job demands my presence.

It's been six days since Talon's betrayal, but he's finally been spotted in a small town in Alaska, hiding under a false name. He might have survived up there if not for Aleric Zadar's connections, knowing that I wouldn't ask our brother to change into him, preferring to kill him with my own two hands.

Two hands...

My gaze drops to the one missing as Varius stands beside

me, studying me to see if I'm okay with going after someone so close.

I clench phantom fingers as I lift my eyes back to my girl. She suffered because of him. I have to live with the memories of hitting her because of him.

My jaw clenches as my anger overrides the pain. "I'll leave today," I tell Varius – the words he wanted to hear.

Talon will undoubtedly be keeping an eye on all of our online presences and will know if I take a plane. He'll be banking on me not coming out to Alaska if I have to travel up there myself. He probably has people watching the main highways, which is going to make it tricky to actually get to him. Unless...

"I'll text Vlad then; he'll be here in a few minutes."

I smile as I turn to Varius. As a born vampire, Vlad has the ability to phase. He can move only about a hundred miles at a time though, so it's still going to be a bitch of a journey given my body isn't made for such travel, but it will be a hel of a lot faster than driving or moving as a shadow and have a much higher chance of success than getting on a plane.

"He volunteer?" I ask.

"I doubt it. He hates you."

"I can't think of a reason why."

He doesn't respond as he walks away. He wasn't much of a conversationalist before, but since Talon's betrayal, he's barely spoken outside of business.

I have found him outside of Micha's room sometimes, just standing there staring at her door. My chest tightens as I watch him disappear down the hall, and I wonder if that's where he's heading now.

Theirs was not a love match, and I doubt Varius feels guilty over doing what he believed needed to be done, but he has always done his duty, and this must be frustrating him, not knowing how to get her to do hers.

But in the end, Micha has been bought and paid for. She can't leave even if she wanted to. Her father would kill her as per the common contract of a runaway bride, and the Blacks are well-known for their assassins. We've hired a few out ourselves a couple of times.

Micha might've been a rising star in their ranks before being sold, but what Maddox did to her... She wouldn't survive a single night.

Then again...maybe she thinks death would be better instead of living without magic.

My eyes fall to my missing hand again.

I lost one and so can still control my abilities.

But Maddox took both of hers.

He didn't cut them off, nothing as quick and clean as that, but he disfigured them beyond use. Mother tried to fix them after, but despite how powerful she is, even she wasn't able to make them work again.

Micha's magic isn't gone like Varius', but attempting to use it will most likely end in her death.

Lifting my gaze, I catch my girl's eye through the open glass door of the living room. Her smile falling, she climbs out of the pool and grabs a towel. She's in front of me a moment later, her hair dripping wet as it hangs across her shoulders.

"When are you leaving?" she asks.

"In a few minutes."

She struggles to control her fear, but it's all over her face, as well as blitzing down our completed bond. Being able to feel it makes me smile. When I started it, I thought it would give me happiness to know she was mine, but I was a fool to think I could imagine how it would make me feel. Like someone fully blind trying to imagine colors. Someone deaf hearing music that makes others weep. Someone with aphantasia able to picture all the scenes in their favorite book.

"When will you be back?"

It's a question that doesn't have an answer, but I know she needs one to cling to. She's been so strong these last few days, trying to overcome her disliking of families to fit in with mine. It helps that she can feel my love for them all, but her mother tore her to pieces for too many years for six days to have fixed.

Cupping her cheek, I kiss her. When I pull back, I press a light one to her forehead. "I'll be back by the end of the week." As long as Talon doesn't run.

As long as he doesn't kill me. Although normally, he wouldn't have a chance, his expertise as a businessman who sometimes gets his knuckles dirty versus mine as a reaper. But I am still recovering from the magic I wasn't able to control. My kidney is mostly healed, but I still only have one working lung and the pain from heating my blood still lingers. My skin is hot to the touch.

Varius has banned me from using magic, but that will be lifted as I hunt Talon, and Scarlett knows it might very well spiral out of my control, consuming me completely this time.

"I'm not dying before I get a lifetime with you, *kira*," I murmur as I rest my head against hers. "I promise I will be back."

She nods mutely, then throws her arms around me. "I'm going to hold you to that."

I smile as I kiss her forehead. "I need to get my mask from upstairs before Vlad gets here."

"Vlad's going with you?" She wrinkles her nose, not the biggest fan of the vampire that was so rude to her while she was grieving.

"Yep. He might not be coming back though."

"Yes he will," Varius says as he enters behind us.

I turn to face him. "It was a joke."

His only response is to hold up his hand, my mask

dangling from his fingers. "He'll be here soo–"

The vampire in question suddenly appears beside us, and Scarlett jumps on a small scream. Maddox comes in from outside, a towel around his waist, a wide grin across his lips.

"Dicktective!" he shouts as he opens his arms to hug the guy.

Scowling, Vlad bares his teeth. "Touch me, and I'll bite you."

"Kinky. I'm all right with that." Turning to me as the vampire glares, he slugs me in the shoulder. "Kill T quickly, okay?"

The temperature in the room drops to zero as I nod sharply. Scarlett squeezes my hand, and I drop a kiss on her lips, then step away. I don't want to linger, to draw out the inevitable.

"I'll be back soon," I promise as I grab the reaper mask from Varius. Vlad places his hand on my left shoulder, and then we phase, my stomach dropping out of my feet as the world disappears around us.

We pop back into existence a hundred miles in the direction of Alaska, my guts churning as if someone twisted them like wet rags. Vomit shoots up my throat, but just as it comes free, we're phasing again, the bastard not giving me any time to adjust.

By the time we're in Alaska, an uncountable number of hops later, I'm curled in a ball, my body shaking from the drain on it. Sweat stinks in patches across my shirt, and my mouth needs a wash, having spat up the entirety of my lunch. Night clings coldly to my hot skin, and I shiver on a groan.

"Stop being such a baby." Vlad nudges me with his foot, and I sink into my shadow, not liking being so vulnerable in front of one who will gladly kill me if given the chance.

Phasing has killed weak sups before, tearing apart their bodies faster than they can heal. It is extremely rare but not outside of the realm of possibility. Born vampires are one of the very few sups whose bodies are made to handle the strain of phasing, so where Vlad is barely feeling any effects, I feel like I've been thrown around a warehouse, my every muscle screaming, my every bone feeling as if it's broken. Phasing a handful of times wouldn't have been too bad, but it's been a day of constant hopping.

Dry heaving, I lie on my back and fall asleep in the safety of my shadows.

Soft light covers the Alaskan landscape when I step back into the world. Vlad is nowhere to be seen, and I wonder if he's left now that his job is done or if he's in the bar across the street, catching up with the locals. His family is from somewhere up here, having migrated down after his sister married into Aleric's family a hundred-odd years ago. He is the only one of his line that remains, and I wonder if he has ever been back in all that time.

A familiar movement snags my attention, and I watch the back of Talon move through the bar, serving drinks to a table of women. For a moment, I think to leave him here, to let him live a life in solitude. We have no ties in Alaska. If he's planning on starting a rebellion or killing Varius, he would need to be a lot closer.

But to leave him alive will be damning the rest of my brothers. They'll wonder what he knows; they might seek him out, might even join his cause when we cannot afford to be divided.

So I pull out my reaper mask, lock down all the years we shared between us, years full of laughter and having each other's backs, and I wait for him to finish his shift.

A few hours later, he's ushering out the last drunken customer and closing up shop. Glancing out the windows, he searches for me with a nervous tic at his jaw, but he doesn't know I'm already inside, seated at a table and waiting for when he turns.

Drawing the door shut, he locks it quickly, then spins on a sigh that lodges in his throat. His face pales as he takes a step back, his hand reaching for the door.

"Don't run, T. Die with more dignity than that."

He stops, his shoulders squaring, and I am very much reminded of a little brother I taught how to throw his first fist.

"Stand side-on; you're a smaller target that way..."

I block out the memories of his little fists clenched tight as he stared ahead with a seriousness that made me laugh. He looked so much like Varius.

"You told Antonio about Scarlett that night in the woods, didn't you?" I ask even though I already know the answer, the mystery having bugged me since then. There's no way he could have smelled me on her, not with only one drop of mine in her veins.

Warmth pours into my chest, a hug from a distance, a squeeze of the hand as my girl comforts me through our bond. I put up a wall, not wanting her to feel how cold I get when I'm about to kill. After...when he is dead and I am crying over his corpse...then I will reach out to her. Then I will fall into her comfort and mourn the brother I lost.

But right now I need to get answers, and I can't do that if she's making me all emotional.

"He wasn't supposed to hurt her."

"Mmm. Just like he wasn't supposed to touch us at the offices," I say, lifting my left arm onto the table.

Sorrow and guilt crush his face in big meaty hands. "He gave me his word."

He sounds and looks so broken, I almost think to spare him the details of what happened, but Scarlett suffered because of him. *I* suffered.

Mom suffered.

Micha suffered.

I will not grant him mercy. Holding up my arm, I say, "He made me beat Scarlett while he jerked himself off. I couldn't live with that. You're not going to either."

Agony hits him hard, crumbling the last of his resolve, and he steps away from the door, from the lure of false safety. Dragging out the chair across from me, he sits down and buries his head in his hands.

For a long moment, neither of us say anything.

Then he lifts his head and nods. "I won't fight you, Kal. I won't make you do that. I didn't mean for any of this... No one other than Varius was supposed to get hurt."

My lips tighten as I struggle to hold on to my calm. "Yes, you will. I will not kill you unarmed, but first I want to know why you did all this. What made you so *stupid*, that you then won't even fight for?"

He shakes his head. "What does it matter? I won't win this fight –"

"You might. I burned up one lung, a good chunk of my kidney is missing, and a lot of my nerves aren't quite right yet. I nearly died in your shadow protecting her."

"You started a blood ritual. She should have been safe."

"We didn't share enough blood at that point. Now. Why did you do it, T?"

He stands up and makes his way behind the long bar. Pulling out a glass of whisky, he uncorks it and brings it back to the table. He doesn't bother with a tumbler. He takes a drink, then sets it down in front of him.

The sweet smell of butterscotch and heat wafts in the air

between us – an insurmountable distance neither of us can cross.

Rubbing a hand over his head, he looks me in the eye. "Because I found out why Dad cursed Mom."

My body stills.

My every hair rises.

"Why?" I ask, the word a sharp demand that verges on a growl. A reaper kills without emotion, and I clench my jaw as I force it back down.

Dad was a piece of shit. He didn't need a reason to curse Mom, and the fact that Talon took his side when he didn't even know the fucker...

My hand clenches beneath the table.

"Varius isn't his son."

"What?"

"Someone raped Mom, and she didn't abort him."

"So you thought it was your right to?"

"He's not even a witch, Khalid. He's a –" He stops, his lips pressing tight as he swigs the bottle back to them.

He has to be a witch. "He has magic. It's just trapped."

"Because Mom cursed him!" He throws the bottle at the wall behind me. I don't flinch, knowing he didn't aim for me. "She cursed him in her womb so no one would know he wasn't Dad's."

"That's not true."

"Why? Because you don't want to believe it? I didn't either, but think about it, Khalid. How else would he be born without magic into one of the strongest families in North America?"

"Shit happens."

"Yeah. Shit does happen." He drags his hand through his hair, a gesture he's had since he was a child – unable to sit still, to control his emotions so no one could read them.

Except he did learn at one point, didn't he?

"He's a dirty fucking hybrid, Kal. Leno should be the one

leading. But instead Mom had you slaughter Uncle Myers and dozens more of our family just for him. And why?" A harsh laugh hits the air.

"Varius can't even conceive. He can't create the next generation. Hybrids are infertile. All those deaths. All those people *you* killed without hesitation. Uncle Myers practically raised us!"

"*Varius* raised us," I say. "He helped you with your homework. He picked you up when Cassey left you crying with a broken heart. He fucking *raised* you, and you want to kill him because of who his father is?"

He glances away, a scoff on his lips. "He stood aside and did nothing when they slaughtered Jackie." His high school crush. The 'bloodbank' the vampires had bled dry on their first date. "He is nothing but an abomination. We're going to war with the Death Hunt because he's making hybrids, and Mom doesn't even tell us there's one living in our own fucking house."

He looks back at me with a shake of his head. "Uncle Myers was right. He shouldn't be leading with the blood of a vampire in his fucking veins."

Shadows form across the table as I pull a twelve-inch knife out of them and slide it over to Talon. I don't know the brother sitting across from me anymore – the one with so much hatred for Varius that he would risk my life and that of someone I love just to kill him. He is a coward who had to make a deal with the devil to have any hope of seeing Leno become Boss, and I am no longer interested in hearing his excuses.

Cursed hybrid or not, the sins of Varius' parents are not his. He is our brother. He has sacrificed so much for this Family. He's given up any future of happiness, carried the weight of our crimes upon his shoulders, and this is the thanks he gets.

A stab in the back over something he doesn't even know

about.

Talon's eyes drop to the blade, and his anger flees under the approach of fear. "You're really just going to turn me into another one of your marks?"

"You did that yourself when you tried to remove me so Antonio could kill Varius, when you told him about my girl, when you threw her into your shadow, almost got Mother killed, and stood aside while Micha got tortured. You are not my brother, but you can take comfort in the fact that I promised Maddox I will kill you quickly."

Ignoring the blade, he shoots a bolt of lightning at me. Anticipating it, I've already thrown up a shield and kicked the table into him. He grunts as it hits him in the stomach, bending over from the force. I jump over the table, sliding across its surface and snap up the knife. I stab him in the side of his neck as I land on my feet.

His fingers sizzle with another spell. His eyes grow wide, then dim as I jerk the blade out of him just like I did with Daniel at Hannah's house.

Blood sprays across the table in a fountain of choices he shouldn't have made. Slumping to the ground, Talon hits his knees, then his face.

I lean down to wipe my blade on his back, cleaning it of blood before dropping it back in my shadow. Closing my eyes, I take off my mask, and with its removal comes a flood of pain that brings me to my knees beside him.

He was my brother.

A traitor or not, he *was* my brother.

I told myself what I needed to in the moment, lied under the protection of the reaper. But with the mask gone and the deed done, I am left with nothing to protect me from my grief. Dragging him onto me, I rub at his skin, making it move, making him move from his eternal stillness. It won't bring him back, I know this, but the grief doesn't care about logic. It just wants my brother back.

I want my brother back.

Curling my arms, I hold him tight against me, my body shaking with each exhale of my breath that highlights the stillness of his.

Talon is gone.

He was gone the moment Vlad arrived at our house.

Was gone when he learned Mother's secret. He just didn't know it yet.

Closing my eyes, I scream out all my pain.

The gentle touch of my girl envelopes me, and I grasp at it with my missing hand. A phantom touch against a phantom touch as a shudder rips through me, and I rock Talon on my lap.

But the movement doesn't make him move.

Nothing will.

Scarlett pushes more love down our bond, convincing me I'm not the monster I am. But a reaper is not a hero. We are not a savior or a protector. We are the hand of vengeance and pain.

More love. More understanding. More acceptance of who I am. She sends it all, sitting with me patiently as I cry clinging to my brother. I hug him tight.

But he does not hug me.

Vlad appears as the night turns to morning, smelling of whiskey and sex. "We have to go," he says. "The owner comes in every morning to have an affair with his sister-in-law."

I don't move for a moment, as still as Talon. Then I squeeze him one last time before dropping him into my shadow. The monsters will tear him apart, returning his magic to where it came.

Without a word, I hold out my arm. Vlad takes it in a

matching silence, for once not being his arrogant self.

The world disappears.

But the pain tearing me apart does not.

We arrive in the middle of the night. The house is asleep. Vlad leaves as soon as he deposits me on the living room floor. I lie curled there for about an hour, masking myself from Scarlett so she doesn't come down, needing to first see my mom alone. Hot shivers rake me as I finally regain the strength to stand. On wobbly legs, I stagger to Mother's room. I don't bother knocking; she wakes the moment I enter – a habit she gained during war and never lost.

"Oh, Khalid." She throws off her covers and comes towards me, but I step back with a shake of my head, the thought of her touch sickening me when she's the one who caused all this. She stops, and I seal her room in *silence.*

She flips on the light, and tears fall down her cheeks as she looks at the blood of her son on me. "Was it quick?" she asks.

I nod.

She wraps her arms around herself, and for a moment, I can't bear broaching the subject tonight.

But I need to know. I do not have the luxury of burying my head in the sand.

"Talon knew about Varius being a hybrid," I say, not bothering to dance around the question of, 'Is it true?' I can see on her face that it is. "You cursed him so he wouldn't have his ascension, blocking his magic as well as the truth of what he is."

"Yes. I didn't realize he wasn't your father's until the day before he was born, when I felt him bite me."

"Does his real father know?" Emotions burn my skin, making me itch with the need to move. I keep my feet rooted, my arms still.

She shakes her head. "And he never will. *No one will.*"

"There is *always* a way to break a curse."

"Not this one."

The curse and how to break it is created by one person. I want to trust her. I want to trust that this isn't going to blow up in our faces, that no one else will find out Varius is a hybrid and try to kill him, ripping apart this family, ripping apart *me* as we all take different sides, but I can't.

I can't...

"You can't guarantee that," I say hoarsely, imagining all the deaths that will be at my hands. "And then he will find out, and what do you think will happen?"

Varius can't step down in the middle of a war. Leno is not strong enough to lead. In the fragile peace we were born into, yes. But not when Antonio comes for us like he has the Blood Fang. Varius' hold on power will both save us and break us.

"I *can*," she says strongly, grabbing my hand. "He will never break it."

"How do you know?"

Her eyes soften as she squeezes my fingers. "Because I know the weight of a first born. He has to fall in love with someone to break it, and that won't ever happen. He will never trust someone enough to be that vulnerable."

Experience thickens her words, her being the first born of the previous generation, but it is not a shock to know she never loved Father. It was clear even as a child that theirs was nothing but a business deal.

Shaking my head, I pull my hand free. "You better be right." Because this will destroy Varius if he finds out that everything he sacrificed for this Family was all for naught, a false crown that had never fit his head.

My jaw locking down all the rage burning inside me, I turn for the door, unable to look at her. Before I pass into the hall, I say over my shoulder, "Talon died because of your lies, Mother. Make sure no one else does."

A pained noise comes from her, but I end it by shutting her door. Standing there, I close my eyes, grief rocking me on my heels. Warmth envelopes me, my *kira* breaking through my barriers, holding me in my pain. Heading for the stairs, I go to her.

She is a balm on my soul.

A treasure I'll forever cherish and never fail to protect again.

When I open the door, she wraps me in her arms. "I'm so sorry, Khalid. I'm so sorry."

Her wet cheek presses into me. Her love envelopes me. And in the comfort of her arms, I break.

CAN VARIUS KEEP HIS THRONE WHEN HIS CURSE BREAKS?

Find out in *Broken Souls.*

He suspected me.
He tortured me without evidence.
And now he demands my forgiveness.

Broken Souls is not for the faint of heart as Micha's torture is shown on page from her POV, and that isn't even the hardest scene.

WANT TO KNOW WHAT HAPPENED BEFORE THE TREATY?

Find out in *Madness Behind the Mask.*

As a woman of the Shadow Family, my only worth is in my ability to breed. But on my wedding day, we're attacked by the werewolves, and I'm kidnapped by the alpha for killing his mate. After stabbing my hands to a tree, Antonio begins to punish me...

AUTHOR'S NOTE

Hello everyone!

Thank you so much for reading *Cursed to be Mine*. These two have gone through hell, and unfortunately, it is not the end of their pain. In *Broken Souls*, book two, Micha teaches *kira* how to wield magic. But although she is a big part of book two, the storyline follows Micha as she is forced to stay married to the man who tortured her. Khalid thinks Maddox did it under orders... But Varius did it himself, wanting to punish her for her sins, and when Khalid finds out, things are going to get heated.

Preorder *Broken Souls* now for lots of groveling. Lots of pain. And lots of CNC breeding...

And jump to the very last page in this book for a fun crossword about the clues leading to chapter 13 ;)

Happy reading,

RESEARCH NOTE

I ended up researching quite a lot about the darker parts of society while writing this book, and there's just something I need to say (TRIGGER WARNING: CHILD SEXUAL ASSAULT RESEARCH).

The pedophiles in schools statistics mentioned are, unfortunately and disgustingly, based on actual reports[1]. Worse, only a couple decades ago, male pedophiles in Germany were actually sought out to be foster carers.[2] Combined with the whole Catholic church and orphanages scandals not too long ago either, and you get an ugly picture of the world when it comes to caring for children. So here are some signs of a sexually abused child:

- Trouble sleeping
- Loss of appetite
- Grades slipping
- Withdrawal into a safe space
- Freezes or flinches when touched or about to be touched
- Suicidal thoughts

So sorry to end on that dark note, but although I enjoyed writing this and I hope you enjoyed reading this book, I did not enjoy the research aspect of it and just needed to get that off my chest.

May we be there for the children in our lives.

---

[1]https://childrenstreatmentcenter.com/sexual-abuse-teachers/
https://www2.ed.gov/about/offices/list/ocr/docs/sexual-violence.pdf

[2]https://www.newyorker.com/magazine/2021/07/26/the-german-experiment-that-placed-foster-children-with-pedophiles

SPOT ANY ERRORS?

Please let me know by emailing me at:
authormirandagrant@gmail.com

WANT TO IMPACT THE REST OF THE SERIES?

Drop me a review!

WANT TO LEARN ALL ABOUT WIPS AND NEW RELEASES?

Follow me on Facebook

Across

3. Khalid _____ whenever he thinks of his girl, yet when talking to Hannah he never ______.

6. What is the name of the thing that marked Hannah for death, which is also the name of Khalid's position in his Family?

7. Khalid went home because his girl was arriving soon. Yet, Hannah didn't arrive until long after he started washing his what?

9. How did Khalid describe his girl's cheeks? (5)

10. I constantly said throughout the first 12 chapters that Hannah was going to ____

11. How many boyfriends did Hannah have?

13. In chapter 1 and 6, Khalid stood outside the glass door to Hannah's house and looked up to see what? (9-7)

16. Khalid would protect his girl first and foremost. Yet, he ignored Hannah in the van while he saved who?

17. At the end of chapter three, I said Hannah was a ____ woman walking.

19. When Hannah stripped to take a shower, what item was the only thing she took off?

20. What pattern of underwear did 'kira' have? Something Hannah likely wouldn't wear given her age and appearance obsession?

21. Khalid said his girl was what? Something Hannah is definitely not?

Down

1. How did Khalid describe his girl's thighs?

2. How many boyfriends did Khalid say his girl have - something he would know all about?

4. Who did Antonio want to play with?

5. Khalid killed Hannah only after Scarlett said she wished she was _____, giving him permission.

8. What did Maddox almost say before Khalid cut him off in chapter 12? 'Killing her m-'

12. What sort of spell did Khalid use on his girl? And what did Hannah say Scarlett was doing all the time?

14. Khalid said his girl loves her family. Yet, Hannah is constantly _____ Scarlett.

15. Khalid said his girl was all alone in this world outside of her family. Yet Hannah was always surrounded by_____?

18. The only interaction Khalid and Hannah shared was super what?

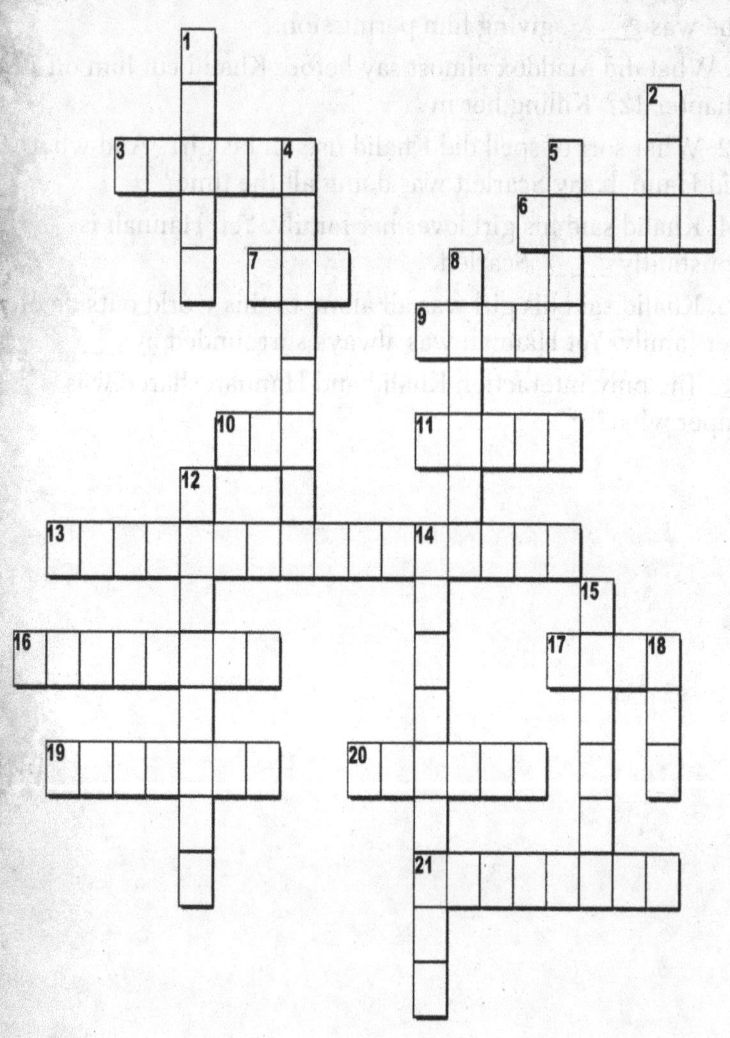